The House of
WINDJAMMER

The House of
WINDJAMMER

Book I

V. A. Richardson

BLOOMSBURY

BLOOMSBURY
CHILDREN'S
BOOKS

Published by Bloomsbury, New York and London
Distributed to the trade by Holtzbrinck Publishers

Library of Congress Cataloging-in-Publication Data

Richardson, V.A.
The House of Windjammer / by V.A. Richardson. p. cm.
Summary: In the fall of 1636, Adam, fourteen-year-old heir to the House of
Windjammer, must find a way to keep his family afloat after his father dies and
tulip fever sweeps Amsterdam.
[1. Amsterdam (Netherlands)—History—17th century—Fiction.
2. Netherlands—History—17th Century—Fiction.] I. Title.
PZ7.B6293 Ho 2003
[Fic]—dc21
2002027818

First U.S. Edition 2003

3 5 7 9 10 8 6 4 2

Bloomsbury USA Children's Books
175 Fifth Avenue
New York, New York 10010

In memory of my father,
John David Benbow Richardson CBE MC.

And for Janie.

The purest treasure mortal times afford,
Is spotless reputation; that away,
Men are but gilded loam, or painted clay.

William Shakespeare, Richard II, Act I, Scene I

Author's Note on Historical Fiction

If I had a time machine I would go back in time and see for myself exactly what happened at the time of the Windjammers. But I don't, and as neither I – nor anyone else lacking Time Transport – can be absolutely sure what happened on a daily basis to ordinary people in the distant past, there has to be some educated guesswork to complete the picture. I believe this is justified in the context of an historical story – even the word *history* incorporates the element of the story and storytelling – but it is important that all historical fiction is set within fact.

As a result I have taken care to ensure that all recorded dates and historical events are in their right order and place. In the writing of this book I have taken great pains to respect the history of the seventeenth century as it is now known and recorded.

On the matter of language, however, I have written the dialogue and narrative in modern prose. This is entirely intentional, because no matter how historically correct it would be to use certain words (such as thee and thou) and pitch everything in the correct style of grammar of the day, after a short while it becomes very tiresome to read. I have taken care to omit from the dialogue words that would very obviously not have been used at the time (such as okay, rocket, hot dog etc.). In the interests of the story, I have tried to strike a balance by giving a flavour of old times within the style and construction of the sentences and I hope this has added to the story rather than detracted.

One final point on the name Windjammer: the term *windjammer* was coined from the habit of jamming sailing ships hard over to catch as much wind (and therefore speed) as possible. By the late nineteenth century, and the advent of all steam-powered ships, it had become commonly used as a term for old sailing ships. It would not have been a word commonly used in seventeenth-century Holland and all connections with any family of that name, either ancient or modern, are entirely coincidental in this the first book of the House of Windjammer ...

Contents

1. Shipwreck

They were lost. All aboard the *Sirius* knew it now.

'Damn and blast this fog!' Lucien Windjammer cursed under his breath.

The *Sirius* rode uneasily on the swell, moving through the fog like a ghost ship. No breath in her sails. Her wooden bones creaking as the current sucked and pulled at her keel.

'Skin your eyes, men!' Lucien Windjammer called up to the lookouts in the rigging and on the forecastle. 'Our lives will depend on your keen eyes this day!'

But it was no longer just pirates and privateers they feared. The fog had brought new terrors. They could smell it in the air: the scent of wet rock and seaweed flinted the thickening mist and drove a chill spike into the hearts of even the most hardened of the crew.

'By the mark – seventeen fathoms!' the ship's mate called as he measured the depth of the water beneath their keel with a plumb-line.

Lucien listened to the splash of the lead weight as Hendrik dropped it over the side and let the knotted line go until it reached the bottom.

Hendrik pulled in the line counting sixteen knots in the rope. 'Rocks – sixteen fathoms.' He swung the lead again: *splash!*

'Much more of this and we'll be food for the sharks,' Lucien said, and nodded to the ship's boy.

Hobe stood ready at the mizzen mast, wide-eyed with the strain of watching and listening. He knocked a signal note from the ship's bell. It made a lonely sound, forlorn and cracked, and seemed to hang over them eerily.

Lucien Windjammer held his breath, listening to the reply that came tolling back out of the mist.

'Are you a ghost ship?' his words misted on the cold of the dawn as he spoke.

He stamped his frustration into the quarterdeck and turned to pacing the deck in front of the mizzen mast. Three steps one way. A turn. Three steps back. Until the sound of Hobe's bell brought him to a pause once more to watch and listen again.

Lucien Windjammer cursed the bad luck that had dogged them. Had all gone well, they should have reached the safety of the little Dutch settlement at the mouth of the Hudson River. By now they should have taken on food and fresh water at the trading-post on that river island they called Manhattan. But all had not gone well – pirates, privateers and a great storm had seen to that.

Almost six months had passed since the *Sirius* had led the ships of the Windjammers' merchant fleet out of the old port of Amsterdam, flags flying. Their mission: to follow the trade winds west to the Americas, to explore this new land and trade with the fledgling colonies there.

They had made a fine sight then. The *Sirius*, *Cygnus*, *Orion* and *Hesperus*: four fat-bellied merchant galleons in the Spanish style, each with three masts, square topsail and main, and twenty cannon apiece. They had sailed with a flotilla of smaller ships, the finest merchant fleet the Windjammers had ever put to sea. Yes, the crowds on the waterfront had cheered them then. But even as Lucien had charted their course across the vast expanse of the Atlantic Ocean on that spring day in 1636, he knew they sailed more in hope of reaching land than certainty.

The storm had blown up suddenly from the southeast, scattering the fleet and churning the waves into mountains of water. The *Sirius* had been forced to run before its fury for days as the storm hurled them to the very rim of the world – that unknown uncharted place on the edge of their maps – and there it had abandoned them to their fate.

'By the mark – fifteen fathoms!' Hendrik's voice broke into Lucien's thoughts.

Lucien strode to the bulwark and gripped the taffrail as he looked out over the side of the ship. Around them the water was ink-dark and restless. Fat waves swirled, sucking in gurgling eddies as a gentle breeze stirred the fog to trick the eye and fill it with phantoms. He judged the speed of the current and tried to make sense of the bell. More than once he thought he heard the sound of surf breaking on a reef somewhere to starboard. And yet still that bell answered their call – urging them to come.

'Steady, lads! We know not her colours!' Lucien was taking no chances. The men stood ready by the cannons on the main deck.

Hobe's bell cracked at the fog once more. Lucien listened – they *all* listened – to the answer that came tolling back out of the fog.

'What do your young ears make of it, Hobe?' he asked.

'Nearer, sir,' Hobe said. 'Much nearer.'

'Rocks – ten fathoms,' Hendrik's voice cut in again.

'If there's a ship ahead of us,' Lucien reasoned, 'then there must be clear water too, by God. A channel through these reefs.'

But even as he spoke the thought aloud, some instinct born out of years at sea told him not to trust his own ears. He strode back to the ship's side and gripped the rail. He caught a fleeting glimpse of something ahead of them in the mist. A shadow in the whiteness, little more. Vague and indistinct. There for a moment, then gone.

Something was wrong, he was sure of it. Something was *very* wrong. His grip tightened on the rail as the answer came to him suddenly.

In three bounding steps Lucien Windjammer crossed the deck to the mizzen mast. He pushed Hobe aside and took hold of the bellrope himself.

'Silence, for the love of God!' he roared. 'Not a man shall speak!'

An uneasy quiet fell over the crew as he struck a note from the bell. The note soared high into the air and seemed to hover, quivering like a delicate bird, before being sucked into the mist.

Lucien stood listening, timing everything by the solid blood-thump of his own heart. He didn't have to wait many beats before he heard the sound of a bell tolling back across the water.

His hand was trembling slightly on the bellrope now as he knocked two sharp notes from the bell in quick succession, sending an unmistakable signal. Again he listened. Again the bell answered: *two* notes. And suddenly it was as if a wave of that dark water had washed right through him, sucking the strength from his bones and leaving him weak.

'An echo!' he gasped. 'It's only an *echo*!'

The full realisation of what it meant sent Lucien staggering back. This was no signal. There was no ship, no clear water. Just rocks and the face of some hidden cliff ahead of them to send the sound of their own bell echoing back to them.

'Hard to port!' he shouted down through the hatch to the two helmsmen straining on the massive tiller on the main deck below.

Too late.

'Reef! Dead head. Rocks!' Harsh cries exploded on the air as a line of dark shapes appeared in the whiteness.

Lucien rang the alarm in a jangle of notes. Feet thumped on the wooden decks. Suddenly everywhere men were shouting and running to their stations, until gradually the noise and confusion died down as one by one they stopped to stare.

Ahead of them the fog parted briefly. As it rolled back the blunt face of a cliff jumped skywards. Sheer and solid. Jutting. Angular. And in that moment all aboard the *Sirius* knew that awesome monument would be their gravestone.

The impact, when it came, sent Lucien reeling across the deck. He slammed into the mizzen mast and for a moment the fog seemed to flood into his head. The *Sirius* lurched as her keel dragged on the reef, the rocks ripping up through her rounded belly, snapping and cracking her timbers. The ship let out a terrible groan and the dark waters rushed in.

'Captain! Captain! Wake up!'

Lucien Windjammer came to his senses to find the ship's boy shaking him by the lapels of his coat. He sat up, still stunned from the blow. He wiped at the blood running from the gash on his forehead and looked around. The *Sirius* had driven up hard on to the reef. Her bow now pointed high into the air, her bowsprit lost in the mist, her decks slanting steeply aft as she began to list to port.

'Abandon ship!' A wail of despair went up from the crew.

Lucien struggled to his feet. Already men on the main deck were trying to launch the ship's boat over the side. Others abandoned all hope and jumped. He could hear men splashing in the churning water. Everywhere there were screams and shouts for help.

'Here, lad, you stay close to me!'

But the *Sirius* was sinking, and sinking fast. With a sound like a cannon shot the main mast cracked. High above, the rigging stretched. The mast swayed violently. The ropes parted to lash the air. Men screamed. The great square sails folded like broken wings and the mast crashed down.

'Captain! Heeeeeeeeeeeeeeeeeeeeeeeeeeeelp!'

Lucien heard Hobe's cry and turned to see the boy slithering helplessly down the slope of the deck towards the hole the mast had smashed through bulwark and rail at the stern of the ship. The boy caught hold of the splintered edge and came to a stop with his legs kicking out over the side.

'Hold on, lad!' He went after him. Sliding down the

deck to catch hold of the bulwark at a point where the rail had not been broken. 'Your hand, lad!' He called down to the boy. 'Give me your hand!'

The boy was wild-eyed with terror, kicking helplessly at the fog as the water seethed and boiled below. Lucien let the rail take his full weight, reaching down into the gap as far as he dared. The tips of his fingers touched the boy's collar. He leaned down further, then further still, and managed to take hold.

'I have you, lad!' And just for a moment he thought he would save the boy. Then what was left of the rail gave way.

Lucien heard the crack and knew immediately he had to find another hold. And yet still he refused to let the boy go. He made a desperate lunge for some trailing ropes of the ship's rigging, but the boy's weight dragged him down. He clawed desperately, snatching only handfuls of air as the sea and the ship turned in a whirl. Then the water just seemed to reach up and take them, wrenching the boy from his grasp as they both fell with a terrible rush.

Some time later, an exhausted boy crawled up on to the sand at the foot of a great cliff. Hobe lay shivering at the water's edge for a while, looking up only when he heard the *Sirius* shift on her rocky spike. With an agonised groan the ship settled back on the reef like the carcass of some great, beached whale. A rush of trapped air blew out from her hull. A dying breath to swirl the mist into ghostly eddies that danced across the dark water. Then the mist settled once more and drew a pale shroud over Lucien Windjammer and the rest of the crew.

2. Amsterdam 1636

A chill breath lifted off the sea. The sudden gust ruffled the furs of the merchants on the quayside and set the men stamping their feet. It swirled on through the city streets, stirring through the branches of the lime trees, shedding leaves like tears into canals, and rattling the glass in the leaded windows of the big houses along the Herengracht.

Deep in the heart of the old house, Hercules Windjammer felt the change and looked up from the ledgers on his desk.

' ... And we await more tar and seasoned oak for the completion of the *Draco*, Mr Hercules,' the clerk Gerrit was saying, unaware he had lost his master's attention to the world outside. 'I placed the last order with the master of the *Alkmaar* ... '

Hercules Windjammer's thoughts flew to his brother Lucien, his gaze drawn irresistibly towards the window. Heavy clouds were sliding their greyness through the watery swirls and bubbles of the glass. He watched as they gradually spread into the colours of the image stained in the middle of the diamond-shaped panes: a globe resting on its great W. The clouds brought darkness to the symbolic mark of the House of Windjammer.

' ... However, our bankers have shown concern at the money the *Draco* is costing to complete,' Gerrit went on. 'I have, of course, given them the usual assurances that the Windjammers will pay in full when the Star Fleet returns ... '

Hercules Windjammer nodded without paying much attention. The noise of the city reached in to him: the rattle of the carriages along the street next to the canal outside, the dull thump of barrels being loaded into a barge, the shouts of the hawkers and herring-sellers. They were sounds he knew well. The sounds of the city. *His* city. Amsterdam. As familiar to him as the canals and bridges and tall ships in the harbour. He had known them all his life and yet something about them suddenly seemed different – *threatening*.

A bell in the tower of the church nearby began to toll the hour. It made a lonely sound, forlorn and flat, and seemed to hang over the old house eerily.

' ... Only that moneylender Hugo van Helsen is demanding higher rates of interest than the rest,' Gerrit said, wrinkling his nose as if the name left a bad smell in the air. 'It's all in the ledgers, Mr Hercules ... '

'Where is Adam?' Hercules Windjammer interrupted his clerk mid-sentence.

'Master Adam?' Gerrit was surprised by the question. He stood washing his ink-stained hands in the air while he thought about it. 'At this hour the boy will be at his lessons with Meister Bloem. Yes, there's little doubt,' he nodded with great certainty, 'he will be in the schoolroom upstairs.'

But Gerrit was wrong about that.

3. Adam Windjammer

Adam Windjammer stood in the mud of the riverbank and looked up. The bow of the ship towered over him, the graceful curve of her hull rising high into the air like some great, unfinished cathedral. The ship stood three-quarters built on the gentle slope of a wooden ramp. The trunks of a hundred cut trees supported her like so many pillars and columns, while on the rickety platforms high above – made insignificant by her sheer size – men worked at the wooden cranes and ropes.

'The *Draco*,' Adam whispered the ship's name.

High overhead a dragon circled. Adam watched it moving through the air and marvelled at its beauty and grace.

The beast had come to life before his eyes, spread its painted wings and taken flight. The watery sunlight caught in glints on its gilded coils as it moved. Its head thrown back, mouth open as if bellowing its new freedom to the sky.

'Pull, men! Pull!' the master carpenter's voice cracked in the air like a whip. 'Put your backs into it!'

A dozen men were straining on the rope that held the beast aloft. They chanted a song now as they hauled on the rope, lifting the wooden figurehead ever higher, then easing it down to where men waited to set it in place on the ship's curving prow.

This was the finest ship the Windjammers had ever built. Sleek and fast in the English style. A merchant galleon with quarterdeck and raised poop. A ship designed to go far – even to the ends of the earth – and she would be a new star to guide the Windjammers' Star Fleet when it returned.

Draco. The dragon. A constellation of stars in the northern night sky had given this ship her name.

Around Adam, the shipyards on the western edge of the city seethed with activity. Skilled men laboured at the skeletons of half a dozen new ships: cutting, shaping, nailing the timbers into place. The air was laced with the smell of sawdust and boiling tar, the smells mingled to sweeten the smell of men's sweat and the sewage stink from the waterfront. But Adam hardly noticed now as he stood in awe of the *Draco*.

High above, the dragon turned gently and settled on to the prow. As it perched, a bell began to toll the hour. A lonely sound, forlorn and flat, each note seemed to hang over the ship eerily. Adam shifted uneasily and looked towards the city. Only as the eleventh note struck and faded did he remember his lessons.

'Meister Bloem!' he gasped, beginning to run.

Adam's feet slithered in the mud. He reached one of the many ladders leaning against the wall and leapt up it, taking two rungs at a time. He reached the top, cast one last look back at the *Draco*, and jumped down on to the wooden walkway that ran along the length of the waterfront. He set off towards the warehouses of the docks and the line of tall ships tied to the spiles of the quayside.

The docks were crowded with merchants, sailors, traders and the like, so he cut up between the warehouses and into the squeeze of the alleys and streets. Here the streets burrowed between top-heavy houses that sagged under the weight of their upper floors and roofs. At every turn more streets and alleys opened to left and right, filled with the smoke of fires and the belch of pewter factories. Through this maze of sounds and smells and houses and streets, he picked his way until he ran straight into trouble.

Cut purses, that's what they were called. Street rats, thieves, robbers, and plenty of other names beside. Two stepped out of a side alley in front of him. They were older than Adam and bigger. Adam saw them and came to a sliding halt. Wild thoughts of trying to outrun them back down the alley set him spinning on his heel, only to be brought up short by a hungry-looking youth who had stepped out of a doorway behind him.

'And w-what have we g-got here, lads?' the hungry-looking youth asked, his tongue tripping slightly over his words.

'Looks like a rich boy, Wolfie,' one said.

'Shut your m-mouth, can't you!' the hungry-looking youth stammered, glaring at his mate. 'How many t-times have I told you not to use my name when we're r-robbing?'

'*Robbing!*' Adam gasped. 'But I don't have any money.'

'Is that the t-truth of it?' Wolfie said. 'Well, we'll be the j-judge of that.'

'But I'm late already!' Adam panted. 'I haven't got time ... '

'N-no *chinks* in his pocket and no t-time to talk to

us neither, hey rich boy?' He shook his head sadly. 'And us only wanting to ask if you'd show a little k-kindness to the poor.'

'But ain't *we* poor, Wolfie?' one of the others started. 'Oh, sorry Wolf ... I didn't mean to ... well ... '

Wolfie glared him into silence, before turning his attention back to Adam. His eyes narrowed. 'I seen your f-face before – you're one of them W-w-w-w-w-'

'Windjammers,' Adam finished obligingly.

'That's what I said!' Wolfie snarled.

One of the others gave Adam a shove. 'Wolfie don't like no one putting words in his mouth.'

'The Devil tied his tongue at birth, see,' the third agreed. 'Ain't that right, Wolfie?'

'Will you t-two put a cork in it before I cut your t-tongues out and make you eat them!' Wolfie was snarling now. 'I ain't n-no different from no one else just 'cos my tongue's not slick with words.'

The others took the hint and fell silent.

Wolfie gave them a look as if to say *that's more like it*. 'Now where w-was I?' His thoughtful look quickly becoming dangerous as he dared the others to say another word. 'Oh yes!' He made a big show of turning out the pockets of his threadbare coat to show just how empty they were.

'But I told you – I haven't got any money,' Adam said, truthfully.

'Do you think I was b-born yesteryear, rich boy?' he said. 'I can smell g-gold at ten paces. It's a g-gift I got from God. That's why I'm g-going to be rich one day. So hand over your *chinks* or I'll sh-shake them coins out of you!'

Wolfie stepped forward and caught Adam by the

collar of his coat. But Adam was ready for him. He ducked low, twisted free and threw all his weight forward. *Ooof!* Wolfie's eyes opened wide with surprise. He staggered back, his mouth making Os at the air, as Adam shouldered him out of the way and set off up the alley at the run.

'G-g-g-g-g ... ' Wolfie gasped for breath.

The others waited patiently, not wanting to put words in his mouth.

' ... *Get* him, you idiots!' Wolfie got the words out at last in a rush.

Suddenly the alley was echoing with the sound of running feet. Adam put on a burst of speed, but they knew the alleyways and short cuts and, despite his head start, they quickly gained on him. Soon he could hear their ragged breathing right behind him. They almost had him when a man pushing a handcart full of pigs' heads started to turn into the alley ahead of them. Adam leapt over the front of the cart before it blocked the narrow alley.

'Oi!' Adam heard the man's startled cry as he ran on. The footsteps behind stopped abruptly and the alley rang with curses, the dull slap of meat and cries of pain.

Adam slid to a halt, gasping for breath. Behind him Wolfie and the others had run into the cart and overturned it. They had fallen among the pigs' heads and offal and were struggling to get away under the relentless assault from the furious cart owner, who was wielding a pig's head like a club.

Adam laughed, waved to Wolfie and ran on.

'I'll g-get you for this, Windjammer!' Wolfie's furious shout followed him. 'You have my oath on it!'

*   *   *

'You're late – *again*, Master Adam!' Meister Bloem said as Adam burst into the schoolroom.

'Yes, Meister Bloem. Sorry, Meister Bloem.' Adam gasped an apology, slipping into his desk by the window. 'I was … '

'*Tsk, tsk, tsk!*' his old tutor clicked his tongue impatiently. '*Qui plura loquitur, is ineptus esse dicitur!*' he scolded him in Latin. 'You must learn to think before you speak, Master Adam.' He paused and glanced up at the window, wrapping the tails of his voluminous cape around himself as if he had felt a sudden chill.

'It seems despite all my best efforts,' Meister Bloem went on, 'not to mention some considerable expense on behalf of your father and mother, that you have achieved the age of fifteen years without learning anything but a love of ships and an unhealthy interest in the common street-hustle.'

'That's not true, Meister!' Adam denied.

'And what of Latin and Greek? What of Virgil, Homer and Herodotus? What of the classics?' his teacher asked loftily. 'What have you learned of these, young master Adam?'

'But this is 1636, Meister! Times have changed,' Adam said. 'There's a whole *new* world out there. A living world. Not a dead one.'

'*Tsk, tsk, tsk!*' Meister Bloem's jowls wobbled as he shook his head impatiently. 'Next you'll be telling me you believe the Earth and all the heavenly planets travel around the sun!' He turned away, muttering to himself. '*Humph!* What does that heretic Galileo know anyway? What do any of these so-called modern thinkers know?' He turned to Adam again. 'As for this *New* World of yours, Master Adam – there's nothing I've heard so far to persuade me that it's any better than this *old* one of ours. You mark my words, no one is *ever* going to want to live in *America*.'

He shook his head, puffing a little with the effort, but as he caught his breath his heavy eyebrows fell into a confusion of a frown over the bridge of his nose. 'What's that confounded noise?'

Adam pushed back his chair and was at the window in a moment.

Below, people had stopped in the streets on either side of the canal. The servants and housemaids of the rich households of the Herengracht had opened windows and come to stand at side doors, water pails and bundles of washing in hand, as they looked to see what was going on. All eyes were turned towards the bridge further along the canal.

'Something's wrong, Meister,' Adam said.

'*Ita fit ut omnino nemo esse possit beatus,*' Meister Bloem said, casting his eyes towards the sky and adding something about people never being happy with their lot in life.

The Windjammers' house stood on the corner at the junction of the narrow thoroughfare known as Deer Street and the street running the length of the canal called the Herengracht. It was the tallest house along the canal and from the window Adam could see clearly over the gabled roofs of the houses on the opposite side. He could not, however, see down to the canals that lay immediately beyond, nor could he see what was happening on the roads and bridges leading to the poor artisan quarter of the city known as the Jordaan.

His gaze was drawn to his right where the masts of the ships crowded into the harbour in the distance. The sails were furled; the masts bare and spindly like a forest of dead trees. He knew instinctively that trouble would come from the waterfront.

Already what had been distant and indistinguishable had become recognisable. They could hear commotion in the streets, a hubbub of voices and the tramp of many feet on cobbles.

'The crowd must be rioting in the Jordaan again, Master Adam,' his teacher wheezed with sudden alarm. 'We must end our lessons at once. Close the shutters! Bar the doors!'

But it was already too late.

Further along the canal a runner had appeared on the road. He was wearing a long blue coat and had a leather bag slung over his back, and was running with his hat in his hand. Moving swiftly, he crossed the bridge and turned down the narrow, tree-lined street between the houses and the canal. His feet rang the alarm from the cobbles with every step.

The messenger was only half-way down the street when a crowd – which had obviously been following him for some way – came streaming down the road after him and started across the bridge. They filled the Herengracht with their noise and sent servants and rich residents alike running inside.

By now the messenger had arrived at the door below Adam's window. The urgent thump of his fist on the wood of the massive front door set off echoes that seemed to boom through the hollows of the house endlessly.

After a short pause, the door opened and the

messenger was ushered in. The door closed quickly again.

The crowd fell silent as it approached, overawed perhaps by the fine, flat-fronted houses lining the canal on both sides. The wealth of the Herengracht seemed to make them uneasy as they gathered in the street outside. The ranks parted and their leaders stepped forward. Then, quietly at first but growing steadily louder, they began calling for Hercules Windjammer to come out and face them.

Adam turned cold. 'They've come for my father,' he said.

4. The Curse of the Windjammers

'Master Adam! Wait! Come back!'

Meister Bloem's shouts followed him down the stairs as Adam raced through the angled landings on each floor. Feet thumping. Heart pumping. Five floors down from the schoolroom, he reached the point where the stairs widened, divided in two and descended in sweeping curves on either side of the main hall below.

Here he paused for breath, gripping the carved banister as if it was the rail of a ship rolling on high seas. Quickly he took in the scene below.

Across the hall the massive front doors were closed and now barred against the crowd outside. Adam's father had come from his library to receive the letter the messenger had brought. Through the open library door, Adam could see Gerrit standing by the desk with an account ledger still in his hands.

'Hercules, what is it?' Adam heard his mother say as she came hurrying out of the large sitting-room at the front of the house. Rose and Viola were right behind her. A frightened servant hovered in the shadows close to the door leading into the kitchen at the back. All now stood quite still, like chess pieces on the black and white squares of the tiled floor waiting for the next move.

Hercules Windjammer read the letter in silence. To Adam he seemed like a giant. Towering. Bearded. He stood a good head and shoulders taller than the messenger waiting in front of him. His sheer size made him seem invincible. But as he finished reading, his head bowed and for the first time in his life Adam saw his father waver. The big man rocked back on his heels, staggering as if he had received a heavy blow.

Adam heard his mother's voice as she spoke quietly to the servant girl. 'Please take Rose and Viola to their room and stay with them,' she said. She looked up at Adam. 'Go back to your lessons and stay there until I say.'

The servant girl gathered Adam's twin sisters and hurried them up the stairs. The girls passed him, their blonde hair and identical white dresses making them seem as pale as ghosts. They looked up at him, the confusion showing in their young eyes, but he didn't speak to them nor did he follow them up the stairs.

With a rustle of her silk dress, Adam's mother moved swiftly to the square beside her husband. They stood together like king and queen. 'Hercules? What is it?' She spoke in English now, knowing the servants would be listening.

'News of our fleet.' He held out the letter. 'Lost. Scattered and wrecked by a great storm.'

She took the letter, read it quickly and looked up. '*All* lost? But what of *Lucien*?'

Hercules Windjammer shook his head. 'It is as I feared. Our ships were overdue even when our man in New Amsterdam penned this letter. Now it can no longer be denied.' He spoke as if a great weight had descended on him. 'My *pride* has brought death and ruin to the House of Windjammer.'

'No, Hercules!' Adam heard his mother's voice rise as she denied it. 'You did not send the fleet to the Americas out of pride and vanity.'

He took back the letter as if it was a lead weight. 'Then why has God punished us so?'

The noise of the crowd outside swelled to fill the silence that followed. Hercules seemed to recover himself a little. A deep breath brought him back to his full height and he made a move towards the front door.

'Hercules! Wait! You cannot face that crowd alone,' she stepped in front of him. 'At least send Gerrit for the city guard! He can go out the side door into the alley and –'

Hercules stopped her with a finger on her lips. 'These are our people, Mary. They had loved ones and friends on our ships. They have a right to know what has happened.'

'Then I'll go with you,' she said.

He smiled. 'I have come to expect nothing less from you, Mary,' he said. 'Have I not always said you are my strength, my beautiful English rose?' The smile faded. 'As the head of the House of Windjammer I must do this alone.'

She hid her tears, pretending to brush away an imaginary speck from his long black coat. She straightened the lace of his collar. In return he touched one of the ringlets of her hair, brushing it back from her face. A silent message passed between them and without another word he moved past her to the door.

A hush fell over the crowd as Hercules Windjammer stepped out to face them alone. Adam saw it all through the open door. His father stood on the steps, shadowy against the light outside. In the street beyond, the crowd had gathered at the foot of the steps that led up to the door, their faces turned up to him now.

Adam looked out at them looking in. The scene seemed strangely unreal. Everything was transformed into shades of light and dark, as if he was looking at a picture – a single moment captured by an artist's brush – a moment when life itself was still.

Then his father spoke.

'Go ring the bell for our dead!' Hercules Windjammer said.

A great wail of despair went up from the crowd when he read the letter aloud for all to hear. They had come fearing the worst, but were stunned to hear that the *Sirius*, *Cygnus*, *Orion* and *Hesperus*, and the rest of the Windjammers' Star Fleet, had been lost.

'And my dear brother too,' Hercules said.

'What's to become of us!' a woman despaired.

'I know not if any have survived,' Hercules said. 'But I give my word to send the *Draco* as soon as I can in search of them. If there are survivors we will bring them back. The House of Windjammer will not rest until this has been done.'

He paused to let this sink in. 'Alas, I cannot bring the dead back to life,' he went on. 'I can only promise that your children will not go hungry this winter. If you are in need, then come to the warehouse on the waterfront. Gerrit will see you have money enough to live. On this I give you the word of Hercules Windjammer and with my word goes the promise of the House of Windjammer.'

'I see nothing here but *pride* and *vanity*!' someone spoke up in the crowd. 'Yes, I say pride and vanity has brought a curse on this house! No good can come of it now.'

Hercules Windjammer paused, clearly shaken. A tall man – dressed entirely in black but for a white collar – stepped forward. He was wearing a wide-brimmed hat with a rounded crown and had a large iron cross on a chain around his neck.

Hercules recognised the man. 'If you are here to preach, Abner Heems – then let your sermon be of the brave men who go to sea!'

'It's true brave men go to sea,' the preacher said, 'but only fools sail to the ends of the earth in search of riches!'

The crowd stirred uneasily. They turned to one another, murmuring.

Abner Heems raised the cross high above his head. 'For does not the Bible say, "And the Lord said unto Satan, whence comest thou? Then Satan answered the Lord, and said, From going to and fro in the Earth and from walking up and down in it"?'

'But does it not also say,' Hercules answered him, '"They that go down to the sea in ships, that do business in great waters. These see the works of the Lord, and his wonders in the deep"?'

'You are blinded by your own folly, Hercules Windjammer,' Abner Heems said. 'Repent of your ways or your greed will bring you down!'

'And I say we will finish building the *Draco* and then I will rebuild the whole fleet,' Hercules said sternly. 'The House of Windjammer will go on. It will grow strong again – because it must. Otherwise all those who have died will have died for nothing. And *that* I cannot bear on my conscience.'

'Then you defy the will of God!' Abner Heems said, causing all those who heard to shift uneasily and murmur to one another. 'For surely God has spoken. His voice was in the storm that wrecked this proud man's fleet.' He shook his head. 'What more proof do you need than this to see the House of Windjammer has been *cursed*? And who here will set foot in a cursed house? Who here will sail in a cursed ship?'

'Not I!' a voice said. 'Nor I! Nor I!' others agreed.

Hercules Windjammer raised his hands for quiet. 'I'll force no man to sail who'll not do so with a good heart, I swear it,' he said. 'Nor would I make anyone do what a Windjammer would not do himself. So if you want to know who'll sail with the next Windjammer ship, I'll tell you – *I* will!'

'Then you'll sail to eternal damnation like your brother and all the rest, Hercules Windjammer.' Abner Heems made his prophecy. 'You mark my words – it is the will of God!'

This brought a gasp from the crowd. Abner Heems turned and pushed his way back through their ranks. The people parted before him. One turned to follow. Then another. The ranks broke suddenly, folding back in on themselves, and the crowd started back the way they had come.

'This is fool's talk!' Hercules Windjammer tried to make them listen. 'We are merchants, nothing more. Seafaring people like yourselves and proud of it. We all know well what the sea can do. The sea gives and the sea takes without paying heed to the ways of simple men.'

But few if any listened now. Even the most loyal turned away. Hercules stood and watched until the last of them had gone, then he stepped back inside and closed the door. To Adam his father seemed to have aged a hundred years.

Somewhere in the distance a lone bell began to toll.

'Gerrit!' Hercules said, bringing the little man running. 'Pay the messenger and clear the Long Table for a meeting.' He turned to go back into the library and saw Adam standing on the stairs.

'Is it over, father?' Adam asked.

Hercules Windjammer shook his head. 'No, my boy,' he said, 'it has only just begun.'

5. The Long Table

'Who are they, anyway?' Adam asked. 'These men coming here, I mean.'

'They are merchants and people of business, as we are,' his father answered him. 'Men who have risked money on our venture hoping for a good return.' He adjusted Adam's coat and pushed back the dark curls of his hair. 'Some of them will take the news well. Others ... ' he paused searching for the right word, then said simply, ' ... Others will not.'

Adam fought against the restrictions of his best clothes. He felt strangled by his new collar. 'But we are *Windjammers* – why do we need them?'

'Because even the House of Windjammer needs support now,' his father said. 'That is why I want you to be at my side today. So you can meet them and know for the future who supported us in our time of need.'

'Our time of need?'

'There is no time to explain further,' his father said. 'So I want you to remember this – one day, when I am gone, you will be the head of the House of Windjammer and this ring will pass to you as it did to me from my father, your grandfather.' He held up his hand so the ring on his finger caught the candlelight and shone dully. 'It bears our mark and stands for everything we believe in. So no matter what happens – whatever is said here today – you must always remember to do what you believe is right and act with honour like a true Windjammer.'

'I won't let you down, father,' Adam promised.

His father stepped back and looked at him. He seemed satisfied with what he saw. His smile was sad and fleeting, however, as he went to greet the men arriving at the door.

Adam stood by the Long Table and listened to the voices in the hall outside. He knew their polite greetings and remarks about the September weather covered the real reason why they had come. Something important was about to happen, but he was not quite sure what. And not knowing left him feeling squeezed inside.

Around him the fire cast its flickering light over the room. It was a room he knew well – the place the family met each day to eat their meals at the Long Table – and yet somehow even that dining-room seemed strange and unfamiliar now.

The table itself was bare except for the candles burning in branching sticks. It stretched away from him down the middle of the room, with high-backed chairs set at intervals along either side. Tapestries hung on the walls, heavy with images of hunting and food, and the curtains were drawn. In the corner near him, where it seemed to have been for all eternity, the heavy globe – the symbol of the House of Windjammer – stood round and solid on its iron legs.

While he waited, Adam looked at the world. The land, as they knew it then, was picked out in ragged patches. The sea was drawn dark and wide around the coastlines of worlds only just discovered. He traced a route to the west until his finger ran over the image of a hideous sea creature devouring ships on the edge of the world. He stared at its tentacles, then a sudden impulse made him set the world spinning and the monster was gone.

'This way, gentlemen, please,' the sound of Gerrit's voice made Adam jump.

Gerrit led the way in, bowing respectfully to the line of men who followed. He continued to bow and bob as he fussed around, finding them suitable places at the table.

Adam watched the men from the shadows. They were mostly dressed for business: white lace collars, long black coats reaching almost to the grey stockings that covered their legs below the knees. The older ones among them wore the shorter tunics of a past style; their heads seemed strangely removed from their bodies by their white ruff collars. Most had moustaches and beards, and many among them had the rounded bellies of once athletic men running to fat. All seemed at ease in each other's company. All but one.

'Hugo van Helsen, sir,' Gerrit addressed him politely. 'Won't you sit here?'

Adam had noticed the man as soon as he stepped into the room. He was taller, slimmer and younger than the others. There was something about him – a polished steeliness, perhaps – that made the others keep a respectful distance. He sat down. His pale eyes swept around the room, taking in the scene as it unfolded. Watching. Calculating at a glance the worth of all around him.

'You all know my brother Augustus,' Hercules

Windjammer said, bringing the meeting to order.

Augustus stood up, clutching a scented handker-chief. He mumbled something no one could hear, then sat down again.

' ... And my faithful clerk, Gerrit,' Hercules went on.

Gerrit bowed, but remained standing.

Hercules beckoned for Adam to step forward into the light. 'But few of you will know my son, Adam,' he said. 'The son who will one day, God willing, take over the business from me.'

Suddenly everyone in the room was looking at him. Everyone, that is, but the man with the pale eyes. Adam followed the line of his gaze and saw he was watching Augustus intently. And then, for the briefest moment, Adam caught a glimpse of the look on Augustus's face. Pale. Drained. Cold. It was the look of a man who had just been given a glimpse of the future and had not liked what he had seen there.

Augustus realised Adam was looking at him and turned away quickly, covering himself by calling for a serving-girl to bring wine. A jug was produced and wine poured into silver goblets. When everyone had been served, Gerrit shooed the girl out of the room and closed the door. By the time he turned to face them again Augustus's face was a mask once more.

Hercules Windjammer stood up to speak from his place at the head of the Long Table.

'Thank you, gentlemen, for coming at such short notice,' he said. 'All of you will have heard the terrible news of the loss of my dear brother Lucien and the Star Fleet.'

The assembly hummed with sympathy, then fell silent.

'As you know, I'm a plain-talking man,' Hercules said. 'So I will speak plainly with you now. The House of Windjammer has lost a son and four of its finest ships. Ships Lucien led west in the hope of rich rewards in trade with the Americas.'

He paused to let this sink in before continuing. 'All of you here have invested money in our venture. Money we used in part to fit out the ships and pay for the expedition. In return for this we promised you a share of the profits, with the largest share owed to the Dutch West India Company.'

Here an old man nodded his agreement.

Hercules drew in a deep breath and gave them the bad news. 'In the light of what has happened, the Windjammer Trading Company can no longer fulfil its side of the bargains struck with you in good faith.'

The men heard the news in silence.

'Nor can we repay our loans to our bankers,' Hercules went on grimly. 'The truth is, the House of Windjammer finds itself short of money and until such time as the *Draco* is finished and we have resumed our honest trade we will be unable to repay what we owe.'

Still silence.

'In short, gentlemen,' Hercules finished, 'without your support here today the House of Windjammer will be ruined.'

A slab of peat burning in the fire settled and sent a cloud of smoke and sparks up the chimney.

'I have spoken openly and honestly with you, gentlemen, because that is my way,' Hercules said. 'I have no need to remind you that my family has traded honourably in this city for over a hundred years. We are not fly-by-night speculators gambling on the price of tulip bulbs like so many do these days.' He shook his head. 'No. We are merchants, and you can be sure the House of Windjammer will reward most generously all those who support us now in our time of need.'

This said, Hercules Windjammer sat down.

A long pause followed. The men around the table glanced at one another. It was the old man who stood up to speak next, introducing himself formally to the meeting as Bartholomew de Leiden of the Dutch West India Company.

'I think I speak for us all when I thank Hercules for being so honest about the state of his business,' the old man said, having offered his condolences to the House for the loss of one of its sons. 'I knew Hercules's father and *his* father before him. Some thirty years ago the House of Windjammer supported the Council of Seventeen with money to help set up the East India Company.'

The importance of this set the men around the table nodding and murmuring.

The old man waited for quiet. 'And thirteen years ago almost to this day, Hercules Windjammer himself supported the West India Company with the money and ships it needed to set up our trading post on the Hudson River.' He looked around at the men assembled. 'The House of Windjammer supported us in hard times and I believe it is only right for us to support it now.'

'I agree!' another said. 'We have all faced losses at sea at one time or another.'

Heads nodded.

'So I think I speak for us all, gentlemen,' the old man went on, 'when I say Hercules Windjammer is an

41

honourable man and his promise to pay when he can is good enough for us all.'

Again heads nodded.

'Then before we leave the House of Windjammer to grieve, let us seal this agreement like gentlemen in the traditional way,' the old man said, raising his goblet.

'*Agreed!*' the others said together and stood up to drink.

All raised their goblets. All but one.

The moment stretched into an awkward silence.

'You do not drink with us, van Helsen?' the old man asked at last.

The man with the pale eyes remained seated, thoughtfully caressing the silver stem of his goblet as if gauging its value by touch alone.

Then those eyes flicked up and ran along the line of faces on the opposite side of the table. The men shifted uneasily on their feet and quickly found some small excuse to look away. The eyes moved on, passing over Adam before pausing and returning to study his face briefly. In the time it took the fire to settle, Hugo van Helsen seemed to calculate Adam's worth as a person.

Adam felt the weight of the man's stare, but he didn't look away. A smile tugged at the thin line of van Helsen's lips as if he recognised something of value in him, then those eyes moved on again to where Hercules Windjammer stood, goblet in hand, in his place at the head of the Long Table.

'Over the years it has served me well to be cautious, gentlemen,' he spoke at last, choosing his words carefully.

'Cautious! Aye! That's *bankers* for you!' the old man said. 'A banker will always offer to lend you a good, thick cloak when the sun is shining on you and your affairs. But he is sure to be *cautious* and ask for it back just as soon as the weather changes and a cold north wind blows!'

He seemed pleased with this and beamed at the company. Some of them laughed politely, but few dared to agree openly. Adam found himself wishing the old man would sit down and keep quiet.

'If Hugo van Helsen has something to say,' Hercules Windjammer said, 'then I think we should all sit down and hear it.'

The men settled uneasily in their places again. The banker inclined his head in a polite bow and stood up. He walked slowly around the table, causing the men to turn and twist in their seats as he passed behind them.

'Like you, sir,' he addressed Hercules Windjammer, 'I leave gambling on the price of tulips to others.' He paused and glanced at Gerrit. 'I'm sure your faithful book-keeper would be the first to agree – in matters of money it pays not to take unnecessary risks.'

'Get to the point, van Helsen!' the old man said. 'We haven't got all night.'

Hugo van Helsen's pale eyes flicked with irritation. Bartholomew de Leiden shrank back a little in his chair and a thin smile flitted across van Helsen's face.

'Of course.' There was a steeliness to Hugo van Helsen's politeness. 'As I was saying,' he went on, 'I am a *cautious* man – and as a cautious man I like to keep my eyes and ears open.' He turned to the others. 'But I am not a superstitious man – no, *I* do not believe those that say this House is cursed.'

'*Cursed!*' the word was repeated around the table. Some of the men even looked around as if they expected to see a warning written large across the walls.

'I do not believe it,' Hugo van Helsen went on, having sown this seed of doubt in their minds. 'Nor do I believe that bad luck comes upon a House like a plague. No, I am far more concerned about the reports of the promises Hercules Windjammer made here today.'

He had their full attention now.

'Yes, gentlemen,' he said, 'the word on the street is that Hercules Windjammer has promised to send the *Draco* in search of his lost fleet just as soon as he can. And while he waits months for the *Draco*'s return he has pledged to support the widows and orphans of the men in his pay.'

'They are my people,' Hercules said simply. 'They need help now.'

The mocking smile returned to the banker's lips. 'A fine sentiment, perhaps, but an expensive promise all the same.'

'What you call sentiment,' Hercules said flatly, 'I call responsibility.'

'And what of your *responsibilities* to your business partners?' van Helsen turned on him. 'We are your partners in business and yet you promise to pay the common crowd before *us*? Surely, once the *Draco* has been launched the ship must be used in trade – not sent on some hopeless mission in search of the dead.'

'But I have given my word!' Hercules said.

'And now you expect further loans from us just so you can keep it?'

Trapped, Hercules remained silent.

The men around the table shifted in their seats and looked at one another. It was clear he had made his point.

'The records of your family's past glories are plain to see,' Hugo van Helsen glanced around at the fine tapestries. He became suddenly brisk and businesslike. 'But the House of Windjammer cannot trade on its past forever. Times have changed. If nothing else, surely the loss of your own brother proves the days of adventuring are over. The House of Windjammer took a risk sending its fleet to the Americas and this gamble has not paid off. Now this House must change its ways or die. You must cut costs. Scale down your affairs. Run the Windjammer Trading Company to make a profit.'

'Are you saying my word is not enough in this matter?' Hercules's tone was dangerously quiet.

Adam could see his father was angry – very angry.

'I merely wish to point out,' Hugo van Helsen said, 'that perhaps you are no longer the right man for the task. You are not as young as you once were. Your ways are the *old* ways. Now more than ever the Windjammer Trading Company needs someone who understands the ways of the modern world. A man of business. A man of money. A man ... '

'A man like you, for instance?' Hercules Windjammer interrupted.

Hugo van Helsen inclined his head slightly in agreement.

A moment of stunned silence followed as it became obvious to everyone seated at the table that the banker was trying to take over. And with that everyone was talking at once.

'For the love of God!' Hercules Windjammer came to his feet suddenly. 'This is the 1630s, not the dark ages! We have found the courage to fight the Spanish for our independence. We have united the northern provinces and made Holland strong! Built cities like Amsterdam on trade and commerce. We have become wealthy and rich in culture and started a golden age. Do you think any of this would have happened if we had all just been *cautious*?'

Hercules strode to the globe and set it spinning on its stand.

'Thanks to risk-takers like us there are Dutch men and women all over the world,' he said. 'Here in the Americas.' His finger stabbed down. 'In New Amsterdam on the river island they call Manhattan. In the Africas too! On the cape of storms where so many ships have been lost.' Again and again his finger stabbed down. 'In the East Indies. In India, Batavia, and the Spice Islands. And who knows one day even in the great, lost land of the south ... *Terra Australis*.'

Hugo van Helsen turned to the others. 'Has Hercules Windjammer become a peddler of myths and bombast? Show me the profit in his grand words and talk of honour! I say it is *gold* that counts in this world and nothing else.'

Hercules Windjammer's face was deathly pale. His jaw set.

'It is time for change at the Windjammer Trading Company!' Hugo van Helsen went on. 'The *Draco* should be used for trade or sold at once to pay us the money we are owed. After that the House of Windjammer can make its living out of the grain trade in the Baltic. The profits are steadier and the risks less great.'

'No!' Hercules appealed to the men around him. 'While there is breath in my body I will not stand by and watch the English, Spanish and Portuguese take our trade. Do you not see – if I do then everything we have worked for will be lost. And Lucien and all the people who have given their lives to make Holland a great trading nation will have done so for nothing. Do you understand – *nothing!*'

'Is it Holland you wish to make great,' Hugo van Helsen's voice cut in, blade sharp, 'or the name of Hercules Windjammer?'

Hercules's eyes narrowed. '*You* have the nerve to ask *me* that?' he said. '*You!* Hugo van Helsen! A mere shadow of a man who sits behind his counting tables making profit out of our labours? A moneylender who does nothing but ride on the backs of others? An opportunist who harbours no other ambition but to advance himself in power above all others? *You!* You dare say that to *me?*'

The banker shrugged off the insults and turned to the others. 'I will not support the Windjammer Trading Company a day longer unless changes are made. Who supports me now? I say we put it to a vote.'

'A vote?' Hercules gasped. He looked to his brother Augustus for support. But Augustus only clutched his handkerchief tighter.

'The grain trade *is* steady,' he bumbled, his chins wobbling.

Hercules gave up on him and faced his adversary alone – an old lion challenged by the young – and everyone around the table waited to see what he would do next.

And when the answer came, Adam knew for certain his father had lost.

'So that's your plan, is it?' Hercules's voice started quietly, but grew steadily louder. 'Very well, then. If you want the House of Windjammer – then take it from me if you are man enough!'

With enormous strength Hercules heaved the globe in its iron frame high over his head and turned to face the men at the Long Table, and as he did so he became even larger than life itself. He stood for a moment like Atlas with the whole weight of the world on his shoulders. Then something inside his great chest just seemed to snap. Adam saw the bewildered look in his father's eyes. He watched him stagger back, swaying dangerously on his feet under the weight of the globe.

'*Father!*' Adam cried as he darted forward to help him.

A flicker of understanding crossed Hercules Windjammer's face. He shook his great head as if to say it was no use. The globe toppled and fell with a crash that sent echoes booming through the hollows of the house. He stood for a moment longer – kept up by the sheer force of his will perhaps – then he clutched at his heart and came crashing down like a broken mast.

And after the noise – *silence*.

6. More Purple than Black

Adam stood barefoot in the shadows. He was dressed only in his nightshirt and he was very cold.

He was standing in the hall at the bottom of the stairs, on the same black square where his father had stood only the day before. In the shadows around him were many doors, but only one was open.

The open door led into a small room at the front of the house. Light came from inside, and he was drawn to it now by the same unseen force that had drawn him from his bed in the middle of the night and down the lightless stairs.

Around him, the house itself was quiet. Silent. Closed up in an armour of shutters. The pictures had been turned to the wall in the tradition of mourning. Only memories and ghosts stirred in a dead house.

'There was little I could do.' An echo of the doctor's voice seemed to ring off the walls. 'His great heart must have failed him.'

' ... Failed him ... failed him ... failed him ... '

He remembered the racked sobbing of his sisters and the way his mother had stood stiff-backed and silent.

Now, Adam's whole body seemed to be moving of its own accord. Drawn towards that light even though he was scared and didn't want to go. His hand stretched out in front of him until his fingers blunted against the studded wood of the door. He pushed at it. The door swung inwards and the light grew stronger.

The coffin had been placed on a table. To Adam it filled the whole room with its sheer size. All around candles burned in iron holders, raising trails of scented smoke that transformed the light into an opaque mist and made the room seem strange and unearthly.

He paused at the door and stared at the coffin. It had stood open all day so those who wished could come and pay their last respects to Hercules Windjammer.

He became conscious of the dull thump of his own heart. It seemed to miss a beat every now and again, leaving him breathless. A faint smell of decay corrupted the sweetness of the incense. It caught in the back of his throat. He was finding it hard to breathe and was beginning to feel light-headed and dizzy.

He had wanted to come earlier. He had wanted desperately to be alone with his father, but Gerrit had been there all day, spinning invisible nets of custom and tradition about the room like a spider. Only now, in the middle of the night, did Adam feel free of it. He took a step into the room. Then another. He felt compelled to go on, creeping towards the open coffin until at last he was standing beside it.

His father was lying on his back with his hands crossed over his chest. His hair and beard were neatly combed. A hint of a smile was frozen on his lips, as if at last he knew the answers to all the great secrets of life. He looked as if he could be woken with a touch.

Adam reached out and touched his father's cheek. The skin felt cold and hard, as if his father had been turned to stone.

'I didn't let you down, father,' Adam's lips worked through the words. 'In front of those men, I mean.'

'Master Adam? What are you doing in here?'

Startled, Adam spun on his heel to see Gerrit standing framed in the doorway. The shadows pooled in the sockets of his eyes, making his face pallid and skull-like.

'I – I – ' Adam tried to find words – any words – to explain that he wanted to be alone with his father.

'The master must rest undisturbed for the night. It is the custom of this House,' Gerrit said.

They heard soft steps crossing the hall and Adam saw his mother appear out of the darkness of the hall.

'I found Master Adam in here, mistress,' Gerrit explained, bobbing into a bow. 'It is quite against the tradition of the House, you understand? The coffin must lie undisturbed after dark on the second day. It has always been so.'

Adam felt the burn of the tears on the backs of his eyes. He tried to fight them, but they welled up and began rolling silently down his cheeks. He brushed them away furiously.

'Thank you, Gerrit,' Mary Windjammer said. 'I know the traditions and I will explain them to Adam myself.'

After a pause, Gerrit bowed and vanished back into the darkness of the hall. Adam waited until he had gone and ran to his mother. He buried his face in her nightdress, breathing in her life and warmth as he sobbed out the terrors in his heart.

The next day the Windjammers turned out to honour their dead at the New Church on the edge of Dam Square.

A carriage drawn by four black horses took Hercules Windjammer's coffin the short distance to the *Nieuwe Kerk*. Adam and his sisters walked behind with their mother, followed by Augustus, the other members of the Windjammer family and Gerrit.

Adam went through it all with a strange feeling of detachment. It was almost as if his soul had left his body and he was able to look at himself sitting in the pew before the great carved pulpit. Around him sat many of the men who had been at the Long Table that evening. He didn't resent them being there. He just watched everything with a numb awareness of the fine words spoken about his father and uncle, and the sad beauty of the simple anthems sung by the choir.

After the service the coffin was carried to the grave-yard beyond the old city walls. There, in a tomb guarded by stone angels and a high wall, they laid Hercules to rest beside a stone marked with Lucien's name.

And suddenly it was all over.

At first Adam felt only relief, then a surge of guilt for feeling that way. He stood beside his mother and sisters to receive the sympathies of the steady stream of people who offered them as they made their way home.

'Terrible business, just *terrible*,' Augustus muttered through his scented handkerchief as he shepherded Adam's cousins, Willem and Angelica, away. 'Both my dear brothers gone and now I alone remain.'

'If there is anything I can do ... ' Bartholomew de Leiden said.

Adam heard his mother speak to each in turn, her voice fading gradually as his thoughts took flight. He longed to be somewhere else. Somewhere far away.

Only very gradually did he become aware that his sisters were tugging urgently at his sleeve.

'He's talking,' Rose said.

'To you, she means,' Viola explained.

'We were out walking,' Hugo van Helsen said as if repeating something he had already said. 'I thought it only right that I should stop and pay my respects to your mother.'

Adam felt as if he had run headlong into a stone wall. He stared at the banker and all the hurt he felt inside seemed to transform itself into pure hatred. But Hugo van Helsen was not alone.

She was tall – almost Adam's height – with long dark hair, tied back. The girl was standing back a little and he looked at her without knowing just how hopelessly the threads of their lives were already entangled. She had lifted the hood of her cloak to cover her hair in a gesture he took as a mark of respect for the dead. He looked at her and she returned his gaze steadily without turning away. And there it was – all the strength and untamed defiance he would come to know so well – captured, crystallised, polished and set in living green.

'This is my daughter, Jade,' Hugo van Helsen introduced her briefly.

Adam looked away only to find his gaze drawn irresistibly back to her a moment later.

'Your father was a good man,' Hugo van Helsen spoke briskly now, as if his time was precious. 'I'm sure you will honour his memory and not be a disappointment to him.'

Adam bit his lip, saying nothing. If he could do nothing else, he would not let this man see he had drawn blood. He felt the weight of the banker's stare – those pale eyes narrowed briefly as if they saw something worth remembering.

'I have a feeling we will meet again, young Master Windjammer,' he said. 'Soon. *Very* soon.' He inclined his head in a slight bow and moved on to speak to Adam's mother.

Jade van Helsen remained stubbornly in front of Adam, looking at him as if she could make sense of the jumble of thoughts in his head.

'I know how it feels,' she spoke at last. 'I remember when my mother died.'

Adam glared at her, saying nothing. How could she – a *van Helsen* – know how *he* felt?

'You must understand, madam,' he heard Hugo van Helsen say, 'it was nothing personal – just *business*, that is all.'

He stressed the word as if it excused everything.

'Then I like not your *business*, sir,' Adam heard his mother's cold reply. '*Nor* do I like your methods.'

'Perhaps not, madam,' the banker replied smoothly. 'But you would do well to remember this is a man's world. The marketplace is hard. No place for a widow.'

'The Windjammers have always traded with honour,' she said. 'Nothing has changed – Gerrit will see to that.'

'We shall see, madam,' Hugo van Helsen bowed. 'Yes, we shall soon see.' He called to Jade.

She stood for a moment longer, then turned away without a word. Adam stood staring straight ahead. He wanted to run. He wanted to scream. He wanted to lose himself in the streets. He fought the impulse until he thought he would burst with it. When he could fight it no longer, he turned to look for her again and saw her threading her way through the small crowd that had gathered around them.

That evening the family met at the Long Table. Adam sat in his place. The twins sat opposite him, wide-eyed with the strangeness of it all. Their mother was flanked by their Uncle Augustus and Aunt Felicia. His cousins Willem and Angelica were there too and some other more distant cousins from Hoorn and Edam. All were conscious of the yawning emptiness of the massive oak chair at the head of the table.

The thunder rumbled, a distant growl that came closer with each flickering stab of lightning. It started to rain.

They ate dinner, picking at their food as they listened to Augustus Windjammer bumbling on about nothing very much in particular. Their mood, like the room itself, was sombre in the candlelight. The fire had been allowed to burn low, the tapestries and pictures had been turned to the wall and the great globe in the corner had been covered with a black cloth.

'The plumes on those horses were more purple than black. Yes, yes, I'm quite sure of it,' Augustus was saying as he waved a napkin around.

'Purple? Do you think so? Perhaps you are right,' Aunt Felicia said, as if it mattered.

In the silence and shadow around the edges of the room, moved Gerrit. He approached the table to speak quietly to Adam's mother.

'It is getting late, mistress,' he said.

The lightning flickered.

'I do so prefer bright colours, don't you? They are so cheerful. Yes, yes, that is why I like tulips ... ' The rest of what Augustus was saying was lost in a crack of thunder.

Mary Windjammer waited for it to roll away across the sky before she called for their attention.

'You know very well we have not gathered here to talk of small matters, Augustus,' she spoke sharply to her brother-in-law before he could begin again.

Augustus Windjammer opened his mouth as if he was about to argue the point, saw the serious look on her face and closed it again without speaking.

'As you know,' Mary Windjammer began, 'it had always been my dearest hope that Adam would finish his schooling before he started work in the Windjammers' business. But now everything has changed, and as the oldest he is the heir and now the rightful head of the House of Windjammer.'

As if to prove it the lightning flickered, dimming the candles and picking out the emptiness of the great chair at the end of the table. She stood up and took Adam by the hand. He had no choice but to follow her to the head of the table. Gerrit moved to pull back the chair and she indicated for him to sit down.

'But it's *father's* place,' Adam said.

'The head of the House of Windjammer *must* sit at the head of the Long Table, Master Adam,' Gerrit insisted. 'It is the tradition of this House.'

Adam glanced at his mother.

She nodded her encouragement. 'Gerrit is right,' she said. 'It was your father's chair and *his* father's before him.'

Adam sat down reluctantly. The wood felt worn and

smooth under him, as if it had been formed and shaped over the years by his father's weight. The Long Table stretched away from him towards the window, leaving him feeling very small.

Everyone in the room was looking at him. Adam caught a glimpse of that same look on his uncle's face. Augustus drained his goblet and wiped his mouth on the back of his hand.

'You are head of the House of Windjammer now, Adam,' his mother went on, and suddenly there was a great weariness in her voice, 'but you are still very young.'

'A mere boy!' Augustus echoed this thought.

She ignored him. 'We cannot expect you to shoulder the responsibilities of this House alone. Especially now – at this, the worst of times,' she said. 'While Gerrit instructs you in the ways of business I see no reason why *I* should not help run the affairs of the company.'

The effect of her words was startling. All turned to look at her in astonishment.

'*You*, dear sister-in-law?' Augustus blurted suddenly.

'And why not?' Mary Windjammer asked stiffly. 'Have I not supported my husband all these years? I know the business better than most.'

'Yes, but, *mistress*.' Gerrit found his tongue. 'Such a thing would be without precedent! *Never* has a woman run a business such as the Windjammer Trading Company. There are many merchants who will never consent to trade with you.'

'Quite so,' Augustus agreed. 'The very thought of dealing with a woman makes me go cold! The Windjammer name will be the laughing stock of the city. Yes, yes, *ridiculed*.'

'And *you* could do better, Augustus?' Mary Windjammer asked doubtfully. '*You* would run this business like Hercules? Working all the hours to make it strong again for Adam?'

Augustus seized his chance. 'I am a true Windjammer!'

The lightning flickered and the thunder rumbled ominously.

Gerrit leaned forward to speak his advice close to her ear. 'It would be more traditional, mistress. And you could guide his hand.'

'And I suppose the traditions must be preserved at all costs?' Mary Windjammer said drily.

'We have little choice, mistress,' Gerrit said. 'Traditions are the rules of the House. We need to be seen to maintain them – now more than ever. For without them people will say we have no order. And without order what do we have? *Nothing!*'

Mary Windjammer considered this for some time. 'Very well then,' she said at last. 'In the interests of this House I will follow its traditions.' She turned to Augustus. 'You will take charge with Gerrit's help, but I wish to be consulted on all important matters, do you understand?'

'Yes, yes, quite so,' Augustus said. His appetite seemed to have returned suddenly.

'How wise you are, my dear,' Aunt Felicia congratulated her. 'After all, we are *only* women and Adam is *only* a boy.'

'Yes, yes – a woman's rightful place is running the household,' Augustus was quick to agree.

'But my uncle hasn't even been to sea!' Adam spoke up now.

'That is true, nephew,' Augustus Windjammer admitted. 'I have indeed always preferred the peace and quiet of my house on the Prinsengracht. It is not as grand as this, but it is much bigger than the cabin of a ship! Nevertheless, let me assure you, God himself fashioned me from the same clay and air as my dear brothers! I am of the same mettle.' He looked down his nose at Adam. 'And I say it is now more important to know how to make alliances than to be able to sail ships we do not have. Yes, yes! I say we first must talk to this banker – this Hugo van Helsen – and bring him on to our side.'

'No!' Adam came to his feet suddenly.

Augustus was taken aback. 'Surely, nephew, you're not saying we can still take on the likes of Hugo van Helsen and win? We have no fleet.'

'We have the *Draco*,' Adam said.

'And no money to finish her,' Augustus pointed out. 'This banker holds the strings of our purse. He is a dangerous man. A wolf, little more. And he is at the door of the House of Windjammer now.'

'We *have* to find a way,' Adam said. 'We have to launch the *Draco* and sail her to the Americas. We have to honour my father's promise!'

'We *have* to be *cautious*,' Augustus disagreed.

The word struck like a note from a bell.

'You must understand, Adam,' his mother said, reading all the danger signs from the look on his face. 'This is much bigger than you alone.' She searched for a way of proving it to him and turned to Gerrit. 'Let him see the ring.'

The thunder rumbled.

Gerrit bowed and went to fetch a box from its place

near the globe. With great reverence he placed it on the table beside Adam.

'Open it!' she said.

Adam opened the box to find his father's ring inside. He picked it up between his thumb and forefinger. The cold flicker of the lightning caught on the symbol of the globe etched into the gold.

'It is the ring of the House of Windjammer,' his mother said quietly. 'It was your father's ring and his father's before him. Now it is yours by right. Put it on!'

Adam hesitated. His mother nodded her encouragement. Adam slipped the ring on to the ring-finger of his left hand, only to find it was too big.

'You see,' she said softly. 'It's a man's ring and, like the House of Windjammer, it does not fit a boy well. That's why you must be patient. That's why you must learn from Gerrit. And in time you will grow into them both.'

'But mistress,' Gerrit spoke up. 'The head of the House of Windjammer *must* wear the ring. It is the custom.'

Augustus coughed politely. 'Then perhaps as I am to be in charge, *I* should ... '

'That will not be necessary,' Mary Windjammer interrupted him.

She reached for the simple chain around her neck, took it off and removed the amulet there. She threaded the ring on to the chain and made Adam bow his head as she carefully placed it around his neck.

'How much closer can it be to your heart than here, Adam?' his mother said softly and slipped the ring down the front of his shirt.

Adam felt the ring drop cold against his chest. Like a dead weight it hung there, heavy and unfamiliar. Little did he know then just how heavy the burden of the House of Windjammer would become.

7. The House of Shadows

In the days and weeks that followed the funeral, the big house on the Herengracht settled into a state of quiet uneasiness. It was almost as if the house itself had taken a deep breath and had held it, leaving anyone who came near with the uncomfortable feeling that it was waiting for something bad to happen.

In strict accordance with Windjammer tradition, a month of mourning began. The shutters were kept closed. The family cloaked their grief in darkness and dressed in black, moving about the house like shadows of happier times. And all the while the house seemed to wait.

As had been decided at the Long Table, Augustus Windjammer took on all matters of business while Gerrit waited for the period of mourning to end so he could begin teaching Adam the ways of business. At first, Augustus came every day to discuss matters of business with Mary Windjammer, but soon he was seen less and less at the house on the Herengracht and more and more lunching and dining with the merchants and bankers of the city. Working hard, he insisted, winning friends for the Windjammer Trading Company.

It was left to Gerrit to account for it all. He worked late into the night by the light of a candle, bent for long hours over his ledgers; the scratch of his quill pen his only company as it whispered into the hollow corners of the small ledger room off the library. And perhaps Adam would have thought little of it, had he not – more than once – heard Gerrit start up suddenly from his desk and say, 'It should not be so,' or, 'The old master would never have allowed it.'

At last, however, the long dark days of mourning were over. The shutters were thrown open again. The pictures and tapestries were turned back to face the light and gradually life returned to the old house on the Herengracht. And there was relief and an end in this new beginning.

Adam peeled off the shadows like old clothes. It would soon be time to start his lessons in business and this new hope made his spirits rise. However, it wasn't long before his suspicions were confirmed that all was far from well with the House of Windjammer.

'We must make savings, mistress,' Gerrit brought the bad news to the Long Table.

'Yes, yes,' Augustus Windjammer agreed. 'You must spend less on your household expenses, dear sister-in-law. Surely it is a small sacrifice to make?'

Money was now very tight. Cut-backs had to be made. And one of the first to go was Adam's tutor, Meister Bloem.

'You know I wouldn't leave you. Not like *this*, Master Adam,' Meister Bloem said at the end of their last lesson together. 'I even offered to come for nothing, at least until times are better for the family.' He shook his old head sadly. 'But who needs Latin and Greek these days? Everyone is too busy making money to see there are even greater riches to be found in learning.'

Adam put a brave face on their goodbyes.

'And if you ever go to America,' Meister Bloem said, 'write to me and tell me what it's like. I understand the people there are tall as giants and, like the peoples of the lost land of Gaora, they have no heads!'

Adam promised and watched from the window as his old tutor walked away down the street and out of his life for ever, little realising that at fifteen his childhood was now officially over.

Meister Bloem was only the first, however. Soon others of the household staff left. One by one Mary Windjammer was forced to ask them to leave and one by one they cleared their belongings from the rooms in the attic and left. Until finally only their old cook remained.

'The old master would never have allowed it,' she was heard to mutter as she stoked the kitchen fire. 'Someone around here is out to spoil the hotpot, or I don't know nutmeg from pepper.'

Adam, meanwhile, had watched the way each change to their circumstances had etched a new line on his mother's face. She looked much older than he remembered and when the sunlight caught her hair he noticed it was now flecked with grey. But if fewer friends came to call than once they had, his mother didn't show it hurt her. She carried on as they always had, while the house seemed to close around them like a fortress. Hollow. Forbidding and sad.

So it took an incident with the twins for Adam to see how bad it had become.

Adam was lying on his bed in his room, holding up his father's ring and letting it swing gently on its chain so it caught the light from the window, when the sound of weeping seeped into his thoughts.

He paused to listen, swung his legs off the bed and sat up. With a flick of his wrist he caught the ring, put it back around his neck and crossed quickly to open his bedroom door. Misery seemed to well up out of the shadows themselves.

He followed the sound along the passage, passing the stairs, and paused briefly to look out of the window down into the street on the north side of the house. He moved on again down the wood-panelled passage. The sounds grew steadily louder as he reached his sisters' door, but their room was empty.

A window overlooked the courtyard garden at the back of the house. It was open and Adam crossed to it and looked out. Some way below he saw Rose and Viola fussing over the withered flowers in the flowerbed where a gnarled plum tree grew up against the high wall of the courtyard. The twins were pathetic in their misery, their sobs rising up the walls like invisible creepers.

Adam leaned out of the window and called to them.

'We wanted them to grow,' Rose said, when at last she looked up and saw Adam at the window above.

'The flowers, she means,' Viola explained.

'But they died.'

'Just like father.'

Instantly Adam felt the full weight of the ring on the chain around his neck.

'Don't you know flowers always grow again in the spring?' he called. He tried to think of a way of explaining this miracle of life after death, but couldn't. 'There'll be just as many, I promise you.'

They considered this seriously for a while before accepting it without question.

'Now dry your eyes!' he called. 'Haven't you got any friends to play with?'

Rose glanced at Viola. Together they shook their heads. Adam began to lose patience with them.

'They won't play,' Rose said.

'Not any more, she means,' Viola explained.

'They say they're not allowed.'

'To come here.'

'Because we're *cursed*,' they chimed together, as if it was carved somewhere on a tablet of stone.

Adam moved through the shadows of the hall. The squares passed under his feet, black, white, black, white. He felt as if some unseen hand was moving him.

In front of him the double doors were partly open. He could see the flicker of the candlelight and hear the murmur of voices.

The door swung inwards to his touch. The Long Table stretched away in front of him, set with platters of food and silver goblets brimming with wine. His mother was sitting in her place at the far end of the table under the window. The twins, his uncle Augustus, aunt and cousins were all there just as before, with Gerrit standing in attendance by the great oak chair at the head of the table.

' ... So I say we seal this alliance, sir,' Augustus Windjammer was saying. 'Yes, yes! In the traditional way, I say!' He raised his goblet in a toast.

Adam realised someone was sitting in his father's place, hidden by the high back of the chair.

'What's going on, mother?' Adam asked. 'That's the

head of the House of Windjammer's chair.'

It was as if a spell had been broken. His mother came to her feet suddenly. He saw the smile fade from Augustus's lips. The twins' eyes grew as wide as saucers. Someone leaned forward in the chair and looked around the high back.

Adam saw the man's pale eyes and gasped. '*No!* What's *he* doing here, mother?'

'You must understand, Adam,' his mother said. 'We had no choice.'

'Yes, yes, nephew,' Augustus said. 'We must be *cautious* now.'

That faint smile flitted across Hugo van Helsen's face. Adam backed away from him into the hall. The doors slammed closed, shutting him out. He spun on his heel and the black and white squares blurred grey beneath his feet as he ran back to the stairs. Then he was climbing, climbing, climbing through the endless shadows of the house. And all the while he could hear his mother's voice calling up to him: 'Wait! Stop! Adam! Adam! Adam ... '

' ... Adam! Wake up!' The voice changed.

Adam came awake with a start. He sat bolt upright in bed. Sweating. Breathing hard. Rolled in a strangle of sheets. His mother was sitting beside him on the edge of the bed, leaning over him.

'No! Stay away from me!' he gasped, struggling.

'It was a *dream*, that's all,' she soothed him. 'You were shouting – crying out in your sleep.'

'But he was sitting in father's chair,' he blurted.

She smoothed back the tangle of hair, her hand cool on his forehead. Gradually the confusion of the dream passed from him and the race of his heart slowed. He lay back on the pillows, only to sit forward again abruptly.

'I don't trust Uncle Augustus, mother! He's not like father and Uncle Lucien.' It burst out of him in a jumble. 'He'll sell us out to that moneylender, I know he will.'

'It's the dream making you say such things,' his mother said, still soothing. 'And do not concern yourself about your uncle. I know his weaknesses only too well.'

'But –'

His mother placed a finger on his lips and wouldn't hear another word on the subject.

'Tomorrow you are to start learning the customs of this House and its business. I am sure Gerrit can answer any questions you have,' she said. 'But he will not approve if you fall asleep over his ledgers.'

She kissed his forehead and picked up her candle, shielding the flame as she moved like a ghost to the door. The candle lit up her face, causing the shadows to pool in the slight hollows of her cheeks. She looked gaunt and drawn as she paused.

'Do not worry, Adam, we will keep your father's word and finish the *Draco*, I promise you that,' she said. 'We will send her in search of our lost fleet. We will lay to rest the ghosts of the past. Then together we will rebuild the House of Windjammer and make it great again.'

And with that she was gone, taking the light with her.

As the darkness rushed in around the four posts of his bed, all Adam's doubts and fears crowded in on him again. He hadn't forgotten the way Augustus had looked at him. He reached for the ring on the chain around his neck – the symbol of the House of Windjammer – but found little comfort there. It only seemed to weigh heavier on him, leaving him breathless. And for the first time in his life Adam knew what it meant to feel true loneliness.

8. The Waterfront

Adam woke from a fitful sleep and lay blinking as the dawn brushed its pale light through the darkness, catching his room in that delicate pause between old night and new day.

He got up and relieved himself in a steady stream into the china pot by the bed. The fire had turned to ashes in the grate and his room felt damp and cold. He rubbed briefly at his teeth with a willow stick, then poured water from a jug into a basin on the table by the window. The icy splash stung the sleep out of his eyes and as his senses came together all his doubts and fears came back. He gripped the sides of the bowl and studied his reflection as it wavered darkly in the circle of water in front of him. The face looking back at him seemed much older than he remembered.

'It's up to you, Adam.' He watched his own lips move as if they belonged to someone else. 'You have to find out what's going on.' His thoughts focused on the *Draco*. 'You *have* to see for yourself.' He scooped up the water in cupped hands and his face vanished back into its rightful place.

It was still early, but already the household around him was beginning to stir. Somewhere in the servants' quarters in the attic he heard a door open and close and realised Gerrit would soon be coming to fetch him. He was determined not to waste the day with Gerrit and a pile of ledgers.

Adam dressed quickly in a white shirt, trousers and leather jerkin. He tied back his hair with a leather thong, stamped his feet into his boots and was careful to make sure no one was about as he slipped out of his room and along the passage. He just managed to duck down the stairs as Gerrit came to fetch him.

'Master Adam?' Gerrit called, knocking at the door.

Adam reached the hall.

The knocking became more urgent. 'Master Adam! Wake up!'

Adam let himself out through the front door and closed it quietly behind him. He took the stone steps down to the street three at a time and ran off towards the bridge. He didn't stop. It felt good to be free of the house at last.

The dawn had washed the length of the eastern sky, low-lighting ponderous clouds and sending out beams of crimson light to blood the roofs and gables of the houses by the canal. Adam hunched his shoulders against the autumn chill and did not look back as he turned up on to the bridge over the Herengracht.

The lanterns glowed feebly on the bridge. The water below was a dark mirror to the wavering points of light as the canal steamed a thickening mist.

He moved on swiftly – driven as much by the simple desire to see the *Draco* again as he was to escape the stifling oppression of Gerrit and the house he had left behind. He crossed more bridges and more canals, in this city of bridges and canals. First the Keizergracht and then the Prinsengracht slid under him. He avoided his uncle's house and turned right when he reached the tight little streets of the Jordaan, heading for the market and the docks that lay beyond.

Night still held on briefly to the narrower streets to his left, lurking in the hollows and crouching beneath the bridges as he passed over them. Around him the city gradually came awake. Chimney smoke thickened the mist and the sweet smell of the burning peat masked the sewer stench that wafted up from the canals. Here and there Adam heard the murmur of voices behind the shutters. The hollow, echoing clop of horses' hooves on the cobbles. The splash of a bed-pot being emptied into the street. Someone somewhere coughed and spat.

He followed the rattle of a handcart to the market square. The stallholders were still setting up their barrows for the day's business. Some stood huddled around iron braziers, warming their hands against the blaze of sparks, their faces distorted and orange beneath the brims of their hats as they watched herrings sizzle and roast in the fire.

Adam paused only once, forced to wait when one of the bridges was raised on its wooden crane to let the water-traffic pass underneath. He heard the bump and pull of oars from the shadows below, then the bridge was lowered again and he moved on.

He was close to the waterfront now. The masts of the ships angled over the streets where the taverns and houses slumped against one another like exhausted prize-fighters. And all the while a hubbub of noise grew steadily louder until at last the twist of the streets ended without warning and he stepped out into the tumult of the waterfront.

'Fresh fish!' 'Get your drinking water here!' 'Clean rooms to let!' 'Hello sailor, want to meet some nice girls?' Laughter and the cry of seagulls burst on the salt air.

The sounds hit him like a wave, then washed over him and surged back around, drawing him into the crowd. Everywhere he looked there was movement and noise. Several merchant carracks and a galleon had arrived on the morning tide. High in the masts above, men climbed hand over hand into the rigging, others clung to the yard-arms gathering up the topsails. And all the while on the quayside the crowd that had gathered to greet them ebbed and flowed like a human tide. Adam felt the excitement of the place in a pure rush.

'What ships are these?' he asked one of the women selling chickens from a wooden cage.

'Traders in from the land of the Turks, young master – and a galleon back from the East Indies,' she told him, but quickly lost interest in him when she realised he wasn't going to buy.

The galleon wore her years at sea in a beard of weed and barnacles on her hull. Her sails were patched and worn. Her foremast broken and spliced. The men aboard crowded at the ship's rail looking down, gaunt-faced and showing all the marks of the scurvy that had tormented them on the long voyage.

Everywhere sailors were beginning to pour from the ships, striding down the gang-planks into the arms of their families that had gathered on the quayside. Their relatives and loved ones thronged around them, thanking God for their safe return. Others still stood waiting expectantly while their children – who had clearly grown bored of waiting for fathers they hardly even knew – took turns at throwing stones at the bloated body of a dead dog floating in the water.

Adam pushed his way along the crowded quayside avoiding the slow swing of the rope and wooden cranes hoisting goods out of the bellies of the ships. The nets of barrels were set down in clusters alongside bags of grain and bales of cloth and other goods, while the merchants of the city gathered on the quayside.

He recognised many of the merchants from that night at the Long Table, and for a while all else was forgotten as he imagined his father there. Standing tall. Agreeing deals on a word and a handshake. But his ships were only the ghosts of the *Sirius*, *Cygnus*, *Orion* and *Hesperus*. His sailors coming down the gang-planks – just phantoms.

And Adam was too busy watching to notice he was being watched.

'Look out, lad!'

Adam ducked out of the way just in time as a wooden cage was hoisted down from the hold of one of the ships behind him under the watchful eyes of some merchants.

The cage swung dangerously. A terrifying roar split the air and a large black bear threw itself at the wooden bars, snarling. The cage thumped down on the quayside and immediately drew a crowd of curious onlookers; people staring in equal wonder at the bear and the men in turbans from the great Ottoman Empire in the East.

The bear's owner – a squat monkey of a man – stepped forward to take advantage of the crowd. He opened the cage and pulled on the chain attached to an iron ring through the bear's nose. The people pointed and laughed as the bear came out and danced for them. And no one seemed to think it might be cruel because to them it wasn't.

To Adam, however, who saw it with fresh eyes, the sight of the bear seemed pitiful. He saw someone step forward to bait the bear, stabbing and jabbing at the bear with a pointed walking stick. The beast bellowed and roared its pain, but the people were caught up in the cruelty of the moment and only laughed louder.

The spell the waterfront had cast over him was instantly broken. Adam felt as if he had been robbed of something precious. Suddenly he noticed the rats and smelt the stink of the bilgewater. Now all he saw was dirt and ugliness. The man raised his stick as the bear reared up on its hind legs. Without thinking, Adam leapt forward and knocked the man's arm so the blow fell wide. The people jeered at him. The man with the stick swore and pushed him aside.

'Leave it alone!' Adam shouted, as if by making the cruelty stop he could have the old waterfront back.

No one was listening. All around angry faces leered at him. Mouths twisted with rotten teeth. Their laughter was like the cry of seabirds. Adam staggered back as he was shoved aside. He tripped and fell. He covered his head, huddling away from the stamp and shuffle of the feet until the crowd moved on, following the bear along the quayside.

The sounds around him began to recede. Gingerly he got to his knees and spat his disgust in the general direction of the man with the stick. He spotted a stone water-trough outside one of the many taverns close to the waterfront and went to wash the mud and filth from his hands. It was while he was bent over the trough that he saw the preacher again.

Abner Heems ducked out under the lintel of the door and quickly pulled his hat down low over his eyes. Adam watched his reflection slide across the water in the trough in front of him and recognised the preacher immediately. He was still wondering what a man of God would be doing in such a hellish place as this tavern called the Trade Winds, when he noticed he wasn't the only person watching.

At a glance, she looked like any other girl on the waterfront. She was wearing a plain brown dress, a dirty white apron and had covered her hair with a tightly fitting white cotton cap and a shawl. He might have mistaken her for a baker's daughter, standing with a tray of dough-cakes, had he not seen the way she hid her face as the preacher walked past.

Jade van Helsen looked up again and their eyes met. She realised he was watching her and moved away through the crowd as quickly as her tray of dough-cakes would allow.

Adam went after her. 'Wait!'

'Leave me alone!' Her eyes flashed like green flints. She glanced around as if frightened she might be seen and recognised.

He tried to stop her by catching hold of her arm and in the brief struggle that followed the tray slipped, spilling the cakes into the mud.

'I'm sorry – I didn't mean to,' Adam said. He bent down and tried to help her pick them up.

'Leave them – they're ruined!' she said.

'What are you doing here?' he asked. 'Why are you dressed like *that*?'

The change was more than just remarkable. Gone were her fine clothes and cloak. He could hardly believe she was Hugo van Helsen's daughter.

'It's none of your business, Adam Windjammer!' she said, dropped the tray and darted away from him again.

Adam went after her, but she soon lost him, leaving him standing alone and mystified in the crowd. He had just given up all hope of finding her when the youths hit him.

Wolfie had been hanging around the corner near the Trade Winds tavern, leaning casually against the wall with his hands in the pockets of his threadbare coat watching everything going on around him with a lean and hungry look. The other two sat on the cobbles nearby rolling dice. Adam hadn't noticed them, but they had noticed him almost the moment he had stepped on to the waterfront.

It all happened so fast. One moment Adam was on the waterfront looking for Jade, the next he had his arms pinned by his sides and was being bundled into a nearby alleyway. They released him with a shove that sent him stumbling ahead of them in the narrows between the backs of the houses.

Adam backed away from them.

'Wolfie wants a word with you,' one said.

'Wolfie?' Adam gasped as he was hit hard from behind without warning.

He went down, sprawling on the ground at their feet. He looked up to see Wolfie standing over him.

'You oughta be m-more careful,' Wolfie said. 'You could hurt yourself f-falling over like that.'

They laughed and dug at him with their worn-out boots, pushing him back down into the dirt each time he tried to get to his knees.

'I heard it said all Windjammers are p-pigs,' Wolfie laughed. 'Maybe that's why he likes crawling around in the d-dung so much!'

The others found that very amusing.

'Well, you'd know all about *d-dung*, Wolfie!' Adam gasped, unwisely.

The smile faded from Wolfie's face. He reached down and pulled Adam up by the collar. 'Now there you g-go upsetting me again, Windjammer,' he said, rifling through Adam's pockets with practised fingers. He found very little worth stealing and gave up in disgust. 'When are you g-going to learn, Windjammer?' he snarled. 'If you want to come down here to *my* waterfront you have to b-bring the *chinks* to pay me.'

'*Pay* you?' Adam gasped. 'Why would I want to do that?'

'Because I s-say so,' Wolfie said. He paused as something caught his eye. 'Well, what have we here?'

Wolfie reached out and hooked the chain up from around Adam's neck with a finger. The ring popped out from under Adam's shirt to dangle in front of his face.

Wolfie licked his yellow teeth. 'I knew I could smell g-gold. I've got a nose for it, see!'

'You keep your stinking hands off!' Adam tried to snatch the ring back.

Wolfie laughed, snapped the chain and fisted the ring. He was older and stronger and he fended Adam off easily, dangling the ring in front of him just out of reach.

'Now maybe you'll see why old Wolfie's g-going

places in life,' Wolfie said. 'Now maybe you'll l-listen, just like everyone else will soon have to l-listen to me. Because I'm going to be rich. And when I am, no one's going to dare say I'm t-tongue tied no more – '

'Leave him alone!' A voice echoed out of the shadows suddenly.

Wolfie froze. To hit and to run at the slightest hint of trouble was his way. He pulled back quickly, hovering on the edge of flight as he looked to see who had spoken.

Adam saw his chance and took it. He snatched back the ring, twisted away sharply and almost broke free. Wolfie slammed him back against the wall and held him there.

'Help!' Adam gasped. '*Please!* I'm being –'

The cold blade of Wolfie's knife touched his throat, silencing him.

'I said – let him go!' the voice said.

Adam swivelled his eyes to see who was speaking and his relief turned quickly to disbelief when he saw Jade van Helsen standing in the narrows of the alley. Wolfie had seen her too. He realised she was alone and his eyes disappeared into famished little strips.

'Stay out of this, g-girlie!'

She stood her ground. 'I won't wait much longer.'

'Sssss ... ' The fury escaped between Wolfie's lips. He glared at her. 'I suppose you're going to make me, are you my p-pretty?'

The others laughed.

'I am not *your* anything,' she said calmly. 'Now, do as I say or you'll be sorry.'

This was too much for Wolfie. He shoved Adam at the others, told them to hold him and stepped out into the middle of the alley to face her.

'Run!' Adam called out to her. 'Go for help!'

If Wolfie had expected her to do just that he was disappointed. She didn't move. He hesitated, frowning. It seemed she wasn't playing the game right at all. Suddenly there was uncertainty in his eyes. He glanced over his shoulder as if he expected to see a whole company of the city guard behind him. But she was alone. The others were watching him. He was beginning to lose face and he knew it.

'Well, well, a reg'lar little f-fire-cat, hey?' he said. His lips peeled back in a leer and he licked his teeth. 'I like girls with a bit of spirit. How about you giving me a k-kiss, girlie ... '

Her chin came up slightly as she dared Wolfie to take another step.

'You touch me and you'll answer to Abner Heems,' she said quietly.

'The *p-preacher*?' Wolfie said, taken aback. 'What's the p-preacher got to do with this?'

'You'll soon find out,' she answered him.

Wolfie shifted uneasily. He looked her up and down. 'You're *bluffen* it, girlie!' he said. 'You don't know the *p-preacher*.'

'Are you fool enough to find out?' the girl asked.

Wolfie glanced at the others.

'We don't want no trouble with the preacher, Wolfie,' one said.

'He'll slit our throats for sure,' the other agreed.

Wolfie hesitated, hovering on the edge of a decision. Then a startling change came over him.

'We was just having a bit of f-fun, that's all. We never meant nothing by it,' he said. The knife disappeared into his belt and he held up his hands. 'See, I'm not g-going to hurt no one – *honest*.' He turned on the others with a snarl. 'Let him go!'

They jumped and let Adam go as if he had suddenly become too hot to handle. Adam didn't hesitate. He pushed past them and quick-walked up the alley. Wolfie glared at him. For a moment Adam was sure he would change his mind, but to his amazement Wolfie just stepped meekly aside and let him go.

'Just keep walking,' Jade said when Adam was close enough to hear. 'Don't stop. Don't look back. And whatever you do, *don't* run until I tell you.'

He nodded.

Jade van Helsen left Wolfie with one final warning. 'If you speak of this to anyone, I will tell the preacher you threatened and insulted me and then you'll be sorry you weren't born a *dog*. Do you understand?'

Wolfie nodded quickly. He understood all right and the fear showed clearly in his eyes.

They walked side by side down the alleyway and turned the corner on to the waterfront.

'*Now* we run!' she said.

And suddenly they were both running. The girl light-ly, her skirt hitched up, her cap blown off and her long, dark hair streaming out behind. Adam followed her lead as she dodged through the crowds and turned up between the houses and into the streets towards the Jordaan that lay beyond.

9. The *Draco*

'I was ... just ... getting on top of them ... ' Adam panted as he patched the rags of his breath together.

'I could see that,' Jade van Helsen answered him with no hint of a smile.

She had led the way through the narrow streets, past a printing shop and a tavern, through the smoke of an alley to a blacksmith's forge where they had ducked behind an old haycart to catch their breath as they waited to see if Wolfie was following them.

Adam looked at the ring and the broken chain.

'It's lucky for you that chain was all he broke,' she said and took the chain. 'I saw them coming – which is more than you did, Adam Windjammer.' She bent the torn links back into shape between her teeth. 'You should be more careful down here – someone could rob you.' She held out her hand. 'Give me the ring!'

Adam hesitated, reluctant to let it go. 'How did you make him do that?' he asked. 'Let me go, I mean.'

She didn't answer. Instead she reached out and took the ring. She glanced briefly at the mark of the House of Windjammer before threading it back on to the chain and handing it back. Adam was surprised to see she had mended the links and he quickly slipped it back around his neck.

'He listened to you,' he tried again. 'They *all* listened to you.'

'Wolfie's a cheap cut-purse, that's all,' she answered him as if it was of little importance. 'There's a lot worse than him down on the waterfront.'

'The preacher for instance?'

She shrugged, then nodded.

'And how do *you* know him?' Adam asked.

'You learn things if you keep your ears and eyes open,' she said. 'Maybe you should try it some time. Maybe then you'd have seen them coming.'

'I'll remember that next time,' Adam said.

She looked at him, a wisp of her hair caught on her lips and cheek. For a moment he thought she was going to say something more, but instead she just turned and walked away. It took a moment for Adam to realise what was happening.

'Hey! Wait! Where are you going?'

'I've lost a tray of cakes,' she said over her shoulder, 'and now I'm late thanks to you, Adam Windjammer.'

Adam followed her along the alley into a small market square and was surprised to see a short, plump woman, holding a basket and a cloak, waiting impatiently for Jade.

'Mistress Jade! Where have you been?' Jade van Helsen's maid greeted her with a mixture of annoyance and relief. She quickly threw the cloak around Jade's shoulders and pulled up the hood to cover her hair. She noticed Adam and began wringing the wicker handle of her basket as if in pain. 'I knew it! Did I not say only trouble would come of this folly, mistress?'

'All is well, Minou,' Jade calmed her affectionately. 'I was delayed, that's all.'

'Then we must return to the house at once!' the maid said. 'Your father will hear of it and then he will know what you have been doing and I will be thrown into a dungeon for allowing it. "Saskia," he will say, "you have betrayed my trust and I will make you pay!"' She was close to tears at the thought. 'Well, I'll have no more of it, do you understand? From now on I will not allow you to go to the waterfront.'

'You *will*, Minou,' Jade used her maid's pet name as she spoke softly but firmly. 'You will let me go because you *love* me.'

Her maidservant remained outwardly opposed, standing stiffly for a few moments longer. She glanced at Adam, then at Jade and relented. 'Hurry then – say your farewells and come quickly,' she said. 'I need to buy vegetables. I will wait for you at Baberon's stall.'

Jade turned to Adam. 'If you cross the market and follow the street on the other side you'll reach a bridge over a canal. That's the Prinsengracht. Turn right and follow the canal – even a *Windjammer* should be able to find his way to the Herengracht from there.'

Adam folded his arms across his chest in an unbudging sort of way.

'What I want to know is,' he said stubbornly, 'why Jade van Helsen – a rich moneylender's daughter – wants to dress up like a poor girl and go sneaking down to the waterfront?'

'That's no concern of yours, Adam Windjammer,' Jade said. 'Now, I must go – Saskia is waiting.'

'Then maybe I'll just have to ask your father next time I see him,' Adam called after her. 'And I'll be sure to tell him the sailors at the waterfront like the dough-cakes you bake too!'

It was the best he could come up with on the spur of the moment and to Adam it sounded weak, but the remark set Jade spinning on her heel. She came back at him – her eyes blazed green fire now.

'If you say anything to my father you'll be sorry!' she hissed.

Only then did he see it. Only then did he realise. Suddenly it was written in the look on her face. It was cemented deep in the beautiful crystal green of her eyes. And with a jolt he realised that this girl – the same person who had just faced down Wolfie and the others – was afraid.

'*Why?*' The question needed no explanation. 'You helped me – maybe I can help you.'

'*You* can't help me, Adam Windjammer!' she said. 'No one can help me unless they have a ship.'

'A *ship*? What do you need a *ship* for?'

'How else am I going to get away from this place?' she said. 'It's all right for you. You're a *boy*. You can do anything you like. Girls are treated differently. We are guarded by maids and kept locked behind doors until someone decides we should be married off.' She shook her head. 'Well, not me! I want to do more than just raise children. I want to see places. I want to sail to the Americas and the Spice Islands in the East. I want to see these places for myself. I want to have adventures and be free. I want to *live* before I die!' She looked at him. '*That's* why I'm looking for a ship.'

'But we *do* have a ship!' Adam said after a moment's thought.

'If you mean the *Draco*?' she said. 'What use is that to me? What use is a ship that's stuck in the mud like a beached whale?'

'Not for long! The *Draco* is nearly built. We'll launch her, just like my father promised, and she'll be the finest ship ever to sail from this port – I swear it!'

She studied his face and then – as if a piece of a puzzle had just fallen into place and she had seen the whole picture for the first time – she seemed to click to some truth.

'You *truly* believe that, don't you?' she said. 'You *truly* believe the *Draco* will sail under the Windjammers' flag.'

'Of course! Why not?'

'*Why not?*' she echoed him in amazement. 'Have you seen your fine ship lately? Have you not heard what's going on there?'

An awkward pause. 'No,' he admitted. 'I was on my way there when I saw you and – '

'Then before you go making promises you can't keep, Adam Windjammer,' she interrupted his explanation. 'There's something I should show you.'

'The men stopped work two weeks ago,' Jade said. 'I know because I overheard my father talking about it.'

'That's not true!' Adam refused to believe it.

'Then look for yourself, Adam Windjammer,' she said. 'Maybe you'll believe your own eyes.'

The *Draco* stood abandoned on her wooden ramp, the dragon on her prow pointing up the slope. Where once fifty men had worked, now only a chill wind blew and a dog scavenged.

They had avoided the waterfront and had cut down between the warehouses, keeping a sharp eye open for any sign of Wolfie and the others as they made their way along the wooden walkway towards the shipyards of the western docks. Adam reached the first of the ladders and started down to the mud of the waterside below. He was almost half-way down before he realised Jade wasn't following.

'Saskia is waiting for me,' she said glancing along the walkway at the maid, who stood fretfully clutching her basket of vegetables. 'I have asked too much of her already. I must go now – I mustn't be seen here with you.'

She drew back from the rail only to reappear a little further along.

'I meant what I said about the preacher, Adam Windjammer,' she said. 'Watch out for him – he's not what he seems.'

With that warning she was gone and Adam was left to descend the ladder alone. His feet sank deep into the mud and ooze as he stepped back and looked up. He caught a glimpse of Jade and her maid moving quickly back the way they had come. Now she had gone all his mistrust of the van Helsens resurfaced. He looked around as if he half expected her to have led him into some sort of trap, but saw only seagulls and the scavenging dog.

Above his head, the bow of the *Draco* curved up towards the grey of the sky. The dragon fixed to her prow looked dull and wooden without the sun. The lines of the *Draco*'s hull were still graceful and proud, but little work had been done since Adam had last stood there and looked up in awe.

The wooden platforms, gantries and rickety workmen's walkways were deserted. Everywhere ropes hung down limply or were looped loosely over wooden pulleys, swinging gently in the breeze. There was something cold and dead about the ship now. Her stillness was stark by comparison with the seething activity on the waterfront nearby. It left Adam feeling strangely uneasy.

He shivered and glanced about anxiously. A ladder led up to one of the wooden platforms above. His gaze climbed the curve of the ship's hull to a line of gunports, then set off again up the uneven, hand-cut rungs of another ladder until he was looking at the ship's rail high above.

Adam placed his foot on the first rung of the ladder. The wooden platform above was distant and small. It hardly seemed big enough to take his weight. Nevertheless, he took a deep breath and began to climb.

Hand over hand, rung by rung, Adam climbed until he reached the top of the first ladder. The platform was loose and he felt it swing gently out from the side of the ship as he stepped on to it. His heart raced as the platform teetered, then moved back to bump against the hull. He breathed his relief and pressed his back against the ship.

From there he could see east along the arm of the inlet as it curved away from the western docks, past the waterfront where the ships were docked, widening as it reached the *Zuiderzee*. He breathed in deeply and noticed clouds gathering on the horizon. The wind had backed into the east. Winter would come soon.

The next ladder drew his gaze right up to the ship's rail. He tested it and found the ladder was securely tied, but it bounced and bent under him as he climbed past the empty gun-ports and up to peer through the scuppers of the bulwark and then over the ship's rail.

The main deck of the *Draco* was deserted. He slithered up and over the rail and stood listening. He could hear the chipping rasp of an adze as someone, somewhere, shaped wood.

'Who's there?' Adam called.

No answer.

He looked around. The decking was only half finished – in some places whole areas were without planking – and as he crossed on the workmen's walkways he could see deep into the darkness of the belly of the ship. The wooden futtocks and staves that formed the ribs and bones of the ship were set in place and bulkheads made a warren around the companionway leading to the decks below. The heel and block were ready to receive her main mast, which – like the foremast and mizzen, rigging and sails – would be raised once the hull had been launched.

'Agh! Quiet your talking, Jacob, and deal them cards!'

Adam could hear men's voices as he picked his way aft. The talk was coming from somewhere at the stern of the ship, and when he climbed the wooden steps to the quarterdeck he saw a sail had been cut and stretched to form a tented roof over a table where three men now sat playing cards.

Only one of the men looked up as he approached.

'If I've said it once I've said it a score of times,' a growl came from one of them. 'There's no work here no more.'

The man who had spoken was wearing a leather apron over an ancient doublet that had once been brown but was now so faded it had little colour at all. His straggling hair sprouted like greying weeds from under a soft cap and he carried a carpenter's hammer and tools on hooks on his belt.

'More cards, Jacob!' he ordered.

The cards were dealt on to the makeshift table.

'Agh!' the carpenter said, having picked them up and looked at them. He hurled them down in disgust. The dealer laughed and dragged the pile of stuviers across the table towards him.

'Now look what you made me do, boy!' the carpenter said.

Adam could hear the steady chipping of the adze and looked to see another man – the biggest of them all – stripped to the waist, working furiously at a wooden timber with the axe-like tool.

'Are you in charge here?' he called out to the big man. The man acted as if he hadn't heard and continued with his labours. Adam looked to the card players. 'Why aren't you working?'

The men at the table laughed and mimicked him. More cards were dealt.

'Where've you been these past weeks, boy – the New World?' the carpenter said, as he shuffled his dog-eared cards into some sort of order. He studied his cards with obvious distaste. He threw them down in disgust and decided to take out his frustrations on Adam.

'Look, you're losing me money, boy,' he said. 'Why don't you just go back to wherever it is you just came from and leave us alone!'

'I asked you a question,' Adam insisted. 'I want to know where everyone is. I want to know why you're not working.'

'Is that so?' the carpenter said, looking at him with new interest. 'And *who* might you be, my fine friend, coming here demanding to know such things?'

Adam told them and noticed the way the big man paused, adze in hand, at the mention of the Windjammer name. As he looked up Adam saw the scar on the man's face. It cut down from his forehead, turning one eye milky white as it curled away across his cheek, dragging his lips into a lop-sided smile.

'A *Windjammer,* is it?' the carpenter said. 'Fresh from your ivory tower on the Herengracht, hey? You see that, Jacob? The Windjammers are sending boys to do men's work now.'

'No one sent me,' Adam said.

'Then you're a brave fool to come here alone,' the carpenter said. He shot a sidelong glance towards the big man, then fixed Adam with a stony look. 'Go, boy! While you still have the chance. We want no trouble here.'

The big man gripped his adze and looked at Adam threateningly. The scar on his face throbbed an angry purple. It took all of Adam's nerve not to turn and run.

'I warn you, boy,' the carpenter said, 'there's some, like Jacob here,' he nodded at the man sitting next to him, 'who'll respect you because of your father. But not Hobe there – not any longer.'

Adam watched Hobe warily. 'What have I ever done to you?' he asked, sounding much braver than he felt.

'We don't want no trouble, Hobe,' the carpenter said. 'He's only a boy!'

'I've got eyes, haven't I?' the big man called Hobe spoke at last. 'I had a boy too once, remember.'

'I don't understand,' Adam said. 'What's going on?'

'Take a good look around, boy,' the carpenter said after a pause. 'Tell me what you see.'

'I see ... the *Draco*.'

The carpenter shook his head. 'This isn't just a shell of a ship. It's *much* more than that. It's a *promise*, see. A word given and not kept. Your *father's* promise.'

'No man here will deny it,' Jacob spoke up from his place at the table. 'We was all there. We was all at that fine house of yours on the Herengracht that day.'

The carpenter nodded. 'Aye! Your father gave his word to finish this ship and send her in search of them poor, shipwrecked fools. He swore to it and with his word, he said, went the promise of the House of Windjammer.'

Adam nodded. 'I heard him say it too.'

'Hark at that! Even a Windjammer says it's true,' the carpenter said, turning to the others.

Hobe's good eye searched Adam's face. His blind eye seemed to look right through him.

'And what of that promise now?' the carpenter asked. 'What have you Windjammers done but bury the old master's given word in the ground with him while the *Draco* is left to rot?'

'That's not true!' Adam denied it. 'Ask *Gerrit*! Ask my *uncle*!'

'Gerrit? Don't make me laugh! What can a book-keeper do but keep books for his master?' the carpenter said. 'And we all know who's master now. That fool of an uncle of yours – Augustus Windjammer.'

'He hasn't the guts to show his face around here no more,' Jacob said.

The carpenter shook his head. 'And he won't come, neither. Not now the rumour's out that the *Draco* is for sale.'

'*Sell* the *Draco*?' Adam gasped. 'No! It's not true!

We would *never* do *that*.'

'Agh!' the carpenter refused to believe him. 'Just look around you, boy! The truth is plain to see.'

Jacob nodded. 'And us with nothing to show for it but a promise to pay what we're already owed.'

And in that instant, Adam truly understood what it meant to be a Windjammer. He realised then he was part of something much bigger than he had ever imagined: part of all that he saw around him and had seen down at the waterfront, just as surely as if he had been chosen for the task, long ago at the very beginning of time.

'Aye, there's a look on your face that says you see the truth of it now,' the carpenter said, turning back to his cards.

After a long pause, Hobe spat on his huge hands. He raised his adze and went back to shaping the timber without a word. Adam watched the curved blade rise and fall. His mind worked only very slowly, but gradually he gathered his wits. He cast around for something to say and his thoughts focused on one man – Augustus Windjammer.

'I'll talk to my uncle,' he said. 'I'll *make* him come here and tell you the truth. The Windjammers would never sell the *Draco*. *Never* – I swear it!'

'You'll forgive us for not believing you,' the carpenter said, sweeping up the cards as Jacob dealt. 'We've had a bellyful of the Windjammers and their promises.'

Adam watched the carpenter as he fanned out the cards in his hand and shuffled them into some sort of order.

'Hobe's different, mind you,' the carpenter went on, without looking up. 'He's sworn to finish the work no matter what. He knows it's hopeless, but what else can he do? His son sailed with the *Sirius*, see.' He slapped down his cards one at a time. 'A boy your age, I'd say. All the family Hobe's got left. But then why should you trouble about such matters? Why would the Windjammers care what became of a simple ship's boy?'

10. A Game of Hide and Seek

'They've been looking for you.'

'Mother and G'rit, she means.'

The twins greeted him on his return to the gloom of the house on the Herengracht. Some time before it had begun to rain, and he was wet through.

'And now *he's* here,' Rose said.

'Uncle Augustus, she means,' Viola explained.

'And something's wrong,' they chimed together.

The twins stood side-by-side in the hall by the front door, one on a white square, the other on a black. Two pairs of eyes blinking at him as he closed the front door.

'Where's Mother now?' he asked, slightly unnerved by the way they were staring at him as if he possessed all the fascination for them of a condemned man.

Two hands flashed up and pointed across the hall to the double doors in the wooden panelling.

'At the Long Table?' Adam was surprised.

Two heads nodded.

Adam approached the doors cautiously. He could hear his uncle's voice and it soon became clear he was talking business.

' ... the moneylender is squeezing us, dear sister-in-law,' Augustus Windjammer was saying. 'Did I not

95

warn you he was a dangerous man? Yes, yes. A wolf at the door of this house and he is beginning to bite.'

Adam shooed the twins away, but they came creeping back to watch and listen as he opened the door and stepped inside. His mother was sitting in her place at the far end of the Long Table as Augustus Windjammer paced to and fro waving his handkerchief.

'I fear we must make more sacrifices,' Augustus went on. 'There have been expenses – *so* many expenses ... ' He paused when he noticed Adam standing in the doorway. 'I see you have returned at last, nephew.'

'Adam! Where have you been?' His mother went off like gunpowder. 'We have been searching for you – Gerrit is out even now.'

'I've been down to the waterfront,' he said.

'Why did you not tell me?'

'You wouldn't have let me go.'

'And with good reason!' Augustus Windjammer interjected. 'Have you no notion of the people who go there, nephew?'

Adam had now.

'The waterfront is not a safe place,' his uncle said. 'It is full of villains and cut-throats.'

'I have to talk to you, mother.' Adam shot a sidelong glance at his uncle. '*Alone* – it's important.'

'It will have to wait,' she said, angrily. 'We have wasted enough time on you today, and your uncle has come to discuss important matters of business.'

'Has he told you about the *Draco* yet, Mother?'

'The *Draco*?' The name left Augustus Windjammer's lips in a hiss of breath. 'What about it?' He clutched his handkerchief to his mouth and took several steps back into the shadows around the edges of the room.

'And what have you heard about the *Draco*, Adam?' his mother asked after a pause.

'The men have stopped work, Mother,' he said. 'The *Draco*'s just rotting in the mud.'

'Is that all?' Augustus said stepping forward, dabbing at his brow with a look of some relief. 'I have already explained the delay to your dear mother. It is only a temporary measure.'

'He's lying, Mother!' Adam said. 'He's going to sell the *Draco*.'

'How dare you!' Augustus Windjammer spluttered, his chins wobbling.

'Ask him, Mother!' Adam insisted. 'I want to hear him say it's not true.'

'I will have no more of this impertinence!' Augustus said, striding towards the door only to find Adam blocking his way. He gave Adam a withering look. 'I suggest, dear sister-in-law, that you discipline this boy with a thrashing before he becomes too unruly to handle –'

'Is it true, Augustus?' Mary Windjammer interrupted him.

'Surely you do not believe him?' Augustus started.

'I want the truth!' Mary Windjammer slapped the flat of her hand down on the table.

'I was about to tell you!' Augustus blurted, clearly shocked. He clutched his handkerchief to his chest and retreated once more. 'Yes, yes – this very day.' He recovered a little of his composure. 'I have not even spoken of it to Gerrit, but I can give a good account of myself. I think I can secure the best price considering the state of the ship. With that money we will be able to pay that devil of a moneylender.'

Adam saw the dangerous look on his mother's face. 'Did I not say,' she went on quietly, 'I was to be consulted on all important matters of business?'

'But I did not wish to worry you until I had more certain news, dear sister-in-law,' Augustus explained. 'Women are the fairer sex – quite unsuited to the cut and thrust of the shipping business ... '

'Enough!' Mary Windjammer came to her feet suddenly, her fury plain to see. 'I am not a young girl to be bullied and patronised!'

'But you do not understand,' Augustus yelped, dabbing at the sweat that had appeared on his top lip. 'Hugo van Helsen will not wait. He is bleeding us dry with his rates of interest. I decided something had to be done to get him off our backs. Yes, yes, I had only the House of Windjammer's best interests at heart.'

'I have begun to wonder recently if it is your heart you care most about or your *stomach*,' Adam's mother said. 'Perhaps if you had spent a little less time eating and drinking and a little more time working over the past weeks things might have turned out better.' She looked to Adam. 'I want to know the moment Gerrit returns. Tell him to come to the Long Table and bring all the month's ledgers!'

'The *ledgers*?' Augustus gasped.

Mary Windjammer paused. She took a long look at Augustus and came to a sudden conclusion. 'There's *more*, isn't there, Augustus? Something you have not yet told us. Something in those ledgers.'

Augustus Windjammer decided he needed a drink and helped himself to some brandy from among the bottles on the table nearby. He drained one glass, poured himself another and glared at Adam as if it was all his fault. He swallowed the spirit at a gulp, slammed down the glass and turned to face them.

'It's true – perhaps I should have listened to Gerrit and not have ordered so many bales of fine black damask and Flemish lace,' he admitted. 'They are expensive luxuries, it's true. But how was I to know everyone would be spending their money on tulips this year? These flowers are the fashion and there is little money for anything else. Colour is the new black, they say! I mean, have you ever heard anything more ridiculous?'

'Yes, I believe I just have,' Mary Windjammer said, slumping back into her chair. She shook her head and spoke her thoughts aloud. 'I must have been a fool to trust him.'

But there was more bad news to come. Gerrit brought it with him, hurrying breathlessly back from the New Market, where he had been looking for Adam, and the civic weighing house known as the *Waag*. His irritation with Adam was soon forgotten, however, when he presented the letter that had been thrust into his hand.

'I was waylaid by a group of merchants, mistress,' Gerrit said. 'They handed me this letter.'

Mary Windjammer read it, then handed it to Augustus without a word. The letter was passed to Adam who read it without fully understanding the implications of the neatly written words. It was sealed on the bottom with wax the colour of blood.

'It is a notice from the Council of Merchants,' Gerrit explained when Adam asked what it meant. 'They are calling on the House of Windjammer to account for the money we owe. It seems an application has been lodged by Hugo van Helsen claiming the Windjammer Trading Company can no longer pay what it owes and now the rumour that this House is close to ruin is spreading through the city like the plague.'

'Then we must put a stop to it,' Mary Windjammer said. 'We have friends on that council, do we not? Bartholomew de Leiden will support us surely?'

'Even the oldest friends of this House fear the banker now,' Gerrit said. 'Hugo van Helsen has grown powerful and the money he lends is like life-blood to many merchants. And I have heard ... '

Here he paused as if what had been said was too painful for him to reveal.

'Go on!' Mary Windjammer prompted him.

He sighed and shook his head. 'I have even heard that some are now saying the House of Windjammer is little more than a House of Cards.' His disbelief was clear. 'Others are saying we are a ship of fools *without* a ship that will sail! *All* now seem to agree it will not be long before we run out of money and are ruined.'

Another long pause.

'Then we have little choice but to raise the money quickly,' Adam's mother spoke at last, sounding as if a great weight had descended on her. 'We could sell this house – it would fetch at least ten thousand golden florins.'

'But we need more – much more!' Augustus said. 'That is why we *must* sell the *Draco*!'

'No!' Adam stepped forward. 'We *can't* sell the *Draco*! We have to keep my father's word.'

'My brother was a fool to saddle us with promises we cannot keep,' Augustus said.

Adam took a step towards him, his fists balled.

Augustus stepped back in alarm, flapping his handkerchief in feeble defence. 'There *is* another way,' he yelped. 'A way to keep the *Draco* and this house *and* my brother's foolish promises.' He turned to Adam's mother. 'I think you know what it is, dear sister-in-law. Do you not?'

There was a long pause before she nodded.

But what it was, neither would say.

'Poor Adam,' his cousin Angelica said. Then she said it again, repeating the word *poor* twice just to be sure he knew how sorry she felt for him.

'Yes, *poor* Adam,' Willem agreed.

Angelica turned around in a sweep of her silk skirts. She looked down at the hem of her dress and was exasperated to see it was getting dirty. She wrinkled her nose at the layers of dust that had settled over everything in the hall.

'I only asked,' Adam said, irritated now. 'I only wanted to know if you had heard anything, that's all.'

He had come to hate these Sunday visits by his cousins more and more. Not just because Willem and Angelica were any more prissy and stupid than they had always been, but because he had the feeling that now the only reason they came was out of pity.

Three days had passed since Augustus Windjammer had hinted at a plan. Three agonising days of waiting – with only Gerrit and his lessons in the right and the wrong ways to keep good ledgers to occupy him – and Adam was now desperate to know what was going on. He would do anything to find out – even be nice to Willem and Angelica for the afternoon.

'*Everyone's* talking about it,' said Willem, managing

to sound just like his father, Augustus. 'Yes, yes! Everyone knows.'

'Knows *what*?' Adam asked.

'Knows how *poor* you are, of course,' Willem said. 'I mean – you don't even have servants any more.'

Angelica agreed. 'Our house may not be as big as this old place,' she said, tartly, 'but at least *we* have servants.'

Adam had to bite his lip.

'Poor Adam,' Willem took it up again.

'Yes, *poor* Adam,' Angelica said. 'Mam-ma says *Pap-pa says* you will lose everything soon – even this dirty, old house.'

'I don't care what *Pap-pa* says!' Adam said, losing patience.

'Then you won't care what *else* he said,' Angelica said, becoming irritatingly coy about what she knew until he had said *please*.

She moved closer and lowered her voice as if she was about to impart some sworn secret. 'Mam-ma says Pap-pa says there is another way to save the House of Windjammer.'

'*How?*' Adam asked through gritted teeth.

Angelica glanced about as if she half expected Adam's mother to be listening. 'An alliance by *marriage*, of course.'

Adam blinked at her. 'What's that supposed to mean?'

'You know – ' Willem explained helpfully, 'marrying someone for *money*.'

'Stop talking in riddles!' Adam said. 'If you know something then tell me!'

Angelica moved closer again. 'Mam-ma said Pap-pa

told your mother that she had no choice,' she said and then sighed dramatically as if she alone could understand such important matters. 'I suppose your mother would have married again some time.'

'*My* mother? Marry *again*? Why? Who?' Adam was as shocked at the thought as he was surprised.

'It's obvious, isn't it?' Angelica said.

'Yes, yes, quite obvious,' Willem agreed.

Not to Adam.

Angelica rolled her eyes as if to say he was being incredibly stupid.

'The moneylender, of course!' she explained. 'Pap-pa told Mam-ma that someone could become very rich marrying into a banking family.'

Adam stared at her in utter astonishment. 'Do you mean ... ? No!' He shook his head violently. 'She would never marry Hugo van Helsen!'

'Why not?' Angelica asked. 'Mam-ma says his wife died a long time ago. Mam-ma says that makes him a widower – and a very rich one at that. I think Pap-pa thinks your mother should marry the moneylender and save the House of Windjammer.'

'I'm not so sure of that,' Willem said. 'I heard Pap-pa asking about the moneylender's daughter.'

Angelica rounded on her brother. 'What's so special about *her*?'

'Pap-pa said it was a daughter's duty to marry well,' Willem defended himself.

'Did not!' 'Did!' 'Did not!' Adam looked from face to face as an argument started and went on.

'Well, Pap-pa doesn't know what he's talking about,' Angelica said. 'Mam-ma says Jade van Helsen is a *strange* girl – not pretty at all.'

'That's enough!' Adam interrupted. But it was more than just anger that made him shout at them now. For a reason he couldn't explain he didn't like them talking about Jade like that. 'You don't even know her.'

Angelica and Willem looked at him in surprise.

'And *you* do, I suppose?' Angelica asked, fixing him with a searching look.

Adam shrugged. 'I don't care what *Mam-ma* says *Pap-pa* says any more,' he said. '*I* say no one is going to marry *anyone* – especially not Hugo van Helsen! So you can tell *Mam-ma* that and then she can tell *Pap-pa*, and then they can both mind their own business and we'll all be happy.'

Angelica sighed. Willem sighed. They both gave him a *you'll-see-we're-right-soon-enough* sort of look, then Willem decided they should play hide and seek.

'Yes, it'll be wonderfully spooky playing in this old house,' Angelica agreed, forgetting everything that had just been said.

Before Adam knew it, the twins had been called down to play. They giggled with delight at being included in something so grown up. Angelica decided Willem would be *it* and then ordered everyone to go off to hide. Willem closed his eyes and started counting to a hundred.

The others vanished upstairs. Willem stood counting, with his eyes screwed up tightly. Adam watched him, surprised to find himself envying this plump, velvet-suited, curly-haired cousin of his. Willem might be stupid, but at least he was happy.

The count was fast approaching one hundred when Adam decided to shake his cousins off for a while. He needed time to think about what they had just said. He slipped quietly in through the nearest door and closed it behind him.

'Coming – ready or not!' Willem's shouts echoed around the hall as he went pounding away up the stairs.

Adam turned, then stood very still. Of all the rooms he could have chosen, he had unintentionally chosen the library. For as long as he could remember this had been a place not to be disturbed. A place of business. His father's place and now, he supposed, Gerrit's.

Through the open door to Adam's right he could see into the ledger-room. It was a smaller room, lined with leather-bound ledgers. Two equally proportioned windows overlooked the small courtyard garden at the back of the house. Gerrit's desk and chair faced a door leading directly on to the street that ran down the north side of the house. Adam could see the doorstep was worn smooth by the feet of the traders and merchants who had come to do business over the years with the House of Windjammer.

He relaxed a little. Gerrit was out. The place was his.

The stained glass of the library window patterned the desk with coloured light. The room smelled of dust and leather and of the soot gone cold in the grate. The sounds of the street outside reached in to him. Inside, the stillness of the room was almost dreamlike.

Somewhere, far away, he could hear laughter echoing through the caverns and hollows of the house. 'Found you! Found you!' Willem's voice was full of delight. 'Oh, you beast, Will!' Angelica squealed her disappointment. But the voices seemed distant and unreal, like voices from another place and time.

Adam moved away from the door, touching things as

he went deeper into the library: running his finger over the lid of his father's sea chest, the high back of a chair, a book of maps by Mercator. He passed through the patterns of coloured light and his father's ghostly image swam out of the shadows around the edges of the room.

Adam was drawn towards the portrait hanging on the wall. His father gazed down at him, posed and stiff in his fine clothes. One hand was resting on the great globe symbol of the House of Windjammer, in the other he held out a parchment. In the distance behind him the ships of the Windjammers' doomed fleet sailed by eternally.

'You would know what to do, father,' Adam spoke his thoughts into the hush of the room. 'You always did. You were always so strong. You knew *everything*.' A feeling of hopelessness swamped him. 'How can I be like you? How can *I* be the head of the House of Windjammer?'

The answer, if there was one, remained painted on his father's lips.

Adam looked at the desk. The inkpot, quill pens and clay tobacco pipes were all exactly as his father had left them. He picked up one of the pipes and puffed at it smokelessly, tasting the bitter residue of burnt tobacco. An hourglass caught his eye. It had not been turned and the sand had run down into the bottom. Time, like the room itself, had stood still.

Suddenly the whole weight of the house above seemed to be resting on that room. The deadness of the place was suffocating. It left Adam breathless, stifled. He put down the pipe and backed away from the desk, only to return to it as a sudden impulse made him turn the hourglass on its head. The sand began to stream down through the nipped waist between the two glass chambers. He watched it pile up, slip and begin to pile up again. The movement brought life back to the heart of the House of Windjammer.

'He must be downstairs!' Willem was calling to his sister. 'We've looked everywhere else.'

'Adam! This isn't fair!' Angelica's voice echoed stubbornly in the high air of the hall.

By the sound of it, they had found the twins and all now were engaged in the hunt for him. Adam knew it was only a matter of time before they stumbled into the library, and he stepped back into the shadows around the edge of the room, camouflaging himself among the shifting patterns of coloured light in the hope that they would only give the room the briefest of looks. And it was while he was standing there, wishing they would leave him alone, that Gerrit returned.

Adam heard the sound of the footsteps as they passed close by under the window in the street outside. Quick and clipped, they were unmistakable. He knew it was Gerrit even before the key rasped in the lock of the side door. There was no time to escape. A moment later the door had opened and Gerrit had stepped in to the ledger-room.

At first Adam couldn't see Gerrit from where he was standing. He only heard the door in to the street being closed and locked, then the jangle of a bunch of keys as Gerrit hooked them back on his belt. After that, nothing happened for what seemed an age.

Adam shifted along the wall. He was hoping to escape back into the hall the way he had come, but he stopped when Gerrit came into view. The clerk was by his desk in the ledger-room, his hat still clutched in his hands, standing quite still as if he had sensed some unseen presence around him.

Gerrit moved at last, placing his hat carefully on his desk before reaching into the pocket of his long coat to pull something out. From where he was now standing, Adam could see something made of leather. But this thing – whatever it was – seemed to have a dramatic effect on the little man. His hands shook visibly as he held it, staring at it as if it filled him with unspeakable horror. Then he glanced about – a look of pure guilt on his face – lifted the hat and quickly hid this hated thing from sight under the brim.

Gerrit seemed relieved now, but his relief was only temporary. He began to pace the length of the ledger-room floor from the desk to the door and back again, wringing his hands and washing them in the air as if the stains on his fingers weren't black ink but red blood.

'I cannot go on!' Gerrit muttered. 'I must tell the mistress.'

Gerrit paused when he reached his desk and crumpled into his chair. He sat for a moment, then leaned back and reached into the pocket of his coat again. This time he pulled out a small velvet bag.

Adam heard Gerrit's breath quicken with the expectation. He saw those long fingers tremble as Gerrit fumbled with the drawstring and pulled open the bag.

'There you are, my beauty,' Gerrit said, his voice sounding as brittle as glass.

His whole body seemed to be trembling as he looked into the bag. Then a moment later he started guiltily and pulled the drawstring tight once more. He put the bag back in his pocket, thought for a moment, then reached for a leather-bound book. Another moment of indecision passed before he snatched a quill from the rack, sharpened it with a thin blade and dipped the nib into the pot of ink on his desk. The words scratched at the ear as he began writing, the quill flying without pause across the page.

Adam took another step towards the door into the hall, but in the quiet of the library even the slightest noise sounded disproportionately loud. A floorboard creaked under his foot. The scratch of Gerrit's pen stopped abruptly.

The clerk looked up, listened, then came to his feet with a scrape of his chair. Adam had just enough time to duck down behind the big sea-chest as Gerrit hurried out of the ledger-room into the library and looked around. It was only as Adam crouched behind the chest, hoping he wouldn't be discovered, that he noticed the sand streaming down in the hourglass.

Gerrit stood peering into the layers of coloured light that shifted with the clouds to trick the eye. Adam knew he would see the hourglass sooner or later and a dozen unbelievable excuses ran through his mind in quick succession. He had just made up his mind to stand up and declare himself, when Angelica came to his rescue.

'We *know* you're in there!' Angelica said as the latch of the library door rattled. The door flew open and she led the others in from the hall.

'What is the meaning of this, Miss Angelica!' Gerrit said, turning on his heel to face them. 'Is the house on fire? Have the Spanish attacked? Why are you looking for me?'

'You?' Angelica sounded unimpressed. 'Why should we be looking for *you*? You're not playing – are you?'

'*Playing?*' Gerrit sounded more confused than ever.

'In our game, of course,' Angelica said and rolled her eyes in that way of hers. '*Hide and seek,*' she explained as if he was being incredibly stupid. She craned her neck and looked around the library. 'But Adam's in here – and that's cheating.'

Gerrit spun around several times, but saw no one and told them so. 'I have been here all afternoon,' he lied, 'and I assure you I have not seen Master Adam.'

Angelica remained unconvinced, and it was while Gerrit was reminding her that the library and ledger-room were out of bounds at all times that Adam took his opportunity and crawled, unseen, into the ledger room. His hopes of slipping out of the side door and escaping into the street were dashed, however, the moment he remembered Gerrit had locked the door.

Trapped, he looked around for a place to hide and, such was his hurry to get behind the door, he knocked Gerrit's hat to the floor as he slipped past the desk. He snatched it up and was about to put it back again when he saw something lying on the floor.

For the briefest of moments Adam thought he had made a mistake, then his surprise quickly turned to horror as he picked it up. His heart raced even faster as he stared at it in disbelief. It was like the shed skin of some monstrous face. A mask made out of leather and sewn on to a skullcap that would have covered Gerrit's hair and ears. Holes had been cut in it to form the eyes and mouth, and it had all been carefully stitched together. It looked like the hood a murderer might wear.

The door into the hall thumped closed as Gerrit managed to shoo Angelica and the others out. Adam flung the mask down on the desk and covered it again with the hat. He slipped behind the door and pressed his back against the wall, listening as Gerrit made a thorough search of the library just in case.

Adam heard a hiss of surprise and pressed his eye close to the crack between the door and the doorjamb. He could just see Gerrit standing staring at the hour-glass. The clerk reached out to touch it – as if he couldn't quite believe his own eyes – and pulled back his hand when he found it was no illusion.

'It's a sign!' Gerrit gasped, glancing up at the portrait of Hercules Windjammer. 'A warning! Yes! A message from the grave.' He stepped back and looked around wildly. 'He's telling me not to wait. He's telling me time is running out.'

Gerrit moved quickly now. All else was forgotten as he hurried back into the ledger-room and dragged the desk to one side. It jarred and juddered as he slid it across the floor. Adam peered cautiously around from behind the door and he saw Gerrit kneeling on the floor, prising at the floorboards with his long fingers. One board came up and then another, until a square hole appeared in the floor. Gerrit quickly reached in and pulled out a money casket bound in iron. With trembling fingers he searched out the key from those in the bunch on his belt and opened the lid.

Gerrit's hand dipped in five times, each time pulling out a bulging leather bag. These he placed in line on the desk, before replacing the empty casket and the floorboards. Adam ducked back behind the door as Gerrit stood up and pulled the desk back into position. He heard the little man's breath catch in his throat and by the time he dared another look, Gerrit was intent on undoing the drawstring around the neck of one of the bags.

The neck of the bag came open and the contents spilled on to the flat of the desk. Gold coins smacked down on to the wood. The coins glinted as they caught the light, some spinning with a fizzing sound until Gerrit's hand passed over them and drew them together into a mass. Some were newly minted guilders with the marks of the Northern Provinces; others were older florins, roughly shaped. With nimble fingers, Gerrit counted the coins back into the bag, drew the string tight about the neck once more, and reached for the next.

Adam watched Gerrit count the contents of all five before tying each securely to his belt and buttoning his coat to cover them. The last of the bags disappeared and Gerrit reached for his hat. As Adam dodged back again behind the door he just caught a glimpse of the mask in Gerrit's hand. Then the bunch of keys jangled and the door was being unlocked.

Briefly the sounds of the street burst in before Gerrit closed and locked the door after him. Adam listened to the footsteps fade, waiting just long enough to be sure he wasn't coming back, then he crept out of hiding and fled back through the library.

'Found you!' Angelica said as he stepped back into the hall.

11. Gerrit

Adam came awake suddenly. For a moment he lay on his back with the sheets crumpled around him, staring up into the thick folds of the darkness that hung with the curtains from the four posts of his bed.

At first he wasn't sure what had woken him. He just lay in the dark listening. In the quiet, the house seemed alive with brittle sounds of night. The slow creak and tick of the timbers as they expanded or contracted. The distant rattle-tap of a loose window-pane. Somewhere in the walls he heard a rat drop, plump and heavy, and begin to scratch. Then he heard the latch of his bedroom door click open.

Adam sat bolt upright in bed, his heart attacking his ribs as he strained his ears. The silence hummed, filled with half-imagined shuffling sounds. He heard the door being closed quietly. There was no mistaking it now – someone was in his room.

The memory of the mask gripped him, sending a shiver through his body that left the flesh crawling on his back and neck. He eased his legs out from under the blankets, shifting to the side of the bed furthest from the door, and slipped out through the curtain. His feet made a soft sound as he landed, crouching, ready for the attack. He held his breath, trying to make out where it would come from, and wished he had a light. But the candle and the tinderbox to light it were on the table on the other side of his bed. Only the moonlight seeped in around the edges of the heavy curtains drawn across the window. Around him was a gulf of darkness.

'Adam!' a breathless whisper clawed out of the darkness.

Adam had to force back the gasp that threatened to escape his lips. He could hear the soft swish of the curtain being pulled back on the other side of his bed and decided he had to do something, and do it fast. He made up his mind. He took several deep breaths and leapt from his hiding-place.

A roaring filled his ears as the air rushed past him. In several bounding steps Adam crossed the room, reached the window and tore the curtains open. He heard a yelp of surprise, quickly followed by a series of screams. Then the moonlight flooded in, rolling back the darkness with its cold green light, and he saw them.

'*You!*' he gasped.

The twins stood side by side: their hair tangled, their nightdresses crumpled. They blinked at him, owl-eyed with fright and lost sleep.

'We saw him,' Rose managed to speak at last.

'From our window, she means,' Viola quickly explained.

'Digging in the garden.'

'In the dark.'

'Burying something,' they chimed together.

Adam lit a candle and held it up. His relief quickly turned to irritation as he looked at them.

'What are you talking about?' he snapped. 'No one goes digging in the garden at this time of night.'

But the twins' heads were full of monsters and fairy-tales. Adam knew what was coming next: the usual talk of *kabouters*, *kabalos* and the goblins that were supposed to come out at night and carry off little children to dark holes under the bridges over the canals. Normally he would have told them to stop acting like babies and sent them back to bed, but now he looked into their huge, night-frightened eyes and understood this fear of the dark unknown.

'And I suppose now you want to sleep in my bed?' he said.

Two heads nodded.

He pretended to take pity on them, but the truth was that, just at that moment, Adam didn't want to be alone either. 'Go on then!' he relented. 'But I don't want to hear another sound out of you.'

Rose and Viola slipped into his bed and, taking his threats seriously, they pulled the bedclothes up under their chins and were soon fast asleep. Adam drew the curtains around the bed protectively, wondering why the ring always seemed to weigh so much heavier on the chain around his neck when they were near.

Sleep was lost to Adam now, however. He put the candle on the mantelpiece, pulled a chair up to the fire-place and stirred brightness into the embers in the grate. He warmed his hands. One thought after another chased through his mind, leaving him feeling slightly breathless. The memory of the mask was all the more vivid now. He tried to push it to the back of his mind, only to find masked faces haunting every shadow. He wondered how Gerrit had so much money, when the Windjammers now had none. And he was still struggling to make sense of it all when he heard the sound of footsteps.

Somewhere deep in the heart of the house a door opened and closed. The footsteps were clipped and quick: Gerrit's footsteps smacking and snickering on the tiles of the hall far below – every sound magnified by the quiet.

Adam crossed quickly to his bedroom door. He listened. The footsteps grew louder, climbing through the turns of the stairs. He opened the door just far enough to see out along the passage and soon a light appeared, growing steadily brighter until at last Gerrit rose out of the inkwell of the stairs, dragging his shadow behind him like a monstrous burden.

Gerrit held a lantern up to light his way, muttering to himself as he moved swiftly on along the passage and started up the next flight of stairs, heading for his bedroom in the servants' quarters. The footsteps faded until at last Adam heard a door open and close somewhere high in the attic of the house. Then all was silent again.

Adam closed the door and was drawn back to the light of the candle. His suspicions of Gerrit only deepened as he wondered what the clerk had been doing out so late. Uncomfortable thoughts filled his head, lodging at the front of his mind one after the other like unwelcome guests, until he was left in no doubt that Gerrit could no longer be trusted.

Adam glanced towards the bed where his sisters lay sleeping. He realised they would need protection if Gerrit was dangerous. He took the precaution of angling the chair so it faced the door and resumed his vigil – wondering what Gerrit might do next.

Some time later, Rose stirred and called out in her

sleep. Viola murmured in agreement. They settled. Then all was quiet again but the house.

'Wake up! Master Adam! Wake up!'

Adam came awake with a start and saw Gerrit leaning over him, shaking him by the shoulder.

Adam was on his feet in a moment, knocking the chair back into the fireplace as he backed away. Still half asleep, he blinked at Gerrit with a mixture of terror and surprise.

Such was his excitement, Gerrit didn't appear to notice that Adam had slept the night in the chair.

'Do you not hear the bells, Master Adam?' Gerrit asked. 'There's no time to waste and business to be done.' He turned quickly on his heel. 'We are being called – the bells! The *bells*!'

He hurried across the room, threw open the window, and a tumult of sound rushed in on a blast of cold air that took Adam's breath away.

'The Muscovy Company's fleet has returned at last,' Gerrit said, taking deep breaths of fresh air. He sounded elated. 'Isn't it a wonderful day? Yes! I think our fortunes are about to change for the better.' He turned again and hurried to the door without noticing Rose and Viola watching him through the curtains around the bed. 'There's no time to waste. I will hail a boat at once.' He disappeared into the passage, heading for the stairs. 'Dress in your best apparel, Master Adam!' his voice echoed back along the passage. 'All men of business must look the part.'

Adam sat in the bow of the boat and watched Gerrit over the curve of the boatman's shoulder. The oars dipped and rose and dipped again. The water swirled gently in ripples as the dark oiliness of the canal slid under them, oozing a sewer stink.

Gerrit had a ledger and a small, wooden writing-box gripped under one arm. The box contained his quills and inks. He was dressed in his usual black, but he was wearing his best hat and coat, and he now sat in the stern of the boat showing all the impatience of someone who wanted to be somewhere urgently.

'Everyone's always in a hurry when the fleet's in,' the boatman grumbled as he strained at the oars. 'The traffic here is something terrible. Mr van *this*, Mrs van *that* – they all want to be somewhere.'

'There's a silver piece in it for you if you pull harder!' Gerrit urged him on relentlessly. 'We must be about our business at the waterfront.'

'I get quite a few merchants in my boat,' the boatman said, cheering up considerably. 'Mind you, most of them don't favour me so well. It's them rich explorers that tip the best. I had that Abel Tasman in my boat once, you know?'

Adam ignored the boatman and watched Gerrit. He had never seen the clerk acting like this before. There was an air of excitement and anticipation about him that bordered on euphoria. It was as if he had succeeded in something and could now go about his business with renewed energy and vigour. The arrival of this great fleet seemed to have come just at the right moment. However, all this new enthusiasm left Adam feeling more uncomfortable than ever and he glanced back longingly at the house they had just left. The windows were ablaze with the morning light. The house appeared to be on fire, burning up from the inside. He remembered the sailor's saying: *red sky in the morning, sailor's warning*. The omens seemed all bad.

Adam had been made to wear the white shirt, black fustian coat and trousers in the style of the merchant businessman. He had tamed his hair and tied it back behind his head with a leather thong and he had break-fasted on dough bread, Gouda cheese and milk.

'I have to talk to you, Mother,' he had tried to speak to her.

But Gerrit had been impatient to leave. Already a boat was waiting on the Herengracht and the boatman had been paid to take them to the waterfront.

'Time and tides wait for no man, Master Adam,' Gerrit had said.

'You can tell me all about it later, Adam,' his moth-er had said and had kissed him goodbye in a sad sort of way – almost as if she was bidding farewell to the boyhood she had tried so hard to protect. Now she was sending him off to do man's work.

The boatman's oars dipped and rose and dipped again. The houses slid silently by on either side. Bridges came and went. And with every bump and pull of the oars Adam's sense of foreboding only deepened.

'Mind yourself, lad!' the boatman said ominously when finally they neared the docks.

He edged the boat to a ladder attached to the slime on the wall. The boat rocked as Adam jumped clear and climbed to the top. Gerrit followed close behind.

They walked the rest of the way. Under a blood-red sky the masts had grown into a forest over the roofs. And all the while the bells of the city tolled out.

'We must hurry straight to the spiles,' Gerrit raised his voice to make himself heard, instructing Adam as they walked. 'I want you to stay by my side at all times and be ready to run errands when I ask. And remember, Master Adam, you must *not* go wandering off. The quayside can be dangerous when the fleet is in. Accidents happen and I do not want you hurt on your very first day.'

The warning left Adam cold. He drew his coat around him again and looked up as they passed under the shadow of the Windjammers' great stone warehouse.

On one side, lines of wooden doors opened into the air over the canal known as the Brouwersgracht. On the other, similar lines of doors opened over the quayside where the ships were lined up at the waterfront. Above each door a hoist jutted like the stub end of a cut beam and everywhere hooks hung down, swinging gently on ropes and chains.

Adam had been to the warehouse many times with his father. Then, it had always been full of movement, the air thick with the sound of men's voices singing as they hoisted the goods up to the doors on ropes. He remembered the swing of the cargo nets and the shunt of the barges on the canal side. And he remembered the lines of horse-drawn wagons loading and unloading on the quayside.

'Why aren't the men working?' he asked Gerrit.

'We have had trouble here too,' Gerrit admitted before adding with all his new-found confidence, 'but all will be well soon, Master Adam – trust me!'

Trust Gerrit? That was just it – Adam no longer could.

It was clear that something was very wrong long before

Hugo van Helsen's shadow fell across the flat top of the spile post in front of them.

'But we had an agreement!' Gerrit was saying to the merchants clustered around a ship's manifest spread out on the flat top of one of the great wooden posts that supported the quayside. A hawser led up to the bow of a merchant ship called the *Alkmaar*, tying her tight to land.

Adam stood back a little and watched the men as they argued. He noticed the uneasy looks that passed between the merchants as Gerrit spoke.

'The goods are clearly listed here!' Gerrit tapped the paper urgently. 'Fifty bags of hard-husked grain, twenty barrels of bee's wax, twenty of whale oil, not to mention the quantities of timber and tar I need at the shipyard.'

'My dear Gerrit,' the master of the *Alkmaar* said. 'The agreements of which you speak were made months ago when Hercules Windjammer was in charge of the Windjammer Trading Company. Now he has gone and, well, his brother ... how can I put it?' He searched for the right words and came up with, ' ... Everyone knows Augustus Windjammer is no man of business!'

'Are you saying you do not trust us?' Gerrit sounded grim.

'This is not a matter of *trust*,' one of the other merchants said soothingly. 'We all know *you* are a man of traditional values, Gerrit. There's none more honest and open in all Amsterdam.' He shrugged. '*But* it has been a long voyage. We have many expenses – a crew to pay.' He waved a hand at the ship in a glitter of rings. 'We are just poor merchants struggling to make a crust. Is it *so* unreasonable to ask to be paid in full before we unload the goods?'

'*Before!*' Adam saw the shock on Gerrit's face. 'But surely the usual monthly terms would apply – '

'Gold will do nicely,' the merchant cut in. He inspected the tips of his fingers casually. 'Of course if the House of Windjammer *cannot* pay now –' He spread his arms wide as if to say there were many others who would buy.

Gerrit couldn't agree their terms. And so it went on. After that, wherever Gerrit turned he was shunned and cold-shouldered by the other merchants. Until it became obvious that a shadow had been cast over them and few, if any, wanted to do business with the Windjammer Trading Company now.

'Times are hard,' Gerrit tried hard to explain it away, 'and when times are hard, trust is a commodity as rare as spice.' He sighed and shook his head, much of his new confidence already gone. 'You cannot blame them for being cautious.'

The word struck like a bell, but Adam sensed there was more to it than just caution. He had seen the way the other merchants were looking at them. He had seen them turn away quickly, only to look back again soon afterwards when they thought it was safe. They seemed to know something – something to scare them off.

And then, with timing that made Adam realise his suspicions were right, Hugo van Helsen's shadow fell over the spile post in front of them.

Adam noticed the change almost immediately. Hugo van Helsen came like a chill breath of wind through the merchants on the quayside. The crowd parted before him as he approached with slow, measured steps. He wore a fine suit of velvet and satin, a fur-lined cape, a wide-brimmed hat trailing a white feather, and he was carrying a walking cane with a silver handle. It was plain to see the impression this outward show of wealth made on the merchants around him.

Adam's heart sank as he watched him come.

'I see the House of Windjammer still has not given up – despite all its troubles, hey Goltz?' Hugo van Helsen said, addressing his remarks to his clerk, who was following attentively close behind. That thin smile tugged at the banker's lips as he looked around. 'But I can't help noticing that trade is *thin*.'

'*Very* thin,' Goltz echoed his master, gripping his wooden writing-box to his chest like a shield.

Gerrit glared at his equal, before turning to Hugo van Helsen with a low bow. 'I am instructing Master Adam in the ways of his father's business,' he said.

'Then I suggest you learn quickly, young Adam Windjammer,' Hugo van Helsen said. 'I fear the Windjammer Trading Company's future will be short at this rate.'

'The Windjammers have traded for a hundred years,' Gerrit pointed out, 'God willing, they will trade for a hundred more.'

'*God* willing?' the banker seemed to find that thought amusing. 'Do you think the fate of the House of Windjammer rests solely in God's hands now?' He turned to those around him. 'Do we bankers matter so little to you?' The merchants laughed. Those pale eyes flicked to Adam. 'And where was this benevolent God when he wrecked your fleet and crippled the Windjammer Trading Company with debts?'

Adam felt Gerrit's steadying hand on his arm.

'We still have the Windjammers' good name,' Gerrit answered him.

'Ah? The famous *honour* of the House of Windjammer,' Hugo van Helsen said. He glanced about him. 'But what can you buy with that here? Tell us what price can you fix on this rare commodity you call *honour*? The price of a tulip? The price of a house? The price of a ship? *Tell* us!'

'There is no price, sir,' Gerrit said. 'For even the richest of men cannot *buy* honour. It can only be earned – as the Windjammers have earned it over many years of honest trading.'

The smile vanished from Hugo van Helsen's face. Gerrit had made a point sharp enough to find a gap between the armour plates of even this banker's skin.

'We shall see,' Hugo van Helsen said. He snapped his fingers impatiently at his clerk. 'The notice, Goltz! *Now!*'

A moment or two passed while Goltz fumbled and juggled with his writing box, until at last he managed to open it and pull out a roll of parchment.

'Give it to the head of the House of Windjammer!' the banker said crisply.

Goltz stepped forward and held out the scroll to Gerrit.

'Not him, fool! *Him!*' Hugo van Helsen hissed, pointing at Adam.

Adam received the rolled-up parchment into his hand without looking at it.

'You will find it all written there,' Hugo van Helsen said, tapping at the paper with the walking cane. 'Or perhaps you should ask your servant to read it?' That smile recovered its position on his lips. 'How things have changed at the House of Windjammer now the tail wags the dog.'

Adam was about to tell him that the only dog he could see around there had been made into a banker's cloak, but again Gerrit gripped his arm.

'It is an unwritten rule of all business, Master Adam, that you must be polite at *all* times,' Gerrit calmed him. He turned to Hugo van Helsen and added in a tone that told everyone he had already guessed what was written there. 'We will read your parchment and let you have our answer.'

Hugo van Helsen seemed mildly irritated not to get a rise out of them in public.

'I suggest you make your appeals to the Council of Merchants,' the banker was curt. 'They meet this very afternoon at the merchants' hall close to the *Waag* to discuss your case.' He raised his voice to be sure all around could hear him clearly. 'Copies of this notice have already been posted on all property belonging to the Windjammers. For I have asked that the Windjammer Trading Company's licence to trade be withdrawn until such time as the House of Windjammer has paid off its debts to me.'

The merchants around him stirred and murmured to one another, and, like ripples on a pond, the news spread out along the waterfront. It was clear that Hugo van Helsen had just confirmed what they had already heard as rumour.

That hint of a smile flitted briefly across Hugo van Helsen's face again as he inclined his head very slightly towards Adam in a polite goodbye. The merchants around him stepped aside to let him pass, his walking cane tap-tapping impatiently as his clerk went ahead alerting everyone to his presence.

Adam turned to Gerrit. 'He can't do *that* to us! He can't stop us trading, can he?'

Gerrit unrolled the parchment and read the notice. He glanced around at the merchants as they moved away quickly to spread the news.

'I think he already has, Master Adam,' he said with a sigh.

By the time they reached the warehouse a crowd of merchants and traders had already gathered to read the notice nailed to the great wooden doors.

'The Windjammer Trading Company owes many people money,' Gerrit admitted as they approached.

Grim-faced merchants stood around, discussing what should be done with the traders and artisans who had come to see for themselves if the rumours were true.

'Did I not warn you?' One voice was raised above the rest. 'Did I not say the House of Windjammer had been cursed? Yes! *Cursed* above all others!' Abner Heems was standing, preaching from the back of an empty cart. 'For is it not written that you cannot serve God and mammon? Is it not written that the grass withereth and the flower fadeth?'

Adam recognised the preacher immediately. The preacher's eyes seemed to seek him out in the crowd, and as they looked at one another Adam felt a chill pass right through him.

'"I have heard of thee by the hearing of the ear: but now mine eye seeth thee!"' Abner Heems called without taking his eyes off him. 'So beware, Windjammer! Yes, beware! For your sins are known to me!'

The preacher raised his hand to point and many in

the crowd turned to look. As soon as they saw Gerrit, the merchants and traders broke from around the door and crowded around, jostling, assailing them with a rush of questions and demands. Gerrit did his best to calm them, but for a while they were caught in the crush on the doorstep, their backs pressed up against the studded wood of the great doors.

And all the while the preacher rained words down on their heads like fire and brimstone. 'Beware the ways of the Windjammers!' he warned. 'Day by day they grow more desperate with their own pride and folly. Wonder not how low they will go. For it is written in their eyes. Satan himself leads them now! Aye! And their servant, Gerrit, too! The Windjammers are full of deceit and dishonour now – that's clear enough.'

The preacher's words had a noticeable effect on Gerrit. He stared at Abner Heems with a mixture of horror and disbelief before he turned and started hammering on the doors with his fists. It took a while longer for the manager to recognise his voice, then the door opened and they were ushered inside.

'Thank God you've come, sir!' the manager said. 'I tried to reason with them – but they're not of a mind to listen to me.'

Gerrit slumped back against the doors.

'Are you wounded, sir?' the manager asked. He was a short, stocky man wearing a leather jerkin and skullcap.

Gerrit looked up, but showed no signs of recognising him.

The manager swept off his leather skullcap. 'It's me, sir, *Borch*.'

'Borch,' Gerrit repeated the name in a faraway voice.

Then he came to his full height suddenly and turned to look at the door. 'What is that *preacher* doing here?' he asked, backing away as if in terror of what lay on the other side. 'He has no right to say these things! No right!'

'It's not the first time Abner Heems has come stirring up trouble,' Borch said. 'He's been spreading rumours among the men. He says the Windjammers are cursed – *finished*.'

'Is that so?' Gerrit's face hardened along with his resolve. 'Then I will speak to the men. But first I must find a way to reassure the people outside. If I do not, before long we will have every tradesman and merchant in the city knocking at our door demanding their money.'

'What did the preacher mean?' Adam asked. 'What's he got against us?'

'Abner Heems hunts witches wherever he can,' Gerrit said grimly. 'I know not why he has taken against the House of Windjammer, but it is sure no good will come of it.'

Adam could tell from the look on his face that Gerrit had left more unsaid than said.

'You must not remain here a moment longer, Master Adam,' Gerrit said. 'There is a back way out. Borch will show you. When you reach the canal you must hail a boat. Give this to the boatman for his trouble and tell him to row you to the Herengracht with all speed.' He pressed another silver piece into Adam's hand. 'Warn your dear mother of the meeting of the council. I will send Borch to find your uncle.' He gripped Adam by the shoulders. His apprehension showed in his eyes. 'Whatever happens a Windjammer *must* speak to the

Council of Merchants or all will be lost.'

'I'll go,' Adam promised.

Gerrit looked at Adam. It seemed the clerk wanted to say more – much more. His lips worked at the words. But for a reason only he knew, it remained unsaid.

'Borch is waiting.' Gerrit turned away abruptly.

Borch took a lantern from a hook on the wall and led the way along the wide passage into the Weighing Room. This was the heart of the warehouse: the place where the goods were first brought after they had been unloaded from the ships to be weighed on the polished arm of the great scales.

As they passed through the cavernous room, Adam remembered his father showing him how the scales worked. The arm had moved constantly, weighing the barrels of spices and bags of grain and other goods under the watchful eye of the manager sitting at the bench-desk on the platform. He remembered the barrels being hauled up in nets through the trapdoors above and stored high and dry on the upper floors. Now, the arm of the scales was still, thrown up as if in permanent defeat. The nets were empty and hanging limply among the hooks and ropes like so much broken rigging. The emptiness around them echoed with the slow drip of water.

Adam looked back as they reached the door on the other side. He could still see Gerrit standing by the great wooden doors. The clerk's head was bowed and he stood wringing his hands as if in silent prayer.

Borch led Adam through a maze of storerooms filled with sacks and barrels, until at last they reached the doors on the canal side of the warehouse. A small wicket gate in one of the doors opened on to the canal, where some stone steps led down to the water's edge.

Borch wished him good luck and closed the door after him. A chill wind lifted off the water as Adam hailed a passing boat and stepped into the stern. The boatman pushed away from the slime on the wall and began to row. Adam drew his coat around him as he looked back at the warehouse rising like a fortress, sheer from the water's edge.

The water made only the faintest of sounds, washing up against the brickwork as they moved steadily away. Above – beyond the edge of the canal wall – he could hear the sound of voices; harsh voices raised against the Windjammers' name. And one voice was raised above them all.

'For does not the good book say,' the preacher ranted, '"He heapeth up riches, and knoweth not who shall gather them?"'

12. Desperate Measures

'They nailed it up,' Rose said.

'The men, she means,' Viola explained.

The twins greeted Adam breathlessly at the door of the house on the Herengracht.

'Mother tried to stop them.'

'But they wouldn't listen.'

'And now something's wrong,' they were chiming in unison again.

Adam tore down the notice. His hands were trembling slightly as he read it: NOTICE OF THE APPLICATION TO THE COUNCIL OF MERCHANTS, it said. ALL TRADE WITH THE HOUSE OF WINDJAMMER TO BE CEASED UNTIL FURTHER NOTICE, it said.

Adam screwed it up and hurled it away. 'Mother!' he called.

Two hands flashed up and pointed across the hall to the door in the wooden panelling of the passage under the stairs.

'The kitchen?'

Two heads nodded.

Adam heard the clonk and scrape of pots as he burst into the stone-flagged passage beyond. He passed quickly down the line of storerooms on either side and went straight to the kitchen where he saw his mother stirring the bubbling contents of a pot that was hanging on a hook over the fire.

'Ah, there you are, Adam.' She didn't seem surprised to see him home early. 'Where is Gerrit?'

'At the warehouse, Mother. There's been some trouble.' He quickly told her about Hugo van Helsen and what had happened.

She nodded as if she had already guessed. 'His men came here too,' she said, turning back to the pot. 'Poor cook was so upset when she read the notice I had to send her to her room to lie down.'

'Never mind about cook,' Adam said. 'We have to go to the New Market. They are meeting in a hall near the *Waag*.'

'We will have plenty of time for that later,' his mother said. She lifted the wooden spoon to her lips, blew and tasted the stew.

'Of course, it could do with some spice,' she said after considering it for a moment or two. She glanced about. 'This kitchen was always so full of spices – pepper and cloves and nutmeg. Ah yes! Do you remember the scent of the nutmeg, Adam? We haven't been able to afford that for some time.'

Adam was beginning to feel a little uneasy. There was a sing-song quality to her voice and a distant look in her eyes. 'Are you all right, Mother?' he approached her cautiously.

'Quite well, thank you.'

'But this is important,' Adam insisted.

'And so is this stew,' his mother said. 'It is almost done.'

Every moment had become an agony of waiting to

Adam. He paced the kitchen at this new delay, turning on the sails of the windmills pictured in the blue and white tiles on the floor. Three strides one way took him to the copper pans hanging on hooks from the ceiling. A turn. Three strides back and he turned again by the beehive-shaped bread oven. And all the while his frustration grew with his mother and the stew she was cooking in the iron pot hanging in the fireplace.

'How can you think about *food* at a time like *this*, Mother?' It burst out of him in the end.

She paused and looked at him, red in the face from the heat of the fire. 'Because I *have* to,' she said simply. 'I am a mother as well as a Windjammer. I have your sisters to think about too, remember.'

She used a cloth to avoid burning her hands as she lifted the heavy pot from the fire and placed it on the scrubbed wooden table.

'First we eat,' she said. '*Then* we will go to the New Market and speak to this Council of Merchants.'

Adam stood before the double doors of the *Waag* and watched the arms of the weighing scales rising and falling. Long ago, this had been a gateway. Now the city had grown far beyond the old walls that had once protected it and the *Waag* had become the civic weighing house and – until the new town hall was built in Dam Square – a meeting-place for the merchants and burghers of Amsterdam.

Adam held his sisters' hands, Rose on one side, Viola on the other. They stood quite still, while the crowds swirled through the market around him, aware that in the hall close by the story of their lives was being laid bare before an audience of men who hardly even knew them.

Adam glanced across the square known as New Market. He could see a clock-tower with a spire, two large bells and four small, and beside that the flat-fronted hall where the Council of Merchants now met in closed session.

'Master Adam!' Gerrit came breathlessly, hurrying across the market square towards them. 'Where is your uncle? Where is your mother?'

They had waited as long as they could. But neither Gerrit nor Augustus Windjammer had come in time.

Gerrit was aghast. 'Your mother went in to face the council alone?' He paced up and down, wringing his hands. 'A *woman*? But that is unheard of! They will not listen. It cannot be!'

'They told us to go away,' Adam said. 'They said we were too young.'

'Wish it were I had the power to be in two places at once,' Gerrit said, cursing the troubles that had kept him so long at the warehouse. 'Borch told me he delivered my message. It seems I relied too much on your uncle getting here in time.' He slapped his fist into the flat of his hand. 'I fear that Mr van Helsen planned to keep me away, but there's little point in fretting over that now – I must go in and support your dear mother.'

It was already too late, however. As they crossed the square and Gerrit sought entry to the hall by the church, the meeting inside was already beginning to break up. Shortly afterwards, the doors were thrown open to reveal the merchants standing around in little groups talking to one another. Some turned to watch Mary Windjammer as she walked out. Her expression was set. Serious. Adam knew at once that the meeting hadn't gone well for the House of Windjammer.

Mary Windjammer silenced their questions, saying it was a matter to be discussed later in the proper place. She gathered up the twins and began to shepherd them back towards Dam Square.

'Mary, my dear!' a frail but familiar voice called after her. She paused as Bartholomew de Leiden detached himself from a group of merchants and came to speak to her. 'I am sorry,' he said. 'I tried my best for you, but they would not listen to ... '

' ... a woman,' Mary Windjammer finished for him. 'And a woman of *English* birth, at that.'

'Alas!' the old man raised his hands. 'I do not agree with them,' he said, 'but I find myself in a difficult position. I cannot go against Hugo van Helsen alone. He has the power to ruin me too. I wish the West India Company was as strong as Anton van Dieman's East India Company, but I fear it never shall be.'

She placed her hand on the old man's arm. 'You did all you could.'

'I wish it were so.' The old man stood stiffly by and watched them go.

Adam followed his mother as she walked – straight-backed and head held high – leading them away. She had never looked so beautiful to him and her serene dignity caused the merchants around to pause. She returned their looks with a steady gaze, until one by one they shuffled their feet and turned their eyes away.

'My mind is made up,' Mary Windjammer said, speaking from her place at the Long Table. 'There is no other way now.'

'But mistress, surely –' Gerrit started.

She silenced him with a wave of her hand. Gerrit obeyed, but his reluctance showed as he stepped back into the shadows around the edges of the room.

Adam looked down the length of the Long Table. To his right the twins sat side by side in their places, kicking their feet in unison until they were told to stop. Gerrit stood back from the table obediently. And if the air felt colder in the dining-room that evening it wasn't just because there was no peat left for the fire.

'I will sign the letter now,' Mary Windjammer said.

Gerrit stepped forward and laid a sheet of parchment on the table in front of her. He had come prepared with his wooden writing-box, but seemed determined to put off the final moment of signing as long as possible, fussing about, taking his time selecting a suitable quill and preparing the wax ready to seal it.

'I will not change my mind,' Mary Windjammer scolded him mildly, 'no matter *how* long you delay.'

Adam fought to control his growing sense of alarm as he watched his mother take the quill, dip the end in the ink and sign the letter. Gerrit took the letter back just as reluctantly. He dried the ink with a dusting of fine sand, folded the parchment and melted some wax on the flame of a candle. The wax fell on the page like drops of blood.

'It is done,' Mary Windjammer said as she pressed the seal of the House of Windjammer into the wax while it was still hot, sealing the letter with the Windjammers' mark. The weariness was in her voice again.

'*What* is done, Mother?' he asked.

'I have made Hugo van Helsen an offer,' she answered him.

'An *offer*, dear sister-in-law?' Augustus Windjammer said, stepping in through the door. They all turned to look at him and it soon became clear he had been standing in the hall listening. 'Can it be that you have seen the sense and have taken my advice at last?'

Mary Windjammer regarded him stonily. She didn't ask him where he had been – she seemed to have guessed that already.

'I think I have a right to be at this meeting, do you not?' Augustus said.

'Gerrit sent for you,' she answered him, her voice flat and cold. 'We waited for you by the *Waag* – but you did not come.'

'Is it *my* fault Gerrit's messenger did not reach me in time?' Augustus defended himself with a flap of his handkerchief.

Gerrit stirred in the shadows, but said nothing.

'No, it is not,' Augustus continued firmly. 'As soon as I received your call for help I wasted no time in finishing the particularly fine plate of beef and onions that had just been served to me and, with little more than a slice of cheese and a glass of brandy to follow, I hurried straight to the *Waag*. I took no account of my own health or the risk of bilious colic from the sudden exercise – only to find I had been called too late.

'But worse was to come!' he went on. 'When I arrived at the *Waag* I was greeted with nothing but rudeness and surly looks as if I was little more than a common debtor. It was terrible. Yes, yes! *Terrible*.'

He assured them only a glass of brandy could settle his stomach and nerves now, and promptly helped himself from the bottle on the side table.

'I spoke to the council,' Mary Windjammer said.

'*You*, dear sister-in-law?' Augustus said, turning with surprise. '*You* – a mere *woman* – have addressed the great and good men of the council?' He remembered the glass in his hand and drained it at a gulp. 'Now I am beginning to see why I was treated so badly!'

'I had no choice,' Mary Windjammer ignored the insult. 'Gerrit was delayed by trouble at the warehouse and *you* ... ' It was clear she wanted to say much more, but refrained. Instead she just shook her head and added, 'They would not listen to me.'

Augustus was not surprised and told them so. 'And now you have decided to follow my advice and make this moneylender an offer?'

'I have.'

Augustus filled and drained his glass once more before he turned to her. 'Have I not always said that a family could grow rich by marrying a van Helsen?'

'*Marrying!*' Adam came to his feet suddenly.

'Sit down, Adam!' his mother said firmly. 'It is time you learnt to listen first and speak later.'

Adam sat back in his chair, overwhelmed by the feeling of his own powerlessness. Strangely, however, the meaning of what was said next only dawned on him slowly.

Gerrit cleared his throat bringing all eyes back to him and the letter in his hand.

'I have drawn up an agreement,' he said. He swallowed, as if the next words stuck in his throat. 'It is ... a proposal ... of marriage,' he confirmed. 'An agreement to unite the House of Windjammer with the banking house of the moneylender Hugo van Helsen ... '

Adam stared down the table, never taking his eyes

off his mother. Her face showed no emotion. Gerrit's voice seemed to become very distant – tiny – fading in a mix of the hiss and thump of the blood in Adam's ears, only to come roaring back suddenly, so loud he thought it would burst his head.

'A marriage between Mary Windjammer and Mr Hugo van Helsen. A marriage that would secure forever the title and rights of the heir of the House of Windjammer and ensure Master Adam's rightful place at this table ... '

Adam heard Augustus Windjammer's glass slam down. After that, he heard nothing but the sound of his own voice shouting: 'Never! Never! *Never!*'

'I would like to speak to Adam alone,' Mary Windjammer said.

Cook was called and the twins sent off to the kitchen with promises of something good to eat.

'If I may suggest, dear sister-in-law,' Augustus Windjammer said, showing no intention of leaving, 'perhaps *I*, myself, should go and speak with Hugo van Helsen tomorrow.'

'*You*, Augustus?'

Adam saw the doubt written all over his mother's face.

'I think you will agree,' Augustus said as he subjected the fingernails of his right hand to minute inspection, 'that my powers of tact and persuasion are second to none. A mastery of fine words and diplomacy will be needed in presenting such a proposal.'

Adam saw his mother's eyebrows rise. Her surprise was evident, but before she could say anything Gerrit stepped forward.

'It *would* be more appropriate, mistress,' the clerk

advised her quietly. 'The tradition of this house dictates that ... '

'Don't listen to him, mother!' Adam interrupted. 'What has Uncle Augustus ever done that's *right*?'

'How dare you, nephew!' Augustus Windjammer erupted with a wild flapping of his handkerchief. 'It is time you learnt to show your elders and *betters* some respect.'

'How right Mr Augustus is,' Gerrit agreed quickly.

Adam hated them both then: the bumbling uncle and the little, ink-stained clerk seemed united against him.

Gerrit overruled Adam's protests, 'Surely the brother of Mr Hercules would be able to present a better case than a humble servant such as myself.' He bowed towards Augustus Windjammer with great reverence.

'Quite so!' Augustus agreed, spiking an evil look at Adam.

'After all,' Gerrit went on. 'A visit from a man such as your brother-in-law would undoubtedly *impress* Mr van Helsen. Mr Augustus could then point out the advantages of a marriage between this House and his bank. For are we not about to offer this moneylender the one thing his money cannot buy' – he paused for the full effect then said '– a *good* name?'

'A fine, *old* name,' Augustus agreed heartily, swelling visibly with his own self-importance.

'Who better than your brother-in-law to impress on Mr van Helsen the great honour we are doing him?' Gerrit said. 'After all, even now the Windjammers will be offering him rank and title far higher than that of a ... '

' ... mere *moneylender*!' Augusutus found the words himself.

'And in return for such an honour?' Gerrit said.

140

'Well ... the money to pay off our debts ... shall we call it a dowry?'

'Yes! Yes! A dowry!' Augustus echoed, getting more than a little carried away. 'Have I not always said a family could grow rich by arranging such a marriage with a banker's ... ' He paused, gave them a look as if he had almost said too much, and hurriedly turned away.

Augustus refilled his glass, drained it and stood for a while with his back turned and head bowed over the bottles on the side table as if he was afraid of turning to face them again.

'I don't trust him, Mother,' Adam said. 'He's up to something, I know he is.'

Augustus shot another venomous look at him out of the corner of his eye. But it was Gerrit who spoke.

'These things must be done properly, mistress,' he reminded her. 'It *would* be in accordance with the traditions of the family for Mr Augustus to go ... '

'Traditions! It's always *traditions* with you,' Adam came to his feet shouting. He felt for the ring on the chain around his neck, pulled it up over his head and sent the ring and chain sliding away down the table towards Gerrit. 'That's what I think of your *traditions*. You can keep your ring! I don't want it – I never did!'

He was surprised how easy it was to cast off the burden. He felt suddenly light, as if a great load had been lifted off his shoulders.

'Have I not always said,' Augustus Windjammer spoke solemnly after a long pause, 'that my nephew is *not* worthy of this House? I think now he has proved me right beyond all doubt. A mere accident of birth made him heir – nothing more. He has not the stomach for it.'

'I have asked you to leave us,' Mary Windjammer said, her face set – grim. She waved Gerrit forward. 'Take the letter and deliver it to Hugo van Helsen tonight.'

'And what of *my* advice, sister-in-law?' Augustus asked.

She hesitated, glanced at Gerrit and saw him nod his encouragement.

'Very well, Augustus,' she said with a sigh of resignation. 'I will entrust you with the task of talking to Hugo van Helsen – but only because Gerrit has recommended it. Do not let this House down. Tomorrow you will have your last chance to prove you are a true Windjammer at heart and make amends for all you have done.'

Augustus's eyes flashed. 'No one has worked harder than I have for the House of Windjammer,' he said. '*No one!* Even though surly looks and complaints are all the thanks I get from some!' He shot a sidelong glance at Adam, then his gaze settled back on her. 'Never fear, I shall prove myself a champion of this House, sister-in-law. I will save it for the good of the Windjammers. Yes, yes. For a *worthy* heir – I promise you that!'

He inclined his head in a slight bow, ignored Adam and, with his nose in the air, walked out.

'Take up the ring, Adam!'

'But I don't want it, Mother.'

Mary Windjammer's fist slammed down on the table.

'You will *never* speak like that again!' For a moment her fury showed clearly in her eyes. 'If you give up the ring then you give up this House. Everything we have worked for will have been wasted. Do you want that? Do you want your dear father and Uncle Lucien – and all the others – to have died in the service of this great House – to have died for nothing?'

'No, but – '

'Then take up the ring and start acting like the heir to this House!'

Adam rose stiffly out of his chair. The ring – the burden of the House of Windjammer – lay glinting dully in the candlelight.

'Why do you listen to Gerrit, Mother?' he asked. 'Why do you listen to him and not *me*?'

'Gerrit has been with us for a long time,' she answered him. 'Your father trusted him and so do I.'

'Well, I *don't*.'

Mary Windjammer lowered her voice. 'There is much you do not understand about that man. You see only his rules and traditions, but he is as loyal to this House as you or I.'

'How do you *know*, Mother?'

'I *know* because I know Gerrit. He is an honest, hardworking man. A man who, many years ago, was saved by your father. He had been beaten and robbed, and left in the gutter to die. Your father helped him. He brought him home. We tended his wounds. Gerrit has been with us ever since – he is sworn to serve and protect us.'

'But he supported my uncle – we both know he's a –'

'I know well what you think of Augustus, Adam. But you must learn not to show your feelings with such openness.'

'How can I keep silent when I think they're planning

something together, Mother? I don't know what it is, but I'll find out,' he said. 'I told you what I saw – Gerrit has money. Gold and silver hidden under the floor. I'll prove it to you if you'll let me –'

'*Enough!*' his mother interrupted him. 'I'll hear no more of this nonsense. Now take up the ring, Adam! I will *not* ask you again.'

Adam fought back his tears of frustration as he walked slowly down the length of the table. The ring of the House of Windjammer seemed to grow to the size of a plate before his eyes. He hesitated – knowing the burden of it would be almost unbearable – before finally he reached out and picked it up. The chain was like a noose as he felt the weight of the ring around his neck once more.

His mother stood up and came down the length of the table to stand in front of him. There was a pause before she spoke. 'No one could ever take the place of your father in my heart, you know that – don't you, Adam?'

Adam looked into her eyes and all the anger and frustration he felt inside suddenly seemed to melt away. 'But how can you *marry* him, Mother? There must be another way.'

'I wish it were so,' she answered him honestly. 'But you heard Bartholomew de Leiden. Even our closest friends fear Hugo van Helsen now.' She took both his hands in hers. 'The Council of Merchants has pledged itself to stop the Windjammer Trading Company trading if it does not pay its debts. We have one week. By noon of Tuesday next we will be ruined and Hugo van Helsen will take everything.' She squeezed his hands tightly. 'What choice do I have? I must gamble on

Hugo van Helsen's own ambitions to save us. He craves nothing more than advancement and power. The Windjammers have always been well respected. Even now we still have a good name. He is no fool. He will see there are advantages in acquiring respectability by an alliance rather than be seen by all to destroy it.'

'But we don't need *him*, Mother. We don't need *any-one*!' Adam said. 'We'll manage, you'll see. We'll start again. We can do it, I know we can.'

She shook her head sadly. 'Do you think a man like Hugo van Helsen will leave anything for us when he has finished? Even after he has thrown us out on the streets we will be in debt to him for the rest of our lives.' For a moment the pain and fear showed clearly in her eyes. 'What of your poor sisters then, Adam? Will they have to grow up in the gutter of the Jordaan? Will I have to watch them die of plague or canal fever?'

The truth tolled over the Long Table like a bell.

'I said today,' she went on after a pause, 'that I am a mother as well as a Windjammer. Perhaps that is why I am prepared to marry the man who has caused us so much hurt. It is the only way I know to protect my family. I am a woman. The merchants will not listen to me. But one day, God willing, they will listen to *you*.'

She let go of his hands and hugged him to her. 'That is why I must marry for money, Adam,' she whispered close to his ear. 'That is why I will do everything in my power to protect your inheritance.' She broke away from him and nodded, the determination reflected in her eyes again. 'That is why I will do this thing.'

13. Gerrit's Shadow

'Gerrit has money,' a small but persistent voice whispered in Adam's head as he paced the floor of his bedroom. '*Lots* of money.'

It was late. The lamplighters had long since lit the torches and lanterns along the Herengracht. Somewhere in the distance a night watchman blew his horn to announce the start of another night hour. Around him only the gentle creak and tick of the timbers disturbed the quiet of the house, leaving him with the strangest feeling he wasn't in a *house* at all, but on board ship: a ship moving slowly on a dark sea, drawn through the mist, blindly heading for the rocks.

'Where did all that money come from?' The voice continued its whisperings. 'Why don't you ask him ... ask him ... ask him ... ?'

'I will!' Adam answered the voice aloud. He strode across his bedroom only to pause before he reached the door, as he had so many times before.

What if Gerrit just denied it? Without proof, Adam realised it would be his word against Gerrit's. His mother would never believe him, but Gerrit would know he had been found out. Yes, *he* would know. Then what would a desperate man do? Wild thoughts of the mask windmilled through Adam's head and set the voice whispering its warnings again: 'He'll come late at night ... while you are sleeping ... It will be easy ... just a stab in the dark ... '

Adam backed away from the door, his heart beating on the drum of his chest. It was with some relief that he remembered Gerrit still hadn't returned to the house.

'How long can it take to deliver a letter?' the voice was relentless. 'Not long ... Not *this* long ... '

'I'll wait for him!' Adam made up his mind to confront Gerrit when he returned. And for a while the voice was silent.

Adam woke suddenly. He sat up, his heart racing as he looked around. He was sitting in the chair by the fire. The candle had burnt low in its stick on the mantelpiece and he guessed he must have been asleep for over an hour. He was just wondering whether Gerrit had returned while he slept when he realised it had been the sound of footsteps on the stairs that had woken him.

He came to his feet and stood listening. The sounds filled the hollows of the house, echoing through the caverns of darkness below him. The footsteps were clipped and quick, but unlike before they didn't bring Gerrit quickly up through the twists of the stairs. Adam heard them stop every so often, the silence filling the darkness with a sense of suspense that was only heightened by the urgency of the steps when they started off again.

Adam blew out the candle and a patch of moonlight slanted in through the window and across the floor. Around it the shadows painted everything in lumpy shades of indigo. He crossed to the door and opened it just far enough to look out.

Gerrit was breathing hard as he reached the top of the flight of stairs. Along the length of the passage, Adam could see him standing holding his lantern, panting as if he had been running. He was still wearing his hat and coat.

Adam watched as Gerrit glanced about and moved swiftly through the shadows to the window overlooking the street outside. He raised his lantern to look out. For a while there was silence, before Gerrit muttered something under his breath and moved on again up the next flight of stairs. Adam heard the footsteps stop when Gerrit reached the floor above and realised the clerk must be stopping at each of the windows overlooking the street. Finally, Adam heard the door into the servants' quarters in the attic open and close and all went quiet again.

Adam waited long enough to be sure Gerrit wasn't about to come back down, then stepped out into the shadows of the passage. A sudden impulse drove him to the window beyond the stairs.

Outside, a lantern hung on a hook over the door from the ledger-room into the street below. The lantern was moving gently in the breeze, sliding its circle of light across the cobbles in front of the side door. Adam pressed his cheek against the leaded glass of the window. As far as he could see, the street below was empty both ways. Nevertheless the fine hairs lifted on the back of his neck as he sensed the danger that lurked in the darkness just beyond the light.

Adam stepped back from the window, only for the same impulse to make him look out again. He watched now, waiting for what seemed an age before a movement caught his eye.

A piece of shadow – a patch of darkness, little more – tore itself away from the rest and moved to the very edge of the light. The lantern swung away, then back again, and as the light reached the full extent of its pendulum motion the circle of its brightness slid up to reveal the features of the man looking up at the house from below.

'The *preacher*,' Adam gasped and ducked back out of sight, but not before that cruel face was burned for ever into his memory.

Abner Heems was just standing there, his hat pulled down low over his eyes, his hands thrust deep into the pockets of his coat and his shoulders hunched against the cold. The preacher had come stealing to their door as quiet as Death.

Adam turned cold as the menace gripped him just as surely as if Abner Heems had reached out one big-boned hand and caught hold of him by the guts. It set him turning on his heel, searching the shadows around him for monsters. He hung back from the window in dread, but in the end he had to look again.

Gingerly Adam approached the window and little by little peered over the sill until he could see the street below. The lantern swung with the breeze. The circle of light moved away. When it moved back again the preacher had gone.

Adam burst into the library and paused, breathing hard.

'Gerrit?' he called. 'Gerrit, where are you?'

No answer.

It was still very early, but he had heard Gerrit's

149

footsteps coming down long before the dawn.

'I have to talk to you. *Now*.' Adam was determined to know the truth.

He moved swiftly into the ledger-room. The portable wooden writing-box was still on the desk. The door into the street was locked. Gerrit had not yet left the house.

What little sleep Adam had snatched had been fitful and filled with phantom images: Hugo van Helsen, the preacher, Gerrit, Augustus Windjammer – one by one they came to trouble his dreams. Each time he had woken in a sweat to lie thinking, each troubled thought leading to the next until he felt as if his head was full of gunpowder and the trail of his thoughts had become a slow fuse burning. It left him feeling burned out and exhausted, but he was determined now to face Gerrit and know the truth.

The ledger-room looked exactly as he had left it. The desk and chair faced the door into the street to his left. The plum tree in the courtyard outside the windows showed only faintly with the dawn. He put down the candle he had used to light his way and threw his weight against the desk. The legs jarred, groaning on the floorboards as he shifted it to one side. He snatched up the candle again, dropped to his knees and studied the gaps between the boards.

The iron brad-nails that fixed the boards to the joists below were as old as the house itself, but he noticed that the ends of three of the boards had been cut to form a square. The joinery had been carefully executed to form the perfect hiding place. With the desk leg placed on top even the most detailed of searches would have missed it. Only the years of use and the scraping of the leg as the desk had been pushed aside left a clue of what might be hidden there.

Adam levered at one of the boards with his finger-nails. It moved. He levered some more and the board came up easily. His hands were trembling slightly as he lifted it out. He placed it carefully to one side and lifted out the section beside it and then the one beside that, until at last he had uncovered a square of darkness in the floor.

A bell in the tower of the church nearby tolled the half hour with a single note as he reached in and pulled out the casket that lay hidden there. He sat for a moment just staring at it. He was surprised to find it wasn't locked and his hands were trembling slightly as he lifted the lid. It was empty.

'Master Adam!' Gerrit's voice cracked at the air. 'What are you doing in here?'

Adam leapt up as if stung by a whip.

The fury showed in Gerrit's eyes. His hands were clasped in front of him, his knuckles showing whiter through his pale skin.

'I found it!' Adam blurted.

Gerrit stared at the open casket, then at the hole in the floorboards, then at Adam. The expression on his face changed as if suddenly he understood. 'You *were* hiding in the library,' he said breathlessly, 'just like Miss Angelica said.'

'Where's the money? It was *here*,' Adam said. 'I saw the bags of gold – hidden in that casket under the floor.'

Gerrit's tone grew harsher. 'You were watching me like a common *spy*.'

'Maybe I was,' Adam defended himself. 'But a spy is better than a *thief*.'

'*Thief?*' Gerrit hissed. 'What are you talking about?'

'I saw the mask,' Adam said, without thinking if it was wise. 'I know what you've been doing. Why don't you just admit it? You're a thief. You've been stealing from us too, haven't you?'

'Stealing from this House – *never*.' Gerrit was clearly horrified by the thought. He cast a hurried look over his shoulder and quickly closed the door.

'Stay away from me!' Adam said, arming himself with a heavy candlestick.

'Master Adam! *Please*,' Gerrit said. 'There has clearly been a … misunderstanding.'

'I don't care what you call it,' Adam said, edging towards the door. 'I knew my mother was wrong about you. She said we could trust you, but we can't. I should have told her. I should have brought her here now and made her see what you're really like.'

'No!' Gerrit blocked his way. 'You must listen to me, Master Adam. You must believe that I would never hurt this House.'

'Then where did all that money come from?' Adam asked. 'We've been living on hotpot and bread and cheese since Father died. You've been telling us we are so poor and we have to tighten our belts and all along you've had bags of gold hidden under your desk.'

'The money was mine,' Gerrit said. 'Saved over the years for my old age. But I would have gladly given it to your mother – every last guilder and florin – had I not needed it.'

Adam would not listen. 'Why should I believe you?'

'Because you *must*, Master Adam!' Gerrit pleaded with him. 'Please! I have my reasons.'

But Adam saw only the guilt that was written all over the little man's face now. His shiftiness. The way he constantly rubbed his hands. He wondered why he had never noticed it when his father was alive.

Gerrit took a step closer as if frightened he might be overheard. Adam watched him warily.

'It is true,' Gerrit started with all the breathlessness of someone confessing his sins. 'I *do* have a secret – a terrible, dark secret. I have kept it from you and your mother out of shame. Even now I cannot believe that I – an honest servant of this great House – have had to stoop so low.' His eyes blazed with a feverish light. 'But I had to do it, don't you see? I *had* to risk my honour and reputation. How else could I save the House of Windjammer? Yes – and stop this marriage too!'

'You want to *stop* it?' Adam could not believe his own ears.

'Of course,' Gerrit said. 'I was against such a thing from the moment your uncle first suggested it at the Long Table.'

'But I heard you,' Adam said, sure Gerrit was lying now. 'You *agreed* to it.'

'It is true,' Gerrit nodded, 'I did advise your mother to listen to Mr Augustus. But I had good reason.' His hands turned over each other almost continuously now. 'I knew her mind was made up. I knew I would not be able to talk her out of it.' He looked at Adam. 'Could you?'

'No,' Adam admitted. 'But why did you let her send my uncle? Why did you let him go to speak to Hugo van Helsen?'

'I knew I could not go myself – I am needed urgently at the warehouse,' Gerrit explained. 'And as for your uncle? It is true I do not trust his ambition. I have seen it grow like a weed in recent weeks. But I also knew I could not stop him from going. So I simply puffed him up with his own self-importance and advised your mother to let him go. I know enough about Hugo van Helsen to be sure he is not a man to be treated with arrogance and contempt. So what better way to make sure this marriage will *not* happen than to send your uncle to speak in its favour? He is, after all, a proud man. And pride, they say, often goes before destruction and a haughty spirit before a fall.'

That part at least made sense to Adam and yet still he refused to believe Gerrit. 'But you delivered the letter,' he pointed out.

Gerrit sighed and shook his head. 'As if my shame has not already plumbed its depths,' he said. 'I could not bring myself to do it.' He pulled the letter from his pocket. 'I will, of course, give it back to your mother later.'

Adam stared at the letter in amazement. 'I don't understand.'

'I wish I could speak openly with you, Master Adam,' Gerrit said, 'but it is not yet safe. I have embarked on a dangerous endeavour. There are some who would stop me. Yes, I have been followed, despite my precautions. So I must be very careful.'

'The preacher?' Adam said.

Gerrit quivered visibly at the name, but said nothing as he drew himself up to his full height. The set of his narrow shoulders now showed his determination.

'I will talk of these things later with you and your mother,' he promised. 'I will tell you everything and expose my shame to the world. But for now, Master Adam, you must trust me a while longer. For the fate of the House of Windjammer hangs in the balance even as we speak.'

And there it was. After all those weeks of darkness and despair – *hope*.

'I must go now,' Gerrit said. 'I fear there will be trouble at the warehouse if I am not there.' He bent down and picked up the casket. He paused to look at Adam. 'I am sorry, Master Adam. I should have seen you more as your father's son and less as a boy. I should have trusted you and suggested you go with your uncle today.' The depth of his regret was in his eyes. 'Now I have no way of knowing what your uncle will say when he goes to see Hugo van Helsen at his house on the Street of Knives. For that, I fear, we must all trust to luck.'

Adam stood in the library for some time after Gerrit had replaced the casket under the floorboards, gathered up his writing-box and had gone. As before, he found himself drawn to his father's desk and the portrait on the wall. He felt surprisingly calm when at last he turned away and climbed the stairs back to his room.

He changed into his business clothes, tied back his hair and gave no hint of what had happened as he descended again to breakfast on bread and water with his mother and sisters.

'I have an errand to run for Gerrit,' he said at last. 'I may be some time.'

Adam moved across the chessboard of the hall. He didn't look at his sisters as they watched from the stairs. His mother kissed him on the cheek and opened the door. He felt the breeze on his face. It stirred the air around him as if the house had breathed in suddenly. The time of waiting was finally over.

14. The Street of Knives

The Street of Knives cut into the heart of the city: a ragged gash of cobbles between the shops and houses that led to a string of market squares, each as busy as the next.

Adam's stomach rumbled as he crossed Bread Street and cut along the Street of Cheeses, where Goudas and cheeses from Edam and many other cities were piled in the windows of the shops on either side. He stood back to let a coach and horses pass, the driver cursing the clumsy vehicle as he negotiated the narrow thorough-fares with difficulty. Across, and some way along on the other side, the Street of Knives opened to him.

The street smelt of blood and rancid fat and saw-dust. Whole oxen, pigs and sheep hung on the hooks outside the open-fronted butchers' shops. The meat was dark with blood and marbled with fat. The butchers and their wives were hard at work, sawing the bones, skinning and laying the cuts of meat on the wooden tables in the front. Ladies accompanied by their maids in white cotton caps and carrying wicker baskets moved from shop to shop looking and buying. And all the while the knives that gave the street its name glinted and flashed in the wintry sunlight.

Adam moved cautiously now, picking his way along

the crowded street, looking up at the houses until he saw a sign and knew he had finally arrived.

Hugo van Helsen's house and place of business stood on the corner at the far end of the street. It was a dark-timbered building with narrow leaded windows and a sign – five golden guilders painted on a black board – hanging over the door. It was by far the biggest house in the street, but still modest by comparison with the ones on the Herengracht. What it lacked in height, however, it more than made up for in presence. It seemed to crouch on the corner rather than stand, hunched over its iron-studded door as if ashamed of what went on in its dark heart.

Adam's plan only went as far as finding the house. He hadn't given much thought about how he was going to get inside or what he would do when he got there. He was just determined to hear what was said when his uncle met Hugo van Helsen and to put a stop to all talk of a marriage. So with little idea of what else to do, he settled back against a wall just across the street where he could watch for a while to see what happened.

He didn't have to wait long. Soon Hugo van Helsen's clerk opened the door. Goltz poked his head out and glanced up and down the street before he stepped back and quickly ushered a tall man out with an impatient flicking of his hand. Adam recognised the man immediately.

'We pay you to preach, nothing more,' Goltz said, still glancing about. 'And don't come here at this time of day again!'

'He was interested enough to hear what I had to tell him,' Abner Heems growled back as he settled his hat on his head and drew the wide brim down close over his eyes. 'I have the *chinks* to prove it.' He tapped the huge pocket of his coat. He paused and fixed the clerk with a hard look. 'Your precious master may not like my methods, but I get the job done. He must be stopped, says he. And that's just what I'll do – *my* way. So you'd best remember that, Goltz. You're mired in this business as deep as me.'

Goltz looked more than just a little uncomfortable as the preacher turned on his heel and strode away. Adam pretended to be looking at the smoked hams, hiding his face as Abner Heems passed close behind him. The door closed with a thump as Goltz vanished back inside. Only then did Adam notice the face at the window.

High up at one of the windows near the top of the house, someone had been watching all that had happened. He could see a face in the darkness behind the window. Someone was standing there, watching, only to draw back quickly when he looked up: the face melting away behind the reflection of the clouds in the diamond-shaped panes.

'Jade!'

If it had been her, she didn't come back. And he was still wondering if it was safe to go on with his plan when events took a hand and Augustus Windjammer arrived.

Augustus Windjammer arrived in some style. He had hired the finest coach – a low-slung, four-wheeled carriage, ornately painted and pulled by two horses – and had ordered the driver to stop right outside Hugo van Helsen's door. The driver announced their arrival from his place on the top. The curtains around the carriage flicked. The cloth door was drawn back. And a moment later Augustus alighted with difficulty. He immediately clutched a scented handkerchief, bordered with the finest lace galloon, under his nose as if the reek of the place was too much.

'Come along! Come along!' Augustus said, impatiently turning back to the carriage. 'It will never do to keep a man like Hugo van Helsen waiting.'

The curtains flicked again as someone else followed him out. The driver whipped on his horses and the carriage moved away to reveal Willem standing at his father's side.

'As I thought,' Augustus Windjammer said, looking up at the house with obvious distaste. 'All money and *no* style.'

Adam watched as they picked their way carefully through the muck in the gutter until they stood at the door. Augustus tossed back his fur-lined cloak, rapped on the door with the knob of his walking-cane and struck a pose designed to make himself look as important as possible while he waited for the door to be opened. His irritation showed when he found he had to knock at least three times more before Goltz opened the door.

'Yes?' the clerk said impatiently.

Augustus Windjammer's nose lifted. 'We have come to see your master.'

'Do you have an appointment?' Goltz asked.

'An *appointment*,' Augustus repeated the word with obvious amusement. 'I hardly think that *I*, Augustus Windjammer, need to make an appointment to see *your* master when I've come on a matter of such urgency.'

The door closed again with a thump leaving Augustus knocking fiercely with the knob of his cane until at last Goltz returned.

'Very well, he will see you,' the clerk said with an audible sigh and stood back to usher them in.

'I should think so too,' Adam heard his uncle say, along with a lot more besides about the clerk's impertinence for leaving them on the doorstep.

Augustus stood pulling his gloves off a finger at a time. As the door closed he was still waiting for Goltz to take his hat and cloak, with Willem standing miserably at his side.

Adam crossed the road to listen at the door. He waited until the sound of the voices receded from the room on the other side before he tried the iron latch. The latch came up easily. He waited. Nothing happened. He pushed open the door and, having taken a quick look to see if Goltz was about, he slipped inside.

The room that opened to him was low and square, with beams turned the colour of ebony by years of soot from the fire and smoke from men's pipes. Goltz's desk and chair stood facing the door, with candles in sticks dribbling wax on either side. A ledger lay open on the desk and the room had the feel of only just being abandoned. A door in the wood panelling to his left was open and he could hear voices coming from the room beyond.

'As I told your impudent clerk, sir, before he left us standing on the doorstep,' Augustus Windjammer was saying, pointedly. 'I have come on a matter of great urgency.'

Adam crept closer until he could see Hugo van Helsen through the partly open door. The banker was sitting behind a large desk with Goltz standing at his shoulder in close attendance. Augustus stood uncertainly before him, hopping from foot to foot every now and again, with Willem cowering directly behind him.

Hugo van Helsen put down his quill and folded his hands in his lap. 'I suppose it must be important,' he said with a hint of a smile, 'if it makes Augustus Windjammer miss his breakfast.'

'Quite so!' Augustus agreed, oblivious of the sarcasm. He took a step or two forward with renewed confidence. 'If I may sit down?' He glanced about hopefully for a chair. He wasn't offered one and was forced to remain standing. 'Hm, er, yes, well ... You, sir, will have received the letter from my sister-in-law, Mary Windjammer, and ... '

'A letter?' Hugo van Helsen interrupted, glancing inquiringly at his clerk.

Goltz shook his head. 'No letter,' he said.

'Surely you are mistaken, sir.' Augustus insisted Gerrit had delivered the letter. 'Yes, yes – last night.'

'*No* letter came,' Goltz said.

Augustus Windjammer asked Hugo van Helsen to make his clerk check again. Goltz took offence, but Hugo van Helsen nodded in a sign for him to go and with sudden alarm Adam saw Goltz slip from his master's side and start across the room towards the door.

'*Master Windjammer*. This way! *Quickly!*' someone whispered from behind.

Adam turned to see that a door he hadn't noticed had opened in the wooden panelling on the other side of Goltz's desk. In the shadows beyond he could just see a woman beckoning to him urgently, entreating him in whispers to come quickly. He recognised her as

Saskia, Jade van Helsen's maid, and only just made it across the room in time. Saskia had just pulled the door closed behind him when they heard the sound of Goltz returning to his desk.

Jade van Helsen's maid placed a finger on her lips in a sign for him to be quiet and indicated for him to follow. Without a word of explanation, she led the way through a series of small, darkened rooms filled with heavy furniture. The furniture was packed into every space and piled high in corners. Tall armoires in the Dutch style carried great weights of blue and white chinaware – jugs, bowls and plates – and the walls were a patchwork of paintings. Adam felt as if he had stepped into an auction house, not a home.

'You don't understand, I have to go back – it's my uncle ... ' Adam tried to explain, but Saskia wouldn't listen.

'Mistress Jade wishes to speak to you,' she said as they stopped at a pair of double doors. She ushered him inside and told him to wait.

The doors closed behind him and Adam found himself standing in a large, galleried room. The gallery – a wooden walkway – ran around the four sides of the room about two-thirds of the way up the wall. It passed over a line of large windows at the far end and came spiralling down into the room in a twisting stair. And there, in pride of place within the room, stood an artist's easel where a canvas had been set and covered by a velvet cloth.

'Jade?' Adam spoke into the hush of the room.

No answer.

He was wasting time. The missing letter would not delay his uncle for much longer and Adam wanted desperately to hear what was said next. His frustration almost overcame him and sent him hurrying back the way he had come, but – for reasons he couldn't explain – he wanted to see Jade van Helsen even more.

With a quick glance over his shoulder at the doors, Adam advanced cautiously into the room. He had the feeling he was being watched and turned slowly as he walked, looking up at the gallery and the lines of carved pillars that supported the roof above. He soon reached the foot of the stairs and found himself standing by the easel. His curiosity got the better of him and he lifted the corner of the cloth to look at the painting beneath. And there he came face to face with Jade van Helsen.

The painting was new, only recently finished and framed in a gold frame – a painting of Jade van Helsen from the shoulders up. He peeled back the cloth for a better look. She stared back at him from a brooding dark red and purple-black background. Some magic of the artist's brush had captured the light and had brought her to life. Her face stood out against the great void of darkness around her, shining – as if effulgent with some inner glow – and the daylight caught on her hair and fell on her lips like pearls. But it was the crystal green of her eyes that brought her image so completely to life and stole Adam's breath.

'What are you doing? Why did you come here?' Jade van Helsen's tone was sharp.

Adam started as if she had caught him spying on her. He pulled the cloth over the portrait, took several steps back and looked up. Jade van Helsen was watching him from the gallery above. She made no sound as she came hurrying along to the stairs, hitched up her long golden skirts and descended the spiral stairs, catching the light like a descending angel.

'Have you lost your senses, Adam Windjammer?' she said, furiously. 'You can't just come sneaking in here to listen at doors!'

'I wasn't *sneaking*,' Adam denied it half-heartedly. 'I followed my uncle, that's all. Then Saskia brought me here.'

'I told her to,' Jade said. 'I knew Goltz would catch you.' She shook her head as if the thought of what would have happened then was too awful to contemplate. 'My father mustn't know you've been here. You have to go, Adam Windjammer. You have to leave *now*!'

Adam refused.

'You don't understand,' she interrupted his explanation about his uncle. 'You don't know what my father's like. He finds out everything. *Everything*. He is already suspicious of my walks to the market. He has even threatened to send Saskia away and promised to employ a new maid to watch me.'

'I can't help that,' Adam said. 'I can't leave – not yet.'

Jade's eyes flashed with fury. 'And I suppose you are just going to march in there and start shouting, are you, Adam Windjammer?'

'If I have to,' Adam said. 'But don't go blaming me for what happens – it's not *my* fault your father's trying to ruin my family.'

He saw a spark in her eyes as they faced each other now, their words honing themselves until becoming as sharp as knives.

'From what I've heard that's not too difficult, Adam Windjammer,' she cut back at him.

'And what's that supposed to mean?'

'It means the Windjammers have only themselves to blame for their own misfortunes,' she said.

'That's not true and you know it!'

'Then why aren't you with your uncle right now, Adam Windjammer? Why is the head of the House of Windjammer left sneaking around listening at doors?' She jabbed her questions at him one after the other.

'I don't have to tell *you* anything.'

They glared, circling one another warily.

'Your father is tearing my family apart,' Adam came back at her.

'No,' she turned his attack aside easily. 'You're tearing *yourselves* apart. Everyone in Amsterdam knows that. And that's why the Windjammers will lose and my father will win.'

'Lies! All *lies*,' Adam counter-attacked. 'Your father hates us just because we're Windjammers.'

'No. My father's a banker – a man of business. Why should he support the Windjammers when they can't even support themselves?' She was remorseless. 'He'd be throwing good money after bad. Your House is like your ships – *lost*.'

She had drawn first blood with the truth and Adam knew it. She had wounded him deep inside and it left an ache somewhere close to his heart. He retreated now.

'I should have known you would be on *his* side.' Adam was blunt. 'I should have known you would support *him*.'

'He's my father – what do you expect?' she said, her words running through him like cold steel. 'And *yes* – I'd support him if only he would let me – if only he'd

165

ask. But he doesn't need *me*. Maybe if I was his son he *would*. But I'm only his daughter.'

'You're a *van Helsen*, that's obvious enough!' Adam threw the name at her like a broken blade.

Jade glared at him for a moment longer, then broke off the attack and turned away. 'How could you possibly know what it's like to be *me*, Adam Windjammer?' she said. 'You don't know anything about me. You're just like all the rest. To you I'm just a girl – a face to be painted. I'll wager you don't even know what this portrait means!'

'It means *nothing* to me,' Adam was cruel now. He had lost the argument and now he wanted to get his own back by hurting her as much as possible. 'You're a *van Helsen* – I'll *always* hate you!'

He saw her flinch as if he had just stabbed her in the back. She hugged her elbows.

It was said. Adam hadn't meant to say it – not like that, at least – but he had. And even though he regretted it immediately, once it had been said it couldn't be unsaid.

'I've wasted enough time already,' he muttered and turned away.

'Wait!' Jade stopped him before he reached the door. She stood for a moment longer with her back to him, then turned to face him. 'If you must do this,' she spoke quietly, 'then at least use your *head*. There is another way and I will show you if you promise to do exactly as I say.'

'You want to *help* me?' He was genuinely surprised. 'But I thought – '

'I have no choice,' she answered him flatly. 'If you go back the way you came Goltz will find you and then my father will start asking questions – *so* many questions. He will find out I know you and then ... ' She shook her head again. 'No, Adam Windjammer, I don't do this for *you* – I do it for *me*.'

'And what do you want in return?' Adam became suspicious.

Jade's eyes flashed. 'I want you to leave me alone, Adam Windjammer,' she said. 'I want you to promise to go and *never* come back.'

Her words stung him like a slap in the face. Adam paused, wished it could be different, then nodded. 'I'll leave you alone,' he said. 'You have my word on it.'

'In there?' Adam was surprised.

Jade pulled a hidden catch aside, opening a narrow doorway in the panels of the wall, and stood back to let him in.

She had not said a word since he had made his promise. Without even looking at him she had led him up the spiral stairs, along one side of the gallery to this door hidden in the panelling.

'I suppose this whole house is full of secret doors,' Adam said.

'I told you to be quiet,' Jade hissed. 'Now do you want my help or not?'

Adam looked in. The chamber beyond was not much bigger than a confessional in a church: tall enough to stand up in, but with little room to move. He could see a stool, but nothing else.

'Sit down and listen,' Jade said. 'You will see and hear all you want.'

Adam heard muffled voices as he squeezed in and sat down. The chamber took the shape of a rounded turret

167

set high in the wall of a room. There was a slit of window without any glass and when he looked through it he was startled to see Hugo van Helsen's office laid out below.

'You can't stay long,' Jade whispered, and closed him in.

From an angle somewhere above Hugo van Helsen's head, Adam could see and hear everything. The room was filled with books, maps and ledgers and several heavy iron chests. The banker was still seated at his desk with Goltz at his side. Augustus Windjammer faced the desk with Willem standing miserably behind.

It was the perfect vantage point and Adam knew this was a spyhole – most likely used by Hugo van Helsen to listen to the talk of the merchants Goltz ushered into his office before he went down to meet them.

'Yes, yes! A great honour,' Augustus Windjammer was saying.

Augustus still had not been offered a chair, as was polite, nor refreshment, as was customary; instead he had been left standing in front of the desk, shifting uncomfortably from foot to foot.

'So you see, it matters not that you did not receive my sister-in-law's letter,' Augustus said. 'For I have come with a proposal that will be of far greater interest to you.'

'I was hoping you would get to the point,' Hugo van Helsen said.

'Of course,' Augustus replied. 'I can see you are a busy man, but I simply wanted to be sure you understood the importance of my ... '

Hugo van Helsen lost patience and turned to his clerk. 'Throw him out, Goltz!'

'What! Well, I ... er ... No, wait! Please!' Augustus spluttered, visibly shaken by this bluntness. He recovered a little. 'Yes, yes. I too like to dispense with the small talk and get right down to business.'

'Then kindly do so,' van Helsen said.

'I have a proposal!' Augustus yelped, mopping his brow with his handkerchief.

'A proposal?' Hugo van Helsen leaned back in an *I'm listening* sort of way. 'What proposal of *yours* could possibly be of interest to me?'

'A proposal of marriage, sir,' Augustus said.

'You wish to *marry* me?'

'Marry *you*?' Augustus gasped, realising the mistake. 'Good heavens, no! The boy! The boy!'

'You want me to marry a boy? Have you lost your senses, man?' Hugo van Helsen came to his feet.

'No, no I don't want *you* to marry *anyone*,' Augustus Windjammer did his best to explain. But it wasn't easy. By now he was in such a fluster the words tricked and tripped his tongue, making polite diplomacy impossible. In the end he gave up with a yelp: 'Your daughter, sir! Your daughter!'

'Jade?' Hugo van Helsen said. There was a dangerous change in his tone. He was defensive now. 'What has she to do with this?'

Augustus was so relieved to have moved on after such a disastrous introduction that he didn't notice the steely edge to the banker's voice.

'I am sure *you*, of all people, sir,' he said, having recovered his breath and a little of his old self-assurance, 'can see the advantages in a match between your daughter and the future heir to the House of Windjammer?'

It took a moment for Adam to understand fully what was being said.

'Admittedly they are young,' Augustus was saying. 'But as you know, in such matters, age is of little importance. Why – such matches are made all the time. Is that not so, sir?'

Adam sat forward in astonishment.

Augustus took Hugo van Helsen's silence for agreement. Only Adam saw the way the banker's fingers clawed into his desk.

'Yes, yes, the union of our two houses will be of great benefit to us both,' Augustus decided. 'It is true that the House of Windjammer has suffered some misfortune recently, but – '

'I am well aware of the House of Windjammer,' Hugo van Helsen said. 'And its *debts*.'

'Quite so.' Augustus made a little cough of embarrassment. 'That is why a marriage will be most suitable to us both. We would, of course, expect our debts to you to be forgotten – call it a dowry, if you will. While you – *you* would gain the honour of being related by marriage to one of the finest families in all Amsterdam.'

Augustus paused. He clearly expected this to be the moment when Hugo van Helsen jumped to his feet and shook him warmly by the hand, thanking him for bestowing such a wonderful honour on him.

Van Helsen didn't move.

'Come, come, sir!' Augustus prompted him. 'What do you say? Do I have your agreement?'

Somewhere nearby a bell began to strike the hour, with a slow, clanging note. The sound so startled Augustus he muffled a little yelp with his handkerchief and looked around in alarm.

Hugo van Helsen leaned forward. 'You said *future* heir,' he said. 'Does not the House of Windjammer already have a head?'

'Ah! As I thought, sir,' Augustus said. 'I knew that would be the part to interest you most.' He puffed himself up to his full height and nodded. 'It is true that my nephew is heir of a *sort*.' He made a big show of shaking his head sadly. 'But he is rude and troublesome, to say the least. Frankly *not* the sort of heir the House of Windjammer needs.'

'And *you* are?' Hugo van Helsen inquired.

'Modesty prevents me from blowing my own fanfare, sir,' Augustus said, 'but there is little doubt that I am far better suited to the position than my nephew, Adam.'

Adam came to his feet just as the door behind him opened and Jade looked in.

'You must go now,' Jade whispered, pulling at his sleeve.

'Not yet,' Adam shook her off. 'I have to hear *this*.'

'All I need is your support against my nephew, sir,' Augustus Windjammer put the finishing touches to his treachery, 'and in return I would gladly allow my only son ... ' he looked around, ' ... where is the boy?'

Augustus turned and almost fell over Willem. There was some confusion while they sorted themselves out and Augustus thrust Willem forward for all to see. Willem cowered in front of them.

'Yes, yes, this fine, upstanding boy is my son,' Augustus said. He noticed the way Willem was standing and poked at him. 'Stand up! Straighten your back, boy!' he hissed impatiently. 'Yes, yes, a fine lad, I am sure you will agree. And with your support, sir, he will one day be the *head* of the House of Windjammer.'

'Where are you going?' Jade asked as Adam pushed his way out past her.

'I'm going to tell my uncle just what I think of him and his *proposal*,' Adam snarled.

'You can't! You promised to leave.' Jade tried to stop him. 'If you go down there now my father will know I helped you.'

Adam was in no mood to think of anyone else. 'You should have heard him. He was trying to marry you off to my cousin – to *Willem*!'

'My father would never agree,' Jade insisted. 'Wait! I'll let you listen some more – you'll see I'm right.'

But Adam had heard enough. He started along the gallery towards the stairs. Jade came after him, but they hadn't gone far when they heard the sound of a door being opened in the room below. Adam stopped and looked over the balustrade just as Hugo van Helsen, Augustus, Willem and finally Goltz filed in. Jade tried to drag Adam back out of sight, but he gripped the rail and would not budge.

'I have something to show you,' Hugo van Helsen said.

'You have commissioned a portrait, sir?' Augustus inquired politely when he saw the easel and the canvas draped with its cloth. 'Of your illustrious self in your prime, no doubt?' He flattered, but deceived no one.

Hugo van Helsen threw off the velvet cover and revealed the portrait.

'Ah!' Augustus said as if a great mystery had been suddenly solved. 'You have brought us here to *see* this daughter of yours? Good, good.' He was the master of diplomacy now. 'It is always important to see the merchandise before you buy, is it not?' He laughed. Coughed into his handkerchief and laughed again. 'Yes, yes! Come and look, my boy!' He dragged Willem forward. 'I hope it is a good likeness, sir!'

'Rembrandt van Rijn seems to think so,' came Hugo van Helsen's terse reply.

'*Rembrandt!*' Augustus sounded impressed. 'Yes, yes, I have heard much of him since he moved to the city from Leiden.'

'Is that so?' Hugo van Helsen said. 'I am a man of business and I have little time for art.' He paused to look at the portrait. 'And yet I have a fancy this Rembrandt will go far ... '

Hugo van Helsen went on, but Adam heard little of what was said next. He gripped the handrail and looked down as his rage boiled up inside to deafen him. He was vaguely aware that Jade had stepped back, retreating some way along the gallery.

'Is she not beautiful?' Hugo van Helsen's voice cut in.

'True. She seems a decent enough sort to me,' Augustus said, appearing to make up his mind. 'Yes, yes. I think this daughter of yours will do – '

'Will *do*,' Hugo van Helsen turned on him with a scowl. 'Do you think I have brought you here for your *approval*?'

'Well ... yes,' Augustus said, 'in the circumstances it is important for me to be sure. After all, you must make certain allowances.'

'*Allowances*,' Hugo van Helsen spluttered, his face darkening. '*Allowances* for the daughter of a mere moneylender, I suppose?'

'Of course,' Augustus agreed, sounding pleased that Hugo van Helsen had grasped the truth so readily. He drew a little closer. 'But a word of advice, sir – there will be no need to remind people of your trade. Your past may have been base and low, but your future is one full of the honour our House will bring ... '

'You bring nothing to me but an ache in the head!' Hugo van Helsen erupted with rage. He let rip with all the pent-up bile he could muster. 'I brought you here so you can see why your proposal is not acceptable. I brought you here to show you that my daughter is worth a thousand Windjammers!' He took hold of poor Willem by the back of the neck and thrust him at Augustus. 'I assure you – ships will fly in the air on wings before this excuse for a boy marries my daughter!'

Augustus Windjammer's mouth fell open in amazement, his slack jaw cushioned on a pile of double chins.

Hugo van Helsen hadn't finished. 'You come here puffed up with your own self-importance, talking as if you are an honourable man, and all the while you are plotting and scheming to save yourself.' He laughed without humour. 'And *where* is the famous Windjammer honour now? The truth is your precious family is no different than any other in Amsterdam – if you scrape off the gilt you find just clay underneath.'

'Am I ... ' Augustus spoke after a long pause, ' ... to take that as a *no*?'

'Get out, you fool!' Hugo van Helsen roared.

'But surely, sir?' Augustus blustered. 'The house of Windjammer ... I mean ... The honour of it all for you ... '

'Enough!' Hugo van Helsen cut him dead. 'Go back

to the Herengracht and call a meeting at that Long Table of yours. Tell what is left of your family that they have one week to find the money I am owed. If I am not paid then I will bring the sheriff and his men and have you all thrown out on to the streets. Do you understand? And then I will take what I want of your *great* House of Windjammer and feed the rest to the crows!'

Augustus retreated before Hugo van Helsen's fury, but he still couldn't quite believe this rejection. He pushed Willem aside, discarding him like a used rag.

'I have a daughter too, sir!' His voice rose in panic. 'Her name is Angelica. She is only young, it's true, but I am sure she would make *you* a good wife in time and I am willing to come to some agreement ... '

'Get out! Get out!' Hugo van Helsen stormed, 'and take this miserable boy with you! One day Jade will indeed be married – but never to a Windjammer. *Never!*' He pulled the cover over the portrait as if to prove that Augustus was no longer worthy even to look at her. 'I swore to my dear wife before she died that our daughter would marry well. Even now I am making arrangements to keep that promise. This portrait will be sent to England and shown to the rich burghers and nobles of London. Yes, I will find her a good husband there. She will marry well and *I* will make an alliance for myself that will be the envy of *all* Amsterdam –'

'*England?*' Augustus gasped, realising he had made a big mistake. 'My sister-in-law is English – '

Hugo van Helsen wasn't listening now. A gleam had come into those pale eyes as he spoke.

'It will not be long before war breaks out between

Holland and England over trade in the east,' he said. 'Already there is trouble. And wars are expensive. Both sides will need to borrow money for ships and men and *I* intend to lend it. Yes, I will grow rich from an alliance by marriage with a good English family –'

'*No!*' Jade's shout rang out suddenly.

Everyone turned to look.

Jade stood, gripping the handrail with all her strength. Her eyes flashed as tears of rage and hurt rolled down her cheeks. 'How could you, Father? How *could* you?'

15. Wolfie

Adam's feet moved him, but he was not conscious of walking or even where he was going, only that he needed to be somewhere else and that his feet somehow knew where.

The Street of Knives blurred past him. He hardly noticed the people around him or the cold, dead weight of the animal carcasses against his shoulder as he barged through them.

He no longer felt angry, just numb and now strangely removed from everything going on around him in the streets. He might have been a ghost drifting through the narrow twists and turns. Unseen. Untouched. Cut off from a city turned suddenly ugly around him.

A series of images had burned themselves into his memory: Jade van Helsen standing on the gallery with tears streaming down her cheeks, the surprise on her father's face as he had looked up and seen them together, Augustus Windjammer with his handkerchief clamped over his mouth in shock, and Willem just grinning with relief.

Everything had happened very quickly after Jade had shouted out.

'Get them down from there!' Hugo van Helsen had

roared. Goltz had come running up the spiral stairs. Adam remembered struggling as he was bundled out into the street with the banker's voice ringing in his ears: 'And stay away from my house. Stay away from my daughter! She will never marry a Windjammer. She will marry a prince not a *pauper*.'

' ... Prince not a *pauper* ... a prince not a *pauper* ... ' even now the words echoed in his head.

Adam's thoughts focused on Jade. She was a van Helsen. Someone to be despised. It should have been easy hating her, but strangely it wasn't. And that made it worse.

He moved through a haze of streets. Bridges loomed and passed. He didn't think where he was going. He didn't care. So it was quite by chance that he stumbled upon the street entertainers.

A crowd had gathered in the market near the old city wall. Before he even knew what was happening he had been drawn in. His feet drove him on, pushing him through their ranks, until he broke free and found himself among the entertainers. Suddenly all around him acrobats were jumping and balancing in a confusion of movement, music and noise. A trumpet blared. Drums thumped and rolled. One man breathed fire. Another stopped, opened his mouth and pushed a sword down his throat. Then a sound tore at his ears, the roaring of a bear.

Vaguely he was aware he had seen the bear somewhere before. The beast was standing tall on its hind legs with a chain through a ring in its nose. Around it, hopping and skipping, danced its master: the small demon of a man now beating a tambourine.

It might all have been part of a grotesque dream. The

crowd jostled for a better look as the bear shuffled by. The people's faces were distorted and ugly. They pointed, leering. Their laughter: the cry of seabirds. And all the while the tambourine flashed and clashed.

Adam stopped as the bear passed in front of him. He watched the bear's owner skipping in circles, shaking the tambourine and making the beast dance to the beat. Around him the people laughed and shouted, 'Dance for us, bear! Dance! Dance! *Dance!*'

And in that instant Adam realised he was no different from that bear. Like the beast he was chained to a ring and being made to dance to another's tune. He turned and fought his way back through people, clawing and snarling in his desperation to be free of them. He tripped and fell, rolling in the filth of the gutter. He scrambled to his feet and ran to the corner where he leaned against the wall and was sick. Breathing hard, he wiped his mouth on the back of his hand and looked around.

And that was when he saw Wolfie.

Wolfie had been hanging around the crowd looking out for opportunities to cut purses, but had been drawn by the cruelty and excitement surrounding the bear. Now, as the bear danced on, he had seen Adam leaning against the wall.

Their eyes met and locked. For a moment they both just stood quite still and looked at each other while all around them there was movement and noise. Then the threads of Adam's thoughts came together, as if they had been unravelled and stitched back in a pattern that began to take clear shape. And in that instant he knew what he had to do.

He took a step towards Wolfie, then another and another. And suddenly he was running across the market square. Wolfie saw him coming and spun on his heel and fled down a nearby alley. Adam didn't stop to wonder if it might be a trap. His only thought now was that somehow Wolfie knew the answers to the questions that burned inside his head.

Their footsteps echoed around the walls as they ran, jinking through the tight turns of the alley, until the chase came to a sudden halt at the edge of a canal. Adam saw Wolfie turn the corner ahead of him and then stop dead, trapped on the edge of a canal with the houses leaning in on either side and only the dark, sluggish water below.

Wolfie paced along the edge like a wild animal, searching for a way out. But escape from that dead end was impossible without a boat. He had little choice but to turn and face Adam.

'So you're ... scared ... of *me* now, are you, Wolfie?' Adam asked, breathlessly.

'I'm not scared of n-no one,' Wolfie growled.

'Then why did you run?'

'That's my b-business.'

Adam shook his head. 'I think it's *my* business now, Wolfie! You know something. I know you do – otherwise you wouldn't have tried to get away.'

'Maybe I d-do and maybe I d-don't,' Wolfie said. 'But I'm not telling *you* – not for n-nothing! You Windjammers are *his* concern now.'

Wolfie paused and looked pained as if he had already said too much.

'*Whose* concern, Wolfie?' Adam asked. 'I *have* to know!'

'D-do you think I'm a fool?' Wolfie hissed. 'If I talk to you the p-preacher will slit my throat.'

'So it's Abner Heems?'

'I never said that!'

'Why does he hate the Windjammers?'

'I'm saying n-nothing more!' Wolfie crouched slightly, his eyes darting as he looked for an escape. 'You can r-rot in Hell for all I care!'

Wolfie leapt forward with startling speed, slammed into Adam and shoved him out of the way. With several leggy bounds he was off, running back up the alley. He stopped when he was safely at the corner and looked back.

'I swear I'm going to make you p-pay one day, rich boy!' he snarled.

Adam had to think fast. This was his one chance to find out about the preacher and he knew it. He remembered the ring, reached for the chain around his neck and pulled it out from under his shirt. He let the ring dangle so it caught the light.

'Remember this, Wolfie?' he tempted him back. 'It's *gold*, Wolfie. *Real* gold, and it's yours if you can take it off me.'

A gleam came into Wolfie's eyes. He licked his teeth, glanced over his shoulder as if he half expected to see the preacher watching him, then greed brought his gaze back to the ring. He was drawn to it irresistibly. He took a step, paused, then another and made a sudden lunge forward.

Adam was ready, but even so the speed of the attack was surprising. In moments Wolfie's long fingers had clamped around his throat and he heard Wolfie's breath hissing in his ears as he felt the squeeze. Adam staggered back, choking, trying desperately to tear those hands away. But Wolfie was full of animal strength. They grappled, turning in circles on the edge. Phantom lights began popping in front of Adam's eyes as he struggled to breathe. Wolfie was determined to throttle the life right out of him. Adam had no choice and made up his mind quickly.

Two steps back took Adam to the edge. Wolfie's eyes opened wide in surprise when he realised what was happening. Then the houses and the canal changed places in a sudden gut-churning whirl and down they went with a tremendous rush.

Adam hit the water head first, driven down deep by Wolfie's weight on top of him. The water closed around them and the shock of the cold stole what little breath he had left. The darkness swamped him. Bubbles broke from his nose unseen. Only slowly did he become aware that Wolfie's grip had slackened on his throat. He twisted, turned sharply and broke free. He kicked hard for the surface, rising up out of the darkness to the light above.

Adam broke the surface in a rush that took him out of the water to his waist. He sucked in a ragged gulp of air. The canal-stink hit him, but at that moment no breath could have been sweeter. He sank back into the ripples, treading water as he looked around for Wolfie.

A moment later, Wolfie came up with a rush. He sucked in water and air and began to choke as he thrashed his arms about helplessly. 'C-c-c-c-c ... ' Wolfie's voice rose to a screech in sheer panic, ' ... c-can't *swim*!'

One look told Adam that Wolfie wasn't lying now. 'Stop struggling!' he called. 'I'll help you.'

Panic gripped Wolfie. He was too frightened to listen. He made a desperate attempt to reach Adam, but the water took him down again as if he had stepped into a hole.

Adam ducked under the surface, swimming down after him, searching him out blindly in the murk. He caught hold of Wolfie's coat and pulled, kicking hard again for the surface. Wolfie came up choking and such was his panic he threatened to drown them both. Adam struck out for the wall of the canal, pulling Wolfie by the collar and it took every bit of his strength to reach the edge.

'N-now look what you g-g-gone and done!' Wolfie gasped, when at last he had caught his breath. He flattened himself into the slime on the wall, stabbing his fingers into the gaps in the brickwork and whimpering with the cold each time they slipped off.

Adam did his best to ignore him and looked around. The walls of the canal rose sheer to the backs of the houses on each side, making it almost impossible to climb out at that point. Nonetheless he was determined to try. He noticed a ledge in the brickwork some way above his head and made up his mind to try and reach it.

'You'll never m-make it up there,' Wolfie said. 'N-no chance.'

The brickwork was slippery with filth, but the mortar between the bricks was poor and crumbling. Adam managed to find a hold, then another, and little by little began to pull himself out of the water. By stretching up as far as he could he just managed to hook the fingers of one hand on to the ledge. He paused, breathing hard, readying himself for the next part of the climb. But as he hung there helplessly, he felt something scurry over his fingers: something warm and furry, something with sharp claws. He snatched his hand away and fell back into the water with a dull slop.

'R-rats!' Wolfie groaned.

Now as Adam looked up he saw them. Big black ship's rats scurrying along the ledge, scuttling over one another as they moved along by the canal.

'I hate r-rats,' Wolfie groaned. '*Help!*' the word burst out of him. 'Heee-eee-eee-eee-eeelp!'

Adam fought back a rising sense of panic.

'No one's g-going to hear us down here,' Wolfie said, giving up. His voice full of their doom. 'I seen it all b-before. People fall in and n-never get out. Why do you think the rats are so *f-fat*?'

Adam tried to think clearly despite the numbing cold. Some way further down the canal he could see the span of a wooden bridge. People were crossing and he was instantly drawn towards the movement.

'I'll go for help,' he said.

'No!' Wolfie squealed. 'I know what you're g-going to do! You're just g-going to leave me here.' He glanced up at the rats, then back at Adam. He was wild-eyed with terror. 'I hate r-rats. I'll t-tell you what you want to know. I'll t-tell you everything – just don't leave me here!'

Adam thought for a moment. Despite the cold and their desperate situation, he realised he would never find a better way of getting Wolfie to talk.

'All right,' he said, cautiously. 'I'm listening.'

Wolfie glanced up at the rats, made Adam promise not to leave him and then let it all out in a rush.

'He's more than just a p-preacher, you know,' Wolfie started. 'Yes, Abner Heems is dangerous, all right – and he can be b-bought too.'

'*Bought?*' Adam asked, treading water. 'What do you mean?'

'I *mean* he'll p-preach what you want him to for the right price,' Wolfie said. 'And someone's b-bought him – paid him to p-preach against you Windjammers.'

'*Paid* him?'

'Yes, you're in big trouble, r-rich boy. I heard stories about the p-preacher that'll make your eyes jump clean out of your head. He's the Devil's own, that's for sure,' he said and lowered his voice. 'Some say he's sailed under the red flag. That means blood – *blood*! That's why the pirates use it and I don't d-doubt it – Heems'll slit your throat as soon as look at you, th-that's for sure.' Wolfie glanced about nervously. 'I'm as good as dead if he finds out I t-talked.'

'The rats will get you first,' Adam said.

Wolfie decided he would prefer to take his chances with the rats rather than the preacher. He swore he wouldn't say another word.

'Have it your own way,' Adam said. He began to swim away from Wolfie towards the bridge.

'N-no! Wait! All right! I'll t-tell you!' Wolfie's terror was plain to hear. 'All I know is, the preacher's been paid to stir up t-trouble against you. That's his style, see. He preaches from the book and people believe him because he makes p-prophecies. He tells people something bad'll happen, then, when the t-time's right, he makes his own p-prophecies come true.'

'*Makes* them?' Adam swam back to the wall. 'How can he *make* them?'

'Don't you know nothing, r-rich boy?' Wolfie said. 'He makes it look like an act of God. But it's *him* all right. He's c-clever. He watches. He waits. Then he strikes. No one sees him so no one can prove anything. Then he stands up and p-preaches – telling everyone that God warned them and now God has struck them down like one of them old kings in the Bible.'

Suddenly it began to make sense. Even there, floating in the freezing cold of that stinking canal, Adam began to see the truth. The preacher was part of a bigger plan. Someone had made the most of the Windjammers' misfortunes and decided to make it even worse. If Abner Heems had been paid to stir up trouble then it had been no accident that he had been in the crowd in the Herengracht the day the news of the fleet reached them – the day Adam's father had died.

'*Who's* paying him, Wolfie?' Adam asked. He had already guessed, but he had to know for sure. 'Tell me – *now*!'

'Work it out for yourself, r-rich boy!' Wolfie managed a sneer despite the cold. 'It's the m-moneylender who's after you Windjammers. It's the m-moneylender who's got most to gain.' He glanced up at the rats and the terror showed in his eyes again. 'Now – I've told you all I know and you swore you'd help me!'

Adam had to prise Wolfie's fingers off the wall to make him let go. Wolfie clung to him helplessly, whimpering like a baby.

Had he not been so cold Adam might have wrung

even more answers out of Wolfie right there and then. But one look at the bluish colour of Wolfie's face told him the rest would have to wait until later. With some difficulty he persuaded Wolfie to lie on his back in the water, and with a supporting hand under Wolfie's chin he began to tow him towards the bridge.

Adam stayed as close to the edge as he could, pausing every now and again to rest, until at last they were close enough to wave and call out to the people crossing the bridge. But it was hard to stay afloat and even harder to make themselves heard.

'We'll have to climb up,' Adam gasped and struck out for the bridge supports.

The underside of the bridge drifted over their heads and Adam caught hold of one of the wooden supports. The water dragged on him. By now his fingers were so numb he couldn't feel them. They slipped off again and again as he tried to push Wolfie up out of the water.

'I d-done it!' Wolfie said, wheezing when at last he managed to pull himself out of the water. He clung to the bridge's cross-support, gasping until he had regained his breath. Then he sat up.

'Give me a hand!' Adam said, reaching up.

Adam saw the look on Wolfie's face and knew then he had made a big mistake.

'You shouldn't oughta have done that, r-rich boy!' Wolfie said, having looked around to make sure there were no witnesses to what he was about to do. 'You shouldn't have made me tell you them things. The p-preacher'll do for me if he finds out. So I g-got no choice now, see!'

He thought about it for a moment and came to a sick conclusion. 'But then maybe I'll be doing him a f-favour,' he said. 'Maybe the p-preacher'll even thank me.' His lips peeled back from his teeth in an evil grin. 'This could be my b-big chance. If I do you it'll prove to everyone that I'm not to be messed with. Maybe then everyone'll stop laughing at the way old Wolfie talks and show some respect like what the preacher gets.'

Wolfie's dripping boot flashed down, stamping Adam's fingers hard against the wooden beam. The pain shot up through Adam's arm and he cried out as he let go.

Wolfie pushed him down into the water again and again, stamping at his fingers each time Adam tried to catch hold, until finally Adam no longer had the strength to try. Wolfie grinned down triumphantly as he watched him begin to drift away.

'You done me a b-big favour, rich boy,' Wolfie said and then began to climb up through the criss-crossing beams to the bridge above.

Adam could only watch helplessly as Wolfie reached the top and slithered over the rail. With only a quick glance back down, he fled across the bridge and was gone.

It all seemed so unreal. Adam could see people on the bridge. He could even hear them talking. But he no longer had the strength even to call out to them. Everything seemed to happen so slowly. He found it hard to think of anything but the weight of the water. The cold gripped him, it seemed to squeeze the breath out of his lungs, crushing his chest. His head filled with a strange sound and he realised it was his own heart beating, *thu-dum, thu-dum, thu-dum*, and he began to wonder what it would be like to drown.

And perhaps Adam would have drifted for all eternity had the sound of his heart not been joined by the steady dip and pull of oars in the water.

'Looks like I gone and caught myself a big'n!' a voice said.

Adam became aware of a hand on his collar. The water rushed off him as he was hauled out and dropped into the bottom of a row boat. He lay there like an exhausted fish.

Thu-dum, thu-dum, thu-dum.

A boatman's face appeared close to his. 'Still alive, then?' He sounded surprised. 'Didn't your mother tell you not to go swimming in canals?'

Thu-dum, thu-dum, thu-dum.

The boatman rowed on until he reached a place further along the canal. There, he dragged Adam out of the boat and up on to the canal side. Few people even bothered to stop and look.

The cold came biting back with the wind. Adam couldn't even gasp his thanks, so he caught hold of the boatman's hand and clung to it.

'Looks like I found you just in time,' the boatman said.

Adam lay back on the cobbles and stared at the sky, his head filled only with the sound of his heart beating: *thu-dum, thu-dum, thu-dum.*

16. Lost and Found

'He's wearing fine clothes.'

'Aye, but no chinks on him.'

'Been robbed, I'll wager. Then thrown in the canal like the rest.'

Adam opened his eyes and saw a woman bending over him. He felt her rubbing his arms and legs and cried out as the feeling came back into his frozen limbs in a rush of warm blood.

'Don't just stand there, you great lump!' the woman said, turning to the boatman. 'Help me get him up. He'll die of cold and the ague if we leave him out in this wind much longer.'

'Aye, but I've a boat to row,' the boatman said, sounding reluctant. 'If I took pity on every boy I dragged out of the canal I'd be a poor man.'

'Or a *rich* one, maybe,' the woman said, as she found the ring on the chain around Adam's neck.

'Now that's the price of a boy's life,' the boatman said. He knelt beside Adam and fumbled with the chain. 'We'll say he lost it in the water if he asks.'

Adam was vaguely aware of the chain being lifted over his head, but was still too weak to resist. His arms and legs felt like wet rope as the boatman dragged him to his feet.

'Walk!' the woman commanded him, slipping a shoulder in quickly under one arm to support him. 'You *must* walk!'

Adam didn't remember much of how they got there, only that the woman and the boatman helped him to a house nearby. They passed through a small cobbled square with a washhouse in the middle where women were kneeling scrubbing clothes on smooth stones.

'Inga will help you,' the woman said as she knocked on a door.

A small, squarely built washerwoman opened the door. She was wearing a white cap and an apron over a dress the colour of sacks. 'What's this?' she greeted them.

'Dirk here found him floating in the canal,' the woman explained.

Adam's teeth were chattering so hard he didn't hear much of what else was said as Inga waved them in and started tugging at his sopping coat. Adam clutched the sodden cloth to him.

'If you don't take off these wet things the ague will set in,' Inga explained. 'Then you'll die of the canal fever most like.'

All resistance was useless. With strength born out of years of hard work, they began stripping him.

'Don't be shy!' Inga teased him. 'You ain't got nothing my boys ain't got – 'cept maybe fleas ... '

They stripped him to the skin, lifted him into the bottom half of a cut barrel and doused him with water warmed by the fire. Before Adam knew it he had been scrubbed, dried, wrapped in a blanket and sat on a stool in front of a fire in Inga's simple kitchen. His clothes had been washed and scrubbed just as vigorously and they were soon steaming gently beside him on a rail while he sat feeling more than just a little embarrassed.

His hand went to his throat, 'Where's my ring?'

'Ring?' Inga said.

'It was on a chain around my neck.'

Inga placed a wooden bowl in front of him and glanced at the boatman. 'He must have lost it in the water, hey, Dirk?'

'Most likely, Inga,' Dirk agreed. 'Happens all the time.'

Inga went away and came back to place a bowl of stew and a loaf of freshly baked bread on the table in front of the boatman.

'Have you a spoon, Inga?' the boatman asked, unable to look her in the eye.

Inga held back the spoon. 'Not until you've paid,' she said.

'*Paid?*' the boatman sounded surprised.

Inga held out her hand and fixed him with a knowing look. 'I only want what's rightfully due.'

'But I saved his life!' the boatman protested weakly.

Inga remained with her hand held out until finally the boatman sighed and reached into his pocket. He pulled out the ring and chain. 'Must have forgot to mention it.'

'You forgot all right,' Inga said. She took it and handed him the spoon.

'My kindness will make me a poor man,' the boatman muttered.

'But a rich one in heaven,' Inga said.

The boatman seemed to prefer it the other way around. He gave Adam a weak smile and bent low over his stew.

Inga held up the ring on its chain, looked at the mark briefly, then dropped it into Adam's hand. He thanked her and slipped the ring back around his neck.

'Now drink up!' Inga said.

Adam sniffed at the contents of the bowl warily.

'It is a brew of herbs and hot water,' Inga said. 'Meadowsweet for the stomach, feverfew for the head, garlic for the cold, and the root of dandelion for the bowels. It's an old potion – it'll help ward off the canal fever.'

Adam took a sip. The liquid was scalding hot and bitter, but as he swallowed he felt the potion warming him deep inside. The second taste wasn't nearly as bad and he had soon finished it.

'I didn't fall into the canal,' Adam started to explain.

'We don't ask questions here,' Inga said. 'God knows, we all have our troubles.'

'I will come back and pay you for your kindness,' Adam promised.

Inga's face lit up as she laughed. 'Aye, you can pay me,' she said, 'just as soon as you've weighed a mortal breath in the scales and told me how much gold a life's worth.'

By the time Adam's clothes had dried and he was fully dressed again, an assortment of Inga's lodgers had passed through the door and had settled to eat their lunch at the table in the kitchen. Men from the local pewter factories, their faces blackened with soot from the fires, and workers from the waterfront nearby. They paid little attention to the newcomer in their midst.

As each arrived Inga placed a plate of fresh herrings

and shellfish in front of them. The herrings had been fried in onions, herbs and butter and the men spoke to each other in low voices as they ate quickly, every so often tearing great chunks of bread from a loaf or slicing Gouda cheese on to their pewter plates, and washing it all down with ale from a wooden jug. Soon the men lit their pipes and sat back to talk.

As he listened, warm in Inga's friendly little kitchen, Adam realised they had accepted him without question. Not one of them had even asked his name. It didn't seem important to them to know he was a Windjammer. It was only later, when he had time to think about it, that Adam realised what it meant: rich or poor, it didn't matter – among these people he was simply *Adam*. And it felt good to be free for a while of the responsibility of being a Windjammer.

'How now, Valentino?' the men greeted a latecomer as he arrived. 'What news from the taverns?'

Valentino was taller, thinner and fairer than the others, and he was wearing a wine-coloured coat over clothes that had once been fashionable and fine. But there was a worn-out, stained feel about him that went deeper than just his outer appearance.

'A thousand apologies, madam!' Valentino greeted Inga, sweeping off his battered hat with a flourishing bow. 'But I have been detained on important business.'

'I know your business well enough to know it never pays the rent,' Inga said, unimpressed.

'Ah! *Money*,' Valentino said. 'A curse when you have it, but an even greater curse when it has gone! And yet – ' he drew up a stool and leaned forward to speak to the men around the table, 'I heard today that a simple clerk bought a rare tulip bulb worth more than 30,000 florins! So you see a clever man can grow rich if he dabbles in the right business!'

'Or poorer like you,' Inga pointed out.

'True, madam, true,' Valentino agreed. 'I have to admit fortune has not smiled on me of late. But never fear – the wheel of fate is always turning and must turn in my favour soon.'

Inga doubted it, but Valentino had spotted the herrings and all else was forgotten for a while as he lavished praise on Inga's culinary skills until she produced him a plateful. It was while he was half-way through cutting a huge slab of bread from the loaf that he noticed Adam.

'We have a guest,' he said, sounding pleased.

'You leave him be!' Inga warned. 'The boy's had enough trouble for one day.'

'Then like me he has fallen on hard times,' Valentino said. He looked at Adam's coat with some interest. 'There's been money with you, I'd say. Can one so young have lost everything? But I was a young man too when I first came under the spell of that rarest of flowers they call the tulip.'

'Pay him no heed, lad,' one of the company said. 'The only spell he's been under is the cudgel of the *kapistan*. And we all know what happens when you're introduced to that judas flower the Turks call *Lale*.'

'I was sold an onion, that's all,' Valentino winced and rubbed the back of his head as if it hurt. 'A heavy blow that brought me here to good Inga's door, it's true. If I'm poorer for it, then I'm wiser too. And I'll prove it one day.'

'If they don't hang you for a rogue first,' Inga said. She turned to Adam. 'You mark my words, for every one that's made his chinks from tulips, there's a dozen like Valentino here who's lost it all.'

And so the talk would have gone on, had the news not reached them of the trouble at the waterfront.

'A mob,' a boy reported breathlessly to the women in the washhouse in the square. From there the word spread fast. 'They've been gathering outside one of the warehouses. They'll burn it down soon, they say.'

Adam looked up sharply when he heard the news. Instinctively he knew which warehouse it would be. He pushed back his stool and followed the men as they went to see for themselves. Only Valentino stayed seated at the table, showing little interest in this new turn of events – it seemed he had seen and heard it all before.

Torches had been lit. Grim-faced men had met to talk and listen, gathering on the waterfront in front of the Windjammers' warehouse.

Adam came to a halt and looked up at the massive wooden doors. By now the early winter evening was beginning to draw a thin, evil-smelling mist in from the marshes to the north. The mist hung in wispy skeins in the air over the waterfront, blurring everything so that the warehouse loomed ahead of him like a ghost ship. It stood silently, with the flickering light of the men's torches licking up the walls to the lines of wooden doors that faced the waterfront.

He had run all the way, cutting through the winding streets of the Jordaan. Now, as he stopped to catch his breath, a slight dizziness swept over him. He bent forward, gripped suddenly by a twinge deep in the pit of his stomach, and breathed hard through the O of his mouth until the feeling passed. Only then did he move on.

'I was there! I heard Hercules Windjammer give his oath,' a voice rose above the heads of the men. 'And is it not so written in the good book? "Better is it that thou shouldest not vow, than that thou shouldest not pay."'

Abner Heems had set himself up on a wooden block to address the men around him. He seemed to float above the crowd as if he had devil's wings. Adam recognised many of the faces there. He saw the carpenter from the *Draco* and Jacob and Hobe. The scarred shipwright stood out from the others, noticeable by his sheer size and the massive long-handled hammer in his hand.

'Up there!' someone called out and pointed.

They all looked up as one of the small doors that opened into the air over the waterfront was thrown open. Gerrit appeared and stood, clinging to the doorframe among the lines of ropes hanging from the hoist above. Just behind him, cowering near some barrels, Adam caught a glimpse of Augustus Windjammer with his handkerchief clutched to his mouth.

'This is a place of business,' Gerrit called down to them. 'By what authority do you come here?'

The preacher looked to the men around him. 'The book-keeper asks for authority and yet he holds none!' he said. 'Why will Augustus Windjammer not speak to us? We know he is in there. We saw him go in. And now he hides like a rat in a trap!'

'Aye!' other voices were raised. 'We want to talk to a Windjammer!' they called. 'Bring him out! Bring him out!'

The torchlight washed over the preacher's face. His eyes seemed to drink in the fire and somehow set his soul alight. Adam saw a woman step forward out of the crowd and hurl something rotten. It fell splat on the Windjammer name over the door. The men around her cheered and surged forward. Many fists beat at the doors until Hobe pushed through them and raised his great hammer. The blow splintered the wood and set off echoes inside the warehouse like distant cannon fire.

The preacher watched with obvious satisfaction, then – his work there done – he leapt down from his wooden block and vanished into the mist that swirled up from the canal.

Hobe stood back as the carpenter cleared the people away from the door, making more room as Hobe readied himself for another mighty blow.

'*Please.* Listen to me, all of you! This is not the answer.' Gerrit appealed for calm.

'Then bring out Augustus Windjammer!' It was the carpenter who answered him now the preacher had gone.

'I understand your concerns,' Gerrit called, 'but please – '

'Oh, that's all right then,' the carpenter said, turning to the others. 'He *understands our concerns.*'

Their laughter was coarse and without humour.

'Then go and tell that coward of a Windjammer to come out!' one called.

'Tell him we wants our money!' another agreed.

Gerrit was shouted down and a moment later disappeared back inside. A short while later the door opened again and Gerrit, not Augustus, reappeared. The men saw him and their mood turned even uglier.

'Augustus Windjammer says you are to go to your homes. He says he will not speak to you under the shadow of your threats.' Gerrit had to shout over the men's booing. He tried to be reasonable: 'It is true that the Windjammer Trading Company has been going through difficult times of late. We have all had to tighten our belts. None more so than the Windjammers themselves.'

'Are we supposed to believe that?' the carpenter asked, 'when the Windjammers still live like French kings in the Herengracht!'

'Aye!' another agreed. 'I've seen Augustus Windjammer – stuffing himself on beef and onions while we go hungry!'

Adam, meanwhile, had been working his way through the crush of men to the front. With every step it became obvious that his uncle would have to come out and face them or they would break in the doors and drag him out.

Hobe now raised his hammer and struck the doors again, with enough force to shake them on their iron hinges. The carpenter called for more support. Adam saw there was no chance of getting in at the front and ducked quickly back out of sight. He wormed his way out of the crowd and slipped away to the canal in the hope that the back way in had been forgotten and left unguarded.

The mist blanketed the canal, swirling up in stinking eddies. It hung heavily over the boats tied up alongside, and the water beneath was like molten night. Adam kept to the shadows and turned the corner. The warehouse rose sheer: a fortress of stone. He kept his back to the wall and crept along the canal side towards the doors.

'Hurry, man! *Hurry!*' Adam heard someone call out in a hoarse whisper. Some way ahead of him a light appeared. 'Go to the boat! Make ready the oars! I will keep watch from here in case we are surprised.'

Adam drew back against the wall and watched as a man broke away from the back of the warehouse and ran through the swirling mist to a boat tied up to the wall of the canal. The water slapped and sucked at the keel as the man stepped into the boat, rocking it violently before he sat down. There was a muffled clunk, then another and the oars were set in place.

'Hurry, Borch!' the same voice called from the safety of the doorway. 'They must not find me here.'

Adam recognised the voice now. 'Uncle!' he called out.

Augustus Windjammer heard him, let out a startled yelp and set off towards the boat at the run. He held up a lantern, the light swinging wildly as he made an ungainly dash to the canal.

'The door, sir!' Adam heard Borch say. 'The door!'

'Blast the door!' Augustus Windjammer said. 'Help me in, damn you! There's someone after me. Out of the way, man! Can't you keep this boat still while I sit down? There. I'm secure. Now *row!*'

Adam reached the edge of the canal soon after the boat had pulled away from the canal side. He could see Borch at the oars and his uncle sitting in the stern, weighing the back of the boat down almost to the waterline as he sat hunched with the lantern at his side.

'Uncle, come back! It's me – *Adam.*'

'*You*, nephew? What are *you* doing here?' Augustus

raised the lantern and looked at him across the water. His voice changed. 'Have you not caused enough vexation and trouble for one day? Yes, yes! You little fool. Thanks to you everything is lost. *Everything*.'

Had he had time, Adam would have argued the point. But time was running out. By now the air was full of the dull thud of the many shoulders that had been brought to bear on the doors at the front of the warehouse.

'You have to tell Gerrit to open those doors, uncle,' Adam said. 'You have to go out and talk to the crowd before they break in.'

'Are you mad?' Augustus was clearly appalled by the suggestion. 'Open the doors? *Me* – go out and talk to them? *Never!* That mob would tear me to pieces.'

'If you don't they'll break in the doors,' Adam said. 'Then who'll listen to the Windjammers? No one!'

Augustus was adamant. 'I have told Gerrit to stay and talk sense into them while I go with Borch, at great personal risk to myself, to fetch the city guard.'

'But it'll be too late by then,' Adam said. 'And anyway they won't listen to Gerrit. I heard the men – they want to talk to a Windjammer.'

'A *Windjammer*, is it?' Augustus said. 'Then why do you need me? *You* are as much a Windjammer in name as I am. *You* talk to them!' He nodded. 'Yes, yes, nephew, by all means tell Gerrit to open the doors and talk to them. See what happens then!'

Augustus Windjammer turned to Borch. 'Lay to the oars, man! Quick now,' he said. The boat began to pull away. The mist swirled and closed around them. 'I will return only when I have a company of the city guard at my back.' His voice came echoing eerily out of the mist. 'Go make your speeches, nephew! But take care, for I'll wager the only talk that mob will listen to is the language of cold steel.'

Adam heard his uncle laughing as the glow of the lantern faded into the mist, growing dimmer with each pull of the oars. Wavelets washed back, lapping up over the steps to wet Adam's boots. He glanced up at the warehouse brooding in the darkness behind him. By the time he looked for the boat again it had gone. He was alone.

17. The Battle of Hobe's Ear

A series of heavy thuds sent echoes booming through the vast spaces of the warehouse.

Adam looked up sharply. He was still standing by the canal, but even from there he could see the wicket gate was open in the great double doors at the back of the warehouse. He glanced into the mist where he had last seen the boat, but his uncle wasn't coming back. He turned away and approached the doors cautiously to peer in through the opening. The fine hairs on the back of his neck lifted. He had the uncomfortable feeling he wasn't alone after all and his every instinct warned him to be careful.

A sudden cramp knotted his stomach in a spasm of pain. He leaned against the door and had to breathe deeply until it passed. He knew it was more than just fear that drove that spike deep into his guts, and tried not to think what it might be as he pushed all thoughts of fever to the back of his mind.

Adam took one last deep breath and ducked in through the doorway. He stood quite still, listening to the sounds that filled the darkness around him. He closed and bolted the door. The darkness was then complete. It swamped him, blinding him, forcing him to feel his way ahead with outstretched hands.

He came up against some barrels, turned first one way and then the other, scraping his knuckles and shins as he fumbled about blindly until he found the way forward again. And all the while his ears rang with the booming thuds and thumps that filled the air, making an enormous drum of the warehouse.

Worse was to come, however. Without warning the noises stopped abruptly. Adam could only assume the attack at the front had reached a critical point and he waited for a cheer or the sound of running feet as the mob broke in. Nothing happened.

If anything the darkness seemed even thicker then. Somehow the silence wove itself into the very fabric of the place and made it seem impenetrable. Adam's ears rang until he could bear that silence no longer and called out to Gerrit. His voice fell dead in the darkness. He gave up hope and was about to move on again when he heard the noise.

Adam's breath caught in his throat. He stood quite still, his heart hammering against his ribs as he listened. It seemed an age passed before he heard the soft crunch of a footstep and the faintest rustle of a coat as it caught and dragged on a sack.

'Gerrit?' he breathed. 'Is that you?'

No answer.

A sudden crash and a cheer from the front left Adam bouncing painfully off barrels as he blundered about with fright. He tripped, fell, stood up and forced himself to stand still again before he lost all sense of forward and back. The noise was deafening after the quiet, but at least it helped him regain his bearings.

He followed the sound as best he could, but he was

still filled with the dread of the footstep he had heard. He was sure now that someone had slipped in through the open door while he had been by the canal. So it was that, with great relief, he saw a light ahead of him at last and found his way into the Weighing Room.

'*Master Adam!* How did you get in here?' Gerrit was astonished to see him.

'It's a long story.'

'You are hurt, Master Adam. You are bleeding!'

'It's nothing,' Adam said, sucking at the blood on his skinned knuckles. He glanced over his shoulder. 'My uncle left the door open to the canal – I think someone might have got in while I wasn't looking.'

'It is the least of our troubles, Master Adam,' Gerrit said grimly. 'The doors are bent and twisted. They will not hold for much longer.'

As if to prove him right, the attack resumed on the front with new ferocity. From where he stood Adam could see the doors at the end of the wide passage. They jumped and trembled with each new crash, and he could see the wooden bar that secured them was cracked and splintered.

'Take a lantern and go back the way you came, Master Adam,' Gerrit said. 'You must escape while there is still time.'

'I'm not leaving,' Adam said. 'We have to talk to them.'

'I have tried,' Gerrit said. 'But their mood only grows more dangerous with every word.'

'They'll listen to a *Windjammer*.'

Gerrit shook his head. 'I begged your uncle. I pleaded with him – he would not do it. He said they would listen to a company of the guard, but I fear bringing them will only make matters worse.'

'Then I'll talk to them,' Adam said.

'*You*, Master Adam?' Gerrit said. 'No! You are too young. It is too dangerous.'

'But I'm a Windjammer – and a Windjammer is what they want.'

'No, Master Adam,' Gerrit refused to contemplate it. 'I could never forgive myself if something happened to you. *I* am not important – but *you* ... *you* are the heir to the House of Windjammer. All our hopes, all our dreams, rest with you.' He made up his mind. 'Go to your dear mother and sisters! Tell them to gather only the most necessary of belongings and to leave the house on the Herengracht at once. I fear this mob will go there next. But I will hold them here with reasoning as long as I can –'

He was interrupted by the sound of the doors being assaulted violently again. The hinges twisted and buckled.

'The doors won't hold that long,' Adam said. 'I have to face them – like my father did.'

'That was different, Master Adam. He was a man. They knew him.'

Another massive blow shuddered through the warehouse.

Adam took a deep breath and pulled himself up to his full height. 'I am the head of the House of Windjammer now,' he said, with as much authority as he could muster. 'If you serve the Windjammers then you *must* do what I say, Gerrit! Now open the doors!'

For a moment it seemed Gerrit would still refuse – his dilemma etched deep lines in his forehead – but his wish to protect Adam was matched only by his instinct to obey. His resistance crumbled and he ducked into a bow.

'As you wish, Master Adam,' he said, then straightened his back and added, 'You are your father's son, sir – there is no doubt of that.'

He started towards the doors, but it was already too late.

Adam looked up at the sound. It was a terrible, grinding noise followed by a sharp *crack!* The doors bulged in under the weight of many shoulders. The wooden bar broke in two. The doors burst inwards and the mob poured in.

'Run! Master Adam! *Run!*' Gerrit cried out as he was swept aside in the rush.

Adam stood as if nailed to the ground. It took all of his courage, every bit of his nerve, just to stay still. He wanted to run. He wanted to hide. But he just stood at the end of the passage and watched the mob come. They swarmed through the door and in towards the Weighing Room. Most were carrying flaming torches and seemed intent on burning the warehouse down after they had looted as much as they could. And it was Hobe – the scarred, half-blind giant – who led them in wielding his great hammer like some vengeful heathen god.

Hobe saw Adam first. He clearly recognised him and stopped. The general advance came to a sudden halt behind him.

'What's going on? What are we waiting for?' The carpenter pushed his way through to the front. He saw Gerrit move quickly back to Adam's side and laughed aloud.

'So this is it!' the carpenter said, turning to the others. 'All that's left of the House of Windjammer – a boy and a book-keeper.'

Some laughed. Others jeered.

Hobe rested the great hammer on his shoulder and looked at Adam. The scar on his face pulsed, livid purple.

'Listen to me, all of you!' Gerrit appealed for calm. 'Let the boy go and I promise the Windjammer Trading Company will soon pay what it owes.'

'*Argh!* We've heard enough of your talk,' the carpenter said.

'Aye!' others agreed.

'I say this ship's sinking and sinking fast,' the carpenter said. 'I say we salvage what's owed to us before she goes under and the Devil take anyone who tries to stop us.'

And for a moment it seemed certain they would surge forward into the Weighing Room and overwhelm them.

'*Wait!*' It was Hobe who stopped them. 'The boy's a Windjammer – let him speak!'

The carpenter turned to Hobe in surprise. 'What's the point in listening? He may be a Windjammer – but he's still only a boy.'

'Aye, no older than my lad, it's true,' Hobe agreed.

'And the Windjammers did for him on the *Sirius*,' the carpenter said. 'He was drowned like a rat along with all the rest of them. This boy don't care. None of them Windjammers do.'

'Then why's he stayed in his uncle's place?' Hobe asked, fixing Adam with his good eye.

'Who knows? Who cares?' the carpenter said. 'I say

the Windjammers are all the same ... '

As the carpenter spoke, Adam tuned out to the sounds around him. The noise of the mob faded and became very small. He heard only the carpenter's voice now.

' ... *Agh!* He's no different from that fool Augustus Windjammer,' the carpenter's words echoed around the walls. 'He'll grow fat on the fruits of our labours just like his uncle. Aye! And live in high style in his grand house on the Herengracht while we struggle in the gutter of the Jordaan ... '

Adam's head filled with the images of his father standing holding the great globe, bowed and staggering under the weight and responsibility of that symbol. He remembered how he had died fighting to save the House of Windjammer, and how he had sworn to keep his word and send the *Draco* in search of the people he called his own – his *friends*.

The image of his father crumbled to dust in his head and the sounds came back with a rush. Suddenly Adam was angry: raging, screaming angry. He wanted to shout. He wanted to make them see the truth. He wanted to prove that his father had lived and died for them just as surely as if he had been standing alongside Lucien Windjammer and Hobe's boy on the deck of the *Sirius*. But when he opened his mouth, the only word that came out was:

'*Father.*'

In the quiet that followed, Adam's voice was picked up and repeated eerily in echoes that came calling back from deep within the warehouse.

The colour drained from Hobe's scar. He looked around, searching the shadows with the look of someone who was expecting to see a ghost. 'My boy?' he murmured.

The echoes faded and died.

Hobe turned back to Adam. His milky eye was fixed, staring. It seemed able to see much more than the bright one beside it.

'This boy lost a father,' Hobe spoke at last. 'I lost a son.' He nodded slowly. 'We are more equal than I thought.'

And with those few simple words Hobe said it all. He had proved the carpenter wrong. The Windjammers were no different from anyone else there. In the cruel game that fate had played with them, they had *all* suffered.

'Aye, Lucien Windjammer was lost too,' someone behind him said.

'He was a good man,' another said, 'just like the boy's father.'

No one moved or spoke for what seemed an age after that. Then at last Hobe grunted as if he had come to a conclusion.

'Where are you going?' the carpenter asked when Hobe turned away suddenly. 'You can't just leave now! What about our money? What about the *Draco*?'

Hobe looked at him. 'I say the dead speak louder than the living here,' he said and briefly searched the shadows with his all-seeing, nothing-seeing eye. He turned and pushed his way back through the crowd.

'I'll have no more part of this,' another said.

Others now saw sense and agreed.

'Then leave now and you will *all* be paid,' Gerrit promised with growing confidence.

Adam hoped beyond all hope it was true.

Gerrit nodded and confirmed it. 'Even you, Jan Wolks,' he said to the carpenter.

The carpenter stood his ground for a moment longer, but support was crumbling around him. '*Agh!*' he grunted. 'Then it seems I'll have to trust you for my money one more day.'

With that he turned back through the crowd. The men around him stirred and suddenly their ranks folded in on themselves as first one, then another and another followed him out. And there, perhaps, it would all have ended – had the soldiers not come.

'They've called out the guard!' The news spread quickly from the waterfront into the warehouse. '*Soldiers* – coming this way!'

They heard the steady tramp of marching feet. Hobe and the others were driven back into the Weighing Room by the press of people around the shattered doors. And suddenly all the mistrust and anger were in the men's eyes again.

'So that was your plan, hey Windjammer?' The carpenter jumped to the wrong conclusion. 'You've been playing us for fools until the soldiers came.'

'*No,*' Adam denied, but it was too late to explain.

'Make way for the city guard!' a soldier bellowed as two lines of soldiers quick-marched in through the broken doors, armed and ready with their halberds resting on their shoulders.

'Stand back, you dogs!' the captain ordered.

The crowd was forced to divide on either side as the soldiers formed two ranks facing outwards. The steel of the soldiers' helmets and breastplates glinted dully in the torchlight. Their halberds were held at the ready now. When the way had been cleared their captain came strutting down between the ranks with his sword drawn. There was a pause before Augustus Windjammer appeared, hesitantly clutching his handkerchief to his nose and mouth.

'Has bloody murder been done yet, captain?' Augustus asked. He saw Adam and a look of disappointment flitted briefly across his face before he made a show of being greatly relieved. 'You're still alive, dear nephew? Thank God! I have brought the guard as I promised I would. Yes, yes! At great personal risk to myself.' He took up a position of safety behind the captain and breathed advice in his ear. 'This needs a firm hand now, captain. You must arrest the ringleaders. You must make an example of them!'

'Who is the leader among you?' the captain asked.

No one answered. The carpenter shrank back, but Hobe stood his ground clutching his hammer.

'*Him.*' Augustus flapped his handkerchief at Hobe. 'Arrest that man! He's one of them, by the look of it. Yes, yes! A treacherous villain, I'll wager my life on it.'

The captain took one look at Hobe and decided to act first and ask questions afterwards. 'Seize him!' he barked, waving his sword.

Two soldiers stepped forward, snatched Hobe's hammer and took hold of him roughly by the arms. But Hobe was as strong as an ox and in the brief struggle that followed he shook them off easily. Immediately the points of a dozen halberds were levelled at him and he was left glaring at the captain.

'So that's how it's to be, is it?' the captain said. 'Then I'll have to teach you a lesson!'

And with one sweeping cut of his sword he drew blood from Hobe's ear.

Stung, Hobe started forward, snatched a halberd from one of the soldiers, and drove the captain back. The men crowded in behind to support him. A soldier lashed out with the butt of his halberd. There was a cry and a man to Hobe's right went down. Suddenly everywhere people were pushing and shoving. It took some time for the soldiers to regain control.

'Bring me that man!' the captain pointed at Hobe with his sword.

'*Wait.*' Adam stepped forward. 'It's the preacher you want, not him.'

'Preacher? I see no *preacher*,' the captain said, looking around. 'I see only looters and troublemakers in this mob.'

'Abner Heems was here,' Adam said. 'He was outside, preaching. He stirred up the trouble.'

'A preacher? A man of the cloth?' the captain sounded doubtful. 'It hardly seems likely a pious man would cause this trouble.'

'But I saw him,' Adam said. 'I heard him.'

'And *who* might you be?' the captain asked.

'Adam Windjammer,' Adam answered him squarely.

'Heir and rightful head of the House of Windjammer,' Gerrit added for good measure.

Augustus Windjammer hid his mouth and nose behind his handkerchief.

The captain frowned, obviously confused. 'But this gentleman said *he* was – '

'*I am*!' Augustus blurted. He mopped his forehead, gave a weak little laugh and saw he needed to explain. 'I mean to say ... I *am* the boy's uncle.'

'Then do you speak for this House?' the captain asked, impatiently.

'No, captain,' Gerrit corrected him. He ducked into a bow and presented himself to the captain. 'Look to Master Adam here.'

Augustus Windjammer hissed through his handkerchief.

The captain gave Adam a doubtful look. 'I had reports of a riot.'

'It was all over until *you* came,' Adam said, glaring at Augustus.

'What Master Adam means,' Gerrit said quickly, 'is that we had just concluded our business when you and your gallant soldiers arrived.'

'*Business!*' Augustus Windjammer showed his astonishment. He addressed the captain. 'Look at the doors! The hinges are riven and the wood stove in. What sort of *business* do you call that?'

'It is true the doors have been damaged,' Gerrit admitted. 'But only through a misunderstanding, and the master of this House will not be pressing charges.'

'*Misunderstanding*,' Augustus Windjammer spluttered. '*Not* be pressing charges? But I ... '

'And I thought the boy was in charge,' the captain said crisply.

Augustus Windjammer retreated behind his handkerchief again and a spontaneous cheer broke from the men around them until a sergeant silenced them.

'It seems I have been wrongly informed,' the captain said with a meaningful glance in Augustus's direction. 'As for you,' he turned to Hobe, 'you are under arrest for a breach of the peace.'

'No!' Adam stepped between Hobe and the soldiers.

'Hobe *helped* us. Hobe stopped them.'

'Master Adam is right,' Gerrit was quick to explain. 'Hobe is a shipwright working on our ship, the *Draco*. He is owed money like others here. We held a meeting to talk it over and he was the *first* to agree to give the Windjammers a little more time. Others here simply followed his good example. Had you come a little later, captain, you would have found them all going home peacefully enough.' He turned to Hobe. 'Is that not right?'

Hobe lifted one great hand to his ear. He looked at the blood smeared on the tips of his fingers, glared at the captain and Augustus, glanced at Gerrit and finally looked at Adam.

Adam returned Hobe's gaze steadily.

'That's right,' Hobe said at last and yielded up the halberd.

'Then there has clearly been a misunderstanding,' the captain said, sheathing his sword.

'Surely you are not going to let him go!' Augustus was appalled. 'Look at him! His face! That scar! His eye! He's a marked man – branded as a villain for all to see.'

'Appearances can be deceptive, captain,' Gerrit said. 'I am sure you will agree – only a fool judges the quality and contents of a scroll by the size and condition of its seal.'

Augustus Windjammer let out a furious hiss.

'It's time you left, uncle,' Adam said. 'You're not welcome here or at our house any more.'

Augustus Windjammer glared knives at him. 'I shall not forget this insult, nephew,' he said. 'You have made me look like a fool. Yes, yes. A fool! *Me!* Augustus Windjammer!'

He glanced at the hostile faces all around him, clutched his handkerchief to his lips and took several hesitant steps towards the door. His nerve didn't hold, he broke suddenly and made a lumbering dash for the door – chased out by a cacophony of whistles and jeers and catcalls.

'Clear the room!' the captain ordered.

The soldiers made everybody file out in a far more orderly fashion than they had stormed in. They passed Adam on the way, their faces turned down as if now they were ashamed they had come at all. Only Hobe refused to move and gradually the soldiers grew nervous around him again.

'I'm leaving, sure enough,' he growled at them. But he stood for a while longer, just looking at Adam as if he was trying to make up his mind about something.

'I won't let you down,' Adam was the first to speak. 'I promised to keep my father's word and I'm going to do it.'

'Then maybe there's hope yet for the House of Windjammer,' the big man said. And – having waited just long enough to show the soldiers he wasn't frightened of them – he followed the others out.

The relief blew out of Adam in a rush. He leaned back against the arm of the great scales and closed his eyes. He felt weak and light-headed now the danger had passed.

'You were so masterful, Master Adam,' Gerrit said, clapping his hands. 'You have *saved* the warehouse!'

He did a little shoe-shuffling dance on the spot, realised he had got carried away, coughed with embarrassment and assumed a disposition more befitting to a serious-minded and sober clerk.

'Why did I not see it sooner?' he asked the question of himself. 'Why did I not see that a boy like you could be a worthy head of the House of Windjammer? How wrong I was to trust in tradition and your uncle. He is a Windjammer in name alone. Not like *you*.' He caught hold of Adam's hand, gripped it tightly and paused. 'But you feel cold, Master Adam – are you unwell?'

'I'm all right,' Adam said, aware of the dull ache deep in the pit of his stomach.

Gerrit wasn't convinced. 'Perhaps it is the onset of a fever. I should call out a physician. He will recommend a potion from the apothecary – '

'I don't need a doctor or a potion,' Adam said. 'I'll be all right if you'll just tell me what's going on. I need to know. If you have a plan to save the House of Windjammer then tell me – *now*, before something else happens.'

'*Please*, Master Adam,' Gerrit shushed at him. 'You must be careful what you say.' He glanced at the captain who still stood giving orders to some of his men nearby, then up into the ropes and the open trap doors above. 'You said yourself you thought you heard someone.' He shook his head. 'If word of this should leak out ... '

The guilt was written all over his face again.

'But I *have* to know.'

'There's a time and a place for everything,' Gerrit said. 'Have I not already promised to tell you and your mother? I will call a meeting. Yes, the Long Table is the traditional place for such talk.'

'I don't care about the traditions anymore,' Adam

217

said. 'I just want to know what's going on.'

Gerrit cringed slightly. He stood for a moment wringing his hands as if whatever it was caused him great pain. He swallowed hard and finally nodded.

'Very well, Master Adam. I will tell you this much now.' He glanced around and moved closer to be sure the captain wouldn't hear him. 'But first let me tell you that I would *never* have done this thing had it not been absolutely necessary. I am a respectable clerk with many years' service and never once have I gambled or taken such terrible risks. I did it only because I was desperate. I did it only to save the House of Windjammer.'

He paused and looked around again. The captain was still occupied with his men. 'I have,' he spoke at last, 'bought a rare treasure known as the Black Pearl.'

'A *pearl*?'

'Shh!' Gerrit flapped his hands. 'We must be careful.'

'But what are you going to do with it?'

'*Sell* it, Master Adam. At a great profit, too.' Gerrit stiffened slightly and looked around. He frowned. 'I feel a sudden chill, Master Adam.'

Thump! A jolt sent a shiver through the warehouse. They looked up at the sound of something heavy rolling across the floor above. Adam caught a glimpse of a wooden barrel as it reached one of the open traps high above their heads. He watched it teeter on the edge, without comprehending what it meant. The barrel lurched forward, hung for a moment among the nets and ropes above, then dropped, turning lazily in the air, as it picked up speed with a rush.

'Look out!' he heard the captain's shout.

Adam caught a glimpse of Gerrit's face, eyes wide, nostrils flared, his mouth twisted with words of warning. Then he felt a violent shove as Gerrit pushed him, sending him staggering backwards out of the way.

A split moment later the barrel hit the arm of the scales, sheared it off, and caught Gerrit a glancing blow. It tore a gasp from the little man's lips and sent him spinning away in a loose whirl of arms and legs. Then the barrel slammed into the ground where Adam had just been standing. It exploded with a thunderous roar that set echoes booming through the warehouse until he thought they would never stop.

And then after the noise – *silence*.

219

18. The Quick and the Dead

Adam held up the lantern, lighting the way through the streets. His head was filled with the sound of the horse's hooves and the wheels of the cart rattling on the cobbles. He forced himself to walk slowly, but all the while he knew time was running out.

The torches had been lit on the bridges, setting the canals beneath alight with points of reflected light. Every now and again shadowy figures appeared at the edges of his circle of lantern light, looming suddenly out of the alleyways around them only to draw back into the shadows to watch as the cart passed by.

They had laid Gerrit's broken body on a plank and had carried him out of the warehouse. Hobe had been outside with the carpenter and it had been Hobe who had shown them to a small apothecary's shop on the waterfront. There, they had placed Gerrit carefully by the fire and – surrounded by the bottles and jars of the pharmacist's trade – had tended to him. The apothecary had brewed a potion against the pain and they had sent for the doctor. But there was little anyone could do.

'Take me home, young master,' Gerrit had pleaded, his eyes burning with his pain.

They had borrowed a cart and Hobe had lifted

Gerrit in his arms and had made him as comfortable as possible. Now Adam tried not to listen to the rattle in Gerrit's lungs as each jolt of the cart's wheels tore a gasp from his lips.

It should be me lying there, not him. The thought turned over and over in Adam's head as he walked in front of the cart.

They had sent word ahead to the old house on the Herengracht. A room was to be prepared: a bed, hot water, fresh bandages. But with each passing moment Gerrit was growing weaker. He was dying and they all knew it.

'They would not trade with us! What else could I do?' Gerrit was raving by the time they reached the bridge over the Herengracht and turned down the street towards the lights of the house where Mary Windjammer was waiting silhouetted in the doorway.

'Be gentle with him now! *Gently,*' she said as the driver of the cart pulled up and Hobe jumped down. 'He is a dear friend.'

'It's a secret! Yes. A secret. Wait! Now is not the moment. I'll pay your price. Gold for a rare pearl!' Gerrit raved.

Gerrit opened his eyes and saw Adam holding the lantern. He beckoned for him to come closer and caught hold of his collar, gripping it with surprising strength.

'It is up to *you* now, Master Adam,' he gasped. 'Only you can save the House of Windjammer. Do you understand? Promise me you will! *Promise* me!'

'I promise,' Adam said, half choked.

Gerrit pulled him closer. 'You must find it. You must find the Black Pearl and sell it ... ' he broke off with a gasp.

'I'll find it,' Adam soothed him. 'Just tell me where to look.'

Gerrit swallowed with some difficulty. 'I hid it under the plum tree. Look for it there,' he said. 'And do not think badly of me for what I have done, Master Adam. I did it for you and your dear mother.' His grip slackened, then tightened again as he arched up in pain. 'Speak not of my shame!' he gasped through gritted teeth. 'For I loved this House more than my own life.'

'He must rest now,' Adam's mother said.

Adam stayed by Gerrit's side as Hobe lifted him out of the cart. The clerk was in great pain and yet strangely a smile played briefly across his purple lips.

'All will be well with the House of Windjammer,' Gerrit said, looking at Adam. Then he sank back as one long, last breath escaped him, misting the air as if it was his soul departing.

Adam burst out of the house into the courtyard and paused, breathing hard.

'Adam – come back!' his mother came after him.

The plum tree was twisted against the wall with shadows. Adam ran to it, slammed down the lantern and dropped to his knees. The soil close to the roots had been freshly turned and he began scooping it away with his bare hands. He clawed at the soil with hooked fingers as the tears burned his cheeks. He rubbed at them, smearing his face with mud. He felt his mother's hand on his shoulder.

'It is not the time for this,' she said. 'Come back into the house.'

Adam shook off her hand and scrabbled through the

soil. His fingers touched something hard and he fumbled with it, brushing away the dirt. His hands were trembling as he lifted the lantern and saw that it was only the bulb of a flower. He hurled it away, slammed down the lantern and began attacking the soil again.

'It isn't here,' he said. 'It's *gone*.' He snatched up the lantern and held it up so the light filled the courtyard. 'There isn't another tree. It *must* be here!'

'Adam,' his mother said, 'Gerrit was delirious with pain – raving. We all heard him – it was probably the pain talking.'

'No,' he gasped. 'Gerrit told me he had bought a pearl. "A *rare* treasure", he said. He told me he had hidden it under the plum tree – but it's gone. *Gone*.'

He punched his fist into the soil in front of him and suddenly all the pain and hurt and frustration overwhelmed him.

'I thought only bad things of him,' he groaned. 'I thought he was stealing from us. But he wasn't. He even died saving *my* life.' He stood up. 'It should be me lying up there in that room under a sheet. *Me*. Not him! It's all *my* fault.'

His mother caught hold of him by the arms and shook him roughly. 'Stop this! Stop this at once!' she commanded him. 'None of this is your fault, Adam. The men told me that the soldiers searched the warehouse. They said the captain said it was an accident – just a *terrible* accident.'

She hugged him to her and spoke more softly. 'We have to stay calm. We have to stick together. *Together* the Windjammers can face anything. Do you understand? *Anything*.'

She stood back to look at him.

'But Gerrit made me promise,' Adam said. He felt so weak now. 'Gerrit said it was up to me to save the House of Windjammer. That's why he bought the pearl.'

'You must face it, Adam – there *is* no pearl,' she said. 'How could there be? And if there was, why would Gerrit bury it there? He was delirious – raving, that's all.'

Adam refused to give up. He dropped to his knees and attacked the tangle of flowers in the bed beside the tree. He tore at them until his breath was ragged and the tears streamed down his face.

'I have sent for your uncle,' his mother said. 'I will talk to him. You go to your room now and try to get some rest.'

'No!' Adam pleaded with her. 'You can't trust him, mother. Not any more.' He tried to explain what had happened at Hugo van Helsen's house on the Street of Knives, but it came out in a confused jumble.

'That's enough, Adam!' she stopped him. 'Augustus is capable of many things, but not such treachery. He is your father's own brother. He is a *Windjammer*.'

Adam shook his head. 'It's not *who* you are, mother – it's *what* you are that counts. If nothing else Gerrit has taught us that.'

Adam paused breathlessly and looked at her for a moment. Then he bent down and started digging again. He heard her turn away and realised Rose and Viola had come to stand by the door. Two pairs of eyes watched him, wide with shock and wonder.

'You shouldn't hurt them,' Rose said.

'The flowers, she means,' Viola explained.

Adam tore up a handful of withered stems. 'They're

224

dead, can't you see? Rotted away – just like *us*.' He hurled the dead flowers at them. 'Now leave me alone!'

The twins retreated behind their mother's skirts as she tried to usher them back inside. Rose broke free and darted forward again. She snatched up the flower bulb that lay discarded on the flagstones and clutched it to her chest as if it was the most precious thing in the world. Then together his sisters turned and fled back into the house.

It had been no accident. If Adam was sure of nothing else, he was sure of that. He didn't care what the captain of the guard said. He knew it was murder.

It was true, the soldiers had searched the warehouse and found no one. The captain had quickly concluded the barrel must have been badly stacked and had broken loose. He decided a tragic series of events had set the barrel rolling to that open trapdoor. It had been a terrible accident, nothing more. 'An act of God,' the captain had said.

A shiver ran through Adam as he lay curled up on his bed. He knew just how easily someone like the preacher could have hidden in the warehouse and slipped out of the warehouse later without being noticed.

Now the darkness surrounded him. He had been too tired to take off his clothes and he was too exhausted and sick to sleep. He just lay in the darkness of his room, alert to the pain in his stomach and lower back. His head ached and he was tormented by a thirst he couldn't slake.

He dragged himself off his bed and over to the jug and bowl on the side table. The jug was empty, but he lifted it to his mouth to catch the last drops. Another huge shiver racked his body and he was drawn to the embers in the fireplace. He sat in the chair and noticed his hands were shaking as he sought out what little warmth was left there.

Crash! The noise was startling in the quiet. Adam looked up, listening. As usual the old house was alive with noises of the night. Its old bones were creaking as if the roof above their heads had become a heavy burden to bear.

A loud thump followed by the sound of breaking glass brought him to his feet and sent him to open the door. He stepped out into the passage and listened. He could hear raised voices – his mother and his uncle were arguing. Then again: *Crash!*

The arguing stopped.

They were the same stairs. The same landings on each floor. The same creaking sounds. Adam couldn't count the times he had been up and down them and yet somehow now they seemed endless, as if he was spiralling down into a dark pit bloated with hidden dangers.

Three floors down he passed the passage leading to the room where Gerrit had been laid out on a bed. He moved on quickly to his mother's room. Her door was half open and he could see her moving around. She had taken something out of a leather box and she was still busy with it when he pushed open the door. She let out a little cry of surprise and turned sharply. The flicker of the candlelight caught and reflected on something in her hand. Adam saw it was the polished barrel of a pistol.

She relaxed a little when she saw him and turned

back to the heavy snaphance flintlock pistol. He could see she had already primed it with gunpowder and tamped the lead ball hard down the barrel, and now she pulled back the S-shaped hammer bearing the flint, ready to strike down and send a shower of sparks to ignite the powder in the firing pan.

'You were right about your uncle,' she said, without looking at him. 'I should have known he would do something stupid. I knew he was a weak man, but I never suspected his ambition and greed.'

'He *told* you?' Adam was surprised.

'The drink has loosened his tongue,' she explained. 'We argued. He laughed at me and said I was weak. Then he told me everything – even the part about Willem. He said it did not matter any more because Hugo van Helsen is going to take everything.' She shook her head. 'How could I *ever* have trusted him?'

'Where is he now, Mother?'

'In the library. He's drunk.' She lifted the pistol, pointing at the wall as she sighted down the barrel. 'I know how to use this. Your father showed me in case the Spanish attacked. It's loaded and primed.'

Crash! They heard the sound of cursing and something heavy being dragged across the floor.

Mary Windjammer picked up a candle and started towards the door. Her face was set and determined.

'I will not let him come up those stairs,' she said simply. 'He is too drunk to listen to reason and I do not trust him. I will shoot him dead if he threatens the girls.'

'I'll go down, Mother.'

'Not alone.'

'But we can't leave him down there,' Adam said.

'Who knows what he might do?'

'Then we'll go together,' she said.

So together they descended to the floor below and soon reached the place where the stairs divided, curling around and down towards the front door on the other side of the hall. This was the point of no return and Adam knew it. Below and to their right, the library door was open and the huge sea-chest had been dragged out into the middle of the hall. To their left the double doors into the dining-room were open and the light from inside spread itself like a mat on the black and white tiles in the hall. Everything else was much blacker for it and Adam realised the advantage lay in the shadows.

He pinched out the candle and they stood for a while just listening.

'He could be in either room, Mother,' he whispered. 'You'll have to stay here – we don't want him to get past us and up the stairs.'

She was still unwilling to let him go on alone, but her determination to protect the twins was just as strong. 'I'll watch over you from here,' she said, gripping the pistol tightly as he crept on down to the library.

Adam first peered cautiously in through the library door, but saw no sign of his uncle so he moved on to the sea-chest. The chest had been badly packed. The lid wouldn't close properly on the assortment of goblets, books and maps that had been hastily crammed inside. Adam guessed Augustus had dragged it as far as he could towards the front door, but had been forced to give up.

'Was it so wrong?' Augustus said. 'Was it so *very* wrong?'

Adam spun on his heel and looked at the double doors across the hall. His mother had heard too, and had started down the stairs towards the dining-room. Adam raised his hand in a sign for her to stop and made his move across the chessboard to the other side of the hall. He emerged from the shadows into the flicker of the candlelight and looked in through the open doors. The Long Table stretched away in front of him to a branching candelabrum laden with dribbling candles.

'Have I not served this House well?' Augustus Windjammer was muttering and mumbling to himself. He was sitting with his back to Adam, slumped in the great oak chair at the end of the table. A black bottle stood on the table in front of him. 'Was it so wrong to want something for myself after all this time?'

Adam felt the pain stab deep into him again. A shiver ran through him, starting somewhere deep under his left arm and shuddering up through the muscles of his back into his neck and head. The pain increased and the dizziness took longer to pass this time.

Augustus Windjammer picked up the bottle and took a long swallow straight from the neck. He wiped his mouth on the back of his hand, breathed through the strong spirit and sensed Adam standing in the doorway with the darkness at his back.

'Well, if it isn't the heir and *rightful* head to the House of Windjammer,' Augustus mocked him with Gerrit's words.

'You're drunk,' Adam said quietly.

Augustus glanced at the bottle. Nodded. Took another pull on the fiery spirit and breathed heavily. 'What if I am?' he slurred. 'I have every right to be drunk after all that has happened to me today.'

'What happened to *you*!' Adam couldn't believe it. 'And what about Gerrit? He's up there now – lying cold under a sheet and you – '

'Gerrit is dead, it's true,' Augustus interrupted. 'And maybe if you had listened to me he might still be alive. But *you* sent the guard away. *You* let that rabble go. So if you are looking to blame someone – blame *yourself*.'

The image of Gerrit's broken body came back to haunt Adam.

Augustus laughed. He knew he had made his point. He took another long swallow and turned to look at Adam for the first time. 'Who will be next, hey?' He pushed back the chair and studied Adam's face. 'The head of the House of Windjammer perhaps?'

'What are you talking about?'

'Come, come, nephew,' Augustus said, with an obvious degree of pleasure. 'We both know that barrel did not break loose on its own. From what I hear it was no accident that it fell where it did. Were you not standing beside Gerrit? Your mother told me he saved you – he pushed you out of the way and so was struck down himself.'

Adam knew it was the truth.

Augustus smiled. 'It seems someone is out to get you, nephew. Yes, yes, time is running out faster than you think. Every day your enemies are growing stronger while this House ... ' he paused and glanced around as if it was a living thing, ' ... *this* House grows weaker.'

He snatched up the bottle and took a long pull, winced and breathed hard into his words. 'The money-lender has given the House of Windjammer a week. But how long do you think you will last once the news of Gerrit's death gets out? The rumours will spread. People will talk. Yes, yes, they are sure to. They will say the House of Windjammer has no hope now and nothing you can say will make them believe otherwise. They will descend on this place like a pack of hungry wolves on a dying deer.' He nodded with great certainty. 'That's why I care little for Gerrit's plight – it's the *living* that should concern you now, not the *dead*.'

Augustus laughed at him. 'It will take more than your father's ring to save the House of Windjammer now,' he said. 'But *I* will not be here when the money-lender comes to call. *I* will not wait for the bailiffs to come knocking on the door.' He shook his head. 'I will take my family and all that is left to me and be aboard a ship that sails with the morning tide. I care not where – the New World perhaps. And when we are safely aboard I will think of you, nephew, sitting in this chair. I will think of you and laugh at your misfortune.'

Augustus stood up with some difficulty, swaying gently on his feet as he looked back at the chair.

'It is true, nephew,' he said. 'Once I did want that place at the Long Table to be mine. Was it so wrong of me to have ambition? Was it so wrong to ask for something in return for all my years I spent watching my brothers win all the glory and acclaim?' He sneered at Adam. 'But you are the eldest – how could you possibly know what it is like to live in the shadow of two brothers?'

He snatched up the bottle, swigged at it and breathed hard.

'This is a scene to make you laugh,' he said as if he was talking to the house around him. 'My brothers were always the strong ones. Hercules the hero and

Lucien the brave adventurer. Me?' He laughed without humour. '*Me?* I was always just Augustus. Augustus the bumbler. Augustus the middle brother. Neither fish nor fowl.' He took another long pull on the bottle. 'Well, I may be a bumbler, but I am *no* fool. I am still alive and I intend to stay that way. And I will dwell in the shadows of this cursed house no more.'

He took another pull on the bottle and hurled it away. It smashed against the wall and dribbled wetly. The raw spirit seemed to ignite flames in his eyes. He snatched up the candelabrum and stumbled away from the Long Table towards the door.

A wave of dizziness washed over Adam and left him leaning heavily against the door. Before him Augustus Windjammer loomed out of the shadows, staggering as if he was trying to tear himself free of the very fabric of the house itself.

'Stand back!' Augustus said. 'Let me pass!' He lifted the flaming candelabrum threateningly and the light fell on Adam's face for the first time.

Augustus paused and raised the light higher, causing Adam to blink and step back.

'You do not look well, nephew,' he said. 'A fever is upon you.' He reached out, caught Adam by the collar and shook him. 'Just as I thought – as weak as a puppy!'

A cruel smile twisted Augustus Windjammer's lips and he pushed Adam back through the door ahead of him, sending Adam staggering out into the half-darkness of the hall.

'Look at you!' he said, thrusting the flaming ends of the candles towards his face. Augustus laughed. 'It could have been so different. But you've ruined everything. *Everything*.' He jabbed the flames at him. 'I have a mind to teach you a lesson for what you've done.'

The flames roared, cutting through the darkness in a blazing flash. Adam staggered back as burning wax splattered across his face. He stumbled over the sea-chest and fell heavily on to the floor. Augustus loomed over him threateningly, the flickering candlelight washing over his face, sending his shadow leaping up the walls to the height of the ceiling. In that moment he seemed to grow to giant proportions: a grotesque, mis-shapen figure with eyes filled with a mad, dancing light as if he was burning up inside with rage and jealousy.

'Yes, yes, nephew, I will teach you to make a fool out of me! I will teach you some *respect*.'

Adam threw his arms up to defend himself as Augustus Windjammer raised the heavy candelabrum high above his head. For a moment he just stood there with the candles blazing above him like some terrible burning brand. And there was no pity in his eyes.

A shout rang out – a warning – followed by a loud click and a shower of sparks as flint struck metal. Then the darkness was split with a bluish flash and the thunderous roar of the pistol.

Mary Windjammer had aimed high and the lead ball hurtled through the darkness over their heads, smashed through the blaze of candles and cracked into the wood of the front doors.

Augustus cried out in surprise and terror. He turned to see her standing on the stairs and hurled the candelabrum at her. It fell, clattering harmlessly at the foot of the stairs. The candles spluttered and died.

Then Adam heard his mother speak. 'Get out, Augustus!' her voice lashed out of the darkness. 'Get out and *never* come back!'

Augustus reeled away from her towards the door. He kicked out at Adam, but missed. Then the darker patch of night that Augustus had become went staggering across the hall. He pulled open the doors and stood on the threshold for a moment with the lights of the Herengracht behind him.

'A curse on you and this house!' he said, and then he fled into the night.

19. To the Grave and Back

The night crawled to an end in the cold grey of another dawn. Adam woke shivering and lay staring at the ceiling. He had slept only for a few short hours, drifting in and out of dreams, until the dawn had brought him to the beginning of another terrible day.

The dizziness washed over him again and again as he dressed ready for the funeral. He knew they would come soon with a coffin for Gerrit and he wondered if he had the strength left to follow the cart to the cemetery. He ached deep in his bones and he was shivering through his own sweat. A rash prickled the skin of his shoulders and neck and he covered it with a high collar. Inga's potion had not worked. The fever was upon him, but he was determined to honour Gerrit by walking behind his coffin.

Adam met his mother and sisters at the foot of the stairs. The sea-chest had been dragged back into the library and the candelabrum had gone, but the floor was still splattered with wax where it had fallen.

'We will walk alone behind Gerrit,' Mary Windjammer told them and explained for the twins' benefit. 'Your uncle and aunt and cousins, Willem and Angelica, are going on a long voyage. They will not be back for a very long time.'

Rose and Viola accepted this without question. It seemed they had seen enough in their young lives to know that nothing now was constant.

It occurred to Adam that he was standing almost exactly where his father had stood the day he had received the news of the fleet. He stared at the black square in front of him. It was almost as if he had been moved – like his father before him – to the very edge of a dark hole. Just one move forward, one wrong step, and he would fall to his doom.

'You will need to be very brave and strong and hold my hands as we go to the church … ' his mother was saying to the twins.

Her voice receded as she explained what simple arrangements had been made for the funeral. When she had finished Adam heard a rustle of skirts and looked up as she came to stand in front of him.

'Not there,' he stopped her from standing on the square. 'Don't stand *there*, Mother.'

She paused and looked down, then up again at his face.

'You look so pale, Adam,' she said. 'You are not well.'

'It's nothing. I'm tired, that's all. I'll be all right.' Adam found his gaze drawn irresistibly back down to the black square between them.

His mother stood for a moment longer, then, quite deliberately, stepped forward. She didn't disappear into the pit. She reached out and Adam felt her hand lifting his chin.

'What are we going to do, Mother?' he asked.

'We will honour Gerrit in the only way we can.'

'What then?' Adam's mouth was dry, his voice hoarse.

'*Then* we will go on,' she reassured him. 'We are Windjammers – we will *never* give up.'

She hugged him to her, but pulled away again and looked at his face. The concern was suddenly in her eyes.

'Gerrit saved my life, Mother,' Adam read her thoughts. 'I *have* to walk behind him today.'

'But you are not well, Adam.'

'It's nothing, Mother, just a bad ague,' he said. 'And how will it look if I leave you to walk behind his coffin alone with the twins? People will see and know something else is wrong. The rumours are already spreading. My uncle was right – the news is already bad enough.'

His mother still hesitated. Her instincts clearly told her he wasn't well enough to go and yet she also knew he was no longer *just* Adam her son, but Adam her son, head of the House of Windjammer.

'Then let us go now and honour Gerrit,' she said, making up her mind at last. 'After that you *will* do as I say and rest.'

A brisk north-easterly was blowing, bringing low clouds scudding in off the sea as they followed the cart to the graveyard outside the city walls. A lone bell tolled in the tower of the small church as they laid Gerrit to rest in the Windjammers' tomb; knowing they couldn't honour him more highly than by treating him as one of their own.

The coffin preceded them with Gerrit's bunch of keys – the symbol of his authority in the house – laid on top. Adam followed the coffin, leading the small procession through the iron gates into the

Windjammers' large burial plot. Around him the stone angels stood guard on the four walls surrounding the graves and tombs where his ancestors lay in silent repose. There they took back Gerrit's keys and laid him to rest, faithful to the House of Windjammer even in death.

Only when it was over – as if somehow this final act had used up the very last dregs of his strength – did Adam feel the full impact of the fever that had taken hold of him. It seemed to descend on him like a lead blanket, driving him down into the ground as the dizziness swept over him in waves that set the angels free from the walls around him. He watched as they took flight and climbed high into the sky to come screaming down at him as if seeking vengeance.

'Stay away from me!' he gasped, reeling back.

He saw his mother look up. She was saying something he couldn't hear. The twins were kneeling side by side in front of their father's grave. They were planting something. Adam saw it was the bulb of a flower. The angels turned in the sky around them as he staggered back, stumbling out through the iron gate. A thickening darkness seeped into his head as he staggered between the graves.

'Adam!'

Through the creeping darkness he saw Jade van Helsen. Vaguely he wondered what she was doing there.

He felt her touch on his arm and leaned heavily on a gravestone. She was talking to him, but the words didn't connect with the movement of her lips. 'You are not well,' she was saying. He heard her call out to his mother. 'He needs help! *Quickly!*'

Adam slipped down to lie on the cold hard earth. The stone behind his head was as grey and cold as the sky. The darkness thickened even further around him, bringing the angels crashing down from the sky like falling stars. The pain faded until at last it became just a strange tingling sensation. The blackness crept in from the edges of his vision, swallowing the light bit by bit. Then the darkness came upon him with a breathless rush and he remembered no more.

Adam was dreaming. He knew he was dreaming now, but he didn't care.

In his dream he was walking in a beautiful garden. He felt warm in the sunshine. Safe. And yet somehow he knew the garden was forbidden to him.

As he walked through the garden he seemed to float on the scent of a million flowers. The colours were dazzlingly bright. Tulips, roses and daisies moved gently in the breeze, red and yellow like an ocean of flame, washed by waves of cool greens and white. And above him the sunlight dripped down through the leaves like liquid gold.

Then the voice came to him in his dream: 'Adam!'

He looked up and saw a man standing some way off, his form made indistinct by the brightness of the sunlight.

Adam shielded his eyes against the glare. 'Father?'

Without a word his father beckoned for him to follow and stepped through an archway in a hedge and vanished.

'Father! Wait!' Adam went after him.

He followed the figure through the arch and immediately high hedges of yew sprang up on either side.

Trimmed and neat. Thick. They squeezed the grass into a path and threw down green shadows in a maze of light and dark.

The figure moved ahead of him, gliding silent as a ghost, turning through the sharp angles between the hedges. Adam called out to him again and again as he followed through every twist of that great maze. Turning, turning, turning ever inwards until the hedges towered over him, the shadows deepened and he had the strangest feeling he was spiralling downwards through different levels into a pit.

Then, quite suddenly, he stumbled into the open square at the very heart of the maze. And there he saw a group of people standing beside a bed.

Adam recognised the bed as his own and pushed his way through them to see who could be lying there. He saw a boy about his age, with sallow face and feverish half-closed eyes, and it took a moment to realise he was looking at himself.

A doctor leaned over him, applying leeches to his skin. Adam watched the slug-like creatures sucking on to his skin and he felt the creep of the soft mouths on his own flesh.

'Is he going to die?' a voice asked.

'Like Father, she means,' another said.

The voices sounded small and frightened.

'No!' Adam gasped. 'No! No! No!' And as he cried out he felt as if he was being drawn back into his body and with a rush he opened his eyes.

Rose and Viola were standing near the door with their mother. Their faces swam before him. He wanted to tell them to stop moving, but when he opened his mouth no sound came out. The heat of the fever gripped him. He felt as if his skin was on fire. He was burning, burning, burning. He tore at the bedclothes, throwing them off only to grip them tightly around him again as a shiver stabbed through him. 'Water!' he pleaded. His throat was parched. His lips cracked. He was suffocating. Choking.

'Did I not say this House was cursed?' The preacher's face loomed terrifyingly close. The preacher laughed, his head back, his mouth wide and showing the rottenness within.

'Stay away from me!' Adam begged.

The faces crowded around him: misshapen and distorted as if by mirrors.

'You can't help me, Adam Windjammer,' Jade van Helsen's face divided into three. 'I want you to go and never come back.'

'The shame of it, Master Adam!' Gerrit's ghost lamented as he drifted through the room. 'I have done a terrible thing. The shame! The shame! Yes, the shame!'

'Stay away from my daughter! She'll marry a prince not a pauper!'

'You silly little fool, nephew! Yes, yes! It's all your fault.'

'Is he going to die?' 'Like Father, she means.' 'News of the fleet. Lost, all *lost*.' 'I have hidden it, Master Adam.' 'She will marry a prince not a pauper!' 'What about the *Draco*?' 'Save the House of Windjammer! Promise me you will – *promise*!' 'Adam! Adam! Adam ... !'

It only seemed a moment before Adam opened his eyes again. When he did the fever had left him.

He lay on his back and stared vacantly at the mantling hanging from the four posts of his bed. Daylight was coming through the window and he guessed it was either early morning or late afternoon. He tried to move, but his body felt weak and limp, drained of almost all its life force.

He turned his head and saw his mother asleep in a chair at his bedside. Her head was resting on his bed. He squeezed her hand and she stirred, still drowsy for a moment before she came fully awake.

'I'm thirsty, Mother.'

'*Adam.*'

There were tears in her eyes when she brought him a bowl brimming with water. He drank it, then another, before he leaned back exhausted by the effort. He tried to remember what had happened, but couldn't.

'You have been stricken with fever,' she explained as she bathed his face with a damp cloth that smelled of lavender.

'When the fever took hold there was little we could do but hope,' she continued. 'But enough of this – you must rest and regain your strength now before the doctor comes to bleed you again.'

And that's what the doctor did – three times.

'We thought we had lost you, Master Adam,' the doctor admitted as he applied the leeches to the veins of Adam's arm. 'But you're a strong lad and it's lucky for you. There are many who've been carried off by the fever before now – and no amount of bleeding could have saved them.'

Adam endured the leeches with horrified resignation as the doctor placed them carefully on the veins of his arms and neck.

'There's nothing like a good bleeding to cleanse the body of too much bad blood,' the doctor said, enjoying his work. 'Beautiful creatures the *Hirudo medicinalis* – that's a leech to you and me. Cures everything from toothache to plague – I swear by them.'

If they were beautiful, Adam couldn't see it. He watched them gorge on his blood with disgust until finally the doctor declared his blood had been cleaned and, with some rest, he would get well again. It was with great relief that Adam watched the leeches being returned to their bell-shaped jars for the last time.

He must have slept for a long time after that because when he woke again it was early evening of the fourth day. Somewhere in the house the twins were chanting rhymes: their voices distant and unearthly, their songs echoing through the hollows and dark places.

'You had a visitor while you were asleep,' his mother said as she brought a potion made up by the apothecary for him to drink.

'A visitor?' Adam was surprised. 'Who?'

'Jade van Helsen.'

'What did *she* want?'

'She came to see how you are and to bring you these herbs from the apothecary,' his mother explained. 'She had heard what happened to Gerrit. She came to pay her respects to us. She helped us get you into the cart. She is a good, kind girl.'

'She's a *van Helsen*,' he said as if that was enough to show Jade must have had reasons of her own to help.

His mother sighed. 'It has come to a fine pass when we can no longer trust kindness. Did you not say yourself – it is not *who* you are, but *what*?'

'This is different,' Adam said, but couldn't explain why.

His mother stood up and turned away abruptly. He saw the way her hands were trembling slightly as she gripped them in front of her. She brushed at her cheek. She stood for a while longer with her back to him and suddenly he realised she was weeping silently. It came as a shock to Adam to see her shoulders heave and convulse. She had always been so strong.

'We'll be all right, Mother,' he tried to reassure her.

She nodded and wiped at her eyes with the sides of a long, slender finger. 'But we have few friends left,' she said, the enormous effort of speaking calmly clear in her tone. 'I have had news of your uncle. He has taken ship with your aunt and your cousins. He has packed all he could carry and left his house on the Prinsengracht. I heard tell the ship is bound for New Amsterdam in the Americas.' She turned to look at him. 'Perhaps we should follow them?'

'And give up, Mother?' he said. 'We can't. We have to try to save the *Draco*. We have to save this House.'

There was a long pause before she spoke again. And all the exhausted weariness was in her voice.

'Then we will go to Bartholomew de Leiden,' she said in a way that told him her mind was made up. 'He is one of this family's oldest and most trusted friends. He is sure to take pity on us. I know he can do little against Hugo van Helsen, but I am sure he will look at the ledgers and advise us.'

She drew new strength from the thought and pulled herself up to her full height again. Her chin lifted and she nodded. 'You will rest and then on Sunday, if you feel strong enough, we will go to the New Church as we always do. Yes, we will prove to everyone that we are not afraid to show our faces in Dam Square.'

'I will be strong enough,' Adam promised, taking a deep draught of the potion.

20. An Unwelcome Visitor

'My dear Mary,' Bartholomew de Leiden said. 'Have you any idea what you are asking of me?'

They were walking away from the New Church, across Dam Square towards the market and the Waag and the boats on the Damrak.

'If you would try to talk to him on our behalf,' Mary Windjammer said. 'We only have two days left, but perhaps even now we can still come to some agreement with this banker.'

'You do not know Hugo van Helsen,' the old man said, his voice cracked and whistling with the effort of walking. 'He will not listen to me and he is a powerful enemy to make at my time of life.'

A lone bell had called the Christian faithful to church that Sunday morning. The Windjammers had made their way to the New Church on foot and had taken their places on their usual bench. There were far fewer of them now: Adam, his mother and his two sisters sitting in a line listening as a sermon about forgiveness had been thrown down from the great pulpit like a challenge. But Adam found it hard to forgive when all he wanted to do was get even.

'You supported us once against him,' Adam pointed out. 'I was there – I heard you speak up for my father at the Long Table.'

'But, Adam,' the old man said with a pained look, '*so* much has changed at the House of Windjammer. Perhaps I could help if I knew I could count on some other merchants for their support. But now even the common crowd has turned against you.' He shook his head. 'The House of Windjammer has few friends now and even if I could find others willing to help I fear they would be too busy spending their money on tulips to spare the money to pay off your debts to Hugo van Helsen.'

Adam's mother stopped walking and turned to him. 'Then I fear it will not go well for you to be seen with us any more.'

The old man's eyes were watery with more than just his age as he reached out and gripped her hand. He lifted it to his lips and kissed it. Adam noticed the furtive looks the merchants and their wives were giving them.

The old man saw Rose and Viola standing politely behind their mother. He smiled indulgently at them and dug some coins for each of them out of the purse on his belt. 'Take these,' he said, 'and buy yourselves some pancakes – the sugared ones are the finest, there is little doubt.'

Mary Windjammer tried to refuse his kindness, but the old man insisted. He pressed the money into the twins' hands, much to their delight. He smiled as he watched them go skipping away to the brightly painted stalls that were lined up around the edge of the New Market. His smile faded. He inclined his head in a slight bow and took his leave of them. He had not gone far, however, before he turned on his heel with a second thought.

'If an old man may be permitted to change his mind,' he said. 'I will come to the Herengracht this afternoon. My clerk and I can look over your ledgers together then. It is the least I can do for old friends.'

In the true spirit of the strange normality their mother now assumed for the sake of appearances, they didn't hurry back to the old house on the Herengracht. Adam was sent to make sure the twins didn't gorge themselves sick on pancakes, while she stopped and chatted here and there, pretending not to notice the uncomfortable looks the wives of the merchants gave her.

By the time Adam arrived at the stall Rose and Viola were grinning from ear to ear, gripping pancakes in paper twists, their mouths covered in sugar.

'Master Windjammer!'

Adam heard someone call out to him and turned to find Saskia standing behind him.

'I have a message for you,' the maid said.

Adam followed the direction of her glance and saw Jade van Helsen standing at a stall some way off. She had her back to him, her silk dress shimmering gold and green in the wintry sunlight, as she pretended to be watching a baker making pancakes on the hot metal sheet over a brazier.

'Why can't she deliver her own messages?' Adam asked. He hadn't forgotten the bitterness of their last meeting.

He deliberately turned his back on her and there was a brief pause before Saskia tried again.

'Please, young sir – just take this note and read it. It's of some importance to you.'

Adam ignored her and bent down to wipe at the

sugar on the twins' faces. Saskia gave up. Adam glanced up when he heard her turn away. He watched Jade's reaction as her maid delivered the news with a shake of her head. Jade's eyes flashed angrily and she glanced at him. He pretended to be helping the twins choose more pancakes, but found little pleasure in this small act of spite. When next he looked up, both Jade and Saskia had gone.

The depth of his own disappointment surprised Adam. He ignored his sisters' excited chatter and couldn't help looking around for Jade. And that was when he noticed her father standing not far away in the square. Hugo van Helsen was talking to a group of merchants, but Adam noticed the way he kept glancing towards the pancake stalls.

'A cake for you, young master?' A baker's wife approached him with a tray of pancakes in paper twists.

Adam shook his head with irritation.

'But it's paid for, young master,' the woman insisted.

He looked at her in surprise. 'Paid for?'

'By the *Miss*,' the woman said. 'The one who was just here.'

Startled, Adam looked around. He couldn't see Jade anywhere, but he felt sure she was watching. He hesitated and reached out to take a pancake.

'You'll find this one will taste sweeter,' the baker's wife said, indicating one that had been set aside by the edge of the tray. 'It comes with more than just sugar.'

She thrust the pancake into his hand, nodded, grinned knowingly at him, and turned back into the crowd around him. Adam looked suspiciously at the pancake. It crossed his mind that it might even be poisoned and he was about to throw it away when he noticed something different about the paper twist that held it. Then he saw the note tucked inside.

A note written neatly in flowing curling letters. A simple warning that struck a cold spike deep into him:

Beware of the preacher – you are in great danger.
                                                    JvH.

Adam read it. Then read it again. And suddenly his fear turned to fury. He forgot all about the twins and pushed his way through the people around him, desperately searching her out among the stalls. He caught a glimpse of Saskia some way off and then saw Jade buying bread at a stall nearby. He didn't think twice. His burning anger blinded him to the folly of it. He didn't even consider that what he was doing might get Jade into trouble.

Jade van Helsen looked startled as Adam appeared suddenly at her side. She glanced around quickly and tried to turn away from him, but he caught her by the wrist and held on tightly.

'What does *this* mean?' he shook the note at her.

'You're hurting me,' she hissed.

'Tell me! I want to know! *Now!*'

Saskia appeared threateningly at Adam's side. Jade stopped her.

'I'll deal with this, Minou,' she said. 'You keep watch for my father.' Saskia stepped back reluctantly to hover close by. Jade pulled her arm free and rubbed at her wrist. 'I mustn't be seen with you.'

'Well, I'm not leaving until you tell me what you know.'

Jade glanced about again – as nervous as a deer

with hounds about – and turned to look at the bread laid out on the stall. She didn't look at him when she spoke:

'I came to warn you.'

'Warn me?'

'I heard what happened at your warehouse,' she spoke softly as if frightened someone might hear. 'I heard about your clerk, Gerrit. I came to the grave-yard. But you were sick with the fever. I couldn't talk to you then.' She paused and took a deep breath before continuing. 'What happened to Gerrit – it wasn't an *accident*, was it?'

'Why don't you ask your father?'

'My father had nothing to do with it.'

'I suppose I should have known *you* would say that.'

'Don't look at me!' she hissed. Then she sighed and shook her head. 'I know my father is a hard man and I understand your bitterness towards me, Adam Windjammer,' she said, 'but he's no murderer and nor am *I* – that's why I came to warn you.'

'And why would a van Helsen care what happened to a Windjammer?'

'Listen to what I have to say, Adam Windjammer,' she said. 'And for *once* try to forget who I am!' She glanced over her shoulder. Saskia was growing restless. Jade turned back to the stall. 'I can't stay much longer.'

'I'm listening,' Adam said, folding his arms.

Jade paused, as if what she was about to tell him made her feel deeply uncomfortable. She swallowed hard and spoke at last. 'It's true – my father did pay the preacher. He was my father's spy at the waterfront.'

'Fine company he keeps.'

Jade did her best to ignore him. 'I said *was*,' Jade

said. 'The preacher used to come to our house, but he stopped coming suddenly. The last time he came there was an argument. I couldn't help overhearing what was said. I heard the preacher tell my father he had pushed a barrel down at the warehouse and it ... ' She broke off.

' ... *killed* Gerrit,' Adam didn't spare her feelings.

'Yes,' she nodded and when she spoke again there was a great weariness in her voice. 'My father was angry – *very* angry. I heard them shouting. I heard him say he hadn't paid the preacher to do murder. The preacher just laughed at him and said if he *had*, his price would have been much higher. My father told him to get out and never to come back, but the preacher swore he'd finish what he had started with or without my father's permission. Then I heard him threaten to kill all the Windjammers and take the black pearl Gerrit had bought.'

'The *black pearl*?' Adam was startled.

'I said, don't look at me!'

'But what do *you* know about the pearl?'

Jade shrugged. 'Only what I've overheard. The preacher had been following Gerrit. He had seen Gerrit buy it. I remember he came to tell my father the same day you came to our house on the Street of Knives. My father wasn't pleased by the news. Later I heard him telling Glotz that Gerrit had taken a gamble that might yet save the House of Windjammer.'

'You've done a lot of listening,' Adam said.

'I *have* to, Adam Windjammer,' she said looking at him for the first time. 'You heard what my father said about finding me a husband. He won't tell me what he's planning – so I keep my ears and eyes open.

Already my portrait has been sent to England and –'

'Mistress Jade!' Saskia interrupted with a warning.

Jade glanced up and was startled to see her father making his way towards the pancake stall where they stood.

'He must *not* see us together,' she said, fumbling with some coins and hurriedly paying for the bread and two pancakes. She took the pancakes the baker served up in paper twists.

'My father paid the preacher to watch you – *nothing* more,' she said. 'But the preacher is an evil man. I fear he is more dangerous now than he was before.'

'Mistress Jade!' Saskia called again.

'So you must be careful, Adam Windjammer.'

'But I *have* to know more,' Adam said.

'I've helped you enough,' Jade said and turned away with the bread and pancakes.

'*Mistress Jade!*'

'But where does the preacher live?' Adam asked. 'Your father must know. You have to find out and tell me. Then we can have him arrested.'

'I have to go,' Jade said. 'My father is already suspicious of me.' She pushed past him, then paused as if she had thought again. 'I'll find out what I can.'

'Where will we meet?'

'Saskia and I always take a walk in the afternoons. Today we will come by the bridge close to your house on the Herengracht. We will be there when the bell strikes three. Come then! Don't be late!'

Adam watched her move swiftly away across the square with her maid following close behind. Jade seemed to glide on the billows of her fine skirts and her long, dark hair shimmered in the sunlight. He saw her meet her father half-way and say something. He laughed as she offered him one of the pancakes she had bought.

Adam was still watching as she took her father's arm and quickly steered him away from the stalls. She was too busy talking to notice the way her father glanced over his shoulder at Saskia. Jade didn't see her maid nod nor did she see the way her father looked back towards the stalls. No, she saw only the smile that had become fixed on her father's face.

Adam watched them until they were out of sight. Only gradually did he become aware that his sisters were tugging urgently at his sleeve.

'I think I'm going to be,' Rose said with great certainty.

'*Sick*, she means,' Viola explained.

'Well, it's lucky Mrs de Hooch has children of her own,' their mother said as they made their way home to the old house on the Herengracht.

'I *was* watching them,' Adam lied.

It seemed Mrs de Hooch was either too nice or too polite to worry about the condition of the twins.

'Mrs de Hooch is here visiting relatives and speaks very highly of Rotterdam.' Their mother changed the subject. 'She says her son Pieter is seven years old and even now is showing promise with paints and a brush.'

As Mary Windjammer found relief in talking about ordinary things, Adam's head was buzzing. His mind was working on what Jade had said. He was sure now that the pearl hadn't just been a figment of Gerrit's ramblings. He had never seen a black pearl, but he had already made up his mind that it must be a rare treasure. All he had to do was find it, and he was just wondering how he would do that when he realised his mother had stopped suddenly.

'What is that noise?' she asked.

They were close to the old house on the Herengracht and she was looking up the steps leading to the front door. Adam listened and heard the sounds of knocking and muffled cries coming from inside.

'It sounds like Cook,' she said, quickly coming to the conclusion that something bad had happened.

She led the way up the steps, pushed open the door and they all paused in the doorway, grouped close together as they listened. The cries for help were coming from the kitchen.

'I'll go, Mother,' Adam said. 'You stay here near the door with the twins just in case. If there's trouble, don't wait for me – go for help. I can look after myself.'

Adam set off towards the kitchen, but was half-way across the hall when he heard other noises coming from the library to his left. He put a finger to his lips in a sign for his mother and sisters to be very quiet and listened.

A muttered curse, a hiss of breath, the bump and judder of furniture being moved, the dry rasp of papers being shuffled about. Adam heard a general rummaging of things as they were picked up and just as quickly discarded.

Mary Windjammer sensed real danger suddenly and drew her daughters to her.

'See to Cook, Mother.' Adam mouthed the words.

Before she could stop him, he had crossed to the library. Gingerly, he pushed open the door. It swung inwards to his touch to reveal that the room had been ransacked. Books, ledgers, papers and parchments had been strewn everywhere. The lid of the oak sea-chest was open wide and the contents thrown out and trampled on the floor. He realised someone was in the ledger-room.

Adam waited until his mother and sisters were safely out of the hall and then slipped in through the door to see who it was. As he crept forward he could see one of the windows in the ledger-room had been smashed. Whoever it was had broken into the house from the courtyard, surprised Cook and locked her in the kitchens so he could steal at will. Adam heard a hiss of breath and dodged back. A tall man was standing with his back to him, pulling down the ledgers from the shelves in a desperate random search.

'Damn that book-keeper! Damn that cook! Damn them all – may they rot in Hell for this!' The man swore under his breath.

In his frustration he swept the ledgers off the shelves with a violent heave of both hands and stepped back. He must have sensed Adam's presence behind him then. Another angry hiss escaped from between his teeth as he turned, coiling himself into a crouching position ready to spring. Adam found himself face to face with the preacher.

'The good Lord has sent a light to shine in my darkness,' Abner Heems said, relaxing a little when he saw Adam was alone.

'What are you doing here?' Adam spat out the challenge.

'I am about the Lord's business.'

'Only if your lord is the Devil himself!' Adam said. 'You're not *even* a preacher – Wolfie told me that.

You're a *murdering* thief, that's all.'

Abner Heems glared at him. 'So that stuttering fool Wolfie's been talking, hey? Well, that's clever and not so clever all at once. I'll deal with him later. But I see now I should have finished you with that barrel when I had the chance. I only meant to frighten you then, but that cursed book-keeper of yours got in the way.' He saw the sick look on Adam's face and laughed. 'Yes, that coward of an uncle of yours was careless – he left the door open and I walked right in when you weren't looking.'

'I'll call the guard,' Adam said.

'You won't get a dozen paces from this room,' the preacher said. 'I'll make an end of you *and* this business. I'm tired of it. The moneylender took fright at what happened. Said he didn't like my methods. Well, I don't like *his* and now I find myself out of pocket. But I know all about the Black Pearl. That's why I've come – for payment. So where is it? Tell me!'

'I don't know what you're talking about,' Adam said.

'Nice try, boy,' the preacher said, 'but I'd advise you not to be clever with me. Now tell me or I'll bring down the wrath of God on your head.'

Adam backed away as Abner Heems advanced towards him out of the ledger-room.

'That book-keeper of yours was clever, I'll grant him that,' the preacher said. 'Yes, he made that moneylender think too – ruined all his precious plans, I'd say. Gerrit only needed to sell it – but he didn't have time, now did he? So it must be here somewhere. Now hand it over and maybe I'll let you Windjammers be.'

'I don't have it,' Adam said. 'That's the truth!'

'*Arrrrrrrrrrrgh!*' The preacher snarled, leapt forward and landed between him and the door.

The door slammed shut before Adam could escape back into the hall. He found himself trapped and was forced to retreat deeper into the library. He managed to put a chair between himself and Abner Heems just as the preacher pulled a knife out of his belt.

'You're a fool, boy,' the preacher said. 'I'll cut you if you don't hand over the pearl.'

Adam bumped up against his father's desk by the window and looked around for a weapon. He picked up the heavy hourglass and weighed it in his hand.

Abner Heems hissed with fury. He even took a step back and studied Adam. His gaze flicked down to the hourglass, then back up to fix on Adam's eyes.

'Don't be a fool, boy,' the preacher said quietly. 'I've slit men's throats for threatening less.' His lips drew back over his rotten teeth. 'And I'll wager my life you're not man enough to risk it.'

But no one had thought about what Cook might do when she was set free.

'*Where* is he? Just you wait until I get my hands on him!' Cook was shouting as she burst out of the kitchen and marched across the hall. 'I'm sorry, mistress, but I've been shoved about and locked in a cupboard and I've had enough.' A moment later the library door was thrown wide open and Cook appeared wielding a copper pan about like a battle-axe. 'There you are. Now you leave Master Adam alone!'

Everything happened very quickly after that. Adam saw his mother appear in the doorway behind Cook. He called out a warning about the knife as Abner Heems turned to face them with a snarl. Then Adam hurled the hourglass with all his strength at the preacher while he was distracted.

The hourglass turned, spinning through the air as it flew across the room. It hit the preacher just as he turned to look at Adam again. It made a dull thud, catching him a blow from his chest to his chin, breaking his rotten teeth and drawing a trickle of blood from his lips.

Abner Heems staggered back with a gasp just as Cook brought down the copper pan on his hand and knife. The pan struck with all the noise of a sounding gong; the preacher cried out and dropped the blade. Adam didn't think twice, he leapt forward and managed to snatch it up before the preacher could reach it again. He swung the knife wildly and felt the blade bite deep into the man's sleeve.

The preacher let out a startled cry and clutched his wounded hand. He retreated into the ledger-room and there was new respect in his eyes now. The speed and determination of the defence had clearly caught him completely by surprise and left him looking around wildly for a way out.

'You'll pay for that with your life, boy!' he snarled. 'No one cuts the preacher and gets away with it. *No one.*'

And with that he leapt headlong out of the broken window into the courtyard. He rolled, came to his feet with surprising agility and leapt up into the branches of the plum tree. He scaled the tree like a ladder and clambered on to the top of the wall, and there he paused, gripping the iron cross that hung around his neck, balancing on the coping-stones as he looked down on them crowded at the broken window.

'"With what measure ye mete, it shall be measured to you." St Mark, Chapter 4 Verse 24,' he quoted ominously, and leapt down into the street on the other side of the wall.

The hourglass still lay where it had fallen. One of the glass chambers had broken in the wooden frame. The sand had spilled across the floor and out through the door on to the black and white tiles of the hall. To Adam it seemed to prove that time had finally run out for the House of Windjammer.

He stood in the library and listened to the crunching sound of the sand and glass under the soles of the men's boots. There were soldiers in the hall, a captain of the city guard was talking to Bartholomew de Leiden. The twins were hanging on their mother's skirts, with Cook looking threatening nearby. They had closed the shutters over the broken window and now the old man's clerk was busy sorting out the ledgers in the ledger-room ready to take them to the Long Table.

'The boy did a brave thing, captain,' the old man spoke quietly to the officer of the guard. 'He chased off this *preacher* before he could steal anything.'

'A preacher, are you sure?' the captain said. 'I have heard tales of this man already from the boy – but I cannot believe this of a man of the cloth.'

Adam had recognised the captain from the warehouse. He was the same soldier who believed the barrel had fallen by accident. His mind was set. There seemed little hope of him changing it now.

'You have the man's description and his knife as proof,' Bartholomew de Leiden pointed out.

'I have, sir,' the captain remained sceptical. 'I will tell my men to keep watch for this *preacher*, but if you ask me there must have been some mistake. No preacher would have done such a thing – and even if he had he will be long gone by now.'

Adam knew the truth, however. He knew the preacher would soon be back and would keep coming back until he found what he was looking for. Adam had decided not to tell the captain – or anyone else for that matter – about the Black Pearl. His own mother hadn't believed him, so why should they?

Adam came to the conclusion it was too dangerous. He knew that if he told them – and they believed him – it would mean admitting the pearl was still lost. The captain, the soldiers, Bartholomew de Leiden, the old man's clerk, Cook – any one of them could have talked. A secret like that couldn't be kept for long. Someone was sure to mention such a rare jewel and the word would inevitably spread. Then every merchant and trader in Amsterdam would be beating a path to the Windjammers' door demanding to know more.

No, Adam had already decided that if he was to have any hope of finding Gerrit's treasure and using it to save the House of Windjammer then he would have to keep it secret as Gerrit had done.

Soon afterwards the captain left, promising to do all he could, but sounding as if he thought there was little to be done. Bartholomew de Leiden then turned and took Adam's mother by the hand.

'There is no need to concern yourself, my dear Mary,' he said. 'I am sure the captain will find this pirate and hang him for the scoundrel he is.'

Adam saw his mother look in through the open door

at him. He wondered if she remembered about the Black Pearl. She turned away again as the clock on the church nearby struck the hour with two lingering notes. The old man remembered the time and called to his clerk. The clerk answered. All was ready. The ledgers were waiting for them on the Long Table.

'Then let us do what we came to do,' the old man said. 'I will need some peace and quiet for a while. If I know Gerrit – he will have written everything down. It should not take too long to see the truth.'

Adam heard the rustle of his mother's skirts as she led the way into the dining-room. She soon re-emerged, leaving the old man and his clerk at work. Cook took her leave and went back to the kitchens, and Adam watched as his mother shepherded the twins away so they wouldn't disturb the men working at the Long Table.

Adam felt strangely resentful of the trust his mother had put in the old man. Even though Bartholomew de Leiden had come to help them, he found himself envying the old man for being able to do what he couldn't. His hand went to the chain around his neck. He fought the impulse to snap the chain and hurl the ring away.

A feeling of utter loneliness and despair washed through Adam then. It left him hollow deep inside as if somehow he had been eaten away from within. The fever had left him feeling drained and empty, but it was more than just that. Only gradually did he come to realise it was the feeling of failure.

After that, Adam roamed around the house for a while, searching in all the places he thought Gerrit might have hidden the pearl. Finally he reached Gerrit's room high in the attic of the house. The room was spartan: a window, bare walls and a scrubbed wooden floor – Adam found little there but an iron bed, a small desk and several suits of black clothes. The emptiness of that room was overpowering. He left it as he had found it and was drawn back down to the life in the house below.

'And here again,' Bartholomew de Leiden was saying as Adam reached the hall. He paused to listen outside the double doors leading to the dining-room. The old man was talking to his clerk. 'I cannot believe it of Augustus Windjammer. Time after time he has paid too much or bought too little. He has shown no under-standing of business at all. And as for the expenses – it seems he spent most of his time at lunch.'

The bell of the church clock struck the half hour with a single note.

Adam noticed his sisters had followed him down from above and were watching him from the stairs. 'What do you want?' he snapped at them and told them to go away.

Rose spoke up. 'We didn't mean to.'

'Cause trouble, she means,' Viola explained.

Adam regretted snapping at them. 'None of this is your fault,' he said.

They seemed relieved and fled back up the stairs. Adam watched them go, then stepped back into the library. The room had changed so much since the game of hide and seek. The colours had faded out of the light, the warm, drowsy smell had gone cold and now the menace of the preacher hung in the air like a bad vapour.

'I could search for a year and not find it.' He spoke the thought aloud. 'I've *one* day left.'

He returned to the ledger-room. With the shutters

closed over one of the windows, half of the room was now in shadow – the half nearest the door into the street – while the other half was bright by comparison. The daylight now fell mostly across the desk. Adam sat down and looked at the scene around him from Gerrit's place. It was like looking through a dead man's eyes. Everything was as he had left it. Nothing had changed.

Adam sat very still and let his thoughts run over all that had happened that morning until they stopped abruptly at something Bartholomew de Leiden had said. '*If I know Gerrit – he will have written everything down.*' The words struck him with the full force of their meaning.

Only then did Adam remember Gerrit's diary.

New hope – like clean blood – surged through Adam, bringing him swiftly to his feet. He wasted no time in dragging the desk to one side and, as he dropped to his knees, he was relieved to see that the floorboards showed no marks of the preacher's knife.

The boards came up one by one until he could reach into the hole. His fingers felt for the casket and he dragged it out. Gerrit had padlocked it and, having spent some minutes in a fruitless search for the key, Adam gave up and picked up a small blade Gerrit kept on his desk for sharpening his writing quills. The blade rasped slightly as Adam slipped it under the catch and gave it several sharp twists. The lock broke on the third attempt and Adam opened the casket. The mask was there and so too was a small leather-bound diary, hidden just where he had hoped he might find it.

Adam took out the diary and put it on the desk. He

had second thoughts about the mask, before deciding it might be useful. He pushed it deep into the pocket of his coat and was careful to replace everything just as he had found it. Then he sat down at the desk to read.

His hands were trembling slightly as he opened the diary. The year AD1636 had been entered on the first page under Gerrit's name. After that, each entry had been marked with a date. Some were long, others short. His heart was racing as he turned quickly through the pages to the most recent entries. And there, written out neatly in the clerk's even hand, he found Gerrit's confession in full.

21. The Bridge over the Herengracht

The church bell began to strike the hour. Adam paused and looked up from the diary, vaguely aware that he had forgotten something. He counted the strikes to three and remembered Jade van Helsen.

He glanced back down at the pages in front of him. He had barely begun, but it would have to wait. He knew Jade wouldn't be at the bridge for long. His frustration showed as he snapped the diary shut, stood up and slipped it into his pocket to read later.

A freshening breeze blurred the reflections in the water of the Herengracht, sending ripples hurrying before the squalls. Purplish-grey clouds weighed heavily on the horizon above the roofs to the north and east, and the daylight was surrendering early to the threat of the approaching rainstorm.

Adam let himself out of the house and closed the front door quietly behind him. He stood at the top of the stone steps and looked both ways. He made quite sure the preacher wasn't watching the house, then he descended the steps, crossed the street to the canal side and ducked behind the trunk of an old elm tree. From there he could study the bridge at a distance.

Few people were about on that cold Sunday afternoon. Those that were had their heads tucked well down into their collars and seemed to be in a hurry to be somewhere else warmer. From where he was standing, Adam had a clear view of the bridge. He could see the entire span was deserted.

'She hasn't come,' he murmured the thought aloud. 'Or I'm too late.'

He moved on again, glancing over his shoulder more than once to be sure he wasn't being followed. More than once he stopped, his heart thumping as someone approached from behind only to hurry on past without a second glance.

It started to rain, a light drizzle falling across the canal in a fine mist. It drew down the darkness of the lowering sky like a veil bringing an early dusk to end the day. Adam reached the approaches to the bridge and hesitated. He pulled his coat about him, checked the diary wasn't getting wet, and wondered what would have made Jade change her mind.

He could see a coach and horses standing in the street on the other side of the Herengracht. While he watched, the coach moved forward and turned awkwardly on to the bridge. The horses were steaming in the rain. The driver cracked his whip, sitting hunched on the bench seat on the top of the coach. He reached the middle of the bridge and pulled back on the reins. The horses and the coach rattled to a sudden stop.

Adam watched it, waiting for the driver to whip up his horses and move on. The driver just sat there with his hat pulled well down over his eyes. The stillness was unnerving. Only the horses moved, snorting and shifting from foot to foot in the traces. No one got in or out of the coach – the curtains over its open frame didn't even flick.

She had said she would *walk*. Adam remembered her words well. Now a small voice in his head warned him over and over again to be careful. He looked up at the sky. It was possible that Jade had seen the approaching clouds and changed her mind and come by coach. He decided to take a closer look and started across the bridge. The horses coughed and snorted. The driver sat hunched over his reins. Adam's every instinct warned him of the trap and yet he told himself that only Jade knew the time and place where they had arranged to meet.

Adam was closer now. He paused and leaned casually against the rail of the bridge, pretending to be interested in the boats on the canal below. But all the while he was watching the coach and its silent driver out of the corner of his eye. Still nothing happened.

Adam moved on cautiously, hoping for a sign. By now he could smell the warm, wet smell of the horses. There was something sinister in the way the driver just sat there staring straight ahead into the rain. One of the horses shook the rain off its mane. The harness jangled and was silent. Adam looked at the thick curtains hanging behind the heavily carved frames that formed the windows on either side of the cloth door of the coach. He was almost close enough to reach out and pull the door back. Still he hesitated.

'Jade?' he whispered.

No answer.

He swallowed hard and reached out. His fingers felt the grainy richness of the material. He steeled himself for what might come and pulled the curtain door aside.

'Jade!' His relief was immediate.

Jade van Helsen sat on the bench seat, pressed back

into the corner diagonally across the coach from him. She was wearing a cape with the hood up over her head. He saw her and the tension blew out of him in a sigh of relief. Then he saw the look on her face and realised something was very wrong.

Adam froze. Someone was sitting opposite her – leaning back out of sight, hidden by the curtains over the carved frame of the window closest to him.

'You are late, Adam Windjammer,' Hugo van Helsen said as he sat forward suddenly. A hint of a smile played over the banker's face. 'Don't you know that you should never keep a lady waiting?'

'Stay away from me!' Adam snarled. 'Just leave me alone!'

He shot a venomous look in Jade's direction – wondered how she could just sit there and say nothing – and spun on his heel. He had to force himself not to run as he set off back across the bridge the way he had come. He hadn't gone far before he heard Hugo van Helsen call up to the driver. The driver cracked his whip and the horses moved forward at the trot bringing the carriage up alongside him.

'Do not blame Jade,' Hugo van Helsen looked out of the carriage, talking over the rattle of the wheels as the driver reined the horses in to a walk. 'She did not betray your confidence. In fact, she denied everything. And for a while I believed her. Then you came.'

Adam strode on without looking at him.

'I have always known that she is a headstrong and disobedient girl,' Hugo van Helsen went on, 'and for some time I have been keeping a closer eye on her than she imagined. Her dear maid, the one she calls most affectionately Minou, has been most helpful in keeping me informed.'

Jade looked crushed, sitting back in the corner of the coach as she stared out through the curtain on the other side.

Adam turned off the bridge and started down the street towards his house. He pulled ahead of the carriage briefly as it was forced to negotiate the turn. The driver whipped his horses on and soon Hugo van Helsen was up along side him again.

'Master Windjammer! *Please!*' he said. 'Do you wish me to shout our business in the street like a fish-seller?'

'I don't care what you do.'

'Very well then, I will,' Hugo van Helsen said. 'Despite how it might seem, I am *pleased* that my daughter has brought us together like this. It gives me the opportunity of talking to you alone.'

'I've got nothing to say to you.'

'But I have decided to make you an offer,' Hugo van Helsen said. 'A generous offer that, should you accept it, will mean you can save this fine house of yours and continue to live here on the Herengracht in peace.'

'Why should I trust you?' Adam said. He glanced meaningfully at Jade as he walked. 'Why should I trust *anything* a van Helsen says?'

Hugo van Helsen lifted his walking-cane and knocked on the roof of the coach with the handle. The driver reined in his horses, the coach stopped. Adam strode on purposefully and started across the road towards the steps leading up to his front door.

'At least listen to what I have to say, Master Windjammer!' the banker called after him. 'I am sure your *father* would have done so in the same situation.'

Those words fired out of the coach and across the street to hook into Adam like barbs into his skin. It was as if invisible reins had been suddenly attached to him, drawing him painfully to a stop.

'I'm giving you the chance to save what is left of the House of Windjammer,' Hugo van Helsen said.

Adam stood for a moment, then he turned and walked slowly back across the road to find Hugo van Helsen waiting for him. A faint smile played over the man's thin lips when he saw he had got what he wanted.

'All right,' Adam said after a pause. 'I'm listening.'

Jade looked away hopelessly.

'Then I suggest you get in out of the rain, Adam Windjammer,' van Helsen said. 'I hear you have been recently stricken by the fever – I would not want you to catch your death of cold on my account. Here, why don't you sit by Jade while we talk ... '

Hugo van Helsen sat back comfortably into his seat, his head protruding from the fur collar of his cloak giving the impression that only the parts of him that were showing had human form. It was easy to imagine him as half-man, half-beast. His pale eyes moved constantly under the brim of his hat and his fingers flexed and settled and flexed again as he rested his hands on the shining silver knob of his walking-cane.

'It may surprise you to know,' the banker began easily, 'that I *admire* you, Adam Windjammer. You have spirit and I like that in one so young.' He sighed and shook his head. 'Ah! The youth of today? They have grown soft on easy living – they expect everything handed to them on a pewter platter.' His fingers flexed, his eyes flicked. 'But *you – you* could go far in life. I knew that from the moment I first met you at the Long Table.'

'Is that so?' Adam was unimpressed.

'Yes,' van Helsen went on regardless. 'It is a great pity your father did not think to start your schooling in the ways of business sooner – as I would have done if I had been blessed with a son.'

Adam sensed Jade stiffen on the seat beside him.

'You've no right to talk about my father,' Adam said. 'He was a bigger man than you'll ever be!'

Hugo van Helsen gave a slight shrug of his shoulders, as if it was of no importance to him what Adam believed. 'You blame me for your father's weakness of heart, that is only natural I suppose. If you were older perhaps you would understand that life is hard and that I am not to blame for the ways of nature.'

'I was there, *remember*. I saw everything. You attacked my father when he was down. You just smiled and baited him like a ... like a ... ' Adam searched for a way of describing it,' ... like a *bear*.'

'It was business, nothing more,' van Helsen said.

'*Business*.' Adam felt sick deep in the pit of his stomach. He turned to Jade. 'And I suppose you believe him?'

Jade said nothing.

'The truth of the matter is,' the banker said briskly, 'after the wreck of the Star Fleet the Windjammer Trading Company was vulnerable to take-over. It was only a matter of time before someone moved in on you. Your father knew it. We *all* knew it. That is why he called us to an urgent meeting at the Long Table. If it had not been me it would have been someone else.

That is the nature of business – the strong will always prey on the weak.'

'It's not true,' Adam said. 'Bartholomew de Leiden supported us. The other merchants were prepared to help too, until *you* stood up.'

Hugo van Helsen's pale eyes narrowed slightly. His lips set in a thin line and for the first time Adam saw a glint of anger in his eyes.

'That cosy little club of fools! They pretend they are men of business, but the truth is they are sheep. They bleat and flock together. They follow a leader of their kind – no matter how weak – and pledge their support for a lost cause even though it makes no sense. I alone could see the House of Windjammer was crippled beyond saving. I alone could see we would be throwing good money after bad.'

'You never gave us a chance. All we needed was time. My father gave you his word he would pay you.'

'Fine words do not pay bills and a good reputation is no guarantee,' Hugo van Helsen scoffed. 'No. I learned long ago that it is only gold that counts in the end.' His lips twisted into a sneer. 'Have you any idea how hard it is to make a living? Have you any idea what it is like to scrimp and save? To go hungry? To see the ones you love grow weak and die from disease and fever?' He spoke quickly as if the words themselves were painful to him. 'To raise a daughter alone?'

Hugo van Helsen paused. He appeared to have said more than he had meant to and controlled himself with an act of great self-will. 'I may not have been born to wealth and privilege like the Windjammers, but I understand how to make money. Do you honestly think I would be a rich man if I had run my business by that old fool de Leiden's rules? No. Only the *strong* can survive.'

'You make us sound like animals,' Adam said. 'But we're not – we're *people*.'

'Ah! You would be surprised, Master Windjammer,' Hugo van Helsen said. 'If you scratch away the veneer of our civilisation you will find we are little more than teeth and claws. The only difference between us is that some of us are born to be the predators.' He smiled, as if the word pleased him. 'The time has come for you to make a choice which you are to be, Adam Windjammer – the *hunter* or the *hunted*.'

Adam wanted to get out. He felt suffocated by the coach – squeezed by its cramped smallness. He wanted to run, gulp in fresh air and blow out the rank smell that seemed to fill his nostrils now.

'It is in our darkest nature,' Hugo van Helsen's pale eyes gleamed and flicked to Jade, 'if we want something badly enough we will do anything to get it. *Anything*.'

'Then what do *you* want?' Adam asked.

Hugo van Helsen didn't answer him directly. Instead he held out his hand, palm up.

'I have the power to destroy you utterly, Adam Windjammer. Your wealth, your health, your happiness – I have them all right here in the palm of my hand,' he said. 'My money gives me that *power* over you – just as it gives me power over de Leiden and those other weak fools. With *power* you can do *anything*. You can make up your own rules.'

'You have *nothing* in your hand,' Adam said.

'Do not be a fool, Master Windjammer,' Hugo van Helsen warned. 'I can crush you as easily as that.' He closed his fingers into a fist. 'I can drive you down into the gutter and keep you there for the rest of your life. Imagine what that would be like! Think of your dear mother and those pretty little sisters!'

'Then what's stopping you?'

Again Hugo van Helsen was evasive. He seemed content to leave his threat hanging in the air for a while like Damocles's sword.

'I admit I was a little hasty to judge you when last we met,' the banker spoke at last. Again he glanced at Jade. 'I can see now that I was wrong to think all Windjammers were like that fool of an uncle of yours. Augustus *Windbag* has fled, well good riddance to him! As head of the House of Windjammer it leaves *you* to make the decisions, does it not?'

Adam nodded.

Hugo van Helsen seemed pleased. 'Then if you are as bright as I think you are, you will see that I can be a better friend than an enemy. Just think what it would be like to save your mother and sisters! Just think what it would be like to save this fine house! All you have to do is listen to what I have to say to you, Adam Windjammer – just listen and I will help you!'

'And why would *you* want to help us?' Adam asked cautiously.

Hugo van Helsen's fingers flexed and settled. 'I have my reasons,' he said. 'Contrary to common rumour, I do not wish to destroy the House of Windjammer just for the sake of it.' He glanced at Jade as if he was saying this for her benefit. 'I know what the other merchants think of me. They do business with me because they have to – not because they want to. I believe it would be to my advantage if I showed myself in a more generous light. If I am seen to be kinder and more understanding their confidence in me will grow and so will my business. This is why I am willing to make you an offer now.'

Adam didn't believe him, but he was careful not to let it show. 'An offer? What sort of offer?'

'I have written it down,' Hugo van Helsen said. He reached into his pocket and pulled out a letter. 'It is quite straightforward – you will agree to hand over the *Draco*, the warehouse and all its contents and what is left of the House of Windjammer's other business interests, and in return I will let you keep this fine house on the Herengracht.' He held out the letter. 'The terms are listed here and require only your signature and the wax seal of the head of the House of Windjammer.'

Adam made no effort to take the letter.

'Take it!' van Helsen insisted. 'You will see it is a fair offer and if you sign it now I will give you my personal assurance that I will spare your dear mother and sisters any more pain. I am not a heartless man. As you will see I have also granted your mother a small annual income.' Then after a pause he added, 'What could be fairer than that?'

Hugo van Helsen's face was a mask, giving no hint of his thoughts or reasons.

'Why are you doing this?' Adam asked at last. 'You said yourself you could take everything we have.'

'That is what I like about you, Master Windjammer,' Hugo van Helsen said. 'You have brains and intelligence. You *think*. You are a natural hunter just like me.'

Jade had heard enough. She made a sudden move towards the curtain door of the carriage.

'Sit down!' her father commanded her. His walking-cane flashed out and jabbed into the wooden frame of the coach, barring her exit. She crumpled back into her seat and a single, fat tear broke out and rolled down her cheek.

'I blame myself of course,' Hugo van Helsen's face took on a pained expression. 'Perhaps if I had remarried and given her a mother she might have turned out differently. But I have always been busy with the harsh realities of my business and I have allowed her to grow up wilful and headstrong. Ah! What a *son* she would have made.'

It seemed that for all his money, Hugo van Helsen was unable to buy the one thing he truly wanted.

'Come now, Master Windjammer,' the banker said. 'We have talked enough – I want your answer!'

Those pale eyes gleamed as Adam reached out and took the letter.

Adam considered it for a moment, then shook his head. 'I don't believe you,' he said quietly. 'There's more – something you're not telling me.'

Hugo van Helsen's face set into a mask. 'I do not have all day, Master Windjammer.'

'Then what are you waiting for?' Adam asked, trusting his instinct. 'You say you have us in the palm of your hand. You say you can crush us. Why don't you?'

Hugo van Helsen made no attempt to answer.

The conviction grew stronger in Adam. 'Go on! *Do it!*'

Still no reaction.

Adam glanced down at the letter. He lifted it up and tore it in half, then half again in front of the banker's face. '*That's* what I think of you and your offer!'

277

Hugo van Helsen didn't move.

'I knew it!' Adam said. 'You won't do anything because you *can't*! You're frightened of something – aren't you?' Adam threw back the cloth door and stepped out of the coach. He let the pieces of the letter flutter down into the gutter.

'You're a fool, Adam Windjammer,' Hugo van Helsen said. 'Let me remind you that you are on your own now. There is no one to help you – not even your faithful Gerrit.'

'*Gerrit!*' Adam said. 'Of course – that's it!' The answer suddenly seemed so obvious. 'It's just like the preacher said! Gerrit took a big gamble and now you're worried it's going to pay off.'

A slight hiss escaped from between Hugo van Helsen's lips. 'You have spoken to the preacher?'

'Yes, he came *calling* on us,' Adam said. 'He was careless. He told me lots of things about you before he left.'

Those pale eyes flashed. 'I warn you, Master Windjammer! I do not take kindly to slanderous accusations. I suggest you think very carefully before you say another word.'

'And I warn you, *Mr van Helsen*,' Adam answered him. 'The Windjammers aren't interested in *you* or your *offer*. We still have time left to pay you and we *will* – in full.'

'Then you have the Black Pearl?' the banker asked.

Adam knew he had to bluff now. 'Yes!' he lied. 'And when we sell it the House of Windjammer will be rich again. We'll be strong, just like before. Then you'll see you have no power over us. *Then* you'll see who's the *hunted* around here!'

'You do not have much time to sell it,' Hugo van Helsen pointed out. '*Less* than two days left.'

'That's enough,' Adam said. He was enjoying the way the banker was squirming in his seat. 'I'll sell it if I have to stand up on the steps of our house and hold an auction. Yes, you'll see – I'll sell the jewel to the highest bidder!'

'*Jewel?*' Hugo van Helsen echoed him.

'It's the biggest you've ever seen.' Adam got carried away.

The banker's eyes narrowed slightly. 'And is this *jewel* ... ' he paused for the full effect, ' ... as beautiful as they say? A pearl fit for the ring on the hand of a king?'

'An *emperor*,' Adam corrected him and with that he turned his back to underline the completeness of his victory.

Adam expected the banker to come after him, begging him on his knees to reconsider. But he didn't. So Adam walked on and reached the steps leading to his front door. He looked back at the sound of the driver's whip. The horses surged forward, pulling the coach away with a sudden jerk. Adam caught one final glimpse of Jade through a gap in the curtains. She just stared back sadly at him. And then he heard the strange, chilling sound of Hugo van Helsen laughing.

22. The Black Pearl

This is the history of my shame.

*On this the fifteenth day of October, in the year of
our Lord sixteen hundred six and thirty, I, Gerrit,
clerk of the House of Windjammer, do hereby commit
to the pages of this diary the full truth of my terrible
deeds . . .*

Adam read Gerrit's diary late into the night by the
flickering light of a candle. His words were like a voice
speaking from beyond the grave.

*Today, as a month of mourning for the old master
draws to a close, all does not go well for the House of
Windjammer. The business of this House has been
wrecked along with our glorious Star Fleet. It has
been my unpleasant duty to ask my dear mistress to
make sacrifices beyond all that I ever believed would
be necessary. She has taken the news as I knew she
would – with strength and determination – and has
asked me to say nothing to Master Adam, Miss Rose
and Miss Viola.*

*She has told me to sell her jewels and precious
things and this I will do with a heavy heart, but she
insists the servants must be paid. They are all to leave*

except Cook who refuses, and myself who will never abandon this House while there is still living breath in my body. However, I fear there is much worse news to come.

17th October. I know now that we have made a grave mistake trusting Mr Augustus. He is not a man of business and things go worse for this House because of him. With each passing day I feel Master Adam's resentment more keenly than ever and it makes it much harder to confide in him.

19th October. I fear we now have no hope of trading our way out of debt. It is for this reason that I have made up my mind and set myself upon a secret and drastic action. Oh! the shame of it. It goes against my true nature. For have I not always endeavoured to uphold the custom and propriety of this fine House? But this is a risk I will have to take if I am to save this House and its good name.

22nd October. Last night, I took all the money I have carefully saved over the years of my service and, masking my face like the kapistan of the taverns, risked it all in a terrible gamble. Yes, now I, like so many others here in Amsterdam, have started living in hope, gambling on the lottery of the bulbs of this flower they call the tulip . . .

Adam paused and went back to read it again just to be sure he hadn't made a mistake. '*Tulip!*' the word burst out of him suddenly. He turned the page and read on, drawn through the pages by events he recognised from a wholly different point of view. And the more he read, the more he realised the terrible mistake he had made.

23rd October. My endeavour has started better than I could ever have expected! I have this day bought and sold the bulbs of three tulips, holding them for less than an hour in my hand before none other than Claes van Hooghelande, the renowned tulip grower, offered me three times what I had paid for them only hours before. 3,000 gold coins! It was an honest trade, but one I could scarce believe. I feel the weight of my shame grows heavier like my purse. Nevertheless, I have set upon this course and I am determined to see it through to the end.

26th October. Once again I have doubled the money I risked. In three days I have bought and sold two more rare tulip bulbs – two <u>Admirals</u> as they are affectionately called – and I have heard of other rare tulips for sale. Do I dare hope that I can raise enough money this way? Yes, perhaps soon I will even be able to pay off our debts to Hugo van Helsen!

27th October. Can it be true? I have managed to buy a bulb of the rare tulip. It is called <u>Viceroy</u> and I have already agreed to sell it for more than twice the price I paid – two thousand gold pieces! A handsome profit, but I fear my good fortune cannot last. Each day it grows more difficult. I fear I will become known in the taverns and that my true identity will soon be discovered. Then my shame will be known

and my good name – and the name of this House –
will be tarnished forever.

28th October. I have fallen under a strange spell
indeed! Yesterday I sold the <u>Viceroy</u> and, no sooner
had I resolved to stop gambling, than I was offered
the rarest of the rare – the bulb of a tulip known in
Latin as <u>Semper Augustus.</u> I could not refuse. Is it not
ironic that this flower shares its name with my old
master's brother? One Augustus to ruin us, while
another to save us!

29th October. A strange thing happened today while I
was in the ledger-room. I felt strongly as if I was
being watched. It was the old master, I am sure of it.
I found the hourglass on his desk had been turned
and yet the library was empty! Is it his ghost come
back to haunt me in my shame? I have taken it as a
sign that my time is running out.

30th October. Last night I think I was followed as I
left the tavern they call the Trade Winds and returned
to the Herengracht. I know not by whom, but I must
be careful. I fear my good fortune cannot last much
longer.

31st October. Oh! How true my last words were. I
started the day in such high spirits. The Muscovy
Company's fleet had returned from the Baltic and I
was pleased to take Master Adam to the waterfront
for the first time. But when we arrived we found
nothing but trouble there. Rumours about the
Windjammer Trading Company are spreading and

few merchants will risk trade with us.

There is worse still! The Council of Merchants has met. My dear, brave mistress faced them alone, but, alas, they would not listen to her. All soon will be lost to Hugo van Helsen unless we pay off our debts. A marriage has been proposed between my dear mistress and this banker, but I have made up my mind that it will not happen. I will go to the taverns again tonight. Yes, I will risk my <u>Semper Augustus</u> in one last great gamble. It must be done tonight. May fortune shine on my darkest deeds!

1st November. I have it! I have risked all I have on this final speculation. I have purchased, with no little difficulty, the rarest of bulbs from the Turkish merchant called Ahmed. He owed me many favours and I called upon them to force his hand. Nevertheless, I paid a high price indeed: four bulbs (one of which was my <u>Semper Augustus</u>) and 5,000 florins. But this is rare treasure indeed. I have a picture of it full grown and a certificate to prove it. I hope it will fetch more than three times the price I paid when I offer it to the highest bidder at the Trade Winds. But I have hidden it this night for I saw the face of the man who has been following me. I know now it is the preacher they call Abner Heems.

After that there was only one last, hurried entry:

My secret is uncovered! Master Adam knows everything. This morning, as I made ready to go to the warehouse, he came to me accusing me of stealing. <u>Me!</u> Steal from this House? How little he *knows me! But I have promised to tell him the truth of the matter. Tonight when I return from the warehouse I will call a meeting at the Long Table and my shame will then be laid bare for all to see. I will yield up my treasure along with the truth and my keys of office, and leave this House in shame. But I pray that my dear mistress will understand and consent to finish what I have started. For I fear only the Black Pearl can save this House now . . .*

The loneliness of Gerrit's position weighed heavily on every line. Adam finished reading and looked at the small watercolour of the tulip sandwiched between the pages of the diary. The petals of the flower were black as night, edged in pinkish white. The certificate was signed and authenticated by the grower.

The mistake was obvious now. The Black Pearl was no jewel, no shining treasure plucked from the mouth of an oyster by a native diver on some distant exotic island, as he had imagined. No. Gerrit's diary had revealed a truth far more puzzling than anything he had expected to find there – the Black Pearl was a *flower*.

23. The Hunter and the Hunted

'*Tulips?*' Bartholomew de Leiden seemed surprised by the question Adam had just put to him. The old man leaned back in his chair. He fixed Adam with a quizzical look. 'You should be careful of those flowers, my boy. Many people have seen them as the easy path to riches only to be sold an onion and led to ruin.'

Adam sat in his place at the Long Table. Their simple breakfast had been cleared away and the ledgers brought out and piled on the table ready for the morning meeting the old man had called.

'I was wondering,' Adam said while they waited for his mother to return from the kitchen, 'how *flowers* could be so valuable?'

'The value of something,' the old man said, 'often lies not so much in the thing itself, but in its rarity. It is this quality, this knowledge that few if any can own what you own, that makes people pay high prices. It might be a rare jewel or a fine horse or a house or even ... the bulb of a tulip. The old man wheezed into a laugh suddenly, 'To think I used to buy them just to plant in my garden. Now, alas, the prices have gone up and up and up.' He pointed an ancient finger upwards as if to prove just how high that was. 'Some of the most rare are of great value. The *Semper Augustus*, for example,' he used the Latin name Adam recognised. 'Why, this year, a bulb of one of these beautiful red and white tulips changed hands for the value of a house on the Herengracht – thirteen thousand guilders!'

Adam had calculated the worth of the Black Pearl to be well over three times as much.

'Yes, these flowers seem to cast a strange spell over people,' the old man said. 'They are sought after by kings. They are hoarded by the rich and coveted by the poor. Not just for their beauty and colours, but for the *money* that can be made by buying and selling them. Greed can be stronger than any apothecary's potion. These days even cautious, sensible people seem prepared to risk everything in order to profit from buying and selling these flowers. They mask themselves for fear of being recognised and robbed, and trade in the bulbs. They are known as the *kapistan* – the hooded madmen who ply their trade in the taverns and inns of the city. It is a trade that stops at nothing. *Nothing!*'

Adam's thoughts took flight and soared on the old man's words, only to come crashing down when he remembered he still had to find the Black Pearl and sell it.

'So beware of the *kapistan!*' the old man finished with a warning as Adam's mother swept into the room and sat down in her place. 'Where you meet with desperate men, there you will surely meet with desperate deeds.'

The night watchman had sounded his horn many times before Adam eventually slept. He spent most of the night staring at the mantling over his bed, his thoughts bridging the chasms and voids of his despair with new hopes. All he had to do was find this tulip called the Black Pearl.

Even now, as he sat at the Long Table to hear Bartholomew de Leiden's verdict on the state of the House of Windjammer, he racked his brain. Fleeting memories of something important haunted him, something lost in the mists of his fever and the events of that terrible night when Gerrit had died. But no matter how hard he tried to remember, the answer remained tantalisingly out of reach.

And now time was running out fast.

Adam wished he had paid more attention to Meister Bloem. 'How many times have I told you to think before you speak, Master Adam?' his old tutor had often said. In one careless moment Adam knew he had given away the advantage and told Hugo van Helsen what he wanted to know: the Black Pearl was *missing*.

'Please forgive me, there is no easy way of telling you this,' Bartholomew de Leiden said, when at last they were settled at the Long Table. The old man looked at them across the ledgers piled up on the table. His face was set. The message in his ancient, watering eyes was *serious*.

'My husband always believed in straight talk,' Adam's mother said. 'So do we.'

'Very well then,' the old man said. 'I have read the ledgers and what I have found there is not good. It is clear that Gerrit did his best, but Augustus Windjammer was not a prudent man. In a few short months he has spent what little money was left on wild extravagances and left the Windjammer Trading Company even deeper in debt. The Council of Merchants was right to question you and I must return

288

to them and tell them the truth. I fear only a miracle could save the House of Windjammer now.'

'Then we are ruined,' Mary Windjammer said.

The old man nodded. 'Unless you can come to some agreement with Hugo van Helsen. Perhaps if you gave him title to the *Draco* and the warehouse he might, even now, agree to let you keep this house?'

Adam said nothing. He couldn't bring himself to tell them that he had already turned down that very offer.

'No,' Mary Windjammer decided after some thought, 'this has gone too far for bargaining. Hugo van Helsen can take everything we have and there is nothing we can do now to stop him.'

A spark came into the old man's eyes. 'Then *I* will talk to him. I am sure he will listen to me – perhaps I can make him see reason.'

'No, old friend,' Mary Windjammer stopped him. 'If you do he will turn on you next. His money makes him very dangerous and you have helped us enough. Your responsibilities must lie with your own family and affairs now.'

The defiant spark faded out of the old man's eyes. His head sank down on to his chest.

'All we can do now is wait,' Mary Windjammer said.

They didn't have to wait long.

Hugo van Helsen's arrival that morning was announced by an urgent thumping on the front doors. Even before the echoes had died in the hollows of the house, one leaf of the great door burst inwards and he blew in like an unwelcome chill. He swept off his hat and stood alone in the middle of the chessboard of the hall – but his victory was not yet complete. He saw them grouped around the Long Table and strode in through the open door. It all happened so quickly, not one of them even had time to move.

'Where is she?' Hugo van Helsen was shouting. '*Where* is my daughter?'

'What is the meaning of this outrage, van Helsen?' Bartholomew de Leiden came to his feet with some difficulty.

'*Sit down*, old man!' Hugo van Helsen stormed. 'And I advise you to be quiet if you know what's good for you! It is all too obvious which side you have chosen in this matter.'

Bartholomew de Leiden remained standing for a moment longer, then he deflated back into his chair. Hugo van Helsen ignored Mary Windjammer and advanced down the table towards Adam.

'I asked you a question, boy,' he said. 'Tell me! *Where* is she?'

'What are you talking about?' Mary Windjammer asked. 'Adam has been here at the Long Table all morning.'

Hugo van Helsen turned on her. 'My daughter is missing and I know your son has something to do with it. I warned him to stay away from her, but he would not listen. Only yesterday he made arrangements to meet her on the bridge. Jade has always been vulnerable to ridiculous notions. Her head has always been full of ideas more fitting to a boy than a girl! And now it seems she has run away to prove it.'

'*Run away?*' Mary Windjammer repeated and looked at Adam. 'Is this true?'

'I don't know, Mother.'

'He's lying.'

Adam denied it. 'But I wouldn't blame her if she has

– he treats her like something to be bought and sold.'

Hugo van Helsen laughed. 'That's rich coming from the nephew of Augustus Windjammer – the same man who came crawling to me offering to sell his own children to save this miserable House for himself!'

Mary Windjammer stopped him, speaking quietly and firmly. 'If my son says he hasn't seen your daughter then I believe him.'

'Then you, like most weak-willed women, are blind to your son's faults, madam,' Hugo van Helsen said contemptuously. 'He is lying – just as he lied to me yesterday.'

'What are you talking about?' Mary Windjammer asked.

'He hasn't told you about our meeting?' Hugo van Helsen said. 'I can understand why. I made your son an offer that would have saved you this house and all that is in it, but he tore it up in my face.'

'Adam?' his mother looked to him for an explanation.

'It's true, Mother,' Adam admitted. 'He was trying to force me into signing away the *Draco*. But I didn't because I had found Gerrit's diary. It's all in there, Mother – *everything*. That's how I knew Gerrit had bought the Black Pearl.' He pointed at the banker. 'He knows what it's worth – ask him!'

'I don't know what you're talking about,' Hugo van Helsen lied.

'That's not true, Mother,' Adam insisted. 'He knows all about the Black Pearl – only it isn't a pearl, it's a *tulip*.'

'A tulip!' Bartholomew de Leiden looked startled.

'He's lying,' Hugo van Helsen insisted.

'I may only be a *weak-willed* woman,' Mary Windjammer said, pointedly, 'but I want to hear my son out.' She turned to Adam. 'Where is this tulip now?'

Adam hesitated.

That smile played over Hugo van Helsen's face. 'Yes! Why don't you show us?'

'I can't,' Adam said.

'You see, madam,' Hugo van Helsen laughed without humour. 'He hasn't got it. The boy's nothing but a common liar.'

Mary Windjammer looked at Adam for a moment longer, then a steely gleam came into her eye as she turned to the banker.

'Adam is the head of the House of Windjammer,' she spoke firmly but politely, 'and if he has turned down your offer, however *generous*, then he must have had good reason. He speaks for us all in matters of business now.' She put an end to the matter. 'As far as your daughter is concerned, perhaps you should ask yourself *why* she has run away from you, Mr van Helsen. Perhaps then you will see that others are not always to blame. If she comes here we will make sure she is safe. But now, please, I must ask you to leave our house.'

'*Your* house, madam?' Hugo van Helsen sneered. 'Yes, it is *your* house for one day longer. But tomorrow on the stroke of the noon bell it will be mine! Yes, mine and everything else with it!' He turned to Adam again. 'If anything happens to my daughter because of you, Adam Windjammer, then I promise I will make you suffer for the rest of your life. You have my word on that. And unlike the *Windjammers* I *always* keep my word.'

292

Hugo van Helsen gave Bartholomew de Leiden one last contemptuous look. He glanced at Mary Windjammer and finally at Adam. Then he turned and walked out past the twins and Cook, who had been drawn to the hall by the commotion and noise to see what was happening.

The front door slammed shut and Adam was left facing his mother.

'You knew of this tulip, Mary?' Bartholomew de Leiden broke the silence at last.

'I thought the talk of this Black Pearl could only be the ravings of a dying man,' she answered him. 'It seems I was wrong.' She held out her hand. 'Please show us this diary, Adam.'

Adam took it out of his pocket and gave it to her. He sat in silence and watched her as she read it, then passed it on to Bartholomew de Leiden. Some time later, the old man finished reading, and pinched the bridge of his nose in a tired sort of way. He looked up and for the first time Adam saw hope reflected in his old eyes.

'Well, Master Adam – what are you waiting for?' the old man said, closing the diary. 'You had better find this tulip they call the Black Pearl – and find it quickly.'

Adam sat in the courtyard garden staring at the plum tree, as if it held the answer somewhere in its twisted branches. They had looked everywhere, but they hadn't found the Black Pearl.

His thoughts turned to Jade again. He had been wrong to think she had betrayed him and he now regretted his snap judgements about her. She had warned him that her father had eyes and ears everywhere. He wondered how she could escape and whether she had found a ship at last to take her far away to the ends of the earth.

'It is over, Adam,' his mother said. 'Even if we found Gerrit's tulip we could not sell it in time. The best we can do now is prepare ourselves for the worst and pack our belongings ready to leave.'

Adam was suddenly overwhelmed by their failure. 'Where will we go, Mother?'

'Bartholomew de Leiden has offered us sanctuary at his house, but I fear it would not go well for him with Hugo van Helsen if we stay there,' she said. 'So we will go to our relatives in Hoorn or Edam. After that? Who knows – perhaps we will go to my home in England. I have not been back for many years, but at least Hugo van Helsen will not be able to touch us there.'

Adam sensed the power the man had over them, it seemed to close around them like a net.

His mother turned away, then pausing stayed to add, 'This is not your fault, Adam. No one could have done more than you to save the House of Windjammer.'

After she had left him, Adam sat for some time before he stood up and walked back slowly through the house. It seemed cold and clammy now, as if the house itself was dying. He crossed the black and white squares of the hall to the dining-room and went to his place at the head of the Long Table. He stood and looked at the great oak chair, then reached for the chain around his neck. He lifted it off and cupped the ring of the House of Windjammer in his hand. He didn't want to bear the burden of it any more. He just wanted to be plain Adam again. Adam the boy. Adam the son. Nothing more, nothing less.

His despair wrapped itself around him like an old, familiar cloak. He looked at the mark of the House of Windjammer and was haunted by his father's last words to him before the meeting at the Long Table.

'I'm sorry.' He spoke to the house itself and carefully placed the ring and the chain in front of his father's chair. He expected to feel the burden of it lift from his shoulders, but he felt no lighter for casting it off at last.

He heard soft footsteps behind him and looked up with a start. His sisters were watching him from the doorway. 'What are you looking at?' he snapped at them. 'What do you want?'

'Someone's come,' Rose said.

'To the door, she means,' Viola explained.

'Why should I care?' Adam asked. 'Tell them to go away! Tell them nobody's in. Tell them the Windjammers have gone and will *never* come back!'

After a short pause, the girls disappeared back out into the hall. He listened and heard them dragging at the front door. He heard them repeat his message word for word and heard the door thump closed again. Only then did he think better of what he had done and went to see who had called.

'We told her,' Rose said.

'The girl, she means,' Viola explained.

'And now she's gone.'

'Girl?' Adam said. He ran to the nearest window and looked out into the street. A wagon loaded with barrels trundled by and as it passed he saw Jade standing across the street by the canal. She was dressed as she had been when he had seen her at the waterfront that day: a woollen shawl up over her head, her long hair tied back, and she was wearing the plain brown dress of a servant girl.

'Jade!' Her name misted the glass in front of him. Then louder, banging on the window with the flats of his hands: 'Jade van Helsen – w*ait!*'

Adam burst out through the front door, took the stone steps down to the street in a single leap and raced after her. She turned away as soon as she saw him and started towards the bridge. He caught up with her and stopped without even noticing that the twins had followed him.

It took a moment or two for him to catch his breath. 'I'm sorry,' he said. 'I didn't know it was you.'

She looked back at him steadily.

'Are you going to?' Rose asked.

'Kiss her, she means,' Viola explained.

'Shut up!' Adam snapped at them. 'Now go home!'

The twins retreated a little way back down the street and stopped.

'I wish it could be different,' Jade said, 'but it isn't.'

He didn't know what she meant. 'Are you leaving?' he asked. 'Have you found a ship? What's going on, Jade? Tell me!'

She looked away without answering him. A man in a long cloak came across the bridge and turned down towards them. She waited until he had passed before she spoke.

'I can't,' she said and suddenly the regret was in her eyes. 'If my father finds out he'll ... ' She left the rest unsaid. 'It's best I go.'

'He was here.'

'I know.'

'If you leave he'll come after you again. If he finds

296

you he'll bring you back – then it'll be worse.'

'What can I do?' she asked the question of herself more than him. 'He wins – he *always* wins. He is going to destroy you, just like everyone else. Not because he hates the Windjammers, not because he needs the money, but because he *can*. It's all a game to him.' She forced a laugh. 'And do you know what the worst part of it all is?'

She paused as if expecting an answer. She looked away at the boats on the canal.

'It's hearing him say, day after day, that he's doing it all for me! Yes, *me*! So I can have a good life unlike my poor mother. I'm no longer his daughter – I'm his *excuse*.' She hugged her elbows. 'Can you understand how that makes me feel, Adam Windjammer? *Knowing* what he does to people?'

The water lapped against the wall of the canal. Somewhere in the distance one boatman called to another. The boats moved closer together. The awkwardness of the moment stretched until Adam broke the silence.

'I could beat him,' he said. 'If only I could find the Black Pearl. All we need is the bulb of that flower.'

He noticed the way she stiffened slightly as he spoke.

Adam moved closer to her. He wanted to put his arm around her. He ached to comfort her – to hold her – but he didn't know how. Instead he just stood awkwardly by her side, watching the boatmen. They were pulling at something in the water. Only as he watched them did he become aware of his sisters talking.

'He didn't believe us,' Rose said.

'About G'rit, you mean,' Viola agreed.

'But we saw him.'

'By the tree.'

Adam looked around at them. And suddenly it was as if a mist had lifted from his mind as he remembered what happened. The events reeled through his mind in staccato images as he spoke: 'You were there. In the garden. I was looking for it. Digging under the plum tree. But I was looking for a pearl – a jewel and you ... ' He paused as an image grew large in his mind's eye: it was of Rose standing clutching the bulb of a flower to her chest as if it was the most precious treasure in the world. '*You* found it,' he said. 'You picked it up, Rose!'

Adam caught hold of his sisters, each by the arm. He crouched down in front of them, sitting on his heels and looked at them. 'Where is it, Rose?' he asked, trying to remain calm. 'Tell me, Viola! What did you do with the flower?'

Four eyes gleamed secrets.

'I promise I'll give you a thousand flowers if you tell me!' Adam said through gritted teeth.

Rose glanced disbelievingly at Viola.

'*Please*,' Adam begged. 'I'm sorry I didn't listen to you before. I promise I always will from now on.'

A pause. Rose nodded to Viola. Viola nodded back.

'We put it there,' Rose said at last.

'In the ground, she means,' Viola explained.

'Where, Rose? Tell me w*here*, Viola!'

'By father's grave,' they chimed together.

Adam hugged them to him and glanced up at a sound behind him. 'Did you hear *that*, Jade? I know where it is ... '

But Jade had gone.

He stood up and looked around. He saw her turn on

to the bridge and start across. She was moving swiftly and he called out for her to wait. She didn't stop.

Adam turned back to his sisters. 'Go back to the house,' he said. 'Tell mother just what you told me. Tell her I've gone to find the Black Pearl and to wait for me here. I'll be back as soon as I can, I promise.'

They nodded, and Adam watched them until they were safely in through their front door. Then he went after Jade. He wanted to tell her it was going to be all right. But something had spooked her. By now she had reached the other side of the Herengracht and was moving quickly down the street. Her shawl had dropped back from her hair and was flying out behind her. She turned down a side street and vanished.

Adam had reached the middle of the bridge when he heard the shout from the canal below. The boats were directly below him now, and as he looked down over the rail of the bridge he saw them dragging what appeared to be a bundle of rags out of the water and into one of the boats. It was heavy and the men struggled with it. The water rushed off and suddenly the bundle of rags was transformed in shape and size. Adam stopped dead and gripped the rail as he looked down on the scene with growing horror.

The men were in the boats, some standing, others craning their necks to see as they sat at the oars. One man was dragging at the bundle in the bottom of his boat. He rolled it over and a hand flopped out over the water, fingers curled up like a dead spider. A moment later Adam saw the face.

'*Wolfie*,' he gasped.

24. The Trade Winds

Adam reached the wall of the graveyard and paused, his breath smoking on the chill air. It was beginning to get dark and beyond the wall the graves and tombs were already lumpy with shadow. It was a clear evening. Already the North Star was showing, a brilliant point of light, and the moon hung close to the horizon, waxing as the daylight faded.

He had run all the way, through streets alive with sounds and sudden movements. People had loomed at him suddenly, quickening the race of his heart as he passed them. Some had even paused to watch as if they could sense the danger. He hadn't stopped. He had run through the belch of smoke and smells, the clash and bleat and harsh voices of the city, until at last he had reached the graveyard.

As he glanced back now his hand went instinctively to the pistol in his belt under his coat. He was glad he had brought it. It hadn't been easy taking the gun from his mother's room without being seen. He had found it by her bed in its leather case. It was loaded and ready to fire. He needed only to prime the firing pan with gunpowder from the powderhorn in his pocket and pull the trigger, and he swore he would use it if he came face to face with the preacher again.

The horror of what he had seen from the bridge over the Herengracht would stay with him for ever. Ever since he had left the house he had been sure someone was following him. Wild thoughts filled his head.

'It's the preacher – I know it is.'

He quickly climbed the low wall of the graveyard to crouch on the other side. His laboured breath sounded loud in his own ears. He held it until he thought his lungs would burst as he listened. Shadowy people passed by in the street on the other side of the wall. Someone stopped close to the wall, looked and listened, cursed, then moved on at the sound of an approaching coach.

It had been the preacher, Adam was sure of it now. He crawled away, then stood up and ran on, jinking between the graves, keeping to the shadows where he could until at last he reached the iron gate in the high wall around the Windjammers' mighty tombs.

The iron was freezing to the touch as he gripped the bars of the gate and looked in at the tombs beyond. Around him the angels stood motionless in the moonlight, looking down sadly on the tombs that lay silent and monochromed in patches of light and dark. The hinges groaned as he opened the gate and slipped in. He wished now he had thought to bring a lantern. The shadows were deep around the tombs and it was hard to see anything clearly. He knelt before his father's tomb, the butt of the pistol digging into his ribs as he felt on the ground about him, digging into the cold earth, his fingers snagging and catching on the sprouting tufts of dead grass. He was still searching blindly when he saw a light in the graveyard behind him.

Adam ducked behind the marble slab of his father's

tomb and watched the light through the bars of the gate. Someone was approaching with a lantern. He watched it, wondering if a night watchman had seen him. He didn't like to think who else might be in the graveyard at night.

The light came steadily closer until at last it reached the iron gate. There it stopped. Adam eased the pistol from his belt. It was a dead weight in his hand. He hid from the brightness as the lantern was raised through the bars. He heard the hinges of the gate groan as it opened and closed quickly. Then the light advanced directly towards him. He steeled himself. He had nowhere to go. Nowhere to hide. Then he saw her face.

'Jade!' he said, coming to his feet suddenly.

She cried out in fright and almost dropped the lantern.

'What are you doing here?' he hissed. 'You scared me half to death!'

She took a moment to recover. 'I ... I had to know,' she said. 'I heard what your sisters said. I just ... well ... ' She paused and glanced uneasily at him. 'I came to help you.'

Adam squinted into the glow of the lantern. 'Were you followed?'

She shook her head quickly. 'I don't think so.'

He saw her staring at the pistol. 'They found Wolfie in the canal,' he explained. 'His skull was beaten in. The preacher said he would do for him. Me too. I'm sure he was there, watching. I'm sure Abner Heems followed me here.'

Jade shifted uneasily and glanced about.

'Don't worry, I know how to use it,' he said, pushing the pistol back into his belt and buttoning his coat to hide it. 'Now bring that lantern over here! We've got digging to do.'

She held the lantern up as he asked. It shed a circle of feeble yellow light on the ground at the foot of his father's tomb. He quickly found the marks where his sisters had dug out the grass and soil, and probed with his fingers, delving into the cold sods of earth until at last he touched the bulb of the tulip. His breath caught in his throat as he dug it out gently and lifted it up to catch the light.

'The Black Pearl,' he breathed its name.

'Are you sure?' Jade asked.

'I'm sure,' he said, brushing the dark earth away to reveal its fleshy greenness. He looked at it in awe. 'How can *this* be worth so much?'

It seemed so small. The bulb was no bigger than a small onion. From the point of its tip it flared, rounded and bulbar, closed tight in a press of scaly leaves.

'What are you going to do with it?' Jade asked, her face pale in the lantern light.

'I'm going to do just what Gerrit would have done,' he answered her. 'I'm going to sell it – tonight.'

'*Tonight?* Where?'

'At a tavern they call the Trade Winds. It's an inn down on the waterfront.'

'I know the place,' she said. 'But it's dangerous – you can't go there!'

'I don't have a choice,' Adam said.

She hesitated, glanced back the way she had come, then sighed. 'Then I'll have to come with you, Adam Windjammer,' she said. 'Or you'll only get yourself into more trouble.'

*　　*　　*

The lantern light set the shadows leaping between the tombs as they wound their way along the uneven paths. A skull face watched them with hollow socket eyes as they passed, grimacing Death, petrified and set crouching on the top of a grave. Those eyeless sockets seemed to follow them, as if the reaper alone could see some hidden truth. They drew closer together and hurried on.

Adam followed Jade over the wall and they dropped down into the street on the other side. A dog barked. They paused to look and listen, then they set off through the wind and coil of the alleyways of the Jordaan.

Smoke thickened the cold night air, turning it soupy and heavy with the smell of the living. Noises, noises, everywhere they heard noises: voices behind the shutters, a burst of song, coarse laughter and every so often the sound of footsteps behind them. They didn't speak or even look at each other as they headed for the market and the waterfront that lay beyond.

Adam stopped suddenly. 'Why are you doing this? Why are you helping me?'

She looked at him. 'What have I got to lose?'

'*Everything*, maybe.'

'I'll take my chances if you will,' she said. 'After all, you have a ship, Adam Windjammer.'

'The *Draco*?'

She nodded. 'If I stay here in Amsterdam my father will find me sooner or later. He'll take me back, then marry me off to some old merchant. I'll do *anything* to get away from a life like that – even help a Windjammer,' she shrugged. 'This way at least I'll *live* a little before I die.'

He looked at her, trying to read the truth from her eyes. Somewhere nearby a tomcat hissed and spat. The screech made them both look up.

'Come on!' she said. 'Before I change my mind.'

They ran now until they reached the market close to the Brouwersgracht. The square was deserted; the wooden stalls, dark and empty. They moved quickly around the edge, keeping to the shadows wherever they could, until they reached the bridge over the Brouwersgracht on the other side. Here they paused to listen again and catch their breath, before moving into the streets around the waterfront. Down the winding maze of streets, past alleyways filled with quick shadows, where men prowled among the women of the night and people drifted between the inns and taverns as if some human high tide had ebbed and left them stranded there like so much flotsam. Until at last they reached the tavern known as the Trade Winds.

The old tavern stood between the waterfront and the canal. Like a ship that had long since been dragged from the sea and left to rot, its floors rose in lines of grimy windows to a roof that seemed to have settled in place as if its torn sails had collapsed and billowed down gently to spread unevenly over the peaks and troughs of the roof joists. A lantern hung over the door and a sign, rusted with salt, declared its name under the points of a compass. The sounds inside were muted, a hubbub of voices and rowdy songs that throbbed out of the old building, every so often bursting on the ear as the door was opened and someone went in or out.

'What do we do now?' Jade asked, abandoning the lantern by the door.

Adam had left Gerrit's diary on the Long Table, but it didn't matter. Those words were burned into his memory along with a name. 'Gerrit bought the Black Pearl from a Turkish merchant called Ahmed,' he said. He dug into his pocket and felt the mask. 'We'll go in and ask if he's here.'

'What if he isn't?'

Adam shrugged. 'Then we'll just have to trust to luck and keep an eye open for the preacher.'

A cloud of steam and smoke belched out like foul breath as they pushed open the door and slipped inside. The Trade Winds was full, thick with noise and tobacco smoke. Along one wall, barrels of beer were stacked up in three rows behind a long wooden table that served as a bar. The tables and benches had been sawn from rough-hewn timbers and rubbed smooth by the generations of people who had stopped to drink there; the wood stained brown with beer and brandy and polished to a patina by countless dirty sleeves. Here and there around the room, red-faced girls served beer in foaming pewter tankards, their once bright dresses stained like the tables, while men drank and laughed and drank some more as the landlord of the Trade Winds smoked his clay pipe and looked on.

Adam saw an empty table and they sat down quickly, huddling close together on the bench. They tried not to draw attention to themselves and watched what was going on until one of the serving-girls stopped as she passed.

'Bit young to be coming in here, aren't you my cherubs?' she said. 'Runaways are we? Young love? Looking for a ship, I'll wager.'

'We're here to meet someone,' Adam said, wishing

she would keep her voice down.

'Oh, are you now?' the girl said. 'And who do you think you're going to meet in a place like this?'

'A Turkish merchant called Ahmed.'

The girl's expression changed suddenly. 'Ain't never heard of such a gentl'man,' she said, but it was easy to see she was lying.

She turned her back on them and made her way between the tables over to the landlord, who now stood drawing beer into tankards from the barrels lined up along one wall. They talked briefly. Adam saw them both glance over. Finally the landlord nodded and the girl took the tankards of ale and disappeared through a ragged sack that served as a curtain over a doorway between the barrels.

Adam watched the curtain and saw several men pass in and out. He nudged Jade and nodded towards it. 'We have to see what's through the back.'

'And how are we going to get past *him*?' Jade asked, looking at the landlord.

He was a big man – at that moment he seemed about the size of a mountain – with dark stubble on his chin. He stood with a clay pipe clamped in his teeth, watching them as he wiped the beer from his hands on the filthy leather apron that stretched tightly over the sag-bag of his belly.

'I'll think of something,' Adam said, not feeling so sure.

He was still thinking when a commotion broke out beyond the curtain. The landlord heard the noise, took a wooden club down from a hook on the wall behind the bar, and quickly ducked through the curtain to see what was happening. He reappeared moments later holding a tall fair-haired man by the collar of his wine-coloured coat. Adam recognised him immediately as Valentino from Inga's lodging-house.

'Is this the way you treat a gentleman?' Valentino cried. 'A man of means?'

'I told you before,' the landlord growled. 'We don't want your sort here!'

'You weren't so fussy when I had money, sir!' Valentino said. At that moment he was being dragged past the table and he saw Adam, recognising him too. 'Don't go in there, my friend! It is the Devil's lair,' he clutched at Adam's coat sleeve. 'Save yourself while you still can!'

The landlord glared at Adam and pulled Valentino away. He dragged him to the door and threw him out, much to the amusement of all those that bothered to watch.

'*Quickly*,' Adam said, taking his chance.

They moved swiftly through the crowd, ducked behind the bar and a moment later they were through the curtain and into the passage on the other side. A guttering oil lamp gave off just enough smoky light for them to see a door to their left and the foot of a narrow wooden stairway to their right. Adam listened at the door.

'In here,' he said, opening the door. 'And stay close!'

As they slipped into the room at the back of the Trade Winds they didn't see the man sitting hidden at a table in the corner, watching, waiting in the shadows.

The room at the back of the Trade Winds tavern was very different from the one in front. There, serious men had gathered to do business. Some sat at the tables in the small wooden booths around the edges of the room, while most were clustered around the tables arranged in the shape of a horseshoe in the middle of the room. All were too busy to notice Adam and Jade as they slipped in and sat down in the empty booth nearest the door.

And there, for the first time, Adam saw the *kapistan*.

They moved in the shadows around the edges of the room: men wearing masks – just like the one Gerrit had made – conducting their trade. Sinister. Disguised. Anonymous behind the masks that covered their faces to their chins. Only their eyes and mouths were visible, glittering now in the lantern light.

'The hooded ones,' Adam whispered, and he couldn't help wondering how many Gerrits were among them, wheeling and dealing furtively in the tulip trade.

The trade was fast and furious. Men sat at the tables, their eyes sharp behind their masks. They watched the deals being chalked up on slates nailed to the wall. Here and there flower bulbs like the Black Pearl were changing hands, valued by their weight in measures of less than a grain – called *perits*. Mostly it was only the notion of the flowers that were being traded in that place. The bulbs themselves were safer in the walled gardens of the growers who held them, cosseted and protected like so many rare jewels held in a distant vault.

'Do you see him – the man called Ahmed?' Jade asked.

Adam shrugged.

'How are you going to find him if you don't even know what he looks like?' Jade hissed.

'I'll think of something,' Adam said.

'Well, you'd better think fast.' Jade glanced up as the landlord came hurrying in. 'I think he's noticed we're missing.'

Together they ducked down under the level of the table top and watched the landlord's legs. The man's knees were like the burls on the trunks of two trees. They came close as the landlord looked into the booth, then moved on.

Cautiously, Adam emerged from under the table. Jade sat up. They were careful now to stay well back in the shadows. The danger had passed, for a while at least, and they were able to watch what was going on around them. Jade nudged Adam and looked towards the table in the corner. The landlord had stopped and had sat down to drink with the man at the table. Adam saw the two men glance in his direction and the lantern light caught on one side of the men's faces.

'He's with the *preacher*,' Adam gasped, pulling Jade back into the shadows.

A stretch of time passed before Jade spoke:

'Do you think he saw us?'

'Even if he did,' Adam said, 'not even the preacher can touch us in here. There'll be too many witnesses. We'll just have to sit tight and hope this man Ahmed comes.'

'And I suppose you're just going to get up and say, "Does anyone here want to buy the Black Pearl?"'

'Something like that,' Adam said. 'Only I'll be wearing this.'

Adam pulled out the mask.

'I always thought you Windjammers were mad,' Jade said.

*   *   *

310

A buzz of excitement passed through the room as the rumour spread that someone important had arrived.

'Make way! Make way for Ahmed the Turk!' one of the *kapistan* shouted as the merchant and his bodyguards swept into the room.

Ahmed the Turk was wearing a turban and flowing robes of the finest pale silk. Way was made for him and Ahmed was ushered to the best chair at the table.

'What treasures have you brought us today, Ahmed?' someone called.

All other dealings were quickly suspended and everyone pressed in around the horseshoe of the table to see what Ahmed the Turk had brought.

'Gentlemen! Please! A little air!' Ahmed pleaded for more room.

His bodyguards pushed the crush of eager dealers back and Adam saw the line of tulip bulbs on the table.

'I promised to bring you something special, my friends,' he said, 'and Ahmed always keeps his word.' He paused for dramatic effect. 'From the far off lands of the great Ottoman Empire in the east, from the slopes of the mighty River Euphrates, I bring you tulips that were once destined for the gardens of the great Sultan himself, may Allah bless and keep him.' He gestured towards the tulips on the table. 'Only the finest quality, of course!'

A murmur rippled through the company. Suddenly everywhere eyes were glittering as the individual tulips were given their European names and chalked up on the board: one *Childer* of 106 *perits* and worth 1,615 florins; a *Viceroy* of 400 *perits* and worth 3,000 florins; an *Admiral Liefkin* and an *Admiral Van der Eyk* worth 4,400 and 1,260 respectively; and two

Semper Augustines ... The auction commenced.

Adam watched in disbelief as the bidders made their bids, marking them on small wooden paddles that were passed quickly around the tables. From hand to hand, the paddles moved with surprising speed. The bids were chalked up and just as quickly rubbed out and chalked again: always higher. And the air seemed to crackle with the tension caused by the mounting sums involved. A house was bid. A house and six white horses. A house, six white horses and some land near Delft. And always florins, thousands and thousands of golden florins, until at last the final bid was made. Only then was the deal struck and, out of respect for Ahmed's religion, sealed with a shake of the hands instead of the traditional cup of wine.

'It's madness!' Jade whispered. '*Madness*.'

Adam's hand went to the Black Pearl in his pocket. Suddenly he felt the thrill of the trade run through him. He could see now why Gerrit had risked so much to buy such a rare tulip. He pulled out the mask and stood up. And in that moment, as he slipped on the mask, he believed – he *truly* believed – he was about to save the House of Windjammer. Then the door opened behind him. A hand clamped over his mouth, and under the cover of all the noise and excitement he was pulled back into the shadows.

25. Greed and Treachery

Adam came to his senses slowly. His head ached as if it had been split open and he blinked at the strange brown fuzziness that surrounded him. He became aware that his face was pressed against some coarse material, and with a jolt he realised his head was inside a sack and the neck of the bag drawn around his throat. He tried to move, but found his hands and feet were tied securely. He fought his rising feelings of panic and forced himself to remain still.

It took all his strength of mind to stay calm and think. He pieced his situation together bit by bit in his head, orientating himself to the sounds of his surroundings. The sack deadened most sounds, but gradually he became aware that he was not alone.

'Did you have to hit him so hard, Abner? You could've killed him and then where would we be?'

'He'll wake with a sore head, that's all.'

'I don't like it, Abner. There's more than just me who saw them come in.'

'Where's the girl now?'

'She's safe enough with Maria downstairs.'

'I don't want her – you can have her for one of your girls.'

'Have you lost your senses? She's the moneylender's daughter!'

Adam could remember very little of what happened. One moment he had been standing up holding the Black Pearl, the next he was being dragged back. After that it was all a blank. Now, he stayed very still and listened. Somewhere below he could hear the sound of many voices and guessed he was still in the tavern. He moved a little and felt the rough coarseness of the sacks on to which he had been bundled and left. He judged from the lumpiness and the smell that the sacks were full of onions, and swiftly came to the conclusion he was in a storeroom high up in the old building.

The ache in Adam's head began to recede and his thoughts focused on Jade. At least he knew she was alive.

I never should have brought her here, he thought. He wished he had been more careful and he wondered what had happened to his pistol.

'This business will go ill for us if the moneylender finds out.' The landlord of the Trade Winds was sounding increasingly worried.

'He doesn't frighten me for all his money,' the preacher replied.

'But we've got what we want,' the landlord said. 'Why not let them go?'

'And have that Windjammer go running straight to the city guard? I don't think so.'

'I'm warning you, Abner! I'll have no murder done in cold blood in my tavern,' the landlord growled. 'You know the soldiers are looking for you. Aye, they've even been here searching. Someone'll talk soon enough and bring the city guard down on us. Then we'll both

314

swing on the gallows in Dam Square, that's certain.'

Adam eased at the cords binding his wrists and ankles, pausing every now and again to listen to the men as they continued to argue over what should be done.

'I'll make you a rich man,' the preacher said. 'A quarter share of the profits when we've sold it will suit you well.'

'*Half*,' the landlord said. 'This is *my* tavern, if you'll recall.'

A pause, then the preacher grunted. 'All right – but you'll do as I say with no argument!'

Adam gave up on the cords around his wrists and attempted to reach the knots around his ankles. His fingers were numb. They kept slipping off. The pain in his head grew worse. He gasped and gave up.

'Did you hear something?' the landlord asked.

The two men listened for a while, then resumed where they left off.

'I want the boy out of here as soon as possible,' the landlord said.

'I'll deal with him, don't you worry,' the preacher said. 'We've got personal business to settle, him and me. He cut me, see!'

The landlord whistled. 'He did that? Then he's braver than I thought.'

'He'll soon end up like that stuttering fool Wolfie. I shut him up, good and proper, and left him where them Windjammers would see I meant business.'

Adam made another attempt to undo the knots around his wrist, but as he bit at the ropes he shifted his weight to one side. He felt the onions begin to move in the bag under him. They were loosely packed and as hard as cannon balls, and the movement became a sudden slide, taking him slithering down to thump painfully on to the floor. He landed face down with his cheek against the sack and the hard wood of the planks beneath.

'So he's awake at last, is he?' he heard the preacher say.

'Take off the hood!'

The hood came off, whipped roughly away. Adam took several deep breaths, but his relief ended there as he blinked up at the landlord of the Trade Winds standing over him. Further away, the preacher was sitting on a stool at a table looking at him. A lantern hung on one of the many beams above his head, drawing down the shadows around the men's faces and filling the sockets of their eyes with utter darkness.

On the table in front of the preacher, Adam could just see the mask along with the rest of the contents of his pockets. He craned his neck for a better look. The preacher grinned and picked up something between his thumb and his forefinger.

'Are you looking for this, Windjammer?' he asked. The light caught on the delicate curves of the Black Pearl as he held it up. He smiled. 'You've made me a rich man this day.'

'Give it back! You stole it!' Adam fought the ropes, but was forced to give up exhausted.

'For it is written in the good book,' the preacher said, ' "God is the judge: he putteth down one and setteth up another." '

Adam looked around him helplessly. He could see two doors. One he guessed led to the stairs, the other, the larger of the two, looked as if it was used for loading the stores up to the storeroom from below. Both were shut. He was alone.

'Where's Jade?' he asked.

'There's no need to fret over her,' the landlord answered him. 'She's safe enough with Maria downstairs.' He laughed. 'Maybe we'll play dice for her later.'

'You hurt her and I'll – '

'You'll do nothing, boy!' the preacher snarled. 'And I'd advise you to keep a civil tongue in your head or I'll cut it out.' He pulled a knife from his belt and jabbed it into the table, leaving it quivering. 'Go fetch us some ale, landlord! This business has given me a thirst.'

'And leave you all alone up here with that fine tulip?' the landlord shifted his pipe and spoke out of the side of his mouth. 'I don't think that would be wise, do you? You might be tempted to make a fool out of me and change it for an onion.'

'Do as I say or it'll go worse for you!' the preacher growled.

'You don't frighten me, Abner Heems. I've met worse than you in my line of work and that's a fact,' the landlord said, pulling aside his tunic to reveal Adam's pistol beside the wooden club he now carried in his belt. 'As you see, the boy came prepared for trouble and I took the liberty of keeping his fine pistol handy. It's loaded with ball and powder, you can be sure of that.'

The preacher pulled his knife out of the table, stood up and advanced slowly across the room. The landlord backed away towards the door, crouching slightly as his hand went to the butt of the pistol.

'I'll cut your throat before you can prime it and pull the trigger,' the preacher pointed out.

The landlord spat past his pipe and moved his hand on to the handle of his cosh. The preacher grinned at him and bent low to speak close to Adam's ear.

'Do you remember this, boy?' he said quietly, but his tone was one of pure hatred. He pulled up the sleeve of his coat and revealed a gash that had been crudely stitched with black thread. 'You took my knife and cut me with it. Well, I have a new blade now and I whetted its edge just for you.'

Adam pressed his back into the sacks as the preacher touched the knife to his throat. The man's breath was foul on his face.

'Leave him be, Abner!' the landlord said, the sweat shining on his forehead. 'We've got to show our faces downstairs like nothing's happened. I'll fetch a bottle of the good brandy – none of that stuff the smugglers bring in. We'll sit down like gentlemen and discuss what we'll do so no one can hear.'

The preacher paused, his eyes sliding a sideways glance at the landlord as if he was an irritation he could do without. However, he seemed to see some advantage in this and nodded.

'I've got a bit of business to attend to with this yellow-livered landlord,' he whispered. 'But I'll be back, you'll see. For it is written: "To every thing there is a season, and a time to every purpose under heaven. A time to be born, and time to *die*."' He grinned and produced the Black Pearl, holding it out close to Adam's face. 'Yes, and "A time to plant and a time to pluck up that which is planted."'

And then he laughed, fisted the Black Pearl and

thrust it deep into the pocket of his coat.

'Now you lie still, lad,' the landlord said. 'Don't cause no trouble if you value your life. There's no use shouting anyway. No one's going to hear you up here.'

The men left in mutual mistrust, taking the lantern with them and leaving Adam in utter darkness and despair. He heard the key being turned in the lock. The light around the door faded with the sound of their boots thumping down the flights of wooden stairs to the tavern below. He thought of Jade and struggled violently against the ropes, but they only bit deeper into his flesh. He gave up, gasping for breath. The air tasted as dry as the dust that covered everything. Somewhere, hidden in the darkness, he could hear the scuffling of a rat. His misery overwhelmed him and he lay with the coarseness of the sack under him prickling his cheek.

A long time passed before he heard Jade calling softly to him.

'Adam? *Adam*, where are you?'

Adam lifted his head at the sound of her voice. He could see light again around the edges of the door now.

'Jade?' he called to her in a hoarse whisper. 'In here! The door's locked. You'll have to find a key.'

But the landlord had been careless. The key was in the lock. She turned it with some difficulty, the door swung inwards and she thrust a lantern in to chase the shadows away to the edge of the light.

'Over here!' he called. The light advanced until he was blinking at its brightness. 'How did you get away?'

'The men are getting drunk,' she said. 'They called for Maria to serve them. She didn't tie me up and I managed to get away when she wasn't looking. We don't have much time, Adam. We have to get out of here – *now*.'

'But the preacher has taken the Black Pearl.'

'That's the least of our worries,' she said. 'He's worse now he's been drinking. I heard him arguing with the landlord. I heard him threaten to do for him and us, and take the Black Pearl for himself.'

She put down the lantern and knelt to undo the ropes around his wrists and ankles. The knots were tight and difficult to unpick. He gasped in pain as the blood flooded back into his hands and feet. He rubbed the feeling back into his skin with numb fingers.

'But I can't leave without the Black Pearl,' he said.

'Don't be a fool, Adam Windjammer!' she said and picked up the lantern. 'Let's get out of here while we still can.'

She led the way back to the door and paused to listen. Only when she was sure there was no one about did she set off down the stairs. Adam followed reluctantly. They reached the landing below. Again they paused to listen. Now they could hear the sound of the men quarrelling in one of the rooms below.

'We can't sell it tonight,' the landlord was trying to be reasonable. 'Not *here*. Someone's sure to start asking questions.'

'I'll take my chances,' the preacher said. 'Like you said – the soldiers are looking for me. I have to be gone by morning.'

'And what of the boy?'

'I'll take care of him. *You* see to the girl.'

'I'll not touch her!' the landlord said. 'It's a bad business – that's for certain.'

'Then lock her up in the attic and keep her there until I've gone,' the preacher said. 'Tell Maria to bring her up. I'll go up first and deal with the boy. And don't worry, I'll make it look like an accident. When it's done we'll sell the Black Pearl to the highest bidder, no questions asked.'

The preacher stepped out of the room and started up the stairs.

'Go back! Go back!' Jade said.

They had little choice but to turn and flee back up the way they had come. They reached the storeroom and Jade took the key and locked the door on the inside.

'That won't hold him for long,' Adam said.

Jade looked around. 'We have to find another way out.'

She pushed past him and threw open the wooden door over the canal. The door swung out and back against the wall. The cold night air came in with a rush to disturb the dust. Suddenly the rooves of the city were laid out in the moonlight before them, stretching away to the south in crooked patterns of light and dark. Below, glittering with reflected torchlight, the dark ribbon of the canal blocked all hope of escape.

'We're trapped!' Jade groaned, reeling away into the room.

She stopped and listened, staring in horror at the door leading to the stairs. They could hear the slow, menacing creep of the preacher's tread coming up. The sudden rattle of the latch brought a gasp to Jade's lips. The door shook violently. There was a curse and a pause before they heard the preacher mutter, 'That fool must've taken the key.'

The footsteps receded once more.

Jade looked back down at the canal below. 'We could jump,' she said.

Adam shook his head. 'Too high.'

Jade noticed the hoist outside, sticking out over the door like a cut beam protruding from the wall. A heavy iron hook swung on the rope that looped up through a wooden pulley at the end of the hoist and came snaking in to curl in circles on the floor of the storeroom.

'Let's hope it's strong enough for two,' she said and tried to reach the hook.

Jade clung to the wooden frame of the door and stretched out as far as she could, but it was just out of reach. Adam tried, with the same result. The hook swung gently in the breeze, curved and wicked against the moonlight.

'I've an idea,' Jade said and she took hold of the rope at the point where it came in through the door and pressed it into Adam's hands. 'Hold on to this! Don't let it go!'

'What are you going to do?'

'You'll see,' she said. She took a deep breath to steady herself and stepped to the threshold of the void.

Before he could stop her, Jade leapt out into the night. The rope went taut in Adam's hands and he took the strain as she swung away into the darkness and then back through the door to land lightly beside him with the hook in her hands.

'Where did you learn to do that?' Adam was impressed.

'I suppose you think girls spend all their time sewing?' Jade said. She pulled in several lengths of the rope and looked around for somewhere to attach the hook. 'Now we can climb down.'

'But we don't know if it's long enough,' Adam said. 'And anyway I've done enough swimming in canals to last me a lifetime.'

'Have you got a better idea?' She picked up a loose onion and dropped it into the darkness beyond the doorway. They listened for what seemed an age before they heard it plop into the water far below.

'What do you mean – you *don't* have the key?' the preacher's voice rose suddenly. 'It can't just vanish into thin air.' There was a pause, then: 'Where's the girl? Where *is* she, damn you!'

'She was here – I swear!' It was a girl's voice that answered him.

A slap smacked at the air. There was a cry and the sound of someone falling to the floor.

'I'll deal with you later, Maria!' the preacher snarled.

Then the footsteps were on the stairs again. Thundering up through the narrow turns until at last the preacher reached the door at the top. The latch rattled. The door bulged in.

'Quickly, Adam!' Jade said. 'Hook the rope over one of the beams.'

Adam took the hook, pulled enough rope through the pulley and let the rest drop, snaking into the darkness outside the door. He weighed the hook in his hand and swung it, ready to hurl it up and over one of the roof beams.

But it was too late. There was a tremendous crash as the preacher brought his boot to bear on the door.

'Go and stand by the door!' he said to Jade. 'Wait until the preacher comes in then try to slip out behind him. If you get through – don't stop for anyone. Go for help. There'll be soldiers on the waterfront.'

'But what about you?' Jade asked.

'I'm going to get the Black Pearl back.'

'But he'll *kill* you!'

Adam shortened his end of the rope and let the hook dangle. It felt heavy enough and he swung it gently like a pendulum. 'He'll have to get past this first,' he said. 'Now go! And don't even breathe or he'll hear you.'

Jade crossed to the other side of the storeroom and pressed her back to the wall by the door. By now the preacher had almost kicked off the lock. The door shuddered with each mighty blow, until at last the lock broke and the door burst in. Abner Heems stood back with a lantern raised in his fist. His eyes narrowed when he saw Adam.

'Where is she?' he growled.

Adam swallowed hard. 'If you mean Jade – I haven't seen her,' he managed an unconvincing lie. 'Maybe she escaped and went for the soldiers.'

'This door was locked on the outside,' the preacher said. 'Someone must have opened it.'

'It's me you want,' Adam goaded the preacher, trying to make him come in. 'I'm here, so why don't you come and get me? Or are you scared I'll cut you again?'

It worked a little too well for Adam's liking. The preacher hissed and took several steps into the store-room. Then he paused, alert to the shadows around him. Behind him, Jade edged towards the open door.

Perhaps he sensed the movement. Perhaps he noticed a tiny shift in Adam's eyes. Whatever it was, as Jade made an attempt to escape the preacher turned, his hand flashed out and caught her by the wrist.

With one easy flick, he sent her spinning away to fall heavily on the floor.

'Jade! Are you all right?' Adam called to her.

She groaned, dazed and winded from her fall.

'How very touching,' the preacher said, kicking what was left of the door closed behind him. 'A Windjammer caring about a van Helsen. Ha! Now I've seen everything. But you're a fool, boy, to trust her. I'll wager she's after the Black Pearl just like her father.'

'Stay away from her!' Adam warned him, swinging the heavy iron hook on the rope. 'I'm not afraid to use it.'

'I have to admit, you've got guts,' the preacher said. 'You were clever to give me the slip at the graveyard, but I knew you'd come here if Gerrit had. Yes, I *knew* you'd come tonight because you had to. All I had to do was wait for you to bring the Black Pearl right to me.'

Jade groaned and sat up.

The preacher pulled his knife from his belt. 'And now I'll kill two birds. *You* for cutting me, Windjammer. And *her* because of what her father has done to me.' His laugh was pure evil. '"Wide is the gate, and broad is the way that leadeth to destruction."'

Terrified, Adam watched the preacher creep forward. His shadow leapt grotesquely into the rafters above their heads. It loomed over them menacingly and seemed to fill the whole room. Adam kept the table between them and watched Abner Heems warily. He swung the hook in a circle at head height and forced the man to take a step back.

'Abner!' the landlord burst in sweating. 'This has to stop!'

'You stay out of this, landlord! You've made trouble enough,' the preacher said. 'You'll get nothing from me now but cold steel in your guts.'

'Is that so?' the landlord said. He drew his cosh and came lumbering into the storeroom.

The preacher was too quick for him. With one swift movement he dodged, ducked low under the landlord's thunderous blow and struck back. The landlord cried out and only just managed to avoid the knife as it flashed out. He retreated a few steps, then turned and fled back to the door.

'And stay away, you lugger!' the preacher snarled. 'This is none of your business now.'

'But the girl's a witness!' the landlord said.

'She'll not have the chance to talk, you'll see.'

'I'll have no part in this murder,' the landlord said. 'I'll not get my neck stretched for you.'

But the fury and madness showed clearly in the preacher's eyes when he turned back to face Adam. He cut the air with the knife as he stood, crouching slightly.

'I'll make you flap your wings like I did that fool Wolfie and I'll throw your girlfriend out after you for good measure.'

'Leave him alone!' Jade said. 'When my father finds out, he'll – '

'He'll do *what*?' the preacher snarled, driving her back into the corner. 'By the time he finds out what happened, I'll be long gone.' He dipped his hand in his pocket and pulled out the Black Pearl. He tempted them to try to take it from him, but all the while he held back his knife ready to strike. 'Come on, lad!' he said to Adam. 'Let's see just how brave you are ... '

The preacher made a lunge with his knife. Adam dodged it easily and defended himself by swinging the hook on the end of its rope, cutting a circle in front of him. Again and again he swung the hook, again and again Abner Heems ducked and dodged it.

'Stand back!' Adam warned Jade. The hook flashed in a wide circle over his head, faster and faster, until he risked all on one desperate throw. He let it go suddenly, aiming the throw at the preacher's head.

Abner Heems ducked and the hook went flying over his head with the rope snaking out behind. It fell harmlessly amongst the sacks. Adam pulled at the rope frantically trying to retrieve it, but the hook caught in one of the bags of onions and stuck fast.

' "The Lord gave and the Lord hath taken away." ' The preacher laughed as he stepped forward.

Adam abandoned the rope and the hook, and backed away as the knife cut the air in front of him. The preacher came on, crouching slightly as he jabbed and jabbed and jabbed again.

'Come on, boy! You wanted the Black Pearl.' Abner Heems held out the bulb. 'I dare you to try to take it!'

The Black Pearl was so close. Adam made an attempt to grab it. *Slash!* The knife went to and fro. *Slash! Slash!* All the while Abner Heems was forcing him back towards the open door over the canal.

'Watch out, Adam!' he heard Jade shout.

Slash! Slash! Slash!

Adam weaved from side to side avoiding the cuts of the knife. Several times he tried to get past it only to be driven back.

' "Vengeance is mine: I will repay saith the Lord." '

As Adam neared the edge, he was forced to look

down more and more often to make sure he didn't fall. And still the preacher forced him back.

'Up here! Help me someone – Heems has gone mad!' the landlord was bellowing down the stairs for help.

Adam saw him grappling with the pistol, trying desperately to prime the pan with gunpowder from the powderhorn.

'I've played with you, boy, long enough,' the preacher said.

Adam had reached the edge. He had nowhere left to go. The preacher had been waiting for this moment. As Adam glanced over his shoulder at the void behind him, Abner Heems leapt forward, stabbing out with the knife.

'Adam! Watch out!' Adam heard Jade's warning just as he caught the glint of the metal out of the corner of his eye.

Instinctively he turned away from the blow, stepping back to dodge it, but he found only thin air behind him. He saw the rope hanging from the hoist and lunged for it as he began to fall. He caught hold and suddenly the rooves were jigging and canting around him in shades of light and dark as he held on.

The preacher filled the doorway now. He was laughing as he leaned out to stab and slash.

'Heems! Stop or I'll fire!' the landlord was shouting.
Slash! Slash! Slash!

A bluish flash. A shower of sparks. A split moment later there was a thunderous roar as the pistol was discharged. The lead ball struck the preacher in the shoulder, the force of the impact sending him spinning around. The knife flew out of his hand and Adam saw it fall away glinting in the moonlight until it splashed into the water below.

The preacher roared and cursed in his pain and fury. He swore vengeance and staggered back into the smoke-filled attic, the Black Pearl still clutched in his fist.

Adam tried to swing in through the open doorway again, but as he moved the rope shifted suddenly, burning out through the pulley of the hoist above his head. He left his stomach far behind as he held on for his life and dropped into the darkness.

Adam went down fast, just managing to catch a glimpse of a sack of onions being dragged off the pile on the end of the hook. His weight on the other end of the rope was pulling it across the floor. Abner Heems heard the rushing noise and looked up in surprise as the sack hit his legs, knocked him off balance and sent him staggering back towards the open door. A moment later Adam came to a sudden halt as the sack was drawn up into the workings of the pulley, releasing a rain of onions down on him and leaving him dangling like a spider on a thread.

By the time he had steadied himself and looked up again, the preacher was clinging to the frame of the door above with one hand. His wounded arm hung uselessly at his side.

He gasped the name of the Black Pearl through gritted teeth. 'I've dropped it. It's mine! Give it to me – it's *mine*.'

Abner Heems made a desperate lunge back inside, but slipped. His fingernails clawed into the wooden frame of the door, leaving deep scratches as he fought to hold on. Little by little he slipped out until suddenly he let out a hideous scream and toppled backwards.

He seemed to hang in the air for what seemed an age, then he fell shrieking past Adam. For the briefest of moments, their eyes met and Adam saw only fury and hatred there. Then the darkness took the preacher, leaving only his scream echoing thinly in the air as he hit the water below.

Abner Heems did not rise again.

26. At the Stroke of the Bell

'Here, lad – give me your hand!' the landlord of the Trade Winds said as he pulled hard on the rope, hoisting Adam back up.

Many hands reached out to him now and swung him in. Adam let go of the rope and collapsed onto the storeroom floor, where half a dozen people now stood, called up to help by the landlord. They stood around and looked at him as he lay there. His whole body ached. His hands were cramped and burned by the rope.

'I had to stop him,' the landlord said, protesting his innocence to those around him. 'As God is my witness – I warned him. You all heard me! But Abner Heems wouldn't listen.'

Adam looked for Jade. 'Did you get it?' he gasped. 'Did you get the Black Pearl?'

She just stood stiffly, her hands behind her back, trembling slightly as she stared back at him lying on the floor.

'Abner had that bulb,' the landlord said. 'I saw it in his hand. He must have taken it down with him.'

'*No.*' Adam groaned and beat his head several times on the floor until the ache came back and made him stop. A feeling of utter failure swept over him. He closed his eyes and was haunted by the memory of the preacher's face.

'I'm sorry, Adam,' he heard Jade say.

His eyes snapped open and he sat up. 'Jade? Where are you going? *Jade*.'

She backed away from him. 'You said yourself my father'll come after me,' she whispered. She had something in her hand. 'You said yourself he'll find me and bring me back. That's why I have to take it to him. I'm sorry, Adam. I couldn't be trapped in a marriage to someone I've never even met.'

'Jade! *Please*,' he begged.

'Maybe he'll see I'm worth as much to him as a son!' She turned and fled.

'Stop her!' Adam shouted as she pushed out through the people who clogged the storeroom and stairs. He came to his feet and went after her.

'Steady, lad! This is your pistol, not mine,' the land-lord pressed the gun into his hand. 'I had to use it, don't you see! Or he'd have done for you. You'll not be bringing charges, against me – I'm just a poor man. I didn't mean nothing by any of it and I helped you, remember. No one's going to mourn for Abner Heems – *no one*.'

'Leave me alone!' Adam shook him off. 'You're all as bad as each other!' He glared his hatred at the faces surrounding him and fought his way out of the store-room, following her down the narrow stairs. But Jade had gone. He ran out into the cold night shouting her name until it echoed endlessly around the ships and warehouses on the waterfront. But she didn't come back.

*   *   *

Dawn of the last day – payment day – found Adam sitting on the rail of the wooden walkway looking at the half-built hull of the *Draco*. He cradled the spent pistol in his hands. He was cold now. Numb.

He couldn't remember how he had found his way there or how long he had been there. He remembered only a blur of the streets and the weight of his despair as he had looked for Jade van Helsen in vain. The preacher's blow explained the ache in his head, but not the terrible ache he felt deep inside him now as he sat there. He wondered if she had planned to betray him all along.

The light brightened along the eastern horizon, turning the widening expanse of the Zuiderzee pink with reflected light, and his thoughts turned to his mother and sisters. He didn't want to go back to the house on the Herengracht, but he knew he had to. He watched a herring-gull riding the breeze, envying its freedom, before he climbed down off the rail, put the pistol in his belt and started slowly back along the wooden walkway towards the ships tied up at the waterfront. He didn't look back at the *Draco*.

At that moment, somewhere on the canal nearby, a boatman had spotted something in the water. As Adam made his way along the waterfront, the boatman was stowing his oars and reaching down to pull at the coat in the water. Adam passed the Trade Winds without a second glance and was turning up into the twist of streets just as the boatman called to another boat for help. 'It's Abner Heems,' the boatman said. Adam stared straight ahead. He neither saw nor heard nor cared.

The old house on the Herengracht was quiet as Adam made his way to the stone steps leading up to the front door. He paused. His weariness almost overcame him. He took a deep breath before climbing slowly to the top and pushing open the front door.

'Adam!' His mother cried out as she came hurrying down the stairs. She had been watching for him, waiting up all night.

'The preacher's dead,' he said, holding out the pistol. 'He fell, Mother. I saw him.'

His mother rushed to him in a sweep of skirts and hugged him to her. There were tears in her eyes and on her cheeks.

'I lost the Black Pearl, Mother,' he said. 'I failed you.'

'Why should I care about anything,' she whispered, 'when I have you back alive?'

A crowd began to gather in the street outside the old house on the Herengracht. Word had spread and many who knew the Windjammers came to witness the end. Adam watched them through the window and remembered the day when the news of the fleet arrived – that day his life had changed for ever.

Just before noon a coach and horses appeared on the bridge. Two lines of soldiers followed the coach: armed men intent on keeping order. The driver of the coach negotiated the turn and set off down the street towards the house. The crowd parted as the soldiers came forward at the run to clear the way. The coach rattled and jolted to a halt and Hugo van Helsen ducked out through the cloth door. His clerk followed him out. Goltz was carrying a wooden writing-box and a sheaf of papers. The banker turned to look back into the coach and beckoned impatiently. After a brief pause, Jade van Helsen stepped out.

Adam watched her from the window. Strangely, even now he couldn't bring himself to hate her. She saw him at the window and for a moment their eyes met. Her chin came up defiantly, but he saw only sadness in the green of her eyes before she looked away.

'By order of the Council of Merchants,' Goltz announced as Hugo van Helsen looked on impassively. 'This house and all that is in it will be forfeited to its creditors at noon of this the tenth day of November in the year of our Lord sixteen hundred six and thirty. Before the appointed hour the Windjammers must pay off their debts in full or prove that the money is pledged ... '

The crowd stirred uneasily, the people shuffling their feet in an uncomfortable fashion as they listened to the formal announcement.

' ... If the money is not pledged or paid by the stroke of the noon bell,' the clerk went on, 'then any here among you who are owed money by the House of Windjammer must make representation to Mr Hugo van Helsen who will listen to the arguments of your case ... '

'It is time to go, Adam,' his mother said, laying a hand on his shoulder.

'She stole the Black Pearl, Mother,' he said quietly. 'Jade stole it from us and gave it to *him*.'

'Would you not have done the same for your father?' she asked.

He denied it, of course. He said it wasn't the same. But in his heart he knew it was true.

'I had hoped Bartholomew de Leiden might be here,' his mother said. She seemed so composed and strong, but Adam detected fragility to her strength now. It was as if she was made of glass and had been cracked. She held out her hand to him. 'You left this on the Long Table.'

It was the ring of the House of Windjammer.

'Take it!' she insisted as he hesitated.

He took the ring back and put the chain around his neck. The ring fell cold against his chest and he was surprised at how light it now felt.

'I will not have it said we were so ashamed we had to be dragged out of this house,' Mary Windjammer said. She waved the twins forward. They abandoned Cook's apron strings and worked into the folds of their mother's dress. 'I want you to hold your heads up and be polite,' she spoke to them. 'We must show the people out there we are still Windjammers, no matter what.'

Goltz paused mid-sentence as the door opened and Mary Windjammer stepped out with the twins. She stood briefly at the top of the steps and looked at the crowd.

'I am sorry if the Windjammers have caused you harm,' Mary Windjammer spoke in a clear voice. 'It was *never* our intention. We tried only to honour our promises, but in the end we could not. I would it had been different and some among you will say it would have been if I had been a man. Perhaps they are right – for I see now there is no place yet for women in business. If I hope for nothing more – I dearly hope that this, one day, will change.'

Adam watched his mother and sisters start down the steps. He took one last look around at the hall. The house was silent now, a shell. Lifeless, without them. He turned away and followed them out.

The faces in the crowd were turned up to him, watching him as he stood on the steps just as his father had done all that time ago. He never felt closer to his father than he did at that moment. He knew many of the faces in the crowd. Borch from the warehouse, the carpenter and Jacob the card player from the *Draco*, and beside them, standing head and shoulders above the rest: Hobe, the shipwright.

Adam wanted to speak to them. He wanted to say so much. He wanted to tell them how the Windjammers had been hounded and betrayed. But he knew there was little point. Hugo van Helsen had won. He had taken everything, but their name.

'This is all *my* fault,' he spoke looking directly to Hobe. 'I'm not strong like my father was.'

He looked around and saw Jade standing by her father. He would never forget what she had done. She had betrayed him to her father. Just the thought of it kindled the fire of his determination again. He felt the slow burn of his anger, but now his anger turned cold. He saw her look away and grew stronger for it, because he knew – even though he had lost everything – he had won some small victory over her. At least there had been no shame in trying. He took a deep breath, pulled himself up to his full height and spoke with new authority.

'But it's not over yet,' he said. 'How can it be while I'm still alive? My father swore he would never give up and nor will I. He promised to make the House of Windjammer strong again and never let it be said that it was all for nothing. Yes, he gave his word and with it he said went the promise of the House of Windjammer. Well, that's *me* too! And even though we've lost the *Draco* and everything else – I'll find a way. I'll never give up! *Never*.' He looked at Jade and added, 'You'll see!'

He tore his hands away from the rail and started down the steps. His mother reached out a hand to him as he came to stand by his sisters. The crowd parted before them, the people stepping back to reveal Hugo van Helsen waiting for them by the coach.

'My dear Mary!' an ancient voice wheezed. Bartholomew de Leiden had arrived late. He pushed his way through the crowd and took Mary Windjammer by the hand. 'I have this moment come from the Council of Merchants. I have spoken to them. Even now they are meeting to discuss your case. I have left instructions for my clerk to send the news by messenger.'

'Thank you, old friend,' Mary Windjammer said. 'But it is too late. You have done all you can. Please do not put yourself more at risk with Hugo van Helsen by supporting us now he has won.'

The old man tried to argue, but she wouldn't have it. She gathered Adam and the twins around her and, with head held high, walked through the crowd to the place where Hugo van Helsen now stood.

The banker greeted her with a slight bow. 'You will understand, madam,' he said. 'I hold no grudge against you personally – this is business – just *business*.'

Adam stared through Jade.

'Adam, I ... ' she started.

' ... *stole* it!' Adam said. 'You stole *everything*.'

'No –' Jade said, only to be silenced by her father.

'If the Windjammers have lost everything then you have only yourselves to blame,' Hugo van Helsen said.

'What is lost, is lost. It is unfortunate but it can never be regained.' He lowered his voice. 'Perhaps now you will see, Master Windjammer, that I know my daughter's mind far better than you.'

And in that moment Adam realised he had used her. 'You let her run away just to get to *me*?'

Hugo van Helsen stiffened slightly. 'How much easier it would have been for me if I had had a son,' he said.

Tdoom. The bell in the tower of the church nearby began to toll the noon hour. It made a lonely sound, forlorn and flat, and seemed to hang over them eerily.

'Make sure the house is empty, captain!' Goltz said to the captain of the guard.

On the captain's orders four soldiers marched up the steps and disappeared inside.

Tdoom.

A soldier reappeared dragging Cook by the arm. She put up a brave fight, but was no match for the soldier.

Tdoom.

'You should be ashamed of yourselves – *all* of you!' Cook shouted, managing to catch hold of the railing at the top of the steps and holding on.

Tdoom.

'I may not know much about the ways of business,' she continued, 'but I know the difference between nutmeg and sawdust! And sawdust is all you'll get from that man!' She looked at Hugo van Helsen.

Tdoom.

'I've seen how much the Windjammers have suffered with my own eyes. They've lost everything! But never once did I hear them say they'd give up or break the old master's word to *you* –'

Tdoom.

'Get her down from there!' Hugo van Helsen hissed.

The soldier pulled her away from the rail and carried her kicking down the steps.

'Leave her be!' Hobe said, stepping forward out of the crowd.

Tdoom.

'Stand back or I'll have the soldiers arrest you all!' Hugo van Helsen shouted.

Tdoom.

The mood of the crowd turned against the van Helsens. The captain of the guard recognised Hobe as a troublemaker and immediately ordered the soldiers to form a line and protect the coach.

Tdoom.

The scar on the giant shipwright's face pulsed an angry purple as they forced him back. 'You treated me well, Master Windjammer, when I gave you good cause not to,' he called. 'I am truly sorry that it has to end this way for you.'

Tdoom.

'The time for such talk is over,' Hugo van Helsen said. 'The House of Windjammer is finished. This is my house now.'

Tdoom ... Tdoom ... The crowd fell silent as the final notes struck and faded.

'The noon hour has struck,' Goltz raised his voice. 'By the rights invested in me, I hereby claim, on the behalf of Mr Hugo van Helsen, all rights and entitlements of the House of Windjammer for outstanding debts –'

Hugo van Helsen stepped forward. Behind him Jade crouched down and whispered quickly to Rose and

Viola. Her father called impatiently to her. She took Rose's hand.

'Leave my sisters alone!' Adam hissed at her.

Jade glanced up at him, then back to the twins. 'Tell Adam I'm sorry. Tell him I couldn't keep it from him forever.' She slipped a folded note into Rose's hand and closed Rose's small fingers tightly around it. Then she stood up and meekly followed her father.

'Your time is over, old man,' the banker said when he found Bartholomew de Leiden blocking his way. 'If nothing else, I have proved that today.' He smiled. 'There is no value in honour now.'

'I am an old man, it's true,' Bartholomew de Leiden said. 'But I may yet live long enough to see you proved wrong.'

It was Hobe who stepped forward first. He took a purse of money from his belt and pushed his way through the crowd to Adam.

'I am not a rich man, Master Windjammer,' he said. 'But you will have need of this if you are to keep your father's given word. I know now you will because you *must*. For your own sake as well as my son's.'

He glanced at Hugo van Helsen, nodded as if to say enough was enough, and without another word pushed his way out through the crowd. It was a moment before Jacob, the card player, followed his example.

'I won it at cards,' Jacob said as he gave the money to Adam.

'Wait! Stop!' Hugo van Helsen said. 'What are you doing? Why throw good money after bad?'

The carpenter sighed and shook his head. 'I'm a fool, they'll say – but as that cook said, I've seen enough sawdust in my life to know it when I sees it.' He took out his purse and pressed it into Mary Windjammer's hand.

And then, one by one, others followed their example.

The old man watched them. 'I never thought I would see the day,' he said, shaking his head in disbelief. 'A simple shipwright has shown me to be a fool and a coward.'

'I warn you, de Leiden!' Hugo van Helsen said. 'Do not do anything you may regret.'

'My only regret is that I did not do this sooner,' the old man said. 'You may have this house, van Helsen, but I promise you this. I now pledge my support for the Windjammers for all to know and hear. The *Draco* will sail. Yes! Under my captain and flag perhaps, but with an equal share of the profits to the Windjammers. I will see to it if it's the last thing I do.'

Hugo van Helsen stared at him, those pale eyes narrowed slightly as if he had seen something to admire in the man for the first time. Then the faintest of smiles drew new thinness into his lips.

It was over. All was lost. Adam sat by the canal and stared at his reflection in the water. He had the ring of the House of Windjammer in his hand – the mark, like a memory set in gold, was all that was left to them now.

A sudden gust sent ripples crawling across the surface to blur and merge his face with the reflections of the city around him. As the water settled again he saw that his sisters had come to stand beside him.

'Leave me alone!'

Rose and Viola hesitated.

'She gave us this,' Rose said.

'The girl, she means,' Viola explained.

'It's for you.'

'She said you should read it and then you'd know.'

Rose held out a letter.

Adam took it without wanting to. Rose and Viola stepped back. He turned the letter over and looked at the unbroken wax seal bearing Jade van Helsen's mark.

'More lies,' he spoke the thought aloud. His fist closed around the letter, crumpling the paper.

Adam opened his hand and let the letter fall, unread. It landed close to his reflection and floated there for a brief time before the breeze caught it and dragged it away. He lingered just long enough to see it sink out of sight, then stood up and walked away.

27. An End and a Beginning

Early in the spring of 1637 the *Draco* was launched.
Six months had passed since Adam Windjammer had
stood in the mud of the shipyard and watched the gilded dragon settle on the beak of her prow. Now he
stood on the waterfront and looked up.

The *Draco*'s three masts rose high against the blue of
the sky. Her decks and rigging were full of movement
and noise. His imagination soared like the seabirds that
wheeled and turned about her crow's-nest. He knew then
that this life – this way of the sea – was in his blood.

He watched the wooden cranes as they lifted the goods
from the quayside and lowered them into the hold.
Captain Lucas was on the quarter deck. He was eager to
finish loading and set sail. A great sense of expectancy
hung over the *Draco* and this trip to the Americas.

'Ah, there you are my boy!' Bartholomew de Leiden
said.

The old man was standing with several other rich
merchants, all of whom were investors in the new venture of the *Draco*. A new company for a new start and
they had called it the Quadrant Shipping and Trading
Company.

The talk was of business and the recent crash in the
price of tulips.

'These are troubled times,' the old man said. 'Fortunes have been lost as I knew they would be. Even your lost *pearl* would have been almost worthless now.' He glanced over his shoulder and took Adam to one side. 'Tomorrow you sail with Captain Lucas ...'

'You chose an English captain, sir?' Adam was surprised.

'Yes,' the old man nodded. 'I managed to buy the *Draco* from Hugo van Helsen, but that does not mean he will leave us be,' he explained. 'I have gambled a great deal and his memory is long. He has much to gain and we have much to lose. I fear the way he *buys* men's loyalty and there is too much at stake to risk sending you to sea with one of his men at the helm. So I sent to England for a man I know I can trust. Captain Lucas sailed as a young man with Henry Hudson. He'll make a sailor out of you and a fortune for us all, I hope. You'll take passengers out with you to the Americas and,' he licked his lips as if tasting sugar, 'I have a fancy the cargo you will bring back will please your sisters too.'

Adam had grown to like and respect Bartholomew de Leiden and not just because of the kindness he had shown to his mother and sisters.

He had found them a small house close to the Old Church. It was modest by comparison with the house on the Herengracht they had lost, but the old man had made sure it was suitable for them.

'Your mother and sisters are comfortable, I trust?' The old man glanced up towards the sky. 'You should have a fair wind tomorrow so you'd best go on home now and see them while you can – I will take care of the rest of the loading.'

Adam thanked him and took off along the water-front through the crowds.

'Fresh fish!' 'Get your drinking water here!' 'Clean rooms to let!' 'Hello sailor, want to meet some nice girls?' Laughter and the cry of seagulls burst on the salt air.

The sounds washed over him and surged back around him as he moved through the crowds. A bear was dancing close to the Trade Winds. He stopped to let it pass and wondered how life could go on just the same for others when so much had changed for him.

'Master Windjammer!'

Adam stopped dead at the sound of Hugo van Helsen's voice.

'I believe you sail tomorrow with the *Draco*,' the banker said. 'I hope your voyage is a profitable one for your sake as well as de Leiden's.' That faint smile played over his lips as if he thought it might not be. He glanced up at the *Draco*. 'She is a fine ship.'

Adam nodded, but said nothing.

Hugo van Helsen began to turn away, paused, gave Adam a thoughtful look and added: 'Perhaps you would like to know that Jade is to go to England. We sail together soon on the *Salamander*. Her portrait was well received in London and we have been invited to the court of King Charles. I have high hopes that she will take the eye of one of the cousins of the king him-self. If not Lord John Stewart, then his younger broth-er Lord Bernard. I believe Lord Bernard is of a most gentle, courteous and affable nature.'

The news came as a shock. 'You're sending her away? But she did *everything* to try to please you – even stole the Black Pearl from me.'

346

'A tulip that turned out to be an onion,' Hugo van Helsen said.

'An *onion*?'

'Yes, I hardly think Amsterdam will be as famous for them, do you, Master Windjammer?'

Adam thought for a moment. 'But that means the preacher had it when he fell.'

'So she says. But it matters little now that tulips have become almost worthless,' Hugo van Helsen said as if he doubted it. He sighed and shook his head, as if Jade was a great sadness to him. His manner became abrupt. 'Jade knows her duty now. We will go to England and I will find her future husband there. She will marry well, I will make certain of it. A good father cannot leave such matters to the choice of a girl whose head has always been full of wild notions of adventure and romance – you never know *who* she might fall in love with.'

Hugo van Helsen gave Adam a hard look, then bowed his head slightly in a polite goodbye.

'We will meet again, Adam Windjammer,' he said. 'I know it. You have strength and ambition. Ah! If only you were *my* son.'

Adam stood and watched Hugo van Helsen go. He hadn't seen Jade since the day she had betrayed him. He had been so sure she had taken the Black Pearl he had never even considered that she might have picked up an onion by mistake. It would have been an easy mistake to make after the preacher had dropped it and the sack of onions had burst.

He shook his head in disbelief. 'She risked everything for an *onion*.'

*　　*　　*

The next day, after going to church to pray for a safe voyage, Adam accompanied his mother and sisters on one last visit to his father's grave. He stood among the tombs of his ancestors and wondered if they had felt as anxious as he did before going to sea for the first time. Only gradually did he become aware that his sisters were fussing over a flower growing close to their father's marble tomb.

Fleshy green leaves were growing up through the soil, new life drawn up by the rays of the spring sunshine. A tight bud had formed and was just beginning to open. Where the green sepals had parted slightly he could just see black petals beneath: black petals edged in pearly white.

Adam pushed his sisters aside and dropped to his knees in front of the flower. 'Where did you get it?' he gasped, cupping the bud in his hands lovingly.

Rose shrugged. 'We found it.'

'When it started growing, she means,' Viola explained quickly.

'But it's the Black Pearl!' Adam said breathlessly. 'We're saved! *Saved*. It's worth ...' He paused, thought for a moment and remembered what Bartholomew de Leiden had said. He groaned. The Black Pearl was worth nothing now.

Adam rolled over and lay in the damp grass staring at the sky. His head filled with images of Jade's letter sinking into the canal – all she had tried to tell him left unread.

And somewhere in the distance a lone bell began to toll.

Postscript

In November of 1636 tulipmania reached its peak. A few months later, in the early spring of 1637, the market crashed and the High Court of Holland was forced to declare all bulbs to be worthless in order to try and restore order and financial stability.

Many fortunes were made and lost at that time, but Amsterdam remains at the centre of a flourishing tulip trade to this day.

Bibliography

Main sources:
Simon Schama, *The Embarrassment of Riches: An interpretation of Dutch culture in the Golden Age*
Christopher Hibbert, *Cities and Civilisations*
Insight Guides: Amsterdam
Hugh Brogan, *Longman History of the United States of America*
Anna Pavord, *The Tulip*
Charles Mackay, *Extraordinary Popular Delusions (and the madness of crowds)*
Donald Macintyre, *The Adventure of Sail 1520–1914*
Philip Wilkinson, *Ships*
C. H. Brown, *Nicholls' Seamanship and Nautical Knowledge*
Main inspirations: seventeenth-century Dutch paintings including works by Rembrandt van Rijn, Frans Hals, Pieter de Hooch and Jan Vermeer.